Copyright © 2016 by Sean F

All rights reserved. This book ~~or any portion thereof~~ may not be reproduced or used in any manner without the express written permission of the publisher.

This is a work of fiction. Names, characters, places, and incidents either are the product of the author's imagination or are used fictitiously. Any resemblance to actual persons, living or dead, events, or locales is entirely coincidental.

(But, seriously, if this book *did* resemble actual events, how cool would THAT be?)

Author Info:

Website: http://www.SeanRFrazier.com
Facebook: https://www.facebook.com/SeanRFrazierAuthor/
Twitter: https://twitter.com/TheCleftonTwain
Email: cleftontwain@gmail.com

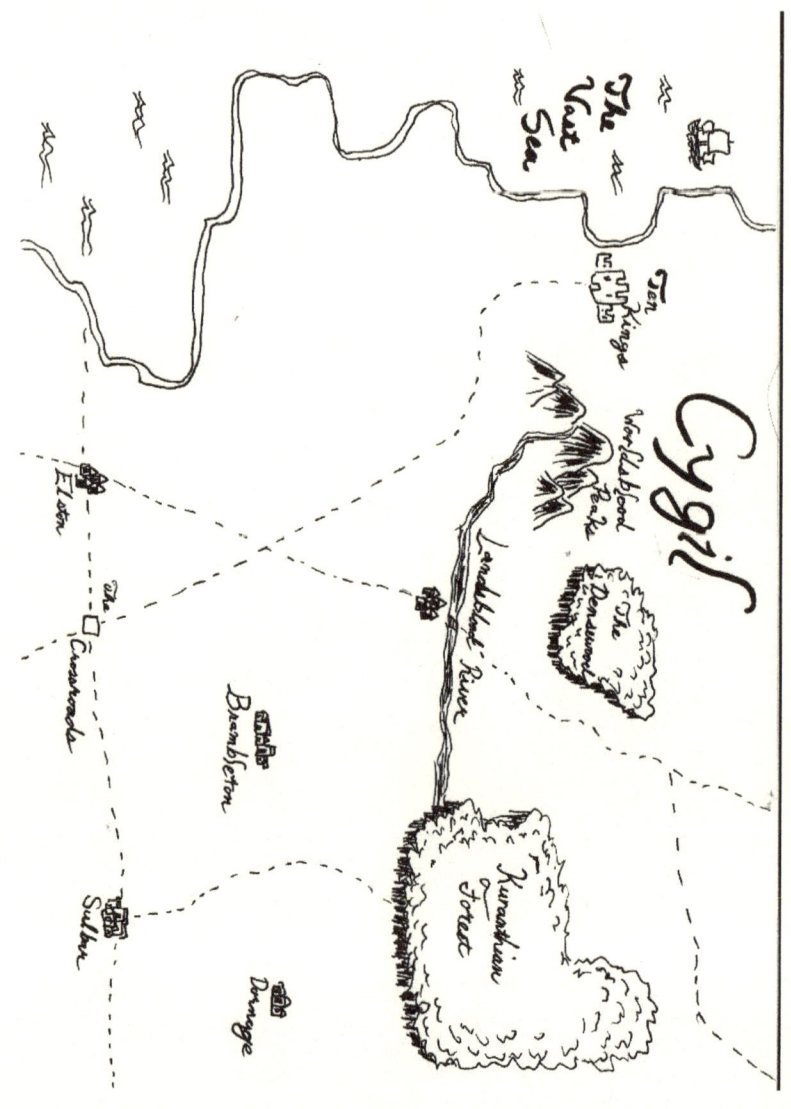

> *"The traveler experiences many wonders, most of which are completely foreign to him. Trust is a difficult thing to assure, especially when one is among the unknown. Trust in yourself as I trust in myself and you will find the answers you seek."*
>
> —Darian, *Out and Beyond*

Chapter 1

Cor'il Silvermoon sat alone at the table, staring down into his mug. He wasn't sure exactly what it was that he had ordered but, after just one sip, he was sure that he did not like it. It was pale and fizzy, with a very bitter taste—almost sour. He thought it was something called "Scorovian Hog Juice." Whatever it was, the rather hairy, barrel-chested man in line before him had ordered it and, rather than stammer with options he did not understand, Cor'il had decided it was best to order "the same,"

He was well past the point of understanding that had been a mistake, but he had begun to realize that he had never really intended to drink it in the first place. This was about trying to blend in—a plan at which he felt he was spectacularly failing. It had started when he first entered the tavern and was promptly knocked to the ground by a group of exiting patrons. After that, Cor'il felt as if all eyes were staring at him. Whether they actually *were* staring was a different story. He wasn't about to find out. He had the hood of his cloak pulled over his head and quietly kept to himself.

You are just passing through, he thought, staring at the tiny, rising bubbles in the mug. The drink *looked* harmless enough—effervescent and tasty. He had hoped it would be similar to the mead he'd had back home. The drink's name should have been a clue. It smelled similar to razorbeast urine.

For a brief moment, Cor'il's thoughts wandered back to memories of his homeland. It felt as though he had been away for years already. But how long *had* it been? Sadly, he knew. He had meticulously kept track of the days and today would be day 42—not even two months since he was run out of his own village by those he had called his friends and family.

And he still wasn't even sure *why* he had been forced to leave his village. He couldn't even explain exactly what had happened. Everyone's stories were completely outrageous, which is why he had not been expelled instantly—it was all very difficult to believe. But, as time went on everyone began to fear and hate him, and more unexplained situations came about. After that, it hadn't taken long for the elders to decide he should be exiled from Kuranthas. Rather than wait until the end of the day and leave with supplies, Cor'il had thought it best to simply leave as quickly as possible. It had pained him to do so, but it had been more painful to stay, knowing he was not wanted.

Kuranthas had always been a welcoming, tightly-knit village where everyone knew one another, and it felt like family. Though he had been raised by his father, he had also essentially been raised by many others—especially Corinne Bailey. Mistress Bailey had been as close to a mother as he'd ever had but, when the time came, even *she* looked at him through angry eyes. It was as if he was now a stranger to her!

Mistress Bailey ran the Seven Hollows Inn. To her, all of the children in town were *her* children. Cor'il remembered many days spent playing Hide and Seek or Catch the Fox in the many rooms of the inn. Often, he and his friends would sneak a pie from the windowsill and gobble it up in the safety of a hiding place. Mistress Bailey swore she had no idea where those pies had disappeared to, but Cor'il suspected that was a lie.

Unfortunately, it was also Mistress Bailey who had pulled him aside one night and convinced him to leave as quickly as possible.

Cor'il fought back a tear welling up in his eye. He had thought a lot about home since he left, and it never got easier. There was still so much he didn't understand! His sadness was coupled with anger. He wanted to throw his mug across the room, to shatter it against a wall and scream at the top of his lungs. He grabbed the mug, sloshing the smelly liquid across the table and dripping it onto the floor.

The odor, mixed with pungent pipe smoke, assaulted his nose again. Surprisingly, his anger changed to quiet laughter as he scooted his chair around the table to avoid the noxious spill.

This really is *the foulest substance I think I've ever smelled,* he thought. He half expected it to congeal into ooze and crawl onto the floor, which evoked more laughter. Without thinking, he instinctively took a swig from the mug and, realizing what he'd done, nearly spat it out. But he caught himself and instead closed his eyes and quickly forced himself to swallow the concoction.

The drink burned as it slid down his throat, causing him to gag. Cor'il was now unsure which was worse—the taste or the smell. *This really is a disgusting drink. Why would anyone actually* want *this stuff?*

It is absolutely dreadful! He had been gripping the mug so tightly that it was a major endeavor to put it down and let go. His hand ached a little as he flexed it, but he decided that the only harm that had been done was probably to his stomach.

He gazed around the hazy taproom. It was nearly full of loud, boisterous individuals, many of whom had probably drunk too much. The stout man behind the bar—the same man who had served Cor'il— was busy cleaning and getting drinks to several different ladies. They quickly dispersed into the crowd while balancing a seemingly impossible number of mugs on trays as they weaved about the room.

So now what? You're on your own, the farthest from home you have ever been, with no friends or family. You are alone.

It was true.

He had never actually strayed from the forest of his homeland before. Kuranthians seldom travelled. And why would they? Everything they needed was provided within the leafy canopies of the towering oaks and the sturdy maples. In fact, he couldn't recall if *anyone* he knew had ever left home.

He never found this to be out of the ordinary. *"Trouble is bad, and the world out there is full of it,"* his father would always tell him. That was a common proverb back home. He heard it at least once a week if not more often. Cor'il often wondered, though, how everyone knew so much about the outside world when none of them had actually ever ventured out into it. Many of them even professed to be experts!

Sure, Kuranthas had its share of visitors from the outside. His village always welcomed travellers with hospitality and wonder. They were allowed into the town and were provided a room at the inn. The majority of travellers stayed away, preferring to stick to the main road. Those who *did* venture into the Kuranthian Forest often were surprised at the warm welcome they received. Several of them said they had been told wild tales of dangerous creatures and mysterious disappearances.

Absurd. All of it. But it was convenient, since Kuranthians preferred not to attract too much attention. Storyweavers and minstrels, however... those individuals were *always* welcomed within the boundaries of Kuranthas. Cor'il, especially, enjoyed hearing their tales and music. Even if the stories they told were untrue, they were still fascinating. It was much more palatable to live out adventures through story rather than... *rather than striking out on your own.*

"Are you callin' me a *liar*!?"

Cor'il's thoughts were shattered when a giant of a man jumped out of his chair and slammed a large knife into the table, where it stuck. His muscular arms looked like bundles of rope as he scowled at another man across the table who, surprisingly, looked as if he couldn't care less.

Silence fell upon the room as several people gasped and everyone stared at the spectacle. Nobody moved, fearing something bad would happen if they did. The man across the table leaned back in his chair, legs on the table, and twirled his moustache between his finger and thumb. He had a huge grin on his face.

"Why no, good Sir Borik," he smirked. "I am calling you a fat, ugly, bone-headed razorbeast."

Silence again befell the room with all eyes transfixed on the altercation. The big man, apparently named Borik, growled low and gritted his teeth. He then picked up his tankard and, putting it to his lips, drank deeply.

"Just checkin'," he laughed, slamming his drink down on the table, causing it to splash. He then returned to his seat. Immediately, the room filled with noise as if nothing had happened. Borik pulled the dagger out of the table and began picking his teeth with it.

Cor'il recognized this man as the one who had been in front of him to get a drink. Apparently, he liked the swill they called Scorovian hog juice. He also noticed the man at the bar discreetly put a crossbow down behind the counter and wipe his forehead with a towel. Cor'il got up, leaving his mug on the table, and approached the barkeep.

"What can I do for you, kind sir?" The man began wiping down the counter with the now sweaty towel. He appeared to be trying to hide the fact that he was nervous but was doing a poor job of it.

"Well, uh..." Cor'il wasn't sure what to call him, since he had never gotten his name.

"Everyn Doyle," the barkeep replied, as if reading Cor'il's mind. "But, around Sulbar, I'm known as 'The Falcon.' You can call me either—it doesn't matter to me. Abyss, I'll even answer to 'Hey You' sometimes!"

The man's face *did* somewhat resemble a bird—it was uncanny. He was stocky and stout. Cor'il wasn't sure if it was muscle or not but, were he a bird, he would never make it off the ground. His nose, however—that was where the resemblance was. It was almost comedic. His hair was thinning atop his head and looked a bit like feathers with its texture and color. Or maybe it was just dirty.

"Did you enjoy your Scorovian hog juice?"

"Uh..." Cor'il stammered. He wanted to be polite but there was no way he could convincingly lie about it. The look on his face probably told the whole story.

"Ha!" Everyn replied with a grin. "Don't feel bad, kid. Truth be told, I was a bit taken aback that you'd actually wanted it in the first place! Borik over there is the only one brave or stupid enough to touch that stuff." Everyn leaned in a bit and whispered. "Just between you and me... I use it to clean the grime off the oven in the back. Works wonders, it does. You really don't want to know what's in it."

Cor'il laughed. That explained a lot. He would most certainly never try that horrible drink again. *I think I will stick to wine next time.*

"So what is it I can do for you, then?"

"I think I will be staying here tonight. Are there any rooms available?"

"Sure are." Everyn cringed as the sound of shattering pottery rang out, followed by laughter. He quickly scanned the room but, seemingly unable to determine what had happened or where, he turned back to Cor'il. "I've got plenty of rooms. Just one night?"

"Yes, just tonight." Cor'il felt the hood on his cloak slipping a little. He quickly adjusted it but tried to disguise that fact by scratching his head. After all, it was summer and wearing his hood up constantly probably looked strange enough. "I'm headed to Elston tomorrow."

"Elston, eh? Great city. King Alzine's seat of power, you know. Quite opulent. I hear he's sparing no expense when planning for the festival." Everyn began piling dirty dishes from the counter onto a cart.

"What festival would that be?"

"Why, the Storm's End Festival, of course. It's going on all summer and is quite the spectacle, I've heard."

Cor'il must have had quite the blank look on his face because it only took a second for Everyn to realize he did not understand.

"The Storm's End Festival is a massive celebration marking the defeat of the Barbarian King 200 years ago. In fact, the Barbarian King himself was killed at the very spot where Elston now stands. It is no coincidence that Elston is the seat of power for the realm. I just assumed that is why you were headed there—the festival."

"To be honest, I am not really sure *where* I am going or why."

"You really don't seem to know much." Everyn scratched his head. Cor'il noticed something—probably dust—fall out in a tiny cloud. "You don't get out much, do you?"

"You could say that." Cor'il felt a bit timid even speaking to this man but, thus far, he was really the closest thing Cor'il had to a friendly ear. "I... I am from a place of great isolation, to the east of here. Kuranthas."

Everyn's eyes widened. He stared for quite a while before shaking it off and, as if he cared not, went back to tidying up behind the counter.

"So... Kuranthian, huh?" He wasn't whispering, but he was certainly quieter than he had been before. "Don't think I've ever met a Kuranthian before. You folks certainly keep to yourselves. But I'd always heard Kuranthians were... well, barbarians. Of course, I've also heard stories that Kuranthians were only a couple feet tall and that some of them had eerie powers of some such nonsense."

"Powers like... what, exactly?"

"What, you've not heard any of the tales people tell?" He scratched his face. A serving maid appeared behind the counter, pushing a small cart. She disappeared through a door, but not before giving Cor'il a strange look. Was she inspecting him or scrutinizing him? It looked like she was more intrigued than anything—maybe attracted? Cor'il had to admit that she was pleasing on the eyes. Maybe she thought the same of him.

"Wha? Oh, yeah. Powers like summoning spirits, or mind reading, or setting things on fire with a stare. Silly tales, I know. But, when you've never actually *seen* a Kuranthian in person, you sometimes believe *anything* is possible. Surely, when you were a child, your parents told you that orcs would come and take you away in the middle of the night if you didn't, say, eat your vegetables or keep your face clean?"

Set things on fire with a stare? For a minute, Cor'il had the urge to turn and quickly leave. A surge of emotions welled up within him, but he fought to push them back down into hiding. He had become good at this of late. Instead, he nervously laughed it off.

"Those tales do indeed sound rather silly," he replied, forcing laughter. "Could you imagine? But, no, we Kuranthians are just like everyone else. From what I've heard, Outlanders often have misconceptions about us."

"I'm sorry, but I am not sure I know what an Outlander is." Everyn had a confused look on his face.

"An Outsider," Cor'il replied. "Someone who does not live in Kuranthas."

"So, then if you don't mind me asking, what are you doing out of your homeland? Tales be tales but I *do* know that your people rarely, if ever, leave the boundaries of Kuranthas."

"That much is true." When this man said it, it sounded different—silly, maybe? Was it silly that nobody he knew had ever actually met an Outsider? Who was the *real* Outlander? "My people are suspicious of everyone and everything outside of Kuranthas's borders. But it seems to have worked for us thus far. We experience no war, no strife, and everything we need, we already have."

"I can't say that sounds half-bad. But you miss out on... um... things like Scorovian Hog Juice!"

Cor'il laughed again. It felt good.

"Oh, right," he continued. "So you wanted a room for tonight! Um... how about The Orc's Den? It's on the third floor. It has a great view and, er, stinks the least!" After a short pause, Everyn started laughing, apparently failing to appear serious.

"It sounds... lovely?"

"And only eight coppers!" he continued. "I'm practically *giving* it away!"

"Well," Cor'il responded, still not quite sure if the man was serious about the smell. "With a promise like that, you might *have* to give it away."

Everyn laughed some more while Cor'il fished out eight copper coins from his money pouch and put them on the counter, exchanging them for a key with the letters "OD" on it.

"There you are, friend. As I said, that room is on the third floor. Head on up the stairs over there." he pointed across the taproom. "Enjoy your stay here in Sulbar!"

"Thank you, sir." Cor'il nodded to Everyn and turned to leave but ran into a wall of muscle and hair. He staggered backwards into the counter as pain shot up his back. Something splashed onto the ground—something foul-smelling.

"Get out of my way, runt," a rather deep, gravelly voice growled.

"Now Borik," Everyn replied. "It was an accident. Calm down and I'll get you another—"

"I said *move*, kid!"

Borik reached out to grab him but was too slow. Cor'il slid to his right and jumped away from the counter, putting a small, occupied table between him and the large man. All eyes fell on the two of them and all conversations stopped. Even Borik's companions were transfixed. Everyn continued to try to talk Borik down but was making no progress.

"I apologize, sir. I was not aware you were behind me." Cor'il scanned the room, looking for an easy way out. He slipped the room key into a pocket in his breeches and nervously put his hand on the blade at his hip. Hopefully, it would not come to that. "Let me buy you a mug of Scorovian hog—"

"Shut up, kid. This shit stinks, and now you've gotten it all over my tunic. I'll be smelling it for *weeks*."

Cor'il couldn't help but wonder why this man drank the pungent liquid if he knew that it smelled so terrible. Maybe, if they ever had a chance to talk, he would ask him. He ducked just in time to avoid the mug which shattered on the ground a mere few feet from him.

Before Cor'il could react further, Borik had moved around the table and was almost upon him. Cor'il jumped backwards, putting a large, wooden support pole between them. *This man is quicker than he looks. I need to find a way out of here.*

Everyn still shouted at Borik who ignored him.

"Hey, Borik!" Borik's moustachioed companion seemed a little more concerned than before.

"Not now, Aleric. I'm busy turning this kid into a dead kid." Borik took a swing at Cor'il who deftly dodged behind the pillar as Borik's fist connected with the wood. Undaunted, and seemingly unfazed, he continued his advance. Cor'il kept the pillar between him and the man, still desperately looking for a way out while patrons nearby scattered to avoid the conflict.

His heart was pounding inside his chest but, despite a shaking hand, he unbuckled his sword and kept his hand near it, just in case. The reality was, even if he could adequately fight this man, his sword would probably not be enough to stop him.

"Well, okay, big guy," Aleric continued. "But, honestly, it's a waste of time to beat up on a child… and not really a brave deed. But we all do what we must… for the good of the Realm, you know."

Cor'il gracefully backed up and rolled over the top of the table behind him, landing on the other side. Borik stopped his advance, his chest heaving with anger. He appeared to be considering his next move.

"Honestly, Borik," Aleric continued, "It's a waste of time. And I doubt the city guard would take kindly to it." He sounded smug, as if he were taking this opportunity to not only try to resolve the situation, but also to poke fun at his companion.

Cor'il stood on shaky legs. He hadn't noticed until now but his sweaty hand had taken a firm grip on his sword and would not let go. The hulking man stood just a table's width away, snorting and grunting. His hands were balled into meaty fists that shook with rage, and sweat beaded up on his forehead. He looked as if he was lost in his own anger. Cor'il wouldn't be surprised if, when this was all over, Borik didn't even remember this encounter. That would be a fortunate happenstance as far as he was concerned.

Cor'il slowly backed away, inching ever closer to the staircase across the room. He wasn't sure what he would do even if he mounted a successful escape. This man looked as though, if he really wanted to, he could knock down a door with just a couple of kicks. Hiding in his room would probably not provide much of a refuge. Cor'il could see Everyn, who looked terrified. He had both hands under the counter, probably gripping his crossbow.

The world stood still, or so Cor'il thought. Nobody moved or made a sound. He wasn't even sure if anyone was breathing. Even Aleric, who earlier seemed relaxed and nonchalant, looked concerned. He was staring at Cor'il, slightly shaking his head and mouthing the word "no." Then he looked at Cor'il's hand on his sword, which was now halfway out of its scabbard.

Shocked that he hadn't even noticed this fact, Cor'il slowly sheathed his blade. Aleric continued staring at him but now he was ever so slightly nodding in approval. Cor'il went further and refastened the strap over the hilt. He put both hands up in front of him and continued backing away.

"C'mon, big guy." Aleric got up and carefully put a hand on Borik's right shoulder. "Let's sit back down and I'll buy you another round. Heck, I'll even pay to have your tunic cleaned! Also, just between you and me… it actually stunk *before* you spilled hog juice on it. I think it actually smells better, now!"

This seemed to work. The transformation was drastic and sudden. Borik blinked his eyes, made his way back to the table with Aleric, and sat down. He resumed talking with his companion, paying no mind to Cor'il who was still slowly backing up toward the stairs. Patrons resumed their clamor.

"It's okay, kid," Everyn urged, visibly relieved. "Go on upstairs. Looks like the fun is over for now." He still had one hand under the counter while the other cleaned the top. Just as with his sword, Cor'il didn't believe a crossbow bolt—even from a sizeable crossbow like Everyn's—would stop a man like Borik. It might not even slow him down.

"Thank you, Everyn. I think I will retire for the night. I've had enough excitement."

Chapter 2

Kendra opened her eyes, stretched, and yawned. Immediately, the pungent scent of horse dung assaulted her nose, ruining the moment. She choked on the odor and sighed, staring up at the dark rafters of the barn. It was still early—the sun had not yet begun to peek over the horizon—but there were faint traces hinting that dawn was indeed near. It was time to go.

She sat up, shaking the stray bits of straw from her hair. It probably looked like a brown rat's nest flecked with yellow and white. She pulled a brush out of her satchel and quickly went to work. Her hair was long enough to get tangled quite easily but she had gotten used to this lifestyle. At first, she'd probably looked like she was homeless and without any coin. While that was the truth, there was no need to look the part. She was much better than that.

She admired the brush, as she did most mornings, before putting it away. It was a thing of beauty—the only object she owned that had value. And the value in this object was not related to the ruby in the steelwood handle or the fine quality bristles. This brush meant something more than that. It always had.

Made of a rich, dark mahogany with a steelwood handle, the brush made her feel regal when she held it. The thumbnail-sized ruby glistened when light shone upon it, and Kendra always made a point to keep it polished. More importantly, it reminded her of her Uncle Sten, who gave her the brush. He had always been her closest family. She missed him.

The animals began to stir. It was as if they thought of her noise as a sign that it was alright for them to rise. *That's my signal*, she thought as she slung her satchel over her shoulder and crept up to the barn doors. They made an obnoxious creaky sound last night when she had snuck in, so she had made sure to prop one of them open slightly so that she could see out in the morning without having to make noise.

Nobody around yet. Kendra had squatted in many a barn and she was surprised to see that this farm family had not risen yet to start their daily routine. Perfect for her. Even with that in mind, she made sure that she took advantage of the situation. She made it a point to choose different spots on most nights. But this one was her favorite. She had even named most of the animals in the barn and sometimes found herself talking to them.

She smoothed out her dress, shaking off more straw, and carefully slipped out of the barn. As the sun's first rays shone, she quickly made her way back to the road that led into town. Hopefully, her luck today would be better than yesterday. It had been weeks since she'd gotten a decent haul and the coin from that one hadn't lasted nearly as long as she had hoped it would. Yesterday, she actually *lost* money—money she never really had in the first place.

It might be time to move on to another town entirely. Even though Elston is a big enough city, I think people are beginning to recognize me. She had known this would happen and was ready to leave if need be. But it was tough to move on when she already knew so many ins and outs of Elston. She had, however, always heard good things about Sulbar. Apparently there were a lot of suckers there.

For the immediate moment, however, she would need to continue her focus on Elston. At the very least, she needed enough supplies to make it to Sulbar. On foot, that was quite a trek. If she was lucky, she might find someone with a cart who would give her a ride. Or, better yet, she might be able to find a horse.

The crown jewel, however, would be Alarantha. If she could go back there, she could set herself up for life without even trying. But that was never going to happen. Although she did consider it from time to time, it was more a daydream than anything else, and she couldn't have that dream. Not anymore. Returning to Alarantha would be a mistake. She'd tried once and it had ended poorly. She never made the same mistake twice because, in her situation, that would end badly.

Never again. Even *she* had her limits, morals… whatever they were called. She had burned every bridge she had in Alarantha—one was an *actual* bridge. A grin came across her lips whenever she thought about that memory. It had been intentional, of course, and Kendra had fled immediately. She had skulked around the outlying farmlands for a few weeks before finally setting out on her own. She wasn't even sure anymore how long ago that was. One thing was certain—it hadn't taken her very long to become accustomed to her current life.

The farm was not too far from Elston proper, so after about 20 minutes, she found herself back at the city gates. The road here was large enough to comfortably accommodate probably 15 horses side-by-side. She approached the city's southern entrance where the ornate gates were wide open. They were crafted from sturdy steel and shone brightly in the morning light. Kendra knew all about them after having inspected them extensively. At first, she had mistaken them for silver and, if they had been, she might have become the first individual ever to actually *steal* a city's gates.

She sauntered carelessly through the throng of people and past the guards, making sure to blend in with the crowd. Kendra always kept her nose clean, even though her activities in town were usually not on the level. She had never been caught doing anything that would land her in trouble with the city guard but always kept an eye out just in case. *Always take the utmost of caution. You can never be too careful, but you can easily be too careless.*

She took a right turn down the first street and opened the heavy, wooden door to the Gryphonwing Tavern. She ducked inside and found her favorite table in the far corner. She sat down facing the door and emptied the pockets from her skirts.

"Five… ten silver crowns and… three gold crowns," she mumbled. "Not a bad haul for my first fifteen minutes in the city this morning."

It was always effortless. Years ago, she had taught herself how to palm small objects. The next logical step was how to lift them from a person's pocket or from inside a coin pouch without detection. To her surprise, she was a natural. Most people were so unaware that they would probably take days to notice anything was missing—if they noticed at all, that was.

She quickly scooped all of the coins into her satchel—into a discreet pocket that zipped shut. She never parted with the bag. Shortly after, a serving maid approached. She must have been new. Kendra did not recognize her as a usual employee. She was thin—almost scrawny—with short blond hair that looked yellow in the dim light of the taproom.

"Can I get you anything this fine morning?" Her voice was high-pitched but soft. Too bubbly. She seemed way too happy, especially for this early in the morning.

"How are the eggs this morning?"

"Same as always."

That was the usual response—what all of the servers said. This one either wasn't new or she learned very quickly. *Leave it to me to scrutinize every detail. Still, it's kept me alive and free this long. Not going to stop now.*

"I'd like… eggs and sausage please. And a pitcher of water."

"Coming right up!" The girl spun around and skipped—she *skipped*—back to the kitchen.

The room was empty except for Kendra. The barkeep wasn't anywhere in sight. Except for the serving maid, Kendra hadn't seen anyone else. But she wasn't alone for very long. Several patrons soon came in and shook the ample dust off of their boots, sitting down at a table close to the door. They looked like travelers from the appearance of their clothes—maybe merchants. One of them carried a dagger on his belt but the rest were unarmed. As if on cue, the serving maid popped out of the door to the kitchen and scurried over to the table to take their order.

Kendra passed the time observing the five men and reading their lips. They were indeed travelers. They had come from the north—from Listerville, a small waypoint along the Landsblood River. Kendra had heard the town's name but had never been there. There was no profit to be had in a town that small.

Once her food was on the table she ate while keeping an eye on the strangers. Several other patrons entered the room but she ignored them. She finished her meal, got up, and put a copper crown on the table.

As she passed the travelers at their table on her way out she stopped and leaned in to talk to them, removing the hair from her face with her right hand.

"Do you gentlemen hail from Listerville?"

"Yes ma'am," the one across from her replied. He looked well built, sturdy. He was probably a lumberjack or something similar. He had bushy eyebrows and a dark mustache that completely obscured his mouth.

"I am headed that direction later today," she continued, running a finger through her hair and pinning it behind her ear. "Is there any place I should visit in particular?"

"There sure is. Drop by the Five-Legged Horse. It's the best inn in Listerville!"

"It's the *only* inn in Listerville!" blurted one of the other men. All five burst out with laughter. They probably told that joke all of the time and it apparently never got old.

"I'll be sure to pay it a visit, then," Kendra continued. "Thank you, kindly."

She pushed open the door and stepped back out onto the street, feeling in her sleeve the dagger she had just lifted off of one of the men. She had only glanced briefly at it while she swiped it. What set it apart from other blades was that the entire weapon was black as pitch. She was well aware that she didn't *need* another dagger. It wasn't the spoils that were exciting; it was the thrill of the acquisition. Most likely she would sell it off somewhere for a few coins.

> "An orc and a goblin sat on a log, gazing at the treasure they had just looted. At first, I thought that there would be a debate about how to split it up fairly between the two. But there was no debate, and the solution was fair and just. The orc got to keep all of the treasure and the goblin got to keep its life."
> —Darian, *Out and Beyond*

Chapter 3

Cor'il stared up at the ceiling, his eyes blurry with sleep. He blinked and rubbed them until his vision cleared enough to make out details. It had been a rough night. Though he had slept soundly, his dreams had been plentiful and disturbing. Yet surprisingly, he found himself unable to recall any specific details from them. Regardless, his head ached with a dull thump as if it was pulsing.

He sat up and rubbed his eyes again. The "Orc's Den," as Everyn had called it, was a comfortable enough room. It was nothing fancy, but Cor'il didn't need fancy. Just a bed was quite enough. Though the room was small, someone had managed to cram a mirrored washbasin and desk into it. True, there was barely enough room to move around but, again, Cor'il did not require it. He did not intend to stay long, anyway. *If this is traditional orcish accommodations, then their life must not be too bad.* He snickered.

The water in the washbasin was cool on his face. He splashed himself a few times, then dried off with a towel. He looked as tired as he felt. He could see in the mirror that his eyes were bloodshot. Looking out the window, he noticed that the sun was halfway to noon already. *How could I have slept that long and still be tired? I feel like I didn't sleep at all.* He normally slept for about four hours each night, but last night may have been an exception.

He looked at himself again in the mirror. And that was when he noticed the book on the desk behind him. He turned and walked around the bed to the desk. *I don't remember that book being here last night.* From what he recalled, the room had been empty except for the furniture.

But Cor'il had been rattled from his encounter with Borik and tired from a full day's worth of travel. He had fallen asleep almost as soon as his head hit the pillow. The room's only light source was a small lamp that he had lit briefly before falling asleep, so he could've easily missed it. But it was odd. It stood out as the only actual object in the room that was not furniture.

The thick tome was bound in worn, brown leather with a design on the front—two circles that contained a series of diminishing pentagons of various colors, with different-colored lines protruding from within. The icon was completely symmetrical, except for the upper-right segment of the outer circle. That segment was missing. Cor'il ran his fingers over the rough cover, feeling the grooves and pock marks. As he did so, his fingers felt warm—a warmth that began creeping up his hand. He jerked away, grabbing his hand and staring at it. The warmth faded quickly.

He touched the book again, instinctively pulling his hand back, but this time he felt nothing. He cautiously ran his fingers over the cover and again felt nothing. Now he wasn't sure if it had actually happened. *Surely I simply overlooked this book last night and I am imagining things because I am tired and don't feel well. Maybe I should go back to sleep?*

He sat and stared at the book for a few moments before he finally picked it up and opened it. To his disappointment, he could not read it. Whatever language in which it was written, it was not in the Common language. *It's just as well. I don't have time to read it anyway.*

That was a lie. Cor'il probably *did* have time. Sure, he was headed to Elston, but he had no real reason to hurry. He had no actual goal or end—he was wandering. He had no real skills or talents and nowhere to live. He was looking for something and didn't even know what it was. Would he know if he found it?

He got up and, grabbing his satchel, checked it to make sure everything was in place. There wasn't much—a money pouch, some dried meat and fruit, flint and steel, candles, and a flask of water.

Sometimes, he felt bitter or betrayed by his exile—especially because *nobody* could actually explain what had happened. But then he tried to consider how he would feel if he was in their shoes. He'd like to think he would be confused and understanding and, for a while, that is the way everyone had reacted. But he guessed they had simply become too scared. They only knew that strange things happened when he was around and yet, he now wondered if his leaving home had actually fixed anything. *What if it's still happening?*

He strapped on his sword, pulled the hood of his cloak over his head, and headed back down the stairs to the taproom which, just as it had been last night, was bustling with activity. He instantly felt his breathing quicken as he scanned the room for that Borik fellow but did not see him anywhere. Breathing a sigh of relief, he headed over to the counter where Everyn stood pouring drinks.

"Thank you for your hospitality, sir." Cor'il put the key down on the counter.

"You're quite welcome, Cor'il. I trust you enjoyed the Orc's Den?"

"Indeed I did, sir." Cor'il again nervously looked around the room. "Oh, but whoever stayed in that room before me left a book on the desk."

"A book, you say?" Everyn looked a little puzzled. "The cleaning maids must have overlooked it. Odd, but not unheard of. I will make sure they take care of it. Thank you."

"You're welcome." Cor'il turned to leave.

"May fortune smile upon you," Everyn continued. "I hope you find what you're looking for."

"Thank you. So do I."

Cor'il stepped out of the inn and onto the walk next to the street. He watched the heavy wooden door shut behind him, making note of several blood stains and what looked like numerous teeth embedded deep within it. The sun was warm and bright and everyone seemed to be out and about enjoying it. And the moment Cor'il entered the crowd, he was swept away into the streets of Sulbar.

He fought the crowd, trying desperately to figure out just which way he was going. He knew he needed to head west once he left the city, but he wasn't exactly sure which way that was. He carefully moved past people, weaving in and out and sometimes walking in the street until he finally found an exit. He hopped up on the curb but was bumped as he did so which sent him tumbling to the ground, spilling the contents of his satchel and landing hard on his right hand.

He grunted and sat up, clutching his hand. It was probably bruised and would be sore for a little while but there seemed to be no damage done. Quickly, he put his things back into his satchel, but stopped abruptly, noticing the book on the ground. He knew that he should get up, lest he be trampled by the crowd, but the only thing he could do was stare at the book in confusion, paralyzed by bewilderment.

He didn't remember taking it—he was *sure* he had left it on the desk. He'd never stolen anything, except for a pie or two from Mistress Bailey. But she had usually *provided* the pies with the intent for Cor'il and his friends to take them. At one moment, he was absolutely sure he had not taken it, though he began to doubt himself. He couldn't deny it—

strange things *were* happening and they did seem to be centered on him. This book was just a piece of it. *Mayhaps I am losing my mind. Or I am just having a difficult time dealing with leaving my homeland.*

He snatched up the book and shoved it in the satchel as he got up and dusted himself off. He'd have to figure out what to do with it later. In no way was he planning on taking it back to the Inn of the Hefty Hammer, especially since Everyn didn't seem very concerned about it. He was accidentally a thief and didn't feel like making that a known fact.

"Goldie!" a young voice called. "Goldie! Get back here or you'll get a whippin'!" Just then, a shaggy, yellow dog ran happily past, trailing a leash behind it. It disappeared into the crowd and was soon followed by a short-haired mass of bulky clothes that vaguely resembled a boy. He waded through the crowd, still yelling after the dog.

Cor'il moved on, walking in the street but keeping to the very edge. Though the streets themselves were not crowded, people on horseback or in carriages would fly by, paying no mind to any obstacles. He was nearly knocked down a couple of times but was able to travel much faster without the crowds. Though he couldn't *see* it, he could hear a marketplace to his right. Merchants yelled out to entice would-be shoppers to view their stock while a band of musicians played a strangely familiar song.

He stopped to listen. It was the exact same tune as "Two Cows in the Water" but the words were about a lost love and a horse. At least, that's what it sounded like. The din of the crowd made it difficult to hear much of anything. Cor'il had always believed his hearing to be superior to most everyone else's, but sometimes this was detrimental—usually in large, noisy crowds. Nobody else he knew seemed to have this problem.

Having no real idea precisely where he was going, Cor'il followed the road. The crowds on the walkways eventually thinned out, allowing for better sight and more room to breathe. He moved out of the street and took the opportunity to purchase some extra food and refill his water flask. He had plenty of money—for now—but would eventually need to figure out either how to obtain more or how to live without it. And where to live. And... pretty much every other aspect of his life. It was daunting, and it weighed heavily on him.

He wondered if his friends Alton, Brand, and Lena missed him. They had been inseparable for as long as he could remember, but even the three of them seemed to think Cor'il's exile was the right course of action. He could tell that they were trying to dodge questions and downplay the things that happened, but in the end, even they had to admit that the past events were a bad omen. He believed they hadn't turned on him, and he hoped that they missed him. He certainly missed them.

Cor'il was in no hurry and he stopped to look at shops, buildings, and people as he slowly walked, still following the street. *You don't need to quickly travel if you have nowhere to travel quickly.* That was something his father always used to tell him. That was a popular phrase back home. It rang true, however, since Cor'il often found himself hurrying toward a destination he didn't actually have.

His head still ached from this morning and he was now getting queasy. By the time he reached the city walls, the sun was setting and Cor'il was ready to bed down for the night. He briefly considered staying at an inn for the night but ultimately decided that it was best to simply move on. He walked through the rather plain iron gates and under the stone archway, nodding to the two guards as he exited. Continuing up the hill, the land around him was grassy but he saw trees in the distance on the right. He preferred to sleep among trees. Maybe it was safer. Maybe it was more shelter. More than anything it reminded him of home. He found that, when he could, he traveled through forests and stayed off the beaten path.

This was usually true. There were times when he avoided certain areas. He remembered the words of Ben Falhar, one of the village elders. He believed that there were areas of the world that should be avoided—areas that shunned the light. He never said exactly what this meant except to say that these areas just felt "cold and wrong." Cor'il took that to heart and avoided any place that he felt qualified. There were countless stories and fables his people always spouted, some of which didn't even make sense. He was pretty sure he remembered once being told never to use a hog bristle brush on a cat. The relevance of that notion escaped him.

He approached the edge of the forest as the sun was just barely visible on the horizon. He took a deep breath as he stepped past the first couple of trees. He could *smell* the forest and the aroma was *wonderful!* A slightly musty smell mixed with dirt and moss. He almost convinced himself that he could build a small house and live here, in these woods. Unfortunately, for all he knew, someone else lived here or it could be infested with wolves or razorbeasts. It was most certainly a tempting thought. But, no, it didn't feel right. He would enjoy it for the night and move on tomorrow morning. Fortunately, he could travel through the forest and, it appeared, follow the road at the same time for a while.

After a few minutes of walking, he found a nice cluster of maples under which he made a small shelter. By adjusting the low-hanging branches so that they braced against each other, he created a crude roof. Though he was tired, he found himself wide awake with a jovial heart. He had missed the nurturing shelter of the trees. In fact, he could almost imagine being back home, making forts much like this one and hiding from his friends. He closed his eyes and listened to the crickets and other night bugs serenade him. This was so much better than a building of stone.

• • •

Cor'il was awakened by footsteps, grunts, and snarls. For a moment, he lay perfectly still on his side staring directly ahead. He could see immediately around him in the darkness but could not make out any detail save for a flickering flame in the trees ahead. It bobbed up and down slightly, heading toward him and soon became apparent that it was a torch being carried by a humanoid creature he had never seen before.

He watched the creature draw nearer when it abruptly stopped and, holding the torch above its head, looked around and sniffed the air.

The flickering light of the torch was not the brightest, but it was more than enough to allow Cor'il to inspect the creature in more detail. It had rough-looking, greenish-brown skin, wore tattered clothing and had a sword on its hip. Matted, unkempt hair fell onto its shoulders and partially obscured its face. If it was a human, it was some strange kind of barbaric human Cor'il had never encountered, but it appeared much more civilized than any normal animal.

The creature looked behind it and motioned with its arm. Several smaller, repugnant creatures emerged from the darkness, huddled around the larger one, and inspected the area. They didn't look as tough or as sturdy as the larger one—maybe a different breed or different creature altogether?

Cor'il wanted to flee—to sneak out and hide somewhere. His head began to throb again, he felt cold and started to shiver uncontrollably, but he was also sweating. He reached over to grab his satchel and his sword but his hand was shaking and he snapped a twig accidentally. Immediately, the larger creature grunted and pointed in several directions while the smaller creatures all spread out, picking up rocks and sticks and licking their lips hungrily.

Cor'il knew that he was about to be discovered. Still shaking, he scurried out the back of his shelter, buckling on his sword belt and slowly making his way toward the edge of the forest. Due to the underbrush, it was impossible to move as quietly as he would've liked but he resisted the urge to run. *Mayhaps their hearing is not very good and I can escape. By The Abyss, what* are *they?*

"I smell something I not smell in... long time," a raspy voice grunted from behind. Cor'il could barely understand what it said. "Tasty flesh! Find it! Track it down! We eat well tonight!"

Cor'il's head pounded now, and he was so cold he could barely breathe. He looked behind him. The creatures were moving out in every direction—quickly. They were hunting him! It was time to leave. But when he turned back around he came face to face with one of the smaller ones. It grinned and snarled at the same time, baring crooked, gnarled teeth. It swung at Cor'il with its rock and missed, but it was enough to make Cor'il back up and trip, falling onto his back. His vision blurred and started to go dark. He continued shivering and sweating profusely, with an intense warmth building up inside him. He remembered this feeling. This is how he'd felt back in Kuranthas when... when he had supposedly set the trees ablaze!

I guess this is how it ends.
Everything went dark.

Chapter 4

Cor'il awoke, choking on thick, sooty smoke. The sky was still dark and the air was heavy, smelling burnt. He sat up and found both his sword and satchel still on his person while charred bodies lay all around him. It appeared as though none of them had made it out alive. Cor'il's head no longer ached and he was not shaking anymore. In fact, he felt pretty good, except for the fact that he had almost died. He *should* have died.

I did this, didn't I? It was me. I must be cursed! But if I was cursed, wouldn't I be just a burnt corpse, too?

This patch of forest was unrecognizable. The trees that had once grown here were now piles of soot or ashes in the shape of logs and sticks, still smoldering—some glowing with residual heat. It was difficult to tell the bodies from the forest itself—everything was ash. The most peculiar thing was how a few of the trees—while ash and cinders—still stood in their original shapes.

Cor'il moved to get up but stopped, inspecting the stumpy, charred remains of the tree next to him. He ran his fingers across it, feeling the smooth, solid wood. *A steelwood tree. Those don't normally burn. I've seen steelwood logs get thrown into a fire and, when it was all over, they were completely untouched. So how is it that this one is nothing but cinders?*

It was true. Steelwood was renowned for being difficult to burn—mayhaps impossible. It was the hardest wood known and very difficult just to cut down. Many an axe had been broken trying to chop down a steelwood tree. They were fantastic, majestic plants unless they grew where you didn't want them to. Cor'il remembered a time when one sprouted up unnoticed right next to the Begelby home. By the time they realized it was there, it had been easier for them to simply move rather than try to cut it down. Their house still stood, but it was being taken over by the tree.

But this tree had been mostly turned to cinder and ash. By what? By him? As unlikely as it seemed, he was beginning to think it was possible. This was not dissimilar from what had happened back home—the last event that had forced his exile. At least, then, nobody had been hurt. The same could not be said for the... whatever creatures they were. Disturbing events, but at least he was still alive.

He ran his fingers over the tree-shaped pile of ash and, this time, it collapsed into a pile.

He breathed a sigh of relief and leaned back with his eyes closed. He wanted to make another shelter and fall asleep. He wanted to put this behind him. But everything that had happened last night confounded and frightened him. He was confused, afraid, and curious all at the same time. *I really should move on. I can't stay here. I don't want to stay here.*

He moved to get up and noticed the book lying under a bush nearby. He leaned over and picked it up. *It must have slipped out while I was trying to escape.* Either that or, at some point after he blacked out, one of… *them* went through his belongings. Except those creatures didn't seem to have any need for a book, let alone a book that Cor'il himself couldn't even read. Cor'il used his flint and steel to light a candle from his satchel. He held it in his right hand and put the book on his knees. Curiosity overtook him.

The binding creaked slightly as he opened it. In the dim, flickering light he inspected the first page just as he had done in the inn back in Sulbar. The text of the first paragraph seemed to shift—the symbols swam through his head and his vision blurred. He watched as they seemed to morph on the page—transforming from gibberish into… not actual *words* but something he seemed to understand.

It made him almost queasy as he read over the words and when he had finished the paragraph, he shut the book and closed his eyes. A wave of warmth washed over him and the world spun. He felt himself slipping into unconsciousness again but fought it and managed to stay awake. When it all had passed, he opened his eyes and gazed upon the book's cover again.

But when he opened it this time, he was confused when he found that he could not, in fact, read the first paragraph anymore. The entire page was gibberish—just as it had been the first time he tried to read it. Had he imagined that he could read it? He was beginning to think so. After all, he couldn't recite anything that he had thought he'd read. His mind was playing tricks on him, or it was stress, or he was just tired. *Maybe all three. In any case, I can't stay here anymore. There might be more of those creatures. This place is no longer safe.*

Slipping the book in his satchel he got to his feet and on still shaky legs, slowly left the barren, charred area. He passed by several piles of ash that once were living creatures. There was nothing left to indicate that any of them had been living at any time.

And then he saw it—one of the creatures was still alive! It was cowering behind a clump of bushes beyond the burnt area, shaking. Cor'il slowly approached it with his sword drawn. He was probably more scared than it was, yet he continued toward it. When he got close enough he could see that it was injured. The entire left side of its body was singed. It didn't try to escape. It didn't try to attack. It was afraid and it was simply trying to *live*.

Cor'il steadied his hand and steeled himself, inching his blade closer to the thing as it convulsed and shivered. It grunted and wheezed in pain while staring up at Cor'il who knew he would have to kill it and put it out of its misery.

But he'd never killed another creature before—not even a chicken for eating. And he found that he couldn't do so now. He stayed his hand, with his blade hovering just a few inches from the creature's throat, unable to force it just a little bit further. Instead, he sheathed it and, before he could turn to leave, the creature breathed its last.

Now that he had gotten a closer look at it, he was certain it was like nothing he'd seen before. *If it is not man, woman, or child, then what is it? The big one had spoken—albeit, poorly. Are the smaller ones less intelligent? They had only snorted and grunted.* It was all very confusing, and Cor'il wasn't certain he was thinking even remotely lucidly yet. There was quite obviously so much about the world outside his homeland that he didn't know and simply didn't understand. He wondered what was next.

And there wasn't even a hint of an explanation as to how exactly this group of creatures had perished. They had burned to ash—that much was apparent. But if he had done it, *how* had he done it, and could it happen again? It was too much of a coincidence to believe that it didn't have anything to do with him. No, he was obviously the commonality. As he stared down at the burned creature he realized that, were he still back home, he could be staring down at a friend or his father.

He felt ill. *It really* is *me. I am a danger to everyone and everything around me, and I don't even know why. Where am I to go now?* He felt compelled to hide deep inside a forest somewhere—somewhere he could live without hurting anyone else. The last map he'd looked at had shown what appeared to be a vast forest north of Elston. Maybe, subconsciously, that is why he felt compelled to head toward Elston in the first place. He thought he'd just randomly picked it, but maybe he had really just used that as an excuse to disappear.

"The Densewood" the map had called it. It sounded as good a place as any to make his new home. His heavy heart lightened a bit and he felt a warm energy course through him, filling him with hope. His legs shook less as he stood tall and walked away from what was now a small, charred clearing. He had a direction. It may not have been an end, but it was certainly more than he'd had before. It sounded lonely—like another form of exile—but, right now, solitude sounded perfect.

After a short trek, he made his way to the edge of the forest. The sun's first rays poked through the trees, and painted fresh sunshine on the grassy fields and the road ahead. Cor'il breathed a sigh of relief as he stared at the scene laid out before him. He looked down the road to his right, now knowing that his future truly lay in that direction. It was going to take time to heal old wounds but they *would* heal. Dwelling on them, though he did from time to time, was not the answer.

To remember is not to dwell. And I shall remember my homeland. I shall remember it fondly. But I have a lot more to think about—more important, dangerous things. And the first thing I have figured out is that I do not wish to be in this particular forest right now.

This was it. His next step felt like a first step. It felt just as important as the first step he had taken outside the forest of his homeland—his first step into the Outsiders' world. And though he'd been in that world for over a month, this felt like a new beginning. Instead of just heading in *a* direction, he was heading in *the* direction. He put his hood down and exhaled the breath he had been unknowingly holding in. He stepped past the tree line and headed toward the road and, hopefully, toward his future home.

Chapter 5

When the sun shone into Arcturas' window he awoke instantly. It had been a long time since he had last greeted the sun, and he tried not to get overly excited. But it was difficult to suppress such feelings on this day. *The drop of water has fallen*, he thought. Soon that water drop would hit the lever that would propel the ball forward and set even more events in motion. It was, in essence, the Great Machine. It reached across the entire world and touched everything—living or not. And even the slightest activity could change the course or alter things. The slightest ripple could cause a tidal wave halfway across the world. The Great Machine was unpredictable in its nature, but it was even more troublesome when it remained still. And it had been still for far too long.

But how long had it been? Arcturas knew not. He had slept through it just as everyone else had. But now, like him, the Great Machine had reawakened. He remembered the day it all just... just stopped. He'd felt empty—as if someone had taken away everything he had ever loved. And, given how long he'd lived, he was unused to that feeling. It was a hopeless existence that the others had felt, too. The world had lost its color.

Some had died from anguish, causing even more grief among his people. But those who survived opted to slumber until, hopefully, the machine started spinning again—*hoping* that it would start spinning again.

And it now had. To sleep had been better than despair. Arcturas and the others had something those who died did not. Faith. He knew how many of his kin were left. He could sense their numbers as they began to awaken. He could feel every one of them regaining consciousness; each one like a pinhole of light springing into existence within him. *Yes. There are many of us left. We will need us—all of us. For if we aren't careful this could be the last time.*

That was not necessarily true. He knew it. The will of a group of people—even *his* people—would never compete with the Threads. They had their own will. If it was meant to be, then the Great Machine would stop as its will dictated. They were servants, caretakers. To think anything else was silly. Nobody questioned their duties. Their purpose was clear.

He rose from his bed and quickly found his journal on his desk—right where he'd left it. He opened it, grabbed a quill and ink, and began recording. He had just finished his thoughts when he heard a knock on his door.

"Come in, Braelus."

The door creaked open and a sheepish, red-haired boy stepped inside, fidgeting with obvious excitement.

"Look at you, Braelus!" Arcturas grinned, setting down his book and quill. "Too excited to run a comb through your hair before coming to see me?"

"Y-yes sir. I mean, I guess, sir."

"Are some of those freckles new?" Arcturas knelt down and, with Braelus' head in his hands, inspected his face. "Why yes, I do believe so. And it appears you've grown a little taller since we spoke last. Come, find yourself a chair and tell me what is so exciting."

The child did as he was instructed, still giddy with energy and anticipation. Arcturas smiled, watching the boy try to keep his composure. He had always been quite the rambunctious youth, but when he applied himself he was absolutely brilliant. His talents may one day put Arcturas' to shame. *If we see that day, it shall truly be a blessing to all of us.*

"So, Braelus," he sat down in the chair at his desk and clasped his hands in his lap. He then reclined slightly, stretching and drawing out the moment to toy with his visitor. "What's on your mind?"

"The Threads, sir!" The boy was so excited he could barely get the words out quickly enough. He brushed the hair from his face and continued. "They're responding again! They're... they're—"

"Malleable, Braelus?"

"Yes!"

And... you have felt this?"

"I have! The moment I awoke I could *feel* them." He bounced in his chair a couple of times. "I could feel their presence and... their power. The Great Machine is churning, isn't it?

"Yes, Braelus. It is indeed. And you have come a long way during our slumber. You seem more in tune with the world around you. That is good. I don't seem to remember you having this connection before The Sleep, yes?"

"Yes, sir."

Braelus had not only been Arcturas' pupil but he had been his *only* pupil. Arcturas believed Braelus would be the individual to take his place in the Ilathri Order someday.

"You are correct, young one. Your feelings are true. The Threads once again bend and the Great Machine runs anew. We have awakened to resume our duties. You are obviously excited, but we must remain focused as always."

"But, sir," the boy interrupted. "Do we know who—"

"We do not. That information is hidden from us—shrouded in a cloak of black. But it will all unfold in the proper way at the proper time."

One of Braelus' shortcomings was impatience. His faith in the Threads was shaky because of it—he wanted to control them, to understand them. But this was neither the way of Ilathri nor the duty of Ilathri. This was a situation that could be rectified merely with experience. He still had a journey ahead of him in order to learn the patience required to trust the Great Machine. He would get there, but the journey had to be his own. Arcturas could instruct him in many things but this just had to be left up to fate, nature, or happenstance.

He remembered his own journey. The memory brought a brief smile to his face. He was a lot like the boy who sat before him, squirming on his seat and forgetting to breathe. *Was I* that *impetuous and impatient? I made the same journey but, yet, I don't truly remember it—not like I should. Mayhaps it's for the best. It's difficult to be rational and calm when one's very fiber wants to be excitable and quick to act.*

"But how will we find him… or her? If we don't know who they are, then we don't know where to look."

"It is different every time, Braelus. What you have learned is based on the instances of the past. But the Great Machine writes its own story. We have but to read that story to find what we require. Tell me, you have often walked the path through the gardens, have you not?"

"I have." Braelus fidgeted, paying attention to his fingers which he twiddled in his lap. "I find walks in the garden peaceful and relaxing. They clear my mind so that I may reflect on your instructions."

"Indeed, they are peaceful *and* relaxing. I have taken many walks myself during my extensive years. But tell me this. With each walk, do you notice things differently? Or is everything—every walk—exactly the same as the last time?"

"What do you mean?" Braelus looked confused, as if the question was thoroughly ridiculous.

"Well, if you took a walk today and then another tomorrow would everything be exactly the same? Mayhaps the sun would be shining at a different angle or possibly a bee might sting you or a fox could scurry across your path. Or mayhaps it would be raining."

"I see your point, sir." Braelus looked disappointed, as if he did indeed understand Arcturas's explanation but did not want to accept it. "You are right... as always."

Arcturas laughed and put his hand on Braelus's knee. "I am afraid I must ask you to exercise patience, young one. For, sometimes, you can do nothing more than sit back, watch, and wait your turn. Fretting over it will do nothing but produce frustration. Take a moment to stop and breathe. Live in the moment."

Braelus closed his eyes and inhaled, then slowly let it out. Arcturas could sense the tension and the forced concentration as his pupil tried to reel in his excitement. Finally, he opened his eyes, seemingly calm.

"We need not seek out the one who has touched the Threads. They will seek us out instead."

The two sat in quiet contemplation for a moment. Both were uncertain about the future but, at the same time wildly excited. The course of the Realm had changed, there was no doubt. But the Keepers of the Threads would tend to their duties as they always had.

"So," Braelus said, breaking the silence. "What does this all mean?"

Arcturas paused a moment. It really could mean *anything*. There was no way to predict the chain of events that had been set in motion. It could just as easily result in something terrible as something wonderful.

"Well, Braelus," he replied, pausing again to gather his thoughts. The recent events could mean a lot of things. It was not their job to predict or control the future workings of the Great Machine. It was not even their duty to worry about them.

"It means... our work has begun."

Chapter 6

When the sun finally peeked over the horizon, Dalinil Thruscar impatiently sat up, letting out an irritated sigh. He had already been awake for a while tossing and turning in an attempt to fall back asleep. He hadn't been overly tired when he bedded down last night so this was no surprise.

Dust sprinkled down as he ran a hand through his short, blond hair. It had been a long night of restless sleep. Nothing new was bothering him that he could think of. He simply hadn't been tired. And, since it was dangerous to travel at night with little visibility, he wasn't about to risk breaking an ankle or falling into an unseen hole.

The ground had been an unforgiving bed. He thought that he'd become used to it by now, but last night proved him wrong. He preferred to sleep on a soft bed of leaves or grass, and this gravel he'd ended up on was definitely not optimal. Still, it was the best he could get when he found himself running out of daylight. He'd seen the pond and thought there might be some comfortable sand nearby. As it turned out, there was not. But he'd not had time to find a different spot. He would have to be more careful in the future. But he was learning. At least the pond was mostly obscured by the trees around it.

The advantage he had was that he could take care of himself if he was in danger. His axe may have only been a simple wood-cutting axe, but it was always at his side, and he was pretty good with it. Though he had not been forced to use it yet, he certainly would if he had to. Basic wilderness survival, on the other hand, left him completely in the dark. He had a lot to learn.

Life had been easy in Ten Kings. It was a nice, large city with plenty of work for a blacksmith of Dalinil's caliber. He'd made a name for himself by the time he'd seen 20 winters which, everyone had agreed, was quite remarkable. That was only three years ago. He was now... *had been* the busiest blacksmith in the entire city. He had jobs set up for at least a year, easy. Coin was not scarce. If only he could've taken it with him because it would certainly come in handy right now, when he needed an inn instead of a gravelly beach.

Though he had to admit that hiding out in the woods made him much more difficult to track down. Of course, he was terrible at it, so maybe that was just his perception. Either way, an inn wasn't an option. A hot bath wasn't an option. *A bloody warm bed isn't an option! I don't even know where I am going!* He knew where he *wasn't* going—back to Ten Kings.

He wasn't sure how ardently he was being pursued, but he felt certain they were looking for him. They would not give up. Whether they were close on his trail, he didn't know. They would definitely have trackers out looking for him—good ones. And they would be asking around cities and towns, which was why he had to avoid them and stick to the wilderness.

He excelled at his trade, yes, but he was terrible at hunting and scavenging. Even if he'd had a bow he probably would've wasted every arrow. That is, if he hadn't somehow broken the bow first. *I just have to keep moving and disappear somehow. It looks like I am going to have to get used to life outside of cities.*

He got up slowly, stretching every part of his body. He could have sworn he heard some new creaks and cracks. Every morning, it seemed, there was a new one to add to his collection. Maybe, if he did this long enough, he'd get used to it. He hoped so, but his body said otherwise.

Picking up his axe, he grabbed his rucksack and headed to the edge of the water where he splashed his face several times. The water was cool and refreshing but smelled a little funny—probably due to some moss or dead fish or whatever. In the city, if the water smelled funny, it was because someone took a shit in it. Out here, there was no telling. Fortunately, he had enough fresh water in his water skin. He'd find a better source to top it off later—this fetid pond certainly wouldn't do. He'd probably be improving the quality if he pissed in it. The Abyss could have him if he was wrong.

After taking one last look around, Dalinil turned to leave. But he stopped and listened, remaining as still as possible. From the trees to the right of the pond he thought he heard something. He wasn't sure what it was but, if it was a tracker, he needed to know. He slowly and, as quietly as possible, made his way to the nearest tree, hiding behind it as best he could. When he peeked out from the right side of it, he saw nothing. He waited to hear something but, after several moments, still heard nothing. He waited a little bit longer before he snuck up to the next tree and then the next, slowly making his way around the pond, gripping his axe tightly in his left hand.

He inched his way around, surprising himself by being stealthier than he thought he could be. At least, *he* thought he was. But he was moving painfully slow. He worked to restrain himself from simply throwing caution to the wind and quickening his pace. If there was a tracker on his tail, he or she would not be alone. And Dalinil didn't relish the idea of taking on a group of people. Not when all he had was his woodcutting axe. At some point, he would make himself a better weapon.

He put his right hand on the axe as well and flexed them both. He was easily strong enough to wield the weapon with one hand but this might require precision. He almost laughed—here he was, a blacksmith caught in the woods, actually pondering killing someone which was the *last* thing he wanted to do! And yet, it was not out of the question. He was not going to get caught. He felt queasy, but continued forward.

And, still, there was no sound from up ahead. Either whatever or *whoever* it was had detected him and was stalking him right now, or it was something harmless like a bird or deer. *Or your ears are playing tricks on you, making you look like a fool as you stumble around the woods, jumping at every sound.*

Caution and paranoia compelled his persistence. There was some curiosity as well. He was pretty certain he'd heard *something*, and it had sounded like more than just rustling leaves or crunching underbrush.

It had sounded like a grunt.

Obviously, there were many animals out and about, probably finding breakfast. But Dalinil was not one to be caught off guard by a tracker, no matter how good they thought they were. Besides, if it *was* an animal, he was hungry, and the food he'd taken when he fled Ten Kings was running low. A nice chunk of venison or wild boar sounded rather tasty right about now. He'd sacrifice a bed for that.

Without knowing just how long he had been stalking this phantom sound, he finally got close to where he thought it had originated. He adjusted his fingers around the axe and his grip tightened when he thought he heard the noise again. This time it sounded like movement and something… wet. It was quickly followed by several grunts that sounded slightly muffled. And it was close.

Dalinil quickly ducked back behind a tree. He felt his hands getting sweaty and he tried to calm himself. He could hear it clearly now—grunting and snorting. At this point, it shouldn't have mattered— it most certainly was *not* a tracker hiding in the brush. Dalinil *should* have moved on and put more distance between himself and Ten Kings. But his curiosity was too strong.

He inched closer. There were no trees large enough to hide behind this close to whatever it was. Dalinil took a deep breath, exhaled, swallowed and quickly walked ahead, axe raised at the ready.

"Let's see what you are," he said confidently. He was trying to make some noise in case this animal was hostile. That way, he may scare it off. "Come out and—"

What he stumbled upon was a humanoid-shaped creature. But it was certainly not human. It had dark green, scabrous skin and was hunched over the half-eaten, mutilated body of a deer. It looked up at Dalinil. Beady yellow eyes staring out from behind a blood-covered face, its maw open to show large, jagged fangs. It growled at him and, without hesitation, leapt into the air.

"Shit!" Dalinil didn't have time to run, or even dodge. Time seemed to almost slow down a bit as he tried to figure out what to do. He wasn't the quickest of thinkers. He was still in shock, trying to figure out what was attacking him.

The creature was in mid-air, just a couple of feet from Dalinil's face when his axe connected a solid blow on the attacker's skull, caving it in completely. Blood exploded everywhere, painting the area in a nasty, dark shade of crimson. The body fell to the ground with a wet splat as blood leaked out onto the forest floor.

For several moments, Dalinil stood over the body, trying both to catch his breath as well as figure out what in The Abyss he had just killed.

He kicked it with his boot to make sure it was indeed dead. *Of course it's dead, you fool. You annihilated its head...* and part of its shoulder. Using his foot, he turned the creature over to inspect it.

It certainly wasn't a wild animal. It looked like a short, misshapen human. *With green skin. Sure... human. What is this thing?* Because its head was essentially gone, it had no face to look at, but it had sharp claws on each of its eight fingers. *Four fingers on each hand? Where is the fifth? What are you, ugly stain?*

He heard the beastly cry and the movement from behind him at the same time he was knocked to the ground face first, sending his axe flying out of his hand. Something was on top of him. It hit him and scratched at his back as he tried to scurry away. He yelled in anger, desperately grabbing at the ground for his axe.

Pain shot up and down his back, which now felt wet. Whatever was attacking him was yelling and screaming in a feral tone. Try as he might, he could not get out from under the thing and get to his axe, just a few feet away.

"Get off of me you bloody—" He screamed as something sharp dug into his back. A warm, raging torrent of anger swelled up within him and he began to scream a string of profanities at the top of his lungs at his attacker. Surprisingly, it stopped its assault. Mayhaps it was scared or confused. Either way, it was now going to die.

With an incredible burst of strength, he pushed off of the ground, flinging both himself and the creature several feet into the air. Dalinil landed on his feet and picked up his axe. The... thing... landed on its back a good 15 feet away. It grunted when it hit the ground and got up slowly, shaking its head.

It looked a lot like the one he had just killed. *Green, scabby, ugly, and about to be dead.* He held his axe at the ready, still furious. It felt lighter, as if it were a mere child's toy in his hand. Though he could feel blood trickling down his back he ignored it. He gulped in air and grunted with every exhaled breath. His vision clouded with a red haze which throbbed with every heartbeat.

Before he could think about what he was doing, he charged at the stunned creature, yelling a horrific, primordial battle cry and liberated the beast's head from its shoulders. The body collapsed in a pulpy heap and the head landed high up in a tree.

Dalinil did not know how long he lorded over the corpse, muttering profanities at it. But when he finally regained his faculties, the sun appeared to be far into its journey toward the other horizon. At some point, he had dropped his axe but his fists were still clenched tightly. He shook out the cobwebs and relaxed his fingers to find his palms were bloody from where his fingernails had dug into them.

He bent down and picked up his weapon. Then, with one last yell, Dalinil buried it into the dead creature one more time. He spat on it and walked away, back to the deer carcass, but he kept an eye out for any more of those things that could be around. He wasn't going to get blindsided again.

The deer, the hind quarters anyway, was not in bad shape. The rest was completely unidentifiable as anything that had ever been alive. He pondered the situation for a moment with hunger finally winning out.

After removing the still intact portion of the deer he carried it back to the spot where he had slept last night. He did a poor job of skinning it but, after all, this was his first time. Thanks to his talent as a blacksmith, he had quite a well-crafted knife to use. While he butchered some of the meat, he had no trouble getting the skin off the carcass.

The fire he built was lousy and, by the time he had finished cooking his dinner, the sun had disappeared behind the trees and probably had set entirely. It didn't matter because tonight dinner was fantastic and filling. He enjoyed it and ate until he was overstuffed. At the very least, the satisfying meal helped take his mind off of the events of the day. While he was perplexed and a bit worried about what it was he had killed earlier in the day, he was relieved that he had not encountered trackers.

Chapter 7

The clouds slowly rolled by in the gentle summer breeze as Kendra watched their lazy parade of various shapes and sizes. Most people who gazed at the clouds saw mundane shapes like an elephant or a cow. She'd heard several children say that some clouds looked like orcs—even though, being creatures of myth and story, they had never actually *seen* an orc before. Many children claimed they had an orc hiding under their bed or in the privy, but she was sure that children's parents always had a good laugh. One day, those kids would be relieved to know that it was all made up to scare them or keep them in line.

Kendra's parents were no different. They had told her the same lies. But the ruse did not last long—she was certainly too crafty for that. True, she had believed it for a little while. She had been a child—she didn't know any better. But it hadn't taken her long to figure it out. Instead of being relieved that orcs were a figment, she was upset that her parents had lied to her. It had been the first in a long string of lies, but it was possibly the one that upset her the most, and she still carried that with her. Her parents had certainly done worse things to her, but this lie had been the first betrayal. *The first is the most painful... and the most memorable.*

She wasn't sure just how long she had been staring up at the sky. This tiny, second-floor balcony wasn't very large or comfortable, and her neck was starting to get sore. It was, however, peaceful and serene. It hadn't taken her very long to tune out the din of Elston's inhabitants below her. This allowed her to focus, even if that focus was used to stare mindlessly up at the sky, which offered no insight this day.

She wasn't looking for shapes or semblances. She wasn't looking for the direction of the wind or whether rain was coming. Put simply, she was looking for peace. If she could clear her mind she could cut out all of the garbage and hopefully find direction or guidance. More often than not, she was very bad at it. *The sky speaks to everyone, but only a few have the ability to determine what it is saying. Isn't that what Uncle Sten always used to tell me?*

A child on the streets below wailed out with excitement. Kendra snapped out of her self-induced trance momentarily, muttering profanities under her breath. She got up and looked over the rail to see a boy, screaming, and being nearly dragged through the street by a large dog. It looked more like a golden streak than a dog, it moved so fast!

This scene brought a smile to her face and she quickly forgot about the interruption. What caught her eye after that, however, disturbed her.

She noticed a man suspiciously following a woman on the street. He was dressed in finery with a hat—brown with a large purple feather in it—obscuring his face. He carried a cane and appeared every bit a gentleman, but his boots gave him away—they were mismatched and falling apart. A detail like that was easy to miss—most people did not look down at someone's shoes.

She watched as he stopped and looked around whenever the lady in front of him paused to look at something. Once she resumed walking, so did he. Nobody else saw this, however. They were not keen on such things—even with regards to this guy who, by Kendra's judgment, was inept. *Bother. I guess this is going to take a little longer than I had hoped. But, as I am pressed for time, I need to get* this *taken care of quickly.*

She sighed and climbed up to the roof of the inn. Once there, she kept low and ran across to the next roof, jumping the gap and landing gracefully on the other side. Every day she was reminded how glad she was that she had traded in her finer clothes for these plain skirts. They weren't anything special, but they were far more durable and allowed for greater movement. Besides that, they were just more comfortable. She even liked the color—dark blue. She hoped whomever she had *borrowed* them from enjoyed the finery that she left them in exchange.

It didn't take long until she was where she wanted to be. The man was slowly closing in on his mark and he appeared to be alone. He stopped and pretended to look at some radishes the moment his intended victim also stopped to browse. Kendra watched him take a bite of one before putting them back and following the lady again. Poor guy. He was trying *really* hard to look normal. If he was hired, whoever hired him probably paid way too much. Though nobody else even gave him a second look, so maybe Kendra's eyes were just *that* keen. She really had a difficult time believing that nobody noticed this buffoon.

Likewise, she wasn't particularly sure why she was about to intervene. None of this was her concern. This was probably some house war started by one man stealing some lady's fork or mocking her hair or something bloody silly like that. But there was the off chance that this woman had done nothing wrong, and was about to be robbed or killed for an even sillier reason. So there was a chance that this would be a noble act, right?

To The Abyss with that. Either way, this is going to be fun.

The lady eventually turned down a smaller, less crowded street. Kendra kept pace with them, ducking behind chimneys and keeping to shadows of taller buildings, trying to stay out of sight. Fortunately, citizens of Elston seemed to never care enough to look up. She had used that to her advantage on several occasions. The city guard suffered from the same flaw.

Looking down the road she saw that, eventually, it ended with a wall to the city's cemetery. Between here and there, she could see a few side streets but not much else. And there were very few people around. She looked closely at the man for any visible weapons. He was not carrying a sword so he probably had a knife. She looked closer and noticed that his right hand kept close to his side and lingered there several times. *A knife it is*, she thought. That would be no problem—as long as she could keep the element of surprise.

He didn't seem to be aware of any of his surroundings. His focus was solely on his mark as he followed her while still failing, in Kendra's eyes, to look nonchalant. The woman he was trailing was making it easier for him by tarrying in secluded areas. The man certainly was taking his time. If Kendra had been in his shoes, this lady would be dead five times already. But she was no assassin.

She leapt across to another roof, slid off the edge, and hung there. Stretching out her legs, she pressed one boot against the wall of each building and, using her arms for balance, basically crawled down to the ground. She then pressed herself up against the wall as the oblivious gentleman passed by. *He's paying attention to his mark and I'm paying attention to my mark. Would it be double irony if someone was stalking me?* She snorted and giggled quietly to herself. However, she quickly looked around just to make sure *she* was not being followed. For some reason, that made her giggle as well. The humor of such irony was not lost on her. She almost wished someone *was* stalking her, just for laughs. No doubt there were many individuals who had good reason to do so.

Of course, the chances of that were pretty slim. She was always very meticulous and careful in her habits. In fact, sometimes she felt she probably went overboard, but her record spoke for itself.

She peeked out from behind the corner of the building. The man was relatively close to the lady, now. He would make his move at any moment. She stepped out onto the street, her soft leather boots barely making a sound, and walked toward them. This particular avenue was relatively empty, save for a couple of men smoking their pipes and a few kids playing a game of "Catch the Gortog."

Then his pace quickened as he approached the woman from behind. His right hand reached under his tunic and produced something shiny. Kendra sped up as well, now just a few feet behind the would-be assailant who stopped and grabbed the lady's shoulder from behind.

"This is a present from Raldin," he muttered as he spun her around. She gasped as his hand reached back and Kendra could see the dagger he had been palming. It glinted in the sun and was tiny enough to be easily concealed virtually anywhere on his person. The woman briefly struggled but was obviously caught off guard. No matter how bad this assassin was, he had still surprised her, and he would be successful.

But Kendra was much better. He never saw her coming. In one smooth motion, she grabbed the black dagger from her belt, stabbed him thrice in the back, took the blade from his hand, sheathed her own weapon, and moved on. She was onto a side street before his dying form hit the ground. The woman then screamed, but Kendra was already gone. There was nowhere nearby with any kind of access to the rooftops, so she was forced to walk quickly through different streets and blend in with the crowd.

It wasn't long before several guards ran past her toward the body, their chainmail armor clinking. She stepped out of the way and watched them pass by, then quickly ducked down an alleyway.

"Well, hello little lady." A tall figure blocked her path. His face was mostly obscured with a bushy, red beard and a wide-brimmed hat that hid the rest. But Kendra could still see his eyes. And, despite the fact that he was trying to appear shrouded in mystery, she instantly recognized him.

"Hello again, Raynar," she replied calmly. She immediately sized him up and inspected everything behind or to the side of him. His right hand was resting on an unbuckled sword that he was obviously trying too hard to show off. He always worked hard to appear dangerous. She knew him well enough to know that it was an illusion.

Her eyes scanned the rooftops and nearby obstacles. The way was clear.

He held grudges. He not only *held* grudges, but Kendra was pretty sure he had made up several against her and probably organized them into a neat list, categorized by severity. But, considering she had bested him every time, it was no wonder he was so bitter.

"Did you come in second again?" She tried to not look behind her. She knew Raynar would think she was showing fear and looking for somewhere to run. He wasn't incorrect about the running part, but she was not afraid. She simply didn't want to fight him—she was no warrior. She stole a quick glance behind her anyway, unable to resist, and was immediately glad she did. Two of Raynar's toadies were blocking the alley's exit, approaching slowly. They looked very cautious—almost as if they were a little afraid of her, which made her grin. They'd probably been told stories about her.

"You have something I want," Raynar said. He was a tall, thin man who grew his bushy beard solely to make himself feel like a tough guy. He had kept it ever since Kendra told him he looked like "a lanky little boy." That had irritated him more than she originally thought.

"And what would that be?"

"You know what it is."

"In all seriousness, I don't. I have *a lot* of things you want, seeing as how I've taken many things from you. So you'll have to be a bit more specific than that." Sometimes she amused herself immensely. Now was one of those times. "Is it green? Does it fit in a carriage? I like this game!" While she did not look behind her again she kept track of the two men by listening carefully.

Raynar was obviously not amused. Kendra saw his hand balled into a fist, quivering just above his sword. She did so enjoy getting under his skin—he deserved it. But she also knew that, if they got into a fight, she would probably lose. He may have been an inferior thief but he was pretty handy with a blade.

"Or is it *this*?" she asked jokingly. She produced the black dagger she had pilfered from the man in the tavern and flipped it over in the air, catching it with ease.

"You know full well that blade belongs to me. Now shut your mouth and hand it over. Or I'll have my two friends behind you there turn you into a pin cushion."

Kendra was more than a little surprised. She hadn't actually known that Raynar desired the black dagger when she had pilfered it on a whim. But what was so special about it? Her mind started racing. Needless to say, she valued it more now, and would never give it up.

She heard the sound of swords being unsheathed behind her. She was unfamiliar with these two goons who appeared to be new to his entourage. She wondered what had happened to the other two.

"I tell you what," she continued, but paused and looked at the dagger. It really *was* unique. She'd never seen black steel before. It wasn't paint or dye—it was truly *black steel*. She lowered her hand, still holding the knife, to her side and paused again, pondering how Raynar came about it in the first place—if he was telling the truth.

"Well?" He was getting impatient. His minions had stopped advancing and, while he was antsy, he looked hopeful. He was relishing his victory! Kendra wondered if he had ever felt this way before and, at that thought, she once again had to suppress an evil grin.

"You can have it. But you've got to go fetch it! Go get it, boy!" She lobbed the knife into the air and watched Raynar's eyes follow the blade as it turned end over end, finally coming to rest on the roof. She took this opportunity to dart past him, knocking him into a pile of garbage as she fled around the corner and onto another street.

"Go get it, you fools!" she heard him shout just before she rounded the corner. She stopped and found a gutter. Without testing its sturdiness, she used it to scale up the wall like a cat up a tree. In no time, she was two stories up, standing on the roof, waiting. And waiting. And waiting.

Eventually, one of Raynar's lackeys made it to the top of the building. Kendra ducked behind a chimney and watched him, now unable to control her giggling. She hoped the bonehead couldn't hear her. He looked around on the roof until he finally found the dagger and grabbed it.

"Here you are, sir!" he yelled as he walked to the edge of the roof and dropped it to the ground. It really *was* too bad. Kendra had really liked that particular blade. Well, in all honesty, she felt that way about *all* of her daggers.

"The Abyss damn that woman! This isn't it! She switched them! Cursed woman!"

Kendra stepped out from behind the chimney, still laughing.

"Yes, Raynar, I'm a thief," she shouted down at the street. She couldn't see Raynar but she knew he must be red with rage. "And I keep what I take. If you want something, brush up on your skills a bit!" She looked at the goon on the other rooftop, waved happily to him, and then hurried off in the opposite direction. A little sleight of hand went a long way.

Once she was out of sight, she stopped a moment to catch her breath. She slid the dagger out from her sleeve to inspect it. Something she noticed when she was toying with Raynar was that it had no blood on it. She had meant to clean it off once she was away from the scene of the crime but was too busy dealing with that idiot Raynar. Looking at it again she confirmed that it was totally clean. Her belt and skirts had some blood on them, though, so that would explain it. *I just might need to find a new set of clothes somewhere... again.* She sighed. This was getting old.

She put the dagger back in her belt and dropped the assassin's tiny blade into one of her pockets. *Well, that was unexpected. I guess I was being followed. Or, more appropriately, he probably was fortunate to have accidentally found me.* Annoying Raynar was beginning to become a hobby of hers.

She sat down on the roof and sighed, closing her eyes and resting for a moment. As fun as it was, she sometimes almost felt sorry for the guy. He wasn't at all *terrible* at their trade, he was just not on the same level as she was. He also wasn't very bright and he made poor business decisions, starting with the idiots he hired to help him. If he wasn't so hung up on getting back at her he may have been mildly successful.

Time to go. She got up and, as she did, something in the sky caught her attention. She looked up and was reassured by a warm feeling washing over her. She dusted herself off, now sure of her direction. *It is indeed* past *time to go.*

Chapter 8

With each passing day Cor'il wished more and more that he had a simple map. But maps cost money, and money was in short supply. At the very least, it would have been nice to know just where the next town was. Cor'il enjoyed walking and being outside, but he was frustrated that everything was so far apart.

Mayhaps he was just being impatient. He really felt drawn to the Densewood. Having lived among the trees of Kuranthas all of his life, he preferred to make his new home in a forest. He was filled with hopeful possibilities and the potential to take control of his own direction in The Realm. Mayhaps he could convince his friends to come and they could all live together. He missed them and longed for everything to be as it was.

The day was particularly hot. Regardless, Cor'il kept the hood of his cloak over his head and, against his better judgment, kept to the road. He had always heard of bad things happening to travelers on the road—everyone in Kuranthas spoke of horrible tales. It was as if they had actually traveled the roads before which, Cor'il knew, they had not. Mayhaps the storyweavers spun memories of bad experiences or mayhaps they had heard stories from someone else. Thus far Cor'il had not had any bad experiences on the road. *Off* the road, on the other hand…

He had encountered many people traveling in both directions. They all had seemed very nice if not mayhaps in just a bit too much of a hurry. He had even seen some local militia patrolling the roads. They hadn't been the most pleasant of fellows but they hadn't bothered him. Regardless, he did make sure not to antagonize any of them, since none of them ever looked cheerful in any way.

The land around him had gradually changed from varied terrain to what was now just plains. Tall grasses covered the countryside, interrupted by an occasional bush. He could often see clumps of trees in the distance but, usually, even any kind of hills were difficult to come by. Every time he asked any travelers how far it was to Elston, he got differing and, sometimes conflicting, answers.

He had also finally lost track of how many days he had been away from home. He had essentially given up counting when he realized that doing so kept reopening a painful wound. He still missed his home but saw no need to constantly remind himself of it. Yet thoughts of Kuranthas still crept into his mind often anyway.

The wagon in which Cor'il currently rode was a bit rickety and bounced a lot but he didn't mind. It was the first ride he had received since he set out on his own. Brandt was a nice man. He was elderly and hard of hearing but had been surprisingly trusting and offered Cor'il transport without being asked. In actuality, it had been Cor'il who was hesitant to accept at first. He had even tried to turn down the offer but Brandt was an insistent man and said that he wouldn't take "no" for an answer. And he hadn't.

This was much better than walking. His legs had gotten used to the daily travel but they were still sore and tired at the end of the day. And this would more quickly get him to Elston and, eventually, the Densewood. Unfortunately, Brandt was heading south at some point and Elston was north of here. But Cor'il would go as far as he could. Besides, it wasn't as if he had never walked before.

The straw in the back of the wagon helped to cushion the bumps and shakes of the road but they still jostled him around a bit. The brown, mangy-looking dog sitting in the wagon with him didn't seem to mind, however. He had found an itch on one of his legs to chew on but was otherwise unconcerned with anything. Cor'il had spent a good portion of the ride thus far keeping his distance from the animal in case it had fleas.

"We'll be at the crossroads in a bit under a half hour!" Brandt yelled to Cor'il. "I'm sorry I can't take you any further!"

"I appreciate it, sir!" Cor'il yelled back. He wasn't sure Brandt even heard him. He'd become used to yelling everything to Brandt just so he didn't have to repeat himself. And Brandt obviously had no idea how loud he himself was.

Cor'il sighed and leaned his head back, eyes closed. He felt the sun shining on his face, trying to peek through his eyelids. He reached into his satchel and pulled out the book, feeling the rough cover under his fingertips. He could smell the familiar, slightly musty scent. The first time he smelled it, back in Sulbar, he didn't care for it. But, now, it was much like a trusty old friend.

He opened his eyes and looked at the first page. For a brief moment, he thought he could read the whole thing, but that moment was fleeting. The page quickly returned to its natural state of gibberish. Or mayhaps it had never been legible in the first place and Cor'il had fooled himself. Cor'il had tried reading it several times since he left the Inn of the Hefty Hammer and, most times, nothing happened. A few times he had the same issue as he did just now. He was beginning to wonder if it was just his eyes playing tricks on him. Or mayhaps it was just wishful thinking.

And now his head slightly hurt. What once was pleasant sunshine, was now just a bit too bright. Cor'il squinted and averted his eyes, mostly looking down at the straw-covered wagon bed. The dog was now peacefully snoozing, one eye cocked open and focused on Cor'il who placed the book back in his satchel. He could feel himself trying to nod off. If they weren't already so close to the crossroads he would have taken a short nap.

Mayhaps I could just rest my eyes, he thought. *It won't hurt anything even if I do nod off for a bit.* He let his eyelids close and leaned his head back again. It wasn't the most comfortable position—he was propped against the side of the wagon—but he didn't really care at this point. Fatigue had, somehow, instantly overtaken him.

The dream started immediately. But to say it was a "dream" would have been the same as saying that random pages of gibberish constituted an actual "book".

Images and snippets filled his mind. At first, he saw a grassy hill leading down to a tree-laden creek where very little light penetrated. He shivered in the sudden cold and wrapped his arms around himself. There was a flash of light and suddenly, there were thin, almost invisible, lines connecting the trees to the ground, water, and stone. The lines shimmered and gleamed—no, they *pulsed*. The cold intensified, and then it all vanished.

After another flash of light, he stood before a city of white buildings, pristine roads made of perfectly-hewn, white stone and silvery gates that looked like they were wrought from lace, not metal. The image quickly vanished.

A storm coalesced. Dark clouds quickly moved in and shrouded the sky in darkness. Within the maelstrom, Cor'il thought he saw two sinister, glowing eyes. They focused on Cor'il. He heard quiet laughter and then a voice spoke.

"There you are." It was a low, guttural whisper. Cor'il couldn't distinguish the voice from the din of the storm. Dark tendrils appeared from the clouds, traveling toward Cor'il.

He bolted upright, breathing heavily and scanning the area. The sun was still shining as the wagon made its way down the bumpy road. The dog eyed Cor'il cautiously but seemed otherwise unconcerned. Cor'il, on the other hand, felt his heart racing.

And then what he saw next made his heart beat even faster. It emerged from behind some large rocks along the road—a cloaked figure—and proceeded to not only keep pace with the wagon, but it began approaching. Cor'il's hand went to his sword but he did not draw it.

The hooded figure seemed in no hurry as it... floated? Cor'il could see no legs! Nor did it appear to have the gait of someone walking! And then, as it revealed its face, Cor'il felt his body go numb. He could not draw his sword. He could do nothing but sit and stare.

Its face was that of a skull. It had no skin and no eyes. Its hands were of bone. And, though there was no possible way it should have had any kind of expression, it appeared to be smiling. Cor'il tried to call out to Brandt but only a slight squeak emerged.

The creature lifted a finger to its fleshless mouth, made a shushing motion, and shook its head slowly. And, though it was now just a few feet from the wagon, keeping pace by floating alongside, it made no other moves. It carried no weapon nor did it take any hostile actions.

Both Brandt and his dog must not have seen the creature because neither one acted any differently. As if to prove this assumption, it floated out in front of the wagon—in front of Brandt—its gaze still fixed on Cor'il. He felt sick and feared he might empty his stomach right there. It resumed its position next to the wagon and kept pace once again, staring at Cor'il.

Cor'il tried merely to look away but he couldn't even do that. He had no notion of how much time had passed with the two of them locking gazes. Even mustering a coherent thought was impossible.

Brandt was yelling something. Cor'il could not concentrate enough to comprehend it. In fact, his hearing seemed to be failing him. Everything sounded as if he were submerged underwater.

And then, surprisingly, the creature nodded to Cor'il. Then it slowly lifted a hand, as if to wave to him before it nonchalantly turned, moved backwards toward a hill, and disappeared behind it.

The moment it broke its gaze, Cor'il regained control. He gripped his sword and drew it but the creature was already gone. Cor'il had no intention of pursuing it. His hair and tunic were soaked and he shivered and concentrated painstakingly on the simple task of sheathing his blade. His body was slow to respond, and he continued to shake.

He wanted to close his eyes, to avoid looking at anything lest that... thing showed itself again. *What was it? And what was it doing? It could have attacked us!* And he would have been helpless to do anything about it. He couldn't kid himself—there would have been nothing he would've been able to do.

And, yet, maybe it had been toying with him?

As he tried to calm himself, he still found it difficult to move any part of his body. The sun should have been warm on his shoulders but he did not feel it. His shaky hand clumsily wiped sweat from his brow and he swallowed, still breathing heavily. He had no choice but to close his eyes and try to relax.

Once he'd closed them, he feared opening them. He concentrated on calming himself by first slowing his breathing and then by flexing his arms and legs. Eventually, he felt his limbs loosening up and his breathing slowed. He once again felt the sun shining down upon him as a slight breeze drifted past his face. He could smell the grass in the air.

With his hand firmly gripping his sword hilt he quickly opened his eyes, ready to draw his blade. He searched the area around him, looking for any sign of the ghostly figure, but found nothing. He was left with many questions and a still-lingering terror.

In fact, it appeared that *every day* left him with more and more questions. And it wasn't just that some of them remained unanswered, but that *all* of them did. Every day threw out new challenges, new elements of Cor'il's very existence that either contradicted what he had been told or just flat out presented unbelievable circumstances.

"Brandt, sir!" he shouted.

"What'cha need, son?"

"Have you heard of any strange beasts or creatures roaming the Realm?" He scooted closer to the edge of the wagon so he had to shout less. He didn't like the thought of excessive noise attracting unwanted attention.

"What do you mean?"

"Well," he stammered. How was he to describe what he'd seen—what he'd fought back in the forest? "Creatures... things I've never seen before."

"Like a bear or something? We've got some pretty big bears around. One of my friends nearly had his entire house destroyed by—"

"No, no," he interrupted. "Not at all like a bear. They... they were brutish, savage creatures. There was a larger one who appeared to be leading the smaller ones, who seemed less intelligent. They had what looked like... small tusks? Or, well, really big fangs."

Brandt belly laughed. It shook the whole wagon and received the dog's attention.

"No, I've not seen anything like that before. Nor have I heard of anyone else encountering anything like it. What you've described sounds like orcs or goblins. Or both. And, as you well know, those are children's stories. My mother told them to me when I was young! Have you not heard those stories?"

"What about... no, never mind."

"What about what?"

"Well, I know it's silly. But I saw something else—something I can't explain. It was skeletal but shrouded in a black, wispy cloak. It floated and I don't think it had—"

The wagon stopped abruptly, shoving Cor'il's shoulder into the front slats of the wagon. Brandt turned to look at Cor'il, concern on his face.

"Son," he said. "It's best you don't go joking about things like that."

"Sir, I am not joking. I saw it."

"Ancient tales tell of creatures called 'skeletal fiends' but, unlike stories of orcs or goblins coming to scare miscreant children, the skeletal fiends were said to appear to those individuals who were going to die. They are an omen, and a bad one at that. These are not just stories."

Cor'il was speechless. *Is that really what he saw? Could this somehow be true?* There was no mistaking how real it was. Dreams were one thing but he was very much awake when that... fiend appeared.

"But, honestly, I wouldn't worry about it. You were most likely just having a bad dream. Orcs and skeletal fiends are just myths—lore. In the 45 winters I have lived to see, I've not once encountered anything like that, nor have I heard of anyone else who has. Besides, ol' Ranger here would've barked up a storm if anything like that had come close." He looked back to the dog who had resumed licking itself. "He's the best guard dog this side of Elston! He may not look like much, but he is!"

The rest of the journey was spent in silence with Cor'il constantly casting glances to all sides. His mind raced the entire time. He repeated the events in his head, trying to make sense of them. Every time he thought of the creature Brandt had called a "fiend," his body shivered. He was dreading sleep tonight for fear of nightmares. *Or maybe I should be worried what might happen while I sleep. Nightmares may be the least of my concern at this point. I'll need a safe place to bed down just in case.*

"Well, this is where we part ways, son." Cor'il looked around, snapped out of his paranoid trance by Brandt's voice. The wagon had stopped off the road near a small building labeled "The Crossroads." He inspected everything he could see, looking for possible danger. "I'll be headin' on south from here. Elston is down that road to the north." Brandt pointed to his right.

This was indeed a crossroads. The four-way intersection was lined with buildings—merchants, houses, and what appeared to be a few of what he suspected were, as Outlanders called them, "brothels." It wasn't a big town—if it was even a town at all—but more of a pocket of existence in the middle of nowhere.

"Thank you, Brandt." Cor'il hopped out of the wagon and walked up to where Brandt sat behind the two horses. "If we meet again, and you need a favor, do not hesitate to ask. I thank you for your kindness."

"Think nothing of it. I enjoyed the company." Brandt was, of course, still talking rather loudly. Cor'il grinned as he shook hands with the man and they parted ways, leaving him to go it alone once again for the rest of his journey. The wagon pulled away and turned left. It crested a hill and, in short order, was out of sight.

The sun was hanging low in the sky and casting long shadows on the ground. The traffic through here was not a steady stream, but it was more people on the road than Cor'il had seen in quite a while. Merchants were milling about, mostly selling things to travelers or, at least, *trying* to. From the looks of it, not many people actually stayed to rest here. Most just came in, got supplies, and continued down the road.

In the 15 minutes Cor'il spent wandering the area, buying supplies, he found this to be true. The building labeled "The Crossroads" was an inn, but it was not very full. In fact, when he'd gone in to take a look, he couldn't find the innkeeper at all, but the taproom had been about half full of patrons. For some reason, he felt uneasy at the prospect of spending the night there, so he decided to move on.

As he left, traveling north, he was passed by several other travelers on horseback. Some were pulling carts but most were not. They seemed friendly enough but none offered him a ride. And Cor'il was too shy to ask for one, so he resigned himself to walking. But, after several travelers got into a heated argument that almost led to a fight, Cor'il decided it was a better idea to maybe not follow the road so closely. At some point, just before sunset, he found a barely visible path that led off the road and toward what looked like an abandoned farm.

And, hopefully, that will be my shelter for the night. Also, hopefully, it would be a peaceful night, for the day had brought only fear and apprehension.

Chapter 9

Kendra's journey out of Elston had been slow—much slower than she was comfortable with. She'd only been on the road for a few days. Merely getting out of the city had been a hassle and had taken several days. Not only was Raynar actively looking for her—and he had more goons than she had originally thought—but the city guard had been alerted to her presence. That was also probably Raynar's doing. It had taken her three times longer to get out and she hadn't been able to leave through the city gates. Fortunately, she still remembered that there were *other* ways in and out of the city. Most of them weren't pleasant. Thankfully, it hadn't taken Kendra long to get most of the dirt off of her.

And now that she was out of the city, traveling became easier but still not carefree. While she had still been within a decent proximity to Elston, she made sure to keep a low profile in case Raynar was really *that* determined to come after her. Either his hired men were really bad or they weren't searching very thoroughly because she had not once been stopped by anyone. And now that she was several days out from the city she could relax her vigilance a bit. Surely nobody would carry a grudge this far.

Still, the journey would be far nicer with a horse. But stealing a mount was a bit more complicated than she cared for and, the one time she'd had a horse, she had been forced to flee from trouble too quickly and had been forced to leave it behind. Plus, they required food, somewhere to rest, and attention every so often. Who had time for that? She was not in the business of looking after any kind of companion. *They only get in the way and slow me down. Well, there's that and all the horse dung. I could do without the smell.*

Of course walking wasn't a whole lot of fun, either. She had turned down numerous offers from various travelers. Many of them looked like lascivious men who merely wanted to steal a grope, or worse. Some of them seemed to be honest individuals but it didn't matter—Kendra didn't trust any of them. They could've been King Alzine for all she cared. She still wouldn't have trusted them. The last thing she needed was to willingly walk into a trap. She'd worked too long and hard to let herself fall for that… again. She shuddered every time she thought about that. But she was much cleverer now.

She hadn't been to Sulbar in a long time. Elston had been so good to her that she'd had no reason to leave. She was sure things would cool down in a few months and she would be able to return safely and pick up where she'd left off. The brief thought of eliminating Raynar crossed her mind, but she dismissed it. She, once again, reminded herself that she was neither a warrior nor an assassin. In fact, it was mildly entertaining having him around. Sometimes, he even made things *easier* for her!

"Hey little lady," a rough voice said. Kendra looked up to see a man on horseback. He was clean-shaven and looked to be about 104 years old. She felt sorry for the poor horse, having to carry this man's weight which was considerable.

"Why yes, dear sir?" She saw no harm in pretending to be friendly. She'd heard and *smelled* him approaching for several minutes but had been optimistic that he would not pay her any attention.

"Anything I can help ya with? Do ya need a ride somewhere?"

"Why, no sir. I am doing just fine, thank you."

The man moved his horse closer to her. Though he tried to hide it, she could obviously see him breathe in deeply to smell her. She also saw into one of his saddlebags.

"You sure? I can be a nice, warm traveling companion! I've even got some prime quality ale and wine here with me." He was missing teeth and his breath was atrocious. Kendra fought back the urge to gag and decided to breathe out of her mouth for the remainder of this conversation. He moved to run a finger through her hair but awkwardly missed.

Before he could try again, she had grabbed his finger and twisted it, feeling it snap in her grasp. She scowled at the man, still holding onto his finger, as he yelped in pain like a five-year-old.

"You're fortunate your finger is the only thing I broke. Now I suggest you move your fat ass on down the road before I decide to break something else." She let go of his finger. He immediately grabbed it with his other hand, wincing and fighting back tears. Quickly, he urged his horse onward in a hurry. She expected him to yell back and insult her but, surprisingly, he didn't. He was probably mumbling them to himself quietly, too afraid to antagonize her further.

It was refreshing. She had been called all kinds of names by all kinds of people. Sometimes, she believed them. Other times, she probably deserved them. She almost felt guilty breaking the man's finger. She *might* feel guilty about having pilfered one of his bottles of "prime quality ale." However, looking at the bottle, the label showed a picture of an elephant. *Elephant Tusk Ale*, she thought. *Just a couple steps above elephant piss.* But it would suffice. She normally wasn't picky. Besides, the price was right.

The sun was sinking low on the horizon and, as always, Kendra did not want to make a camp anywhere near the road. Even if Raynar's men weren't looking for her, any number of things could happen. However, there were no trees or rocks around to help conceal her. She waited until she crested a hill and got a better view, at which point she instantly spied a decaying barn of some kind in the distance.

That looks absolutely perfect, she thought. *It looks like nobody has used it for years. Easily-defended, too, just in case.* She looked up in the sky. It would be getting dark in an hour or two. She did not need to look at the watch in her satchel to tell her that. She grinned and set out toward the barn.

• • •

The sun was casting long shadows by the time Kendra reached the dilapidated building. There were many spots where boards had fallen off the side. The ceiling was caving in at one of the corners and there were no doors at all. This particular structure was looking less appealing by the second. The stalls were still mostly intact but the loft was in shambles. She already missed the "extravagant" barns from around Elston.

I must be a barn expert, she mused. *No, this barn won't do. It's much too drab. Mayhaps some shutters for the windows... what? You say that's not a window? It's a hole in the wall? Tsk tsk. That just won't do! I'll hang a painting over it!* She laughed. It was better than nothing, she had to admit—but not by much. *Sure, it'll protect me if it rains—if it doesn't collapse from a few drops of water.*

After inspecting all of the stalls, she cleaned some debris and rat droppings out of the stall that looked the nicest and put her satchel down for a pillow. But, first, she wanted to look around and hopefully find dinner. There were obviously rodents around, but that was the least palatable option. She'd been down that path before and only considered it as a last resort. Rat was stringy and greasy. Mayhaps she could find some berries or nuts in the trees outside.

She stepped out into the waning light and entered the woods nearby. Hopefully, if things went her way, she could catch a rabbit or a squirrel. She had brought some food with her but she preferred a nice, cooked meal to dried beef. The crickets were just starting to sing their nightly songs and she could hear water running from somewhere up ahead.

It was dark underneath the leafy canopy—to be expected, for sure. None of the sun's waning rays penetrated to the forest floor. Kendra saw a creek running through a small dell up ahead and descended the hill. Where there was water, there was usually game. She was no nature expert but she had spent enough time hiding out in various areas that she figured some things out after trial and error. Only fools saw mistakes as a bad thing—mistakes were experience, no matter how good or bad.

As she approached the creek she slowed down, moving more quietly so as not to scare off any wildlife. She could feel a chill in the air as she stepped closer to the water. She slowed her pace down considerably as she squinted through the increasing darkness. The crickets got much quieter down by the water which made her very conscious of her the sound of her own footsteps. The leaves and underbrush were making it very difficult to walk quietly.

When she finally reached the creek, it was much chillier than when she had first entered the woods. She took a deep drink of the creek's refreshing, chilly water. At this point, she could now barely see her hand in front of her face. If there were any animals around they would be nearly impossible to find, let alone kill.

She heard a rustling noise off to her left and immediately headed that way, her hands reaching out to the trees to both guide her and keep her balance. The sun must have set by now and had left this place cold and dark. Hopefully she would be able to find her way back to the barn. She would still need to build a fire and cook whatever it was she was about to kill.

The rustling was followed by a snort. *Ah, a wild pig*, she thought. *I could live off one of those for days.* Her mouth watered at the thought. *Hopefully I can get the thing up the hill once I've killed it.* She heard it again. It must be rooting around the forest floor for food. It sounded closer now and didn't seem to either hear her approach or care. If it was big enough, however, it would probably be too dangerous for her to handle.

She drew a dagger in her right hand and held it steady at her side. She might only get one shot at this and would probably be almost upon the beast before she could even see it. She despised moving slowly. She grew impatient quickly but was methodical enough to not make stupid mistakes. She had once been told that she could probably sneak up on someone staring right at her. Maybe she would get the chance to try that out and see if it was really possible.

Two grunts now—one ahead of her, the other to her right. This could be easier than she thought. She continued toward the sounds ahead, still making more noise than she was comfortable with. The one in front of her was very close. She could hear it sniffing around and saw a dark shape just in front of her.

She stabbed into the darkness, her dagger solidly connecting with the animal. It did not squeal. It did not cry.

It yelled.

She stabbed again but, this time, found nothing. Without warning, something leapt from the darkness, knocking her to the forest floor and sending her weapon skittering off into the blackness. It jumped on top of her, banging her head into the ground, and began to wildly claw at her. She screamed as a clawed hand ripped into her left arm.

Kendra's vision blurred as she struggled against her attacker. It landed several blows but she managed to kick it off of her and drew a blade in her left hand.

The second, shadowy figure emerged. They were short, squat creatures that were shaped like humans but with oversized jaws full of sharp teeth. Their eyes seemed to almost glow red in the darkness. The world spun as Kendra backed up into a tree, trying to catch her breath as she clutched her left arm. *There is no way I can win this fight. Though I'm not sure I can escape, either.* She did not often get worried but right now, she was *very* worried. She continued backing away up the hill, shooting occasional glances behind her but otherwise keeping her assailants in view at all times.

Her left arm was bleeding pretty badly. She could feel the warmth of blood on her right hand as she clutched her wound. The pain was beginning to make it difficult to think her way out of this. Both creatures were mostly shrouded in darkness only a few feet away. She could hear their footsteps and their guttural noises in front of her, and their dark shapes continued to slowly follow her up the hill. Her head was spinning and it took all of her concentration to focus and stay upright while slowly backing up the hill.

She was able to make it halfway up the hill before she heard what sounded like a body hitting the ground. *I must have injured the one pretty badly. I may just make it out of here. Too bad I am not simply running from Raynar. But what* are *these things?* Certainly, were it Raynar, it wouldn't be difficult to escape, even with the condition she was in. But these... things... they were savage and brutal. Kendra's legs were shaking a little. She knew that she had to get to safety quickly.

In the darkness, she heard something scurrying away from her, followed by silence. She continued backing away and was almost at the top of the hill when the creature cried out. It sounded almost like agony and sadness. Then it yelled out in what almost sounded like some kind of language. *Shit. I must've killed its friend*, she thought. Kendra tried to move faster but her legs fought her at every step. They were failing. She almost fell twice before she finally exited the tree line, when she eventually *did* fall.

Crawling on hands and knees, she scurried out of the trees toward the barn. The sky above was aglow with the vibrant colors of the sunset and the last remaining rays. Nausea swept over her as she climbed to her shaky feet, staggering forward. Keeping her balance was the only thing she could focus on. She was about 20 feet from the blur that was the barn when she was knocked to the ground by the remaining creature.

She screamed and hit the ground hard, knocking the wind out of her. The beast was on her instantly, thrashing wildly and yelling with primal rage. Its claws tore at her; its fists pummeled her. Though she tried to fight back with the dagger in her hand, her blows did nothing. Darkness quickly overtook her as she desperately struggled. Just before she slipped into unconsciousness, she felt no fear. She was angry—disgusted with her reckless actions.

Chapter 10

Dalinil exited the forest about an hour before the sun rose in the East. Unfortunately, since the day he'd fled Ten Kings, his nights were filled with fitful sleep and terrible dreams. He woke up at least half a dozen times each night, sure that there would be a tracker or assassin standing over him. And his encounter with those brutish creatures yesterday didn't help the situation. He was even more cautious now than before.

He needed somewhere he could disappear. Mayhaps somewhere where he would be forgotten or assumed dead. He would've liked to believe that would work. *I would be fooling myself if I thought they would give up. You don't just kill a Lord in Ten Kings and get away with it when they know who you are. The best you can do is live out your life in hiding or die trying.*

He could easily make a new life for himself. He could grow a beard, create a new name, and move somewhere else—Dejarnaya mayhaps. That was pretty far south. He thought about leaving Cygil altogether. There were other Realms out there. He'd heard that the city of Alarantha was nice. *That's in Sorloth, I think—no, it's in Darovinia, isn't it? If it's a large city, and far enough away, that might suffice.* Or mayhaps he could pay for passage on a ship to another land entirely—across the Vast Sea. *How far are they going to go to hunt me down?*

The truth of the matter was that he wasn't even sure if anyone *was* tracking him. He was operating off hearsay and rumors he had heard when similar situations had happened to others in the past. So he simply assumed he was being hunted. It was better to be too cautious than not at all. He had been absolutely sure at the outset but, sometimes, he doubted whether anyone was actually looking for him. No matter how much doubt entered his mind, he would have to be sure not to let down his guard. *Always assume the worst. Then you'll be prepared if it happens, and pleasantly surprised if it doesn't.*

Currently, to the best of his knowledge, he was headed south. He wasn't following any of the roads—that would be foolish. The terrain so far had been fairly easily traversable, with mostly hills and plains. But if what he'd heard was true, traveling off the roads got more difficult to the east. If he was to flee to Sorloth he would need to eventually follow a road. Or so he was told. *By The Abyss, I have no idea. I will just keep heading south until... until I don't. Scorovia is to the south. Mayhaps I'll go there.*

The sun reached out over the horizon as he walked. He had always lived his life within the confines of a city and had never really observed anything about nature. The open sky was something he had never noticed—fantastic, vibrant blue everywhere he looked. And the birds sang wonderfully. It was a much welcome change from the noise of people all day with their horses, carts, and even the clanking metal of his hammer and anvil. If he stopped and concentrated, he could focus on just how quiet it was out here amongst the trees and hills. He found that he quite liked it. Nothing could replace life in a bustling city full of activity and promise; this was true. But it certainly was a pleasant change to be out in the wilderness. An even better change would be if there weren't people who wanted to kill him.

Every time he found something pleasant, his mind returned to the one thing that drove him—staying alive. He couldn't get his mind off of it. If truth were told, he wasn't sorry for Lord Emory's death—not one bit. The man was an oppressive, abusive, insufferable ass and that was a well-known fact to every person in the city. Death was final, however, and it was sad that it had happened.

Along the way, Dalinil passed several farms around which he skirted, hoping not to be seen. He kept his eyes open for any abandoned buildings that could serve as a place to stay for the night or, if remote enough, a home. To his disappointment, he was not finding anything suitable. *It's impossible to find something when you've no vision of what you're looking for. It was much easier, waking up in Ten Kings every morning, knowing what I had to do each day.*

Even more troubling was the fact that he couldn't trust anyone or, at least, he didn't know *who* to trust. For the right amount of coin, just about anyone would change their stance on anything. Dalinil had been on both ends of these situations and was as guilty as the next individual. It had usually been very easy to persuade him to finish someone's order ahead of someone else just by promising a little something extra for the work. For quite a while, Dalinil saw no problem with this. His pockets filled faster and everyone still got what they wanted. Some customers simply got theirs a little later.

But, after a while, those same customers became more demanding and simply *expected* Dalinil to bend over backwards for them regardless. The first time he refused, he got an earful from the man who just *needed* a sword by next week. And this customer threatened Dalinil with his life if he didn't meet his wishes.

    Needless to say, that man was thrown out of the shop and told never to come back. That was the moment Dalinil began to question certain things. That had been a tough pill to swallow and he never forgot it.

    He heard a scream come from somewhere to his right. It was faint and distant but Dalinil heard it clearly. Immediately after, he heard another yell or two and the sounds of weapons. *That's coming from the road*, he thought. He instinctively grabbed his axe from its belt loop and ran in the direction of the commotion. Soon, there were several crashing sounds followed by more yells.

    He stopped. *What if it's Lord Emory's men? Or, if not, what if I help and the people involved later encounter Lord Emory's men?* He resumed his direction, walking now, trying to puzzle it all out. The urge to help was strong but the urge to save his own skin was just as strong. *Maybe I am too suspicious. Lord Emory's men can't be everywhere at once. And even if they get some information on me, I will be far from here by the time they pick up a trail. Piss on it.*

    He quickened his pace, lumbering through the tall field grass and dodging rocky ground. He could still hear the sounds of combat but there was something else—a sound that he was sure he hadn't heard before. At first, he thought it might be more of those green beastly things from back in the forest but this sounded… different. These noises were louder, fuller, and more savage.

    As he topped a small hill, Dalinil gazed down a grassy slope that led to the road below. *What in The Abyss is that? It's most certainly not what I fought back in the forest!* His left hand instinctively clenched tighter around his axe. And he stared in wonder at the scene before him, unsure of what to do. Fear washed over him as he paused a moment.

    On the road below, three men battled a very large creature. Long, stringy hair hung off its head and stuck to its scabrous, green skin. It swung a club wildly at the group and howled angrily, standing over two dead horses and an overturned, shattered carriage. The road itself was lined with a few trees but the men had no real cover to hide behind.

    Dalinil started to descend the hill but then hesitated again. Fear kept him glued to the spot even though he felt an overwhelming urge to help. These were certainly not Lord Emory's men and, even if they could not be trusted, they still needed help. But that monster was *huge*! *How do you fight something like that? Swords are like needles to it!*

Indeed, the men down there did not seem to be faring well against the brute. It swung wildly with the club in one hand and threw large rocks with its other hand. He couldn't believe what he was seeing! It had to be over eight feet tall, and its legs were as thick as tree trunks. It was then that he realized it wasn't holding a club. It was holding an uprooted tree!

One of the men cried out as he was crushed by the monster's weapon, now covered with gore as the creature pulled back and swung again. It missed its targets this time. The two remaining men screamed as they stabbed at it with their swords, poking it in the legs. From here, Dalinil could not see if they were actually wounding it, but he doubted it. They were mercilessly hacking away at it but the creature didn't seem to notice. Dalinil once again felt the urge to charge down the hill and help them, but he still couldn't bring himself to do it. Instead he simply watched from the hill.

It may have originally been fear, and that might still have had something to do with it. More than anything Dalinil realized that if three men could not bring this thing down then he wasn't going to make much of a difference in their odds. From the looks of them, they were not warriors. But neither was he. Blacksmiths made things. They weren't soldiers by trade.

He couldn't bring himself to turn away, either. The urge to help still nagged at him. He tried desperately to think of a way to help them, but his mind came up blank. *It's holding a tree! By The Abyss, a tree! How do you bring down something like that? Certainly not with an axe like mine, no matter how good quality it is!*

It was indeed a quality axe—sturdy and sharp. Dalinil had made it. It was, in fact, the first thing he had ever made for himself when he first started his smithy. But, even if he could get close enough to this thing, he didn't see any way of defeating it.

Looking around, he couldn't find anything that would help. The few trees by the road would not provide much cover. He could sift through the carriage and check for any other equipment but, if indeed there was anything to use, he figured the men would already be using it. Other than the trees, the wrecked carriage, and dead horses, there was nothing to use to his advantage. A trained soldier would probably think differently.

The rest of the fight did not take long and the creature easily overwhelmed the men. Dalinil emptied his stomach as he watched the beast grab one of them and bite into him like he was a piece of ripe fruit.

Blood sprayed into the sky as the man's body fell to the ground. The remaining victim screamed and ran but was quickly crushed underfoot by the giant.

Dalinil backed up over the hill as the creature yelled in triumph and began eating both horse and man. He wanted to cry or scream or destroy something. Instead he ran away from the road, only stopping when he was too exhausted to run anymore. He collapsed to his hands and knees, still gripping his axe in his left hand. Gasping for breath, he tried to vomit again but produced nothing.

His mind couldn't understand what he'd just seen. Growing up in Ten Kings, he was no stranger to violence and death but never before had he laid eyes upon a creature like that! Although he still had no comprehension about them, the beasts he faced in the forest were somehow easier to accept. This monstrosity, however, was completely alien to him. He wondered if anyone had fought one and lived. *I doubt if anyone else has so much as* seen *one and lived.*

He stood, his shaky legs barely supporting him, and staggered back away from the road some more. Hopefully, whatever it was would continue its meal and not go hunting for anything—anyone—else. He continued heading south. He wasn't sure he wanted to camp under any sort of shelter—the woods hadn't been very kind to him last time—but the trees at least offered him somewhere to hide. They also, however, offered other things the same comfort.

While he wanted to keep moving, Dalinil still felt sick. He needed to rest and think over everything he had just seen. More than anything, though, he wanted to feel safe so he pushed himself onward, headed for what appeared to be a clump of trees in the distance. He kept replaying the horrific scene in his mind, even though he tried to forget about it.

• • •

By the time Dalinil reached the woods, the sun had barely passed its noon point, but he was already exhausted. He dragged himself into the company of the trees and, though he simply wanted to sit down and rest, he walked further into the woods, afraid that he'd be discovered by someone… or *something*. He had almost forgotten about the fact that there still was probably at least one person tracking him! *You can't overlook something like that. Don't slip up and make stupid mistakes. Other people aren't your only enemies now—don't forget that.*

Once he had traveled further into the forest, he let his rucksack slide to the ground and dropped his axe next to it. He then slumped against a tree and closed his eyes, trying to relax. He focused on the sounds coming from the trees—mostly birds, but also some light scurrying sounds from the brush nearby— probably from squirrels or rabbits. Enough tension melted from his muscles to where he could finally breathe easy. And when he opened his eyes he could think clearly again.

He was still horrified by what he had seen, but he was calm now. He tried not to think about it. Instead, he looked around, letting the area's peaceful serenity soak into him. The city had its beauty with its buildings, streets, statues, and fountains but the woods had their own unique appeal as well. The realization struck Dalinil suddenly—how he felt safer here. Maybe it was the fact that he was more concealed or simply the fact that he was the only person around.

Something caught his eye in the distance. It almost looked like a building of some sort. From here it was difficult to tell, but something definitely was out of place. With all that he'd been through, Dalinil was hesitant to simply get up and go exploring but, eventually, his curiosity got the better of him. After standing up and dusting off, he put his axe back on his belt and cautiously walked further into the woods. His gaze darted all around him, looking carefully for any danger. He stopped several times to listen when he'd thought he heard something, but when no danger emerged, he carefully continued.

As he approached, he could see what was definitely some kind of building. Further scrutiny revealed it to be much different than anything he was used to. The buildings to which he was accustomed were made from brick, stone, and wood. This was made of wood but it appeared that it was shaped from the tree itself. It also sat at least 10 feet off the ground at its lowest point and stretched upward. He marveled at not only its beauty, but at the way it was... sculpted? Grown?

The tree seemingly grew through the center of the structure or mayhaps it simply widened to form the building? Further scrutiny revealed what looked like a window. *Is this a house of some kind? How was it created? I need to get up there and get a closer look.* Not only was Dalinil burning with curiosity but he also suspected that this would be a safe place to rest.

But there was no way that Dalinil could find to reach it. He looked around for a ladder, rope, or stairs but came up empty. Climbing the tree was out of the question—it was a very wide trunk with no low-lying branches. There were other trees he could climb, but none of the branches reached close enough. In fact, all of the branches looked as if they *avoided* this structure altogether. Most branches grew nowhere near it and, those that did, grew at strange angles so as to miss it.

"Hello!" he called. "Does anyone live in there?" There was no answer except for the normal sounds of the animals around him. He knew that he shouldn't be calling attention to himself by yelling, but he felt reasonably safe in the middle of a forest.

Filled with bewilderment, he walked deeper into the woods and was soon greeted with the sight of more strange but beautiful structures. Some were larger than others but they were all similarly inaccessible, perched in the trees. He noticed a large, thick branch that grew from one tree and *into* another! It was as if both trees *shared* the branch! *How can this be? What strange magical place is this? There must be at least 50 of these!*

Each tree-building was shaped differently. Some were taller than others. The taller ones looked like they might be two floors. He thought he saw chimneys protruding from several roofs, and most of them had leafy branches sprouting from their very walls.

Once again, he was unable to reach any of them so he continued to look for ways to climb. He yelled out again but, as before, there was no reply. Oddly enough, Dalinil could easily see himself hiding out in one for however long he had to. In fact, he thought he might actually like to *live* in one. He'd have an entire city in the trees to himself!

He wasn't sure he had the time to linger here if anyone was indeed pursuing him, but he found it difficult to ignore his curiosity. Brimming with wonder and frustration, he grabbed his axe and swung at one of the mighty trees. But his axe found no purchase within the plant. It bounced off of the trunk and violently flew from his hand. He inspected the spot where he had connected and could not find anything but a slight blemish.

Steelwood trees, he thought. *This place is truly unique. If someone or something made these buildings out of steelwood, then they were very gifted in arts that I cannot even begin to understand.*

Dalinil had only seen steelwood twice. He had tried to work both pieces and create weapons from them but was thwarted at every attempt. He had never seen an actual steelwood tree before, though. The trees themselves were impressive enough but, assuming the buildings were made from steelwood as well, that feat was unfathomable to him. He was now more determined than ever to see these up close.

Chapter 11

The rising sun flooded through the window as Gavin Forstal sat up in bed and stretched. He scratched his head and tried to focus his sleepy eyes. Today was going to be a busy day. From the looks of it, his wife Felina was already up and moving. She normally didn't let him sleep in. There were always chores needing to be done, but today was the day they would hopefully finish up the final alterations on King Alzine's and Queen Elania's attire for the Storm's End festival. They had been working on the garments for over a year and had gone through several different designs and materials. Though it had been a long, laborious endeavor, Gavin was pleased by the end result.

He hoped the King and Queen would also be happy with their craftsmanship. It was unusual for something like this to be asked of a couple of relatively unknown tailors in a small hamlet. There were plenty of skilled laborers in the city proper, but Gavin had once had the good fortune of a positive encounter with the royal couple.

The King and Queen and their entourage had been traveling east back to Elston when one of the carriage's wheels nearly fell off. They had stopped in Illusk for repairs and, when the King and Queen stepped out, Gavin had noticed a tear in her highness' dress. He and Felina quickly asked for permission to fix the tear and did so with the utmost of speed and grace. Of course, he wasn't about to ask for payment from the King and Queen, nor did they offer. Mayhaps this was their way of rewarding him. He and his wife had taken great care to perform their finest work.

The Storm's End festival was near. In mere days, the month-long celebration would begin in Elston. Gavin was working on finishing up King Alzine's robes while Felina was putting the finishing touches on Queen Elania's gown. He had to admit, these were possibly the finest garments they had ever created. There were no requests for anything fancy—no jewels adorning any lapels; no fancy lace and such. But these were anything but plain.

Gavin slid out of bed, found his slippers, and walked outside, standing on the small, stone path leading from his front door to the road. He squinted in the bright sun, and took a deep breath.

The town was abuzz as usual. While Illusk had mayhaps only 100 residents, it covered a lot of area so there was plenty of room for the town to stretch out. This made for longer walks in between destinations but the heavily wooded town was serene and Gavin never minded much.

Felina was down the road a bit, talking with... Amelia Tipton? Gavin squinted. His eyes weren't what they used to be, and they were still adjusting to the bright sunlight. The morning summer air smelled sweet and robust, with just a hint of humidity mixed in. Gavin was thinking about heading to Ben Lack's farm to get some fresh milk when he nearly lost his balance. He caught himself before falling forward onto the path but stood cautiously, resting a hand against the house. It took him a moment to realize that the ground was trembling.

He grabbed onto one of the wooden supports holding the awning above his head but, even then, it was a struggle. He looked out at the town and saw everyone else had either fallen down or was staggering, fighting to stay upright. The ground shook for a few more seconds and, then, all was calm again.

Fear raced through Gavin as his thoughts turned to his wife. He immediately caught sight of her as she came running back to the house, frightened.

"Did you feel that, dear?" she asked, grabbing him and holding him tightly. Her Scorovian accent was still thick even after all of these years—one of the many things he loved about her. Sometimes he feigned confusion and asked her to repeat herself just to tease her.

"I did. It felt like tremors or a quake. It looks as though everyone is okay, though."

"We've never had a quake here." She was concerned. Gavin could see it in her face.

"It's probably nothing," he reassured her. "It looks like our house is fine and we're both unharmed. It will pass."

"I hope you're right."

"Would you like me to fetch some milk?"

Before Felina could reply, the ground shook again—this time, more violently than before. Dust floated down from the awning and the house groaned. They both stumbled, holding each other and using the house as support. Fifteen seconds later, the shaking finally stopped. Gavin and Felina clung tightly to each other, even after it was over.

"This is not normal," he mumbled. Looking around, this time he could see minor damage to some buildings and several people were on the ground.

"You're right," Felina whispered. "It's not. What's going on?"

"I wish I knew."

The house creaked once more and the front window shattered as the ground shook again—more violently this time. They covered their faces and fell to the ground. They heard screams mixed with bending metal and splintering wood.

Gavin got to his feet and clumsily dragged Felina into the yard while she struggled to get up. He again fell to the ground, covering Felina with his body. Immediately thereafter, he heard their house collapse behind them. The ground continued to shake for what seemed like minutes as they both lay in the grass. His heart sank as he looked back at the remains of their home, which had mostly collapsed.

When the ground finally stopped shaking, they both looked up to see the horror it had caused. Not one house or shop stood. People—friends—lay everywhere—wounded, unconscious or, possibly worse. Gavin had a lump in his throat as he took in everything around him. He couldn't believe it.

The ground shook again but, this time, it was different. It wasn't so much *shaking* as it was… moving. He and Felina clutched each other, watching helplessly.

More people screamed from down the street and around the corner as the ground itself split open, tearing the town asunder! Felina cried and Gavin swore under his breath, absolutely unable to do anything. What was now rubble was swallowed by the ground as more cracks opened, making terrible sounds that Gavin had never heard before. People began to fall into fissures that appeared beneath them, their screams quickly being silenced as they disappeared.

"This is horrible!" Gavin sobbed. He closed his eyes and bowed his head, hoping they would be safe. "Why is this happening?" Felina cried by his side, shaking uncontrollably. And, then it was over, and there was nothing but silence. No birds chirped, no children played and the ground was still. It was as if all of the life had been sucked from the town.

Gavin could barely bring himself to gaze upon the ruined town through blurry, tear-filled eyes. Felina was still quietly sobbing, her face buried in her hands.

There was nothing left of Illusk. Every building was either leveled or had been swallowed by the ground itself. Trees had fallen—some of the large, older trees had been snapped like twigs. No one moved.

"I think it's over, Felina," he whispered, tears streaming down his cheeks. "I think we're safe." He gently ran a hand through her hair and whispered. "It's over," he repeated.

And it was at that moment that the sky rained fire.

Chapter 12

Kendra's head pounded with not only a massive headache but what could only have been a bruise. Her left arm also throbbed and stung. As she opened her eyes, the first thing she recalled was the events that had caused these wounds. She tried to move and was rewarded with pain for her efforts. Her vision was distorted—probably from the blows to her head—but she could see something, or someone, hovering over her and she immediately panicked.

It made noises that sounded vaguely like someone speaking but she couldn't understand any of what it said. She tried to speak—she wanted to yell threats and profanities—but, instead, her words slurred and sounded like muffled gibberish to her. Her heavy eyelids closed and she slipped back into the darkness.

When she next opened her eyes, her vision had cleared a bit. She looked up at the ceiling and recognized the rickety barn. The dark rafters flickered with the light of a crackling fire that emanated heat from her right. Her eyes darted around the room but she could see nothing else. She was afraid to move and give away the fact that she was awake.

Everything still hurt, but not as much as before. Kendra couldn't be sure of anything without moving but, until she knew who was in the barn with her, she wasn't about to give away anything. But she couldn't see much, either. *I can't even check to see what equipment I've got on me.* If the individual in the barn with her meant her harm, they had her right where they wanted her. Kendra could do nothing without giving herself away.

"Oh," a man's voice said. "I see you're awake." Whoever it was, he was trying to be quiet. He did not sound menacing. In fact, his voice sounded rather meek.

"Yes," she groaned, sitting up slowly. Running her hands through her hair, she took a deep breath and looked around. The man she had expected to see in the room was actually a boy—thin and spindly with brown hair down to his jaw. She herself was probably barely older. His tunic and breeches were simple, brown attire. He was sitting on a rotting bale of hay, reading a book which he now closed and slipped into a satchel underneath a black cloak next to him. A sword lay nearby.

"Careful," he said in a quiet voice, leaning forward with his elbows on his knees. "There is no need to hurry. There is no immediate danger, so you should rest."

She looked at her shoulder which now had a piece of cloth from her dress wrapped around it. Her clothes were torn and bloody in spots. She adjusted and tried to cover up as best she could, even though there was nothing scandalous to see. Besides, this... boy... didn't really seem to be the peeping kind.

Modesty quickly gave way to severe irritation when she remembered her failure. She was very happy to be alive—that much was true—but she had been saved by a mere *boy*. While she was grateful, she was also ashamed of herself.

"I'm fine," Kendra replied, starting to get up. Her legs shook and she leaned against one of the stalls to steady herself. "Maybe I'm not as fine as I thought," she said as she sat down by the small fire. Irritation turned to anger. It had become very apparent to her that she still needed help.

"So," she continued, keeping her gaze at the ground. "I guess I need to thank you for helping me out with... whatever that thing was." She pinned her hair behind her ears nervously. It wasn't in her nature to be in this position. It felt... foreign. She had been stupid and reckless—possibly allowing herself to be drawn into a trap. *How could I have been so careless?*

"Oh," he replied, sounding surprised. "You're welcome. But, uh, I didn't really save you from anything."

"What do you mean?"

"It was already dead. I found *this* stuck in its throat." He produced one of her daggers and handed it to her. She quickly snatched it out of his hand and turned it over a few times in front of her. "The beast was lying on top of you. I moved you into here and bandaged your arm. You looked hurt pretty badly and I was worried."

She slid the dagger back into the sleeve of her blue dress. Her shoulder stung in the process.

"Oh, well... thank you for helping me, then." She felt both relieved and a little awkward. She finally made eye contact with him. "I really appreciate it. My name is Kendra, by the way."

"I am Cor'il... by the way." He smiled. It was an innocent smile—pleasant and harmless. Her keen eye focused in on the side of his head—one of his ears. It appeared somehow misshapen—longer, mayhaps. She quickly turned her eyes toward other things.

"It's... it's nice to meet you, Cor'il." Kendra got up slowly—her legs were slightly more stable now—and carefully walked over to the body outside. It lay face down in the dirt about 20 feet from the barn doors, right where she had fallen. With significant effort, she rolled it over with her boot. It was covered with its own blood and caked with dirt, its face frozen in a twisted scowl.

"What *were* you?" she whispered, staring into its empty, motionless eyes. "Certainly not an animal," she continued.

"I was going to ask the same thing." The boy was behind her. She hadn't heard him approach. He stood a good hand taller than she—somewhere over six feet, and he was lanky.

"I killed its friend in there," she pointed into the woods. "But this second one," she kicked the corpse again but this time, much harder, "got the jump on me. I've never seen anything like them." She turned to face Cor'il. "You always hear the tales of goblins stealing children in the night or, when you can't find something in the house, 'the goblins took it!' As daft as it sounds, I would dare to call these... *goblins*."

"I've thought about it a lot—"

"You've seen them? Before now?"

"Yes."

The fire in the barn cast very long, flickering shadows this far outside. It was probably a couple of hours short of midnight. *I wasn't out of it for very long. And if there are more of these... goblins... nearby, we should not stay here long.*

"I encountered several of them a while ago," he continued. "They were led by a larger creature. Something I can only liken to an—"

"An orc?" Kendra laughed. But it wasn't really funny. The notion was both outrageous and frightening.

"I guess. But, I mean, goblins and orcs are things out of legend—they're not real. They're not *supposed* to be real."

"I thought the same thing up until earlier when two of these 'not real' creatures attacked me." She had *almost* said "nearly killed" but she censored herself, not wanting to think about that anymore. "Just calling them goblins and orcs doesn't make it so, though, right?"

"I don't really know. But surely there are others who have encountered such beasts. *Someone* must know what these things are." Cor'il looked a little fidgety and kept staring into the trees. Kendra was going to ask him if something was wrong, but thought better of it.

Instead, she started back toward the barn. She didn't wish to stand outside where more of those monsters might be brave enough to venture out of the woods again. But she stopped and came back. After a couple of minutes of rolling it with her boot, the goblin's body disappeared back into the woods.

When they got back into the barn, she pulled up to the fire another rotting hay bale and sat upon it across from Cor'il.

"I had really been hoping that you knew what they were," he said. He was fidgeting with his fingers and staring into the fire. "I simply figured, since I had never strayed from Kuranthas, that I—"

"You're from Kuranthas?" Kendra nearly burst with excitement. She had never met a Kuranthian before. Actually, *nobody* had met a Kuranthian before! At least nobody she'd ever met had. But she had heard all sorts of crazy rumors about them. "So why don't any of you ever leave?"

"Well, I think it's because—"

"And what is it like living in Kuranthas?"

"It's not much diff—"

"And I heard that Kuranthians have all kinds of eerie abilities and powers!" She inspected the boy again. Then she remembered his left ear and withdrew, regaining her composure. "Oh my. I'm... sorry. I got a bit excited, there. That was rude of me." She could feel her face warming up and suspected it was quite red.

"I left because I was told to leave." He said solemnly, staring at the ground.

Her excitement was replaced with embarrassment and she fell silent. At this point, she didn't know what to say or how to get herself out of the hole that she had just dug.

"Well, now I feel like a real horse's ass," she said. "You helped me out and all I did for you was bring up some painful memories. I apologize."

The two of them sat in awkward silence. Kendra didn't know what to say, and she figured it would be wise to just not even say anything at all. After a few minutes, though, Cor'il looked up from the ground.

"It's okay," he said. He didn't sound particularly happy but he wasn't crying, either. "It's just something I am going to have to get used to."

Kendra almost told him that she was in much the same situation, except that she had willingly left Alarantha—her home town—many times before, coming and going as she pleased. She knew what to expect from the world outside, but Cor'il apparently didn't. She wasn't sure she could accurately compare herself to him.

"So I should thank you again for helping me. I was fortunate that you came along."

"I am sure you would have done the same for me if our situations were reversed."

Sadly, Kendra didn't believe that to be true. Most likely, she would have taken anything he had and moved on. She had learned long ago that befriending or helping strangers could get her into trouble. This just happened to be a situation where she had no choice in the matter.

"So." A subject change was most certainly in order. "Where are you headed? Or do you now live around here and simply enjoy pulling people out from under dead goblins?" Even as she cracked a small smile, she shuddered at the world "goblin."

"I am headed to Elston."

"Oh?" She perked up a bit. "What business do you have there? Oh, I'm sorry. I'm being nosy again."

"To be honest," he didn't seem to mind her question, "I'm not really sure. I have never been anywhere. It is all new to me. But I feel most at home within a forest."

"There aren't exactly any forests in Elston. You would probably have to go north to the Densewood. However, after recent events, I think I will be avoiding forests for a while—just in case. But you will probably enjoy Elston. It's large and has its share of problems, but it also has its own charm. And the Storm's End festival is coming up soon—10 days, I think."

"Where are you heading?"

"I was thinking about Sulbar."

"I passed through Sulbar. It was the first big city I encountered once I left my homeland. It seemed like a nice place."

"I have never been to Sulbar." Kendra could feel her eyelids getting heavier. She stifled a yawn and eyeballed the stall she had previously chosen for her bed, hoping her satchel was still in it. "I hear it's nice, but I don't think it's as big as Elston." *It's also a bit rougher, thick with thieves and assassins.*

"I didn't see a whole lot of it but it seemed like a pleasant city. Though, obviously, I don't have much knowledge of Outlander living areas." Cor'il also appeared to be getting sleepy. He had yawned several times in the span of only a couple of minutes.

"Outlanders?"

"We call anyone from outside Kuranthas 'Outlanders' or 'Outsiders.' It is not meant to be derogatory but we do not have any other classification. I don't think most Kuranthians know much about the rest of the Realm, despite the tales we tell."

"I suppose I should get some sleep. It's been a rough day and I am pretty tired... and sore." Kendra headed over to the stall where her satchel still lay. Normally, she would quickly rifle through it to make sure everything was there but, for some reason, she trusted this boy.

"A good idea," she heard him say. "I am going to sleep out here and keep the fire going. "Oh, wait." He appeared outside the stall and handed her his cloak. "You might want this in case it gets chilly—you know, this far from the fire." Summer nights usually stayed pretty warm but she took the cloak anyway.

"Thank you, Cor'il."

Kendra threw the cloak over her and laid her head back on her lumpy satchel. She stared at the ceiling, now wide awake for some reason. The shadows danced among the rafters, playing tricks on her eyes. Or maybe it was just her reaction to the events of the past day. No matter. The glowing eyes that she thought she saw were certainly not there. They belonged to two dead creatures lying in the woods. She felt her confidence returning.

Tomorrow she would continue toward Sulbar. Once she arrived, she could start anew in a city where she had no reputation. Mayhaps she could get in good with those like her and be set up somewhere for a while. That was assuming that she could tolerate working alongside others. The last time she had tried doing that, it hadn't worked out so well. She could maybe even get a job of some kind—if she found work that suited her, of course.

After a few minutes, she could feel herself slowly slipping into sleep. The ache in her shoulder had dulled a bit but still bothered her, and it screamed any time she tried to move. *I will take a look at it tomorrow morning. I am sure the bandages will need to be changed anyway. I'll also have to find some new clothes. I think this dress is more holes than actual cloth.*

As she began drifting off, Kendra suddenly snapped awake when she heard the whispering. She immediately had a dagger in each hand as she sat up, trying her best to ignore her shoulder. She absolutely loved feeling like this—alive and ready for action. Her entire body tingled, longing for payback against these goblin-things. The fear was there; she couldn't deny it. But, this time, she was ready. She wondered if Cor'il heard it too. Mayhaps he was asleep already.

She quietly crawled to the edge of the stall and peeked out, but she couldn't get a good view of the entire barn entrance from where she was. She leaned out to her right to get a better look, but she saw nothing.

Yet she still heard the whispering. It was sporadic and included maybe only one or two words at a time, though she didn't understand any of it. Frustrated, she crawled out to the first stall and peeked out from behind its rotting wall. Her eyes widened.

Cor'il sat on the bale of hay, hunching forward with his elbows resting on his knees. He was cupping his right hand within his left, staring at them intently. He mouthed some words quietly, making barely a sound.

A small flame burst to life *in his hand*! It danced around on his palm before flickering and dying out. Again, he whispered and the flame reproduced itself only this time, it was blue and quite a bit larger. He toyed with it briefly, using his left hand to push it around on his palm, before tossing it into the air. It landed in the waning fire on the ground, bringing it back to life.

Kendra gasped and retreated back to her stall. Hopefully he hadn't heard her! She laid down and shut her eyes, pretending to sleep just in case. Her mind was abuzz with thoughts and questions. She was still tired but now found it absolutely impossible to sleep. Between the goblins and what Cor'il had just done, Kendra had a lot to think about.

Am I so different? She shifted, cracking an eye to see if Cor'il was checking on her. Nothing but flitting shadows. *Surely this can't be a coincidence, can it? Can all Kuranthians do that? Why doesn't it burn his hand? How does he do it?* There was so much she wanted to ask him. But Kendra also knew not to push it—she had already intruded earlier this night. Besides, she had the sneaking suspicion he didn't want to talk about it. *I certainly wouldn't want to talk about it. But, then, I am not the sharing type. My business is just that—my business.*

As she slowly drifted to sleep, the whispering stopped and any noise from elsewhere in the barn ceased. In fact, it was eerily silent outside. The woods should have been teeming with animals and insects but, yet, there came nothing. All the better. It was easier to sleep without all of the racket.

● ● ●

When she awoke later that morning, it took Kendra a moment to remember where she was. Waking up in a barn was nothing unusual for her, but she didn't recall the past night's events until a few moments had passed. She sat up and sorted through her satchel, finally finding the pocket watch she was looking for.

Ah, what a find you were, my friend. She rolled it over a couple of times in her fingers, feeling the gold, cool and smooth in her hand. She pressed the button on the edge and it popped open. The face glowed with a dull, blue light and she could see that it was nearly 5 in the morning.

Watches and clocks were rare items. It was said that very few individuals possessed the knowledge to create them. Many people, confident they could recreate the wonders, had tried to take apart the devices, only to accidentally destroy them in the process. They swore up and down on a bitefly's wing that the timepieces were somehow rigged to self-destruct if tampered with. Some unfortunate individuals had supposedly perished in the ensuing explosion. Kendra didn't understand any of it, nor did she care. She had liberated this beauty from its owner quite a while ago, and she had been careful to make sure it was taken care of. There was no winding necessary, however, and she wasn't sure what powered the device. *That's probably a large reason why people try to disassemble it.*

She closed it up and slipped it back in the bag. *I think it's time I was on my way,* she thought. Life was complicated enough as it was. No sense adding to it by adding a companion.

The dying fire's embers cast an eerie glow about the room, creating bizarre shadows. Cor'il was asleep on the uncomfortable-looking hay bale as Kendra carefully crept over to him and returned his cloak, covering him with it. She quietly nodded at him before slipping out into the morning air.

Okay, Sulbar. Let's see what you've got to offer me.

Chapter 13

Arcturas stood on the small, golden dais in the center of the pentagonal-shaped speaking floor, looking out at a Council Hall that was only two-thirds full. He gazed up at the seats that rose up around him, longing to see those who were absent. *We have lost more than I had suspected. The Threadwoe takes its toll, I suppose. Yet, it is still sad to see how many have departed. This is all the more reason to do all we can, as stewards of The Great Machine, to make sure it doesn't happen again.*

His five High Councilors stood around him, behind lecterns at each corner of the pentagon. They, too, nervously looked around the room, noticing the same thing as him. The room this time was a brilliant shade of blue—a nice contrast to everyone in their white robes. The men and women who filed into the chamber were all present to hear Arcturas speak and they sat with obvious looks of apprehension and hope on their faces. He spotted Braelus in the audience. He was his usual, overly-exuberant self, unable to sit still in his chair. Everyone else appeared to be settled in, awaiting Arcturas' words.

"Welcome, friends," he began, his voice carrying perfectly throughout the room. The crowd fell to complete silence the moment he spoke. It was no different than previous times, but Arcturas found that he never quite got used to it. "I am happy to see that you are all well, and yet I am sad to see so many empty seats. Let us remember our friends and family who have been reclaimed by the Great Machine and are no longer with us."

Everyone remained in silence for a moment and bowed their heads in quiet reflection. Arcturas bowed his head with them and focused on those who were no longer connected to the Great Machine. He could not remember the names of most of the individuals who had passed—it was as if they simply had never existed. He had never understood why this was, except that they faded from memory quickly. Few were ever replaced, so every loss was momentous.

"The Machine has once again been set in motion," he resumed. Everyone in the audience nodded and mumbled to each other. *Good. They have felt it, too. That shall bring us all hope and comfort despite our losses.* "Indeed, it is wonderful. We have all awakened to find what we'd hoped we would. This is truly a day to remember—a day of significance."

The audience clapped their approval. He could almost feel their joy and was, himself, filled with confidence and happiness. His people's special connection to the Threads and, ultimately, to the Great Machine was only partially understood by Arcturas. In its presence he felt warmth, hope, happiness, and sometimes, despair. But in its absence all he felt was emptiness, grief, and loneliness. It wasn't fully understood why some of his people perished when the connection was severed but, because it had happened before, Arcturas had to believe that it was normal—sad, but normal. *But it still feels different this time. I don't think the Great Machine has ever completely stopped before, has it?*

"Yes... yes, you all feel it, don't you?" Many members of the audience nodded happily. "As do I. As do I." He turned to view another portion of his people. "We have done excellent work thus far. I am proud of you all."

There were not any new children this time around and it concerned him. *Nobody to replace those who perished when the Machine stopped. This is troubling.*

Braelus was the youngest of all of them. The Great Machine had delivered him to them after the last time it had stopped—an event that Arcturas himself barely recalled, now. It was troublesome that there were no new additions this time.

"And, I know, many of you are wondering when *he* will arrive."

As if everyone did so in unison, there was a large gasp throughout the chamber.

"Yes, *he*—a Threadweaver. A boy this time. It has been quite a while, hasn't it?" Arcturas watched as Braelus jumped out of his seat in the excitement and nearly tumbled down the stairs. But he caught himself and grinned, full of anticipation.

"Yes, he is out there. Some of you may have felt him. This is indeed encouraging news. But I would suggest caution. There is... something else."

"What do you mean?" he heard from the audience. There was concerned mumbling for a moment.

"I have felt it, too, sir." Braelus stood up. "I thought it was just me—that I was imagining things."

"Ah," Arcturas replied. "You are more in tune with the Threads than I at first suspected. This pleases me." Braelus beamed, obviously proud. "Yes, there is something beneath... something that surprises me—something I have not felt for a long, long time."

"What is it?" Braelus asked.

"Balance. I believe it is balance."

"Is balance not a good thing?" A woman stood up. Her name was Tia. She was a record-keeper and as old as Arcturas if not older.

"An astute question, Tia. Yes, balance is good in all things. But, sometimes, it comes with a price. Let us not dwell on this for too long. We have more important things to attend to. *He* will come. The pull is too strong. And, when he arrives, we will be ready to assist in whatever ways we can. It has happened before; it shall happen again. It just... appears to have taken quite a bit longer this time."

"How can you be sure?" Lod, a rather tall and spindly man, stood up. "The fact that our sleep was *much* longer this time around is worrisome. And you yourself didn't seem to expect it."

"You are correct, my friend. None of us can know everything. We never stop learning—even me. However, I know what I have said to be true. He *is* drawn to us this very moment. Every day brings him closer to us. I trust many of you have felt it. This is certainly a time to rejoice. But, first, we must prepare."

The audience clapped and soon everyone left the auditorium. Arcturas slowly walked back to his dwelling, his mind clogged with thoughts, ideas, and fears.

He was hopeful, above all else. Back when The Sleep started, he was concerned that another Threadweaver had not been provided. In the past, they had never gone more than maybe a year without one. But this drought had lasted much longer. He, and everyone else, had gone to sleep not knowing if they should ever wake—not knowing if the Great Machine would ever move again. Now, however, some of their questions had answers.

There was certainly cause for caution and fear. Just as he reveled in the new dawn, there was an unseen bit of night trying to creep in. It was the sweet smell of a rose combined with the threat of a thorn.

It bothered him. Not only were some things different this time, but there was uncertainty. With the hope of balance came the danger of even worse discord than before. This would require thought—no, more than just thought. *Mayhaps I can discover the true meaning if I look to the Threads themselves. But that will most certainly take more time than we have. Nevertheless, I must do what I can to uncover the truth.*

It was indeed a time to rejoice but it was also a time for caution.

Chapter 14

Dalinil awoke abruptly to primal sounds outside. He gazed up at the ceiling and, for a moment, could not remember where he was. But his mind quickly cleared as he looked around at the empty room and recalled the tree houses he had found. It had taken him a while, but he had finally managed to get into one of them.

More growls and strange noises from outside piqued Dalinil's curiosity. *Whatever it is, at least it's not someone looking for me. Well, unless something out there is in the process of eating a tracker. If so, good riddance.*

He got up off the floor and made his way over to one of the circular windows, resting his hands on the smooth surface. Carefully peeking over the edge to keep himself concealed, he looked out into the trees with hesitation. On the ground below, a bear was fighting something he'd never seen before. It was a grey, four-legged creature with glistening, scaly skin. It was thin—almost emaciated—with leathery wings and a slender tail that ended in a barbed, bony knot. Its head sat at the end of a long, slender neck, and it had no face! Its mouth was filled with sharp teeth but it had no eyes, nose, or anything else!

Dalinil looked away, thoroughly repulsed and feeling shaky. He had expected to see a couple of animals fighting it out. He had not expected to see such a hideous creature. He peered out the window again, shivering and sweating in fear. The bear was standing on its hind legs, snarling as the other creature lunged. The bear swatted it out of the air, knocking the creature sideways and sending it rolling on the ground.

But the attacker was undeterred. It was on its feet instantly and pounced on the bear who, being larger, deflected the creature once again. This went on a couple times more, with the bear getting the upper hand every time. It growled and roared, advancing on the enemy with confidence.

Dalinil tried to calm himself, to control his irrational fear. The creature was hideous and frightening, but he could not let his fear overtake him.

As the other creature struggled to stand, the bear charged suddenly, lumbering across the ground and snarling angrily. Dalinil thought he could feel its heavy footsteps shake the ground.

As the bear pounced, the other creature disappeared! It vanished! The bear's claws found nothing but the forest floor. Then, just as quickly as it had vanished, it reappeared behind the bear. It turned and lashed out with its tail, striking the bear in the back. The bear roared again, but this time in pain, and turned to face its enemy again.

For a while, both the bear and the other... thing... squared off, posturing and snarling, with neither creature making a move to attack. The bear seemed to be slowing down as if it might be getting tired. *Or maybe it was poisoned.* Dalinil wished that he could get a closer view of the monster. He thought he saw something dripping off of its tail but couldn't be sure from this distance. Plus, the foliage partially blocked his view.

Regardless, the bear looked to slowly be losing ground. Dalinil didn't think the fight would last a whole lot longer, and that *thing* was going to win. He was worried, since he had no idea how to escape from the monster below. A bear was one thing. *This* was quite another. *If it can vanish and reappear like that, then what's stopping it from just popping in here?* And there was only one way out of this home—one door... that had virtually disappeared when he had passed through it.

He'd tried not to worry about that fact until now. It had been relatively difficult just to get up to the house in the first place. After an exhaustive search, Dalinil had been able to find a tree that he could climb. But that tree was quite a distance from this area. He'd had to use branches to get from tree to tree, which had been no easy feat. He was shocked when he'd finally gotten back to the first of these houses—*this* house—and there had been no door.

He had run his hand across the smooth, flawless surface several times until, suddenly, he felt an odd tingle in his hand and a hidden door revealed itself, opening for him. Once it shut behind him it became, again, completely undetectable. Dalinil had spent 10 minutes searching for the edges of the door and trying to open it again but it did not yield.

Dalinil stepped away from the window as the battle continued down below. He looked around the empty room—devoid of any furniture or objects. On the wall opposite him, a staircase spiraled up to the level above. Dalinil had investigated it yesterday but found just as much nothing upstairs as he did down on this level. The staircase, however, was a work of art! It looked as though it had been created from the very wall itself, much like this house looked like it had been made from the tree. Dalinil could see no seams, no nails, and no supports for anything.

In the middle of the room, the massive tree trunk jutted up from the floor, through the ceiling to the room above, and on through the roof. There were no branches off of the trunk inside, but the structure itself had leafy branches coming from it on the outside. *Steelwood trees are incredibly difficult to chop down, so how does one go about making a building out of one? How is this possible?*

    Outside he could hear the two combatants still going at it. Part of him wanted to watch, but that faceless beast was too revolting. It also scared him more than he liked to admit. He felt as though it could still see him even behind these wooden walls—without eyes! It gave him the chills.

    For now, however, he simply needed to find his way out. If the bear could keep that thing busy for long enough, he could possibly escape undetected. But, to do that, he first had to figure out the door. Now that the sun shone light through the various windows, he could see better. However, after several moments searching the walls, he was no closer to finding the door. *Well, now, why is that not surprising? It took a lot of effort just to get in so, of course, it is just as difficult to get out! And, if that thing down there finds me, I'll have bigger worries.*

    He could no longer hear the fight below him. He crept back to the window and gazed out to see that the bear had indeed lost. It was twitching and wheezing, lying on the ground while the victor tore it open, eating it alive. Blood briefly sprayed into the air as Dalinil turned away and gagged. It was definitely time to leave.

    He looked back out the window to make sure the creature had not seen or heard him. It was preoccupied with its feast and seemed to actually be *reveling* in its kill. *Sick son of a… freaky whatever in The Abyss you are*, he whispered.

    The creature shot its gaze up at him and, without eyes, seemed to stare right at him. *There is no chance that thing is actually blind. It can see just as well as I can.* He rested his trembling hand on the axe at his side. The creature's gaze did not shift. It opened its mouth in what could only be described as a primal grin, blood dripping from its maw.

    "I see you, boy… tasty."

    "Shi—" Dalinil fell backwards onto the floor, his hands over his ears and eyes squinting shut. He had never experienced such fear until now. He could barely move.

    "There is plenty of time left for us to get acquainted."

    "No!" he shouted. He got to his feet and frantically started searching for a way out. *The Abyss, I am not going to just wait for that thing to find its way in! I need to find the way out!*

He was as successful as the last time. And with every moment that passed, he got more desperate. His heart was pounding out of his chest and he gasped for air.

"What's the rush?"

He realized that it wasn't *speaking* to him—he heard it inside his head! He slumped against the wall and slid to the floor, holding his hands over his ears and keeping his eyes shut. He tried hard to concentrate, to calm himself down. *Just get out of here. If you can get far enough away, you should be safe! But you've got to get out of here first. And you can't do that if you're sniveling like a little child! Pull yourself together!*

Dalinil took a deep breath and exhaled slowly, still sitting up against the wall with his eyes closed. He could no longer hear the creature inside his head but he knew it was still out there, eating. *Just relax. You got in here, surely you can get out... even if you have to cut your way out. Either way, you're going to escape. You have simply got to keep calm and concentrate.*

Another deep breath. Dalinil could feel his heartbeat slowing down, his confidence returning. He envisioned the forest yesterday— serene and beautiful, peaceful and calm. The birds' songs repeated themselves in his mind, combined with the sound the wind made when it whistled through the leaves. He had never experienced these things before now—before he fled Ten Kings. *This* was his calm, his escape. He felt a tingly warmth wash over him as he exhaled slowly and opened his eyes.

He was alone in his head... for now. *It's time to get out of here and away from that thing.* Upon standing, Dalinil felt renewed strength. He clenched his fists and felt the muscles in his forearms tighten. He removed his axe from its belt loop and held it ready while inspecting the wall again. Still, there were no cracks, no sign of any door. He refused to give up. He also refused to panic. Instead, he closed his eyes, laid his palm on the wall, and relaxed, keeping his mind clear and calm. This time, he envisioned a pristine field. The grass gently swayed in the warm summer breeze and lazy clouds floated overhead. He had traveled through this prairie shortly after leaving Ten Kings. He had marveled at the beauty and seclusion. And, now, the serenity permeated him through and through.

Despite the chilly goosebumps on his arms he felt warm and his fingers began to tingle slightly. He could almost smell the grass and feel the wind.

And then the wall moved.

Dalinil's eyes shot open and he watched as what he had thought to be a solid wall shifted and almost melted away into an exit—different than last night but a welcome sight nonetheless. He gasped and brought his hand back as the exit finished forming.

Quickly—before it closed again—Dalinil scurried outside into the sunlight. Surprisingly, the door did not immediately close behind him as he had feared. It's what had happened when he finally got into the house yesterday, after all. However, as he stepped further away, the door did indeed melt back into a wall as if it was never there.

Now he stood upon a large branch, looking out at a vast forest. The ground was difficult to see due to the foliage, but Dalinil knew that it was a long fall should he slip. He still felt the calm inside him—like a still pond without a ripple—as he looked around for any way down, but found nothing. In fact, down was probably not where he wanted to go. That *thing* was probably still down there. *Of course, it has wings... and blinks around. I doubt I am safe anywhere.*

He put his axe back on his belt and gingerly walked out on the limb, holding onto whatever he could for support. While he still felt calm inside, his feet were shaky and he moved very cautiously, trying to keep his balance. He slipped twice before he had gotten far. There were several other branches nearby but he was unsure how to reach them.

The branch underfoot had some spring but he wasn't sure it would support a jump without bending too much. It was already giving considerably under his weight, and he wasn't confident he could go any further. He gazed across the gap at the next branch, wishing he could just reach it. He scooted out a little further and felt himself slipping! He waved his arms and grabbed wildly but his hands found nothing to grasp.

Just as he was about to tumble, the opposite branch grew out to catch him! He stumbled onto it and, once he regained his footing, he hurried to the trunk of the next tree. Gripping it tightly, he frantically caught his breath, afraid to look around him or, worse, down. But he was also confused. He had not imagined it—he knew what he had just seen. *This forest is enchanted... or cursed. But why have I heard no tales of any of this? Ten Kings is a big city. I would've thought* someone *would have experienced this before and told a story.* No storyweaver had ever mentioned anything close to this. So why was *he* seeing weird creatures and moving trees? The branch shrank behind him, returning to normal.

He stepped to another limb and then to the next, carefully sliding out once again on the branch but, this time, it instantly extended to reach the nearest branch from the next tree. In fact, the branch he was standing on widened and seemed to flatten to make a walkway of sorts! The next branch he tested did the same thing. At first he trod with caution but, after he had moved across a few branches, he gained confidence. In fact, he quickened his pace until he was almost running from tree to tree, laughing!

While in the trees he noticed more houses, hidden amongst the trunks and the leaves. And they were *everywhere*—both above and below him. There were a few on his level but he passed them by, eager to put distance between him and the creature on the ground—wherever it was now.

This continued for probably 10 minutes or so, until Dalinil decided it was time to get his boots back on the ground where he could move faster. He found a branch beneath him and, confidently, leapt off his current branch, landing safely below. *No—it caught me, didn't it? How can this be?* That was certainly what it had felt like. He hadn't merely landed on it—the branch itself seemed to rise up to meet him!

Again, he jumped off a branch and landed safely on the one below. He awkwardly swung onto another one that extended downward, allowing him to move to another branch that grew out to meet him. He continued his descent until he hopped down onto the forest floor and kept running. He hoped he was headed south. *I will be able to tell once I get out of here. I just hope I don't run into anything else like that thing.* Between that faceless beast and the giant brute that he'd avoided on the road, traveling had become a lot more dangerous than he had ever expected.

Once he felt relatively confident that he was out of danger, he slowed his pace to a jog. The forest was still beautiful but, obviously, it held unseen dangers as well as fantastic mysteries. *I will have to explore this place more if I ever make it back here. But, I wonder, what other encounters are in my future?* Part of him was afraid to find out while another, growing part of him was becoming more and more curious and excited. One thing was clear—it didn't seem he had a choice in the matter.

As the trees thinned and eventually gave way to hillier, rocky terrain, Dalinil grinned. Elated and refreshed, he traveled cautiously, but with a newfound confidence. He'd faced massive danger twice in as many days and once even before that. While it was terrifying, there was something else there—something... exhilarating. Maybe it was the prospect of battle more than actual combat itself. After all, he'd fled from the last two situations. But killing those beasts back by the pond in the woods had apparently awakened something inside him. It was something primal. Did he crave battle? Or was it just danger? He felt the conflict inside him but couldn't figure it out.

He exited the forest and confirmed, based on the sun in the sky, that he was indeed still headed south. The trees were thin but he stuck close to them, using everything he could to hide himself from view. It wouldn't be long before he would need to start looking for somewhere safe to bed down for the night.

Chapter 15

Cor'il awoke to not only the sound of rain on the battered barn roof but also to the dripping water pooling on the ground under the various holes in the shelter. He lay on the ground next to the remains of the small fire, somehow avoiding all of the leaks. It was a rather chilly, humid summer morning but not uncomfortably so. Certainly there had been worse mornings. At the very least, Cor'il wasn't soaking wet. Well, not *yet*, anyway.

He stretched out on the hay bale and yawned, feeling something in his left leg pop. It had not been the most comfortable of beds but he had wanted to stay close to the fire last night for protection. And he had stayed close to the barn's entrance just in case.

Looking outside, he could not tell what time it was because of the clouds. He was never one to sleep too late so he guessed somewhere around seven or eight in the morning. He got up and briefly walked outside to get a better look. Upon seeing only dark, solid gray in the sky and getting wet he went back inside the barn and sat down on one of the partial hay bales to have breakfast. *Ah, dried meat and an apple. Hopefully I will be able to purchase or hunt something soon.*

Cor'il had always been a proficient hunter and scavenger. Both would take time, however—time he felt was better spent traveling. He badly wished to get to the Densewood as soon as possible.

Still, it would be nice to eat something different for a change. There would be nothing roaming about in this downpour, however, and from what Kendra had said, the woods outside the barn were not safe. Though Cor'il suspected, if there was anything savage milling about that they probably would have encountered it at some point last night. Cor'il had not stayed awake all night to stand watch, but he was a light sleeper and would've heard something approaching. He'd stirred three or four times during the night as it was, and awoken to find nothing.

He took a bite of his apple and placed some of the hay in the ashes of last night's fire. He added a couple of dry branches on top and sat back down on the hay bale, holding his right palm open.

"*Miliam D'thorsoric,*" he whispered, blowing into his palm which instantly burst into purple flame. Cor'il admired it for a moment before tossing it onto the sticks which quickly caught fire.

That comes easily now, he thought, taking another bite of the apple. But fear instantly struck him when he remembered he was not alone. *The Abyss! I forgot about Kendra! What if she saw that? What would she think?* Cor'il knew what *he* would think if he saw someone do what he just did.

He rose and walked over to the stall where she was sleeping, only to find that she was gone. His disappointment rivaled the relief he felt when he realized that his secret was safe. He wondered why she would leave without at least telling him so. She seemed a tiny bit aloof last night, but Cor'il had assumed that was because she was hurt or nervous. Maybe she was afraid? No, he doubted that. She very much seemed to be perfectly capable of handling herself.

Cor'il, however, had told a lie when he explained how he had found her, and he felt a bit guilty. No, she had certainly managed to stab the goblin in the neck and it most definitely would have died eventually, but Cor'il had decided to...help it along so that he could get her to safety sooner. She seemed...vulnerable, and the last thing he wanted to do was make her feel more so. Regardless, he felt a tiny bit guilty about it. *Maybe I'm making something out of nothing.*

He returned to the fire and pulled the book from his satchel. Thumbing through the pages, it dawned on him that he had read more of it than he had realized. He must not have been paying attention. The script on the first 25 pages was completely illegible. However, now, he could comprehend the next few pages. He read through them, devouring the information at a phenomenal rate. Leaning back against the rotting barn wall, he sat in quiet reflection, smelling the fire's smoke and listening to the wood pop and crackle.

The fire seemed to burn hotter than a fire of that size should. The book had instructed him on how to produce the flame, but it had not explained anything else about it. Cor'il had discovered its properties only by observation and experimentation. By combining words *Miliam D'thorsoric* and blowing onto his palm, he somehow created the flame and could control it in certain ways. *Magic words*, he thought. *A spell? With everything I've seen up until now, why would this be any more ludicrous than goblins and orcs? Which begs the question—what* else *is there to discover?*

Everything he had heard from storyweavers as myth and legend was becoming reality. His father had told him stories, too, as had others in Kuranthas. But he could always tell that nobody *truly* believed them. Even storyweavers seemed to spin a tale merely for entertainment rather than historical purpose. Cor'il, when he was young, had asked most everyone who passed through his town whether they had ever seen an orc or a goblin. They had all chuckled and told him something silly like "run along and play." A few outright told him "no" and looked at him like he was a strange little boy.

But, for as far back as he could remember, his childhood had not been normal. He tried to get along with everyone, but there were those individuals who shunned him—even his own father at times. Sure, there were those who befriended him and treated him kindly, but he always suspected, deep down, they had their questions and suspicions. Secretly, they *wanted* to dislike him. He often wondered whether he was merely too suspicious and lacked trust.

So when he was forced out of his home he wasn't completely shocked. He had often let his mind wander, making up wild scenarios sometimes and imagining the worst, but he never really expected any of them to come to pass. He had been unprepared for this one. Still, looking back, it was rather apparent what the outcome would be. The circumstances were suspect at best and Cor'il really didn't know how he would have reacted if he could switch places with one of his friends, and nobody had called him names or been violent with him. If anything, they looked frightened and confused, but had not appeared hostile or belligerent.

But if he saw someone with their hand on fire like his was, that would certainly tip the scale toward uneasiness. And what would he do, then? He certainly didn't think it was normal, and *he* was the one who could do it! Fortunately, he was beginning to understand it. Not just understand, but he felt it as if it was almost a part of him—as if this was the way things were *supposed* to be.

Turning the book's page, he gazed at the symbols on the thick, worn paper. As with every other page, the script on the paper shifted between letters and symbols, rearranging themselves while he watched and absorbed their meaning. This no longer caused a headache or dizziness. In fact, Cor'il had become accustomed to it. And it took a mere moment for him to obtain the knowledge instead of over an hour.

He turned the page and, soon after, turned to the next one. Several pages later, the script was still and unresponsive, at which point he slipped the tome back into his satchel, leaned back, and closed his eyes. He relaxed and enjoyed the familiar rush. It felt as if the knowledge he had just gained absorbed into his mind and body, permeating every part of him. He understood more, too. *Okay, let's try this.*

He looked around the barn one last time to make sure nobody was around. It made him laugh—being this suspicious—but he barely knew Kendra, and mayhaps she was still around, playing games with him.

Once he had satisfied his suspicions, he walked to the back of the barn, under the half-collapsed hayloft where the flickering firelight was dim. Cor'il put his hands at his side and exhaled, trying to calm his mind. He closed his right hand in a fist and flung it above his head, opening his hand as if he was throwing something into the air.

"Illuminate!" he shouted. And a minute ball of light appeared above his head, hovering a couple of feet up. Suddenly, the barn was as bright as daylight. Cor'il concentrated briefly and the orb floated higher above his head. As he concentrated, he changed its size, shrinking the ball down to a spec that still produced just as much light as before. He moved it down and then several feet in front of him. Then it winked out and the barn went dark again.

Illuminate. That will come in handy. Except he hadn't said "illuminate," had he? "*D'rosoco!*" he whispered. And threw the mote of light into the air. "*Illuminate!*" he whispered. The previous light died and was replaced by another one. He repeated the action several times, using both words to make absolutely sure they were interchangeable. Indeed, they *were* interchangeable! *That was unexpected.* He still wasn't sure he was understanding everything correctly, but he made a mental note of what he'd learned.

I should really be going. He gathered his satchel and buckled his sword on his belt, then stopped in front of the fire. Cor'il waved his hand and the flames died instantly, without any smoke whatsoever. He put his hood up, nodded approvingly and stepped out into the rain, leaving the barn behind. The road was sloppy and wet and difficult to traverse so Cor'il stayed in the grass, still trying to keep himself as concealed as possible.

The rest of the day was uneventful, with rain coming down in varying intensities. Cor'il found some rocky terrain a short distance from the road and used a small outcropping as shelter. He sat under the rock and watched the rain come down. There were probably several hours of daylight left but the weather was so oppressive that Cor'il simply didn't feel like slogging through the rain. Even with his cloak he was cold and wet. At least, this way, he was guaranteed a dry place to sleep tonight.

• • •

When Cor'il awoke the next day, he did so to another gray, cloudy sky. Whereas the previous day had been a chilly downpour, today was a warm, humid drizzle that permeated everything and made his clothing uncomfortable. His boots squished in the saturated ground as he walked a few feet off the road. There were more travelers today but they all kept to themselves, obviously wanting to get to their destinations quickly. Even the horses seemed depressed with their heads bowed. Maybe Cor'il was imagining things.

Today, his satchel felt heavier. He kept his cloak up over his head even though the air was uncomfortably warm and damp. He had grown accustomed to wearing it, and he decided that he would be better off if he could remain as anonymous as possible. He found that he cared less about the rain on his face than he did about staying out of trouble.

It was nearly midday—or so he estimated—when two men on horseback heading south stopped next to him. One was bald and had markings on his head—a tattoo. Since leaving Kuranthas he had seen several of them, but he still wasn't quite used to them. The other had short, curly brown hair and wore spectacles. They both looked like huntsman, judging from the bows they had slung over their shoulders.

"You there, boy," the bald one called. Cor'il had the urge to simply keep walking or maybe to dart off, running away from the road. But he had done nothing wrong and was able to remain calm. He had to keep reminding himself of that. *You'll have to get used to conversing with strangers sooner or later.*

"Yes, sir. May I help you?" He stopped walking and looked up at the two men.

"Aye, hopefully you can." The bespectacled man looked slightly uneasy. He remained silent. The tattooed man, however, was quite confident. "We are looking for a young man who may have come this way."

"He has hair shorter than yours," the other man piped up. "Blond...blue eyes."

"We were," the tattooed man interrupted, "wondering if you had seen him? We believe that he may be headed this way. He is wanted for—"

"He is about 21 winters." The other man interrupted, adjusting his spectacles and apparently scrutinizing Cor'il who shifted his hood nervously in response.

"I am sorry, good sirs," Cor'il stammered. He had done nothing wrong, yet these two were making him feel as though he had. "I have not seen anyone who fits that description. Mostly I have seen merchants and travelers—older than you describe."

"Very well," the tattooed man sighed. "If you do see anyone suspicious who fits that description be sure you alert the town watch or anybody nearby. He is dangerous. He carries a wicked axe that is rumored to be sharp enough to split a hair right down the center." The tattooed man made a chopping motion with his hand. Cor'il expected him to start laughing, as if it was meant to scare him, but he kept a straight, very serious face.

"There might be some coin in it for you," he continued.

The two men wasted no time and urged their horses forward, continuing south along the road as Cor'il continued north. Soon, they were out of sight and Cor'il was alone once again. The drizzle continued as he made his way north, now a little more cautious in case he should encounter this individual. He figured that the odds of that happening were nearly nonexistent, but Cor'il never knew what to expect from the Outsider world. It had been unexpected, surprising, and frightening so far.

When it came time to bed down for the night, the drizzle had mostly stopped but the air had only gotten more oppressive. Cor'il couldn't tell where the sun was but he was tired enough not to care. The road passed through a forest which, Cor'il decided, was where he would stop for the night. *I should definitely find something away from the road—especially if there is a dangerous individual on the loose.*

After several moments of indecision, Cor'il opted to head into the forest but kept the road in sight. That way, if he encountered any more orcs, goblins, or whatever, it might be easier to escape. In fact, he didn't really know what he was doing and simply decided he felt safer being able to see the road. *Mayhaps I can stay out of sight of monsters and men*, he thought. He longed for the safety of Kuranthas and the comfort of the familiar oaks, maples, and steelwoods.

Cor'il found a decent spot next to a small stream where he could still see a tiny bit of the road. After he refilled his water skin, he was able to construct a simple shelter by bending branches and using grass and weeds to tie them together. He did so without harming the plants themselves. His father may have been a cruel man, but some of his lessons stuck with Cor'il. "Learn to live *with* nature, not despite it," he would say. Cor'il remembered several times he had been punished when he was younger for digging up plants or breaking branches off of trees.

If any significant moisture fell, the shelter wouldn't do much to keep Cor'il dry but, if it was this same drizzle he would be fine. The canopy of the forest itself did a decent enough job of deflecting much of the rain, so his shelter was probably not of much use. Cor'il settled in and ate a small dinner of dried meat. He tried to relax, but felt anxious to get to where he was going, even though he didn't know what he'd do when he got there. He would have a whole new conundrum once he actually arrived.

Several travelers passed on the nearby road and either did not notice his camp or did not care. Cor'il sat in serene contemplation, inspecting the book and absorbing more of its information. With the dim light available, he could only barely make out some of the script. Regardless, he was able to comprehend the information easily. By the time he was done the sun was setting. The misty drizzle had subsided—for now—and it would be dark in a half hour or so. He closed the book, taking joy in the creaky, rough leather bindings. As with every other time he read the book, he felt a wave of invigoration and excitement, both of which were eventually replaced by fatigue. He'd no idea how long he had been reading but it was probably a decent part of the afternoon.

Slipping the book back into his satchel, he lay down on the damp bed of old leaves and new foliage, staring at the roof of his shelter. He was becoming wary of not having a home and always traveling. Yes, it would definitely feel good to finally start a new life, even if he still longed for the old one. He laced his hands together behind his head and breathed deep.

The sound of movement snapped Cor'il out of his light slumber. The clouds had apparently moved out, giving way to the night sky and some moonlight that shone through the trees, producing small rays of illumination in the slightly foggy air. And it was cold—cold enough that Cor'il could see his own breath. *It's summer. This is not normal, is it? Surely, weather outside of Kuranthas cannot be so drastically different.*

"It would be wise to avoid unnaturally cold or dark places," he whispered. Ben Falhar's words resonated in his head.

He sprang to his feet, grabbed his sword from the ground, and unsheathed it, stumbling around a bit as his eyes adjusted. The small motes of moonlight were like beacons and they allowed him to see, but not as well as he wanted.

"Illuminate," he whispered, touching the blade of his sword. Instantly, it glowed with a blue light, allowing him to see a good 10 feet around him. *Even though I'm not sure I thoroughly understand it yet, being able to do that certainly is handy. Now I hope it's just a deer or rabbit out there making noise.* He shivered. The area around him seemed to almost devour the light from his sword.

But it wasn't a deer or a rabbit. It was one of the smaller creatures—a goblin, and it was running full steam at Cor'il with a knife in its grubby right hand. But, to Cor'il's surprise, it paused a few feet from him, squinting, growling, and wildly thrashing its knife in the air. It looked as though it didn't like the light—maybe it hurt the creature's eyes. Cor'il wondered if *all* light had the same effect. The creature hadn't seemed bothered by the moonlight.

Cor'il didn't hesitate. He swung his sword, slashing the goblin across its chest. It howled at him but was silenced when he forced his long, slender blade through its sternum. It gurgled and fell to the ground as he pulled his weapon away.

I killed it. I... I can't believe...

Cor'il stepped back, mouth agape, with his sword pointed at the ground. He had never killed anything other than game while hunting. But, in this case, he hadn't even thought twice. He had simply cut down the goblin as if it was a minor pest. *You killed the goblin back at the barn. Remember? But it was going to die anyway. That's different... isn't it?*

It was going to kill me—just like the last one. But... I killed it. He looked over at the two goblins that had just emerged from the trees on the other side of the stream, squinting and trying to shield their eyes. They stared at their fallen comrade, its body lying still in the blue-hued light, and hissed. *But I've killed things before, I... I didn't know what I was doing, did I? The world is dangerous. I couldn't let it kill me!* His grip on the sword tightened. He didn't *want* to kill. But the goblins did. And they were advancing.

He heard something off to his right but, when he turned to look, he saw nothing but the trees. The goblins were crossing the stream. Cor'il's breathing quickened, misting in front of his face. He shivered. He wasn't terribly proficient with a blade, nor did he enjoy having to use it. The skills he had learned thus far had been what Brand had been able to teach him. But Brand was certainly no expert, either.

Cor'il swung his sword wildly. He hoped it would scare the beasts but, instead, it appeared only to incite them. Though they still seemed cautious, keeping to the fringes of Cor'il's light, they began to howl and grunt. Mayhaps they had more intelligence than Cor'il had originally thought. And they were working together to try to flank him.

What worried him more was whether there were others out there. He thought he heard other noises from further in the forest.

The goblin on his left lunged at Cor'il with its curved blade. Even in this sketchy light he could tell it was probably dull and rusted. He easily dodged it. But the goblin also dodged his clumsy counterattack. Then, both goblins attacked at the same time. Cor'il jumped back, barely avoiding both of their blades. He tried to utter the words to summon fire that he could throw at them, but he was flustered and he couldn't remember them. He stuttered out a bit of gibberish but was quickly interrupted as both goblins attacked again.

Cor'il blocked the attack from the goblin on the right and kicked it, sending it tumbling backwards into a rock. The second goblin's blade, however, slashed Cor'il's arm. He yelled in pain and struck at the goblin who dodged his sword and... laughed at him? The other beast was getting back up and trying to shake off the haze. Cor'il struck again with his sword, then again. His second strike grazed the goblin's leg but it came at him, throwing him off balance.

He staggered backward, parrying a blow and dodging another until he backed into a tree. He quickly ducked to the side as the goblin's blade hit the tree, throwing the creature off balance for a brief second. Cor'il took the opportunity and ran his blade through its neck. Ichorous fluid sprayed out as the goblin dropped to the ground and choked to death on its own blood.

Cor'il immediately turned to face the other attacker, only to find Kendra removing a dagger from its eye socket. She had the dagger cleaned and concealed before its body hit the ground.

"Uh," Cor'il stuttered, "hi. This is—"

"A little unexpected?" she laughed. "Yes, I suppose it is." She stepped over the body and approached Cor'il. "I killed two more a little bit further out in the woods. They apparently liked your... light... even less than these two. Nice sword, by the way."

"Thank you." That was about all Cor'il could muster. Everything had just happened so fast and he was still surprised to see Kendra.

"Does it always glow like that?" She grinned as she brushed some strands of hair from her face.

Cor'il wasn't sure what to say or do. He obviously couldn't deny that his sword glowed. How much did Kendra know about what he could do?

"Um, no." Cor'il had no idea how to explain. But he knew that he was going to have to.

"Don't worry, treeboy," she laughed. "Your secret is safe with me." She put her arm around him. "Besides," she whispered, "I saw what you did with the fire the other night. Pretty impressive."

Now he had *nothing at all* to say. He simply nodded, wiped the sticky goblin blood from his sword, and headed back to his shelter. Kendra followed.

"I can't say that I understand what it is you do," she continued. "It's obviously not normal, and a little creepy."

"Neither can I," he laughed nervously. "But I know it's rather out of the ordinary."

"It looks like magic to me, but that's silly, right?"

"Ordinarily, I'd agree."

"Not to worry. We all have our secrets. You only need worry about those that are dangerous."

"You may choose to run. You may choose to hide. Your past cares not, for it always has a way of catching up with you." —Lady Alscoradon of the ruling house of Alarantha

Chapter 16

When Cor'il opened his eyes, he expected to be alone again. He was surprised to find that he was, in fact, not. Kendra was already awake and thumbing through his book.

"May I have that back, please?" he asked, sitting up. The dull pain in his arm immediately reminded him of last night. The cut from the goblin's weapon had not been very deep but it had bled for a while. Cor'il had eventually stopped the bleeding with leaves and weeds.

"Oh, you're awake?" Kendra shut the book and handed it back to him. "I was bored, waiting for your lazy bones to wake up, so I figured I would indulge in some light reading."

"Thank you." He put the book back in his bag. "I don't normally sleep this much. It must be the stress from last night. So, was it interesting?"

"The Abyss if I know," she laughed. "What language *is* that, anyway? Kuranthian? Gibberish? Orcish?" She stopped laughing when she uttered the last one. That was apparently still a tender subject, given recent events. Cor'il could feel the instant unease.

"To be honest," he tried to keep the conversation moving even though he would have preferred not to. There was no telling how she would react to even more oddities. "I'm not even sure it *is* a language. I assume you could not read any of it at all?"

"No. Wait, that's not true. I think I could make out the letter 'A' somewhere, once."

Cor'il smiled and relaxed a little. Since leaving his home he had become a very private person—mayhaps excessively so.

"At least the book didn't give you a headache when you tried to read it."

"But you *can* read it?"

Cor'il fidgeted. He hadn't meant for this conversation to delve this far into what he considered his little secret. Or mayhaps he had. He wasn't very keen on sharing for obvious reasons, but it was refreshing to be able to get it off his chest. And Kendra obviously knew he was uneasy. Was she grinning?

"Sometimes," he replied, picking the flower off a weed. He twirled it between his thumb and forefinger a few times until the stem broke and it went limp in his fingers. He tossed it aside. "But it's not so much *reading* as it is... knowing. I know that sounds weird."

"Kind of like a glowing sword?"

"Well, yes." Cor'il scratched his head and looked at the ground. He laughed nervously. There was no easy way to explain anything.

The two of them sat in silence for several moments. Cor'il was unsure about what to say, but Kendra wasn't budging. She wasn't going to let this go, apparently. Not that he expected she would. He probably wouldn't if their situations were reversed.

"It's... some kind of power. I guess you could call it magic."

"Magic? Just like the tales storyweavers tell—like goblins and orcs."

"Yeah."

"Well, now that clears it all up!" She laughed and threw a handful of weeds at him. "At this point, something like that doesn't surprise me in the least. Honestly, stories and tales are all we have to explain everything that has been happening, so why not just keep using them for that purpose?"

"I suspect you have a point."

"You're damn right I have a point. If a beanstalk were to grow out of your head, at this point, I'd probably think nothing of it."

"Really? Has someone told you a story about a beanstalk growing out of someone's head? I must have missed that one." Cor'il was amused. He found it very easy to talk to Kendra.

"No," she replied. "But I'd tell *my* kids about it some day!"

Cor'il threw a handful of weeds back at Kendra, hitting her in the face. She laughed and spat dirt, wiping it off her face. They paused in silence, listening to the water trickling through the creek. Somewhere, out in the forest, were several goblin bodies. Kendra had a small stick she was using to make marks in the dirt.

"Besides," she continued, "I think magic is wonderful!"

"It's why I had to leave home."

"What?" Kendra looked up, surprised. "What do you mean?"

Secrets were a burden. Some secrets *had* to be kept, but Cor'il had the inexplicable urge to tell someone.

"At first, I wasn't sure what had happened. I didn't know what I could do. I *still* really don't know. It just sort of happened. Sometimes I would feel this... energy building up inside me, like a bubble of heat. When I let it out, it was just a flash of light. One time I got angry and all around me, everything floated into the air—books, forks, chairs."

"And you didn't know it was you?"

"Not at the time. I mean, at first I certainly did not know. After similar bizarre events happened more and more often and... every time I had that odd feeling inside I began to suspect. But I didn't know *why* or *how* it was happening—only that I was probably the cause." He paused a moment, picking a few blades of grass out of the ground. "It makes more sense to me now."

"So you left your home?" Cor'il could see sorrow in Kendra's eyes. But she also was extremely curious. He didn't understand why he had opened up to her so easily.

"No, not yet. I was told to leave by... well, most everyone. My friends Alton, Brand, and Lena remained silent. I could tell they would miss me but that they were also afraid of me. *Afraid!*"

"What had you done?"

"I accidentally burned down several large, old trees. I passed out and, when I woke up, there were just piles of ashes where the trees once grew." Cor'il ran his finger through the dirt and leaves. It felt good to tell someone, but it was also painful to recall. He hadn't thought this much about it since, well, since he had been told to leave. In fact, he barely remembered the events themselves. "I was deemed dangerous—whether accidental or not—and told to leave." *Wait. There was something else, wasn't there? Am I forgetting something?*

"That's understandable." The moment Cor'il looked up at Kendra, probably with a shocked look on his face, Kendra gasped. "No no no! I mean, I can understand why they were afraid. They didn't know any better."

"I suppose." Cor'il returned his gaze to the ground. A red and black caterpillar was slowly making its way across a leaf. It stopped to eat a little, then continued its trek. "I very much understand, but that makes it no easier." *How many trees did I destroy? Four? But I only remember three missing. Or maybe it was four. By The Abyss, I can't even remember what I was doing before it happened.* His limited memory of the event not only irritated him to no end, but it also concerned him.

"With everything new I learn from this book," he continued, trying to take his mind off of the painful memories, or lack thereof, "I find that I gain more control and a deeper understanding. So I think any more accidents will be rare—hopefully." He remembered most of his "accident" in the forest the first time he had encountered the orc and goblins, but the details were still hazy and that memory, too, was incomplete.

Kendra got up and shook the dirt and grass off of her dress. She'd found a new one—a red one. It was a little shorter than the blue one and looked as though it barely fit her. But he was sure it was better than a bloodstained, ripped garment.

"Are you still heading to Elston?" she asked, picking up her satchel and slinging it over her shoulder. She adjusted her skirts a bit and pulled her sleeves down, apparently waiting for him. "Are you going to get up so we can leave?"

"I suppose so." Cor'il stood up and brushed a couple of leaves off of his breeches. He adjusted his hair over his ears but left his hood down. "I think I'm heading for The Densewood. It sounds like a good place to live."

"You can't take the trees from the treeboy," Kendra snickered. "Why, exactly, did you pick The Densewood as your preferred location?"

"No real reason," Cor'il shrugged. "But, as you have pointed out, I feel more comfortable among the trees. I'm not sure I could live in a city. Sulbar was more than—"

"Sulbar is burning, actually." Kendra started walking back to the road.

"Wait," Cor'il hurried to catch up to her. "What do you mean—burning?"

"I mean that buildings are on fire and people are dead."

"Wait, how?" Cor'il grabbed her shoulder and turned her to face him. "I was told that there are strange beasts from outside the city walls."

"Orcs and goblins?"

"Probably. But some of the descriptions sounded quite a bit different. It was all hearsay—information from merchants traveling from Sulbar, and I'm pretty sure they hadn't actually seen anything for themselves. But—"

"But, as you and I know, these things are real."

"Yes."

"And if someone has seen something... worse than what we've seen—"

"Then there is probably truth in it. Yeah, I can understand that. I don't particularly want to accept it, though." Kendra turned and continued walking out of the forest.

He hadn't known Kendra long, but this was the first time Cor'il had seen her remotely concerned about anything. It worried him a little.

"So, yeah, I'm not going there after all, I guess." She pushed aside some branches, ducking and weaving around plants of various sizes. "Besides, you most likely need my help. And you, treeboy, need to think about settling down somewhere besides a forest. You don't get bitten by ticks in the city. Well not usually, anyway." She turned and stuck her tongue out at Cor'il, then laughed.

Cor'il wasn't quite sure how to take that, so he laughed a little and walked beside her. He was better at dodging the plants and rocks than she was. She didn't seem to be paying attention or maybe she just didn't care.

"But from what I hear," she eventually continued, "things are relatively under control and I am sure the guards have been increased along Sulbar's walls. Elston should be much more organized and far safer. The Densewood, on the other hand, probably isn't so safe if just this little forest has goblins running around in it."

She had a point; he had to admit it. But living in a city still did not sound appealing. There didn't seem to be room to stretch out and certainly there were few trees in cities if Sulbar was any indication.

"It would seem that even cities aren't safe."

"Well, you have your normal scum in every city—a lot like me!" She laughed. "No, wait... worse than me. But cities are pretty organized. Like I said, I don't think Sulbar will have a problem once they put out the fires. Close the gates and post guards along the walls and you've taken care of the problem. An entire invading Barbarian Horde was defeated 200 years ago. A few orcs or goblins should be of no consequence."

It wasn't much longer before they found the road and began following it, once again walking beside it to stay out of the way of travelers on horseback or wagon. The trees grew close to the road here and Cor'il enjoyed walking beneath the canopy, surrounded by familiarity. He kept a vigilant eye toward anything that might be dangerous. Kendra didn't seem to be bothered. She had a playful spring in her step, having obviously come to terms with the attack on Sulbar.

"I'll be truthful." She riffled through her satchel while walking. "I'm not really looking forward to going back to Elston."

"Why is that?"

She stopped looking in her sack and glared at him a moment. "You really *are* nosy." Cor'il wasn't sure what to say to that. About the time he finally tried to respond, Kendra started laughing. "I'm kidding, silly! Let's just say there are several individuals in Elston interested in finding me. And maybe a couple of actual businesses and organizations... the city guard and watch, and probably King Alzine himself. I was originally headed to Sulbar to start over fresh." She resumed searching her satchel.

"And make new enemies?"

"You catch on fast—quicker than I expected. Ah, here it is." She pulled out a watch and inspected it, squinting. "Looks like it's about... 8 o'clock or so."

"May I look at that? I've never actually seen a watch or clock up close before."

"Sure, but don't go and break it." She handed it over. "That was half a day's work."

The watch was smooth gold with a slightly scratched glass face. There was a part at the top that may have, at one time, held a gold chain, but it was twisted and broken now. Other than that slight blemish and the scratches on the face, it was in good condition, and truly a work of art! There were intricate patterns engraved on the back and tiny gemstones were inlaid on the face of the watch. The 12 was a diamond, the 3 was an emerald, the 6 was a ruby and the 9 was what appeared to be a sapphire.

"Is it true," Cor'il inquired, "that if you try to open a clock or a watch it might explode?" He handed it back to her.

"It's what I've heard," she replied, slipping it back into her satchel, "but I've not seen it happen. Nor do I wish to test that theory. I kind of like this watch and don't wish it to explode."

"I agree."

"So what do you plan on doing when we actually get to Elston?" Kendra inquired, after having walked a few minutes in silence. "If you were to stay in Elston, that is."

"I don't really know. I don't think I have any particularly useful skills. It's one more reason for me to move on. No, the Densewood is definitely where I should be. I can make a new life there."

"You do really love your trees." She kicked a rock into the air. It skittered across the dirt road and into a bush on the other side.

"It's pretty much all I know." He swatted at a bitefly, but it was persistent, and continued buzzing around his head. "So much is changing that I simply wish to find something familiar and safe."

"So... how much of that book have you... er... absorbed?" She smirked.

"I think about half of it. Ironically, once I've looked at a page and understood it, I often cannot go back, look at it again, and gain anything from it. If I try to reread something, it looks like gibberish."

"It sounds like a headache waiting to happen." Without warning, her hand darted out and closed in front of Cor'il's face. Before he could say anything, she opened it and a dead bitefly fell out. "I can't stand those things. They truly have no purpose except irritation."

"I agree with you about that."

They walked in silence for a while. Cor'il had a lot to think about. *What if The Densewood is really too dangerous? Or what if it's not what I thought it was?* The idea of trying to live in a city, shoulder to shoulder with so many people, was certainly not appealing.

I guess I will just have to see what the situation is like when I arrive. No sense worrying about it until I get there. Dogs shouldn't worry about how to fly until they grow wings. For the longest time he had not understood that phrase. It was popular back home. No matter how silly it sounded, it summed up the situation perfectly.

For now, he was happy to have a companion with whom he could travel. He had become accustomed to being alone and fearing all strangers. There was still apprehension any time he met someone, but at least Kendra seemed to be understanding and, most importantly, was not afraid of what he could do. Still, he would have to be careful. He hadn't meant for her to find out in the first place. He suspected many people would not take the same attitude.

As they walked, he felt a sense of peace. Not only was he enjoying walking amongst the trees, but he enjoyed the companionship. He had a sense of direction—The Densewood. To him there was absolutely no question. He couldn't explain it. With everything else he had recently discovered—both good and bad—this feeling did not seem wholly illogical or crazy. Certainly it was no crazier than orcs or creating fire in his hand.

Chapter 17

Where am I even going? And what am I supposed to do when I get there—wherever there *actually is?* As of late, Dalinil's travels had not been what he'd hoped. He couldn't settle in a town—not if there were trackers out looking for him. He often told himself he was simply being overly cautious—that certainly nobody would track him across the entire realm. But he had heard many stories from trackers who came into his smithy regaling him with their exploits and feats. They were a proud lot, but they had a right to be. Tracking was a high demand skill and a good tracker was not easy to come by. Some would say that tracking wasn't actually a *skill*—that it was more of a mystical ability. Dalinil knew not of such things, but he *did* know that he was not going to make it easy for them. They hadn't found him yet. With any luck, they wouldn't *ever* find him. *Some say that luck doesn't exist, but I'll believe in it if it keeps me safe.*

He was still homeless and that wore on him. Additionally, he was running low on supplies. Water was easy to find, but food was much less so—especially for someone without much knowledge of nature. He'd been fortunate and had managed to sneak up on a rabbit or two. He'd found some fruit along the way, but he was certainly no hunter. Ten Kings had always been his home and he'd never seen a reason to step outside its walls.

He'd had to follow the road for a little while at one point. It made him nervous, but it was the only way through the rocky bluffs he had encountered. Fortunately, nothing had come of it. He decided to push east a bit when he began encountering more of those little brutish, green things. Only, this time, some of them were bigger and more savage. He'd surmised that, mayhaps, they were coming from the South but, at this point, he was simply guessing. When he had no actual direction in the first place it didn't really matter which way he traveled. So he headed east for a while. It was all new to him, so what did it matter? In any event, he'd managed to avoid conflict—both human and beastly.

Several times, he thought about simply going back to the treehouses in the forest and hiding there. But, every time, he talked himself out of it, deciding that it simply wasn't far enough away from Ten Kings. He felt that distance was probably the best thing to have at this point. Distance gave him more time to think. Regardless of whether he was actually correct, it made him at least *feel* safer.

So, now, he stood at the edge of a lake, looking out at the water and at the trees beyond. The sun had not reached the Noon point, yet, and the morning air was still fresh. He picked up a smooth, gray pebble from the rocky beach and turned it over in his palm. It was warm in his hand and felt pleasant and... real. He closed his fingers around it and shut his eyes for a moment, listening to the water lap gently onto the shore. Then he threw the stone into the lake. It skipped across the water several times before sinking to the bottom. *Well, I guess I will just go... this way.* He turned to his right and followed the shore of the lake.

The gravel crunched beneath his boots and, for a moment, he wondered if he should try to be quieter. At first he was worried about trackers, but his fears quickly turned toward whatever else might be lurking about. At this point, however, he was skeptical that he could constantly travel quietly and in hiding. New, unexplained dangers were definitely a cause for concern, but Dalinil refused to live in fear or, well, *complete* fear. Fear was just like any other emotion—it was a tool to be used and controlled. Fear could keep him out of danger. Caution was necessary, but he was trying to get accustomed to just how much caution he should take. He wasn't used to thinking about every little detail. *Mayhaps that is why I'm in this mess in the first place.*

He felt stupid—being surrounded by an entire world about which he was completely naïve. He had always thought of himself as a clever individual, but each day outside city walls humbled him just a little bit more.

A few ripples appeared at the point where the stone had sunk into the lake. Not wanting to run into another unexpected, unsavory confrontation, Dalinil moved away from the shoreline, keeping the lake to his left. *Now you're just paranoid. That was probably a fish or turtle. Not everything out here is dangerous.* But no matter how much he tried to convince himself otherwise, he had a tough time believing his own words. The savage brute he saw on the road—the one from which he had fled—was not something he was likely to forget.

After walking for a bit, he relaxed and lost all concern about making noise. He was either certain that nothing was going to happen or he didn't care. He'd done well for himself up to this point and, even though he was learning at every turn, he was gaining knowledge and confidence. The problem was, he didn't know what he didn't know. Until he'd encountered that thing in the forest he was fairly certain he could handle himself, but he wasn't at all sure how to fight or escape from something that could uproot a tree with its hands.

But I did. I did escape from it. And I killed the two small creatures by the pond. I may be a city boy but I'm getting the hang of it. I just wish I knew where I should be headed. A flock of geese alighted onto the lake, settling about 20 feet from the shore. Dalinil half expected something hideous and awful to jump out of the water and devour them all, but nothing did. He watched them for a moment, still waiting for something terrible. *So I am both surprised and disappointed to see that nothing happened. What does that say about me? Or about the world?* He had a good laugh as he made his way slowly around the lake but he still kept his wits about him and shot a glance to the water occasionally.

Dalinil threw a few more stones into the lake, scattering the geese that returned moments later. A stiff wind caught him from behind and traveled past, into the trees beyond. They swayed and it was at that moment that he saw something there, something within the forest. It glinted in the light, he thought. He did not know *what* it was, but he *knew* something was there. When the trees were still again, it was gone. *Well, now, I guess I know exactly where I'm going. Let's see where this takes me.*

He didn't know why, but he *knew* he had to find out what lay ahead. At that moment, nothing else mattered.

But when he finally approached the tree line, he peered inside and saw nothing unusual. He slowly entered the forest, frantically looking around, but still found only the forest itself. He swore to himself under his breath as disappointment washed over him.

He crept further in, still curious. He was absolutely sure he had seen *something* among the trees—a glimpse of something white among the green and brown.

"Am I seeing things now?" he whispered. He grabbed his axe, gripping the handle tightly. Anger began to replace curiosity. The lake was no longer visible behind him. "This is ridiculous. It was clearly not this deep into the woods when I saw it." He delved deeper, now unconcerned with stealth.

When further investigation *still* turned up nothing, Dalinil began to get furious. Sweat broke out on his forehead and he could feel heat rising within him. He was wasting his time chasing shadows and illusions, and he was already tired of running and hiding. He delved further into the forest, almost at a run, muttering to himself.

But, still, he found nothing.

He stopped, raised his axe in the air, and yelled as loud as he could, producing a deep, rage-filled scream. Then he flung his axe into the forest and watched it embed itself in a tree. He wasn't sure how long he stood, grunting and staring, but he snapped out of his trance when the tree came crashing to the ground. It took him a moment to calm down enough and remember where he was and what he was doing. He walked to the tree and inspected it. It wasn't a huge tree—maybe about as thick around as one of his legs—but his axe had cut almost completely through it.

At first he thought maybe it was dying and rotting but upon closer inspection, it clearly was not. *I cut down a tree simply by throwing my axe. I don't understand how that could happen.* He picked up the axe and inspected it, but there was nothing unusual about it. Likewise, he inspected the fallen tree with the same result. He flexed his fingers several times, staring at them in confused disbelief.

He closed his eyes and concentrated on the rhythm of his breathing. He'd always had a nasty temper, and this was an effective technique to calm himself. He could feel his muscles relaxing, starting with his arms and chest, and flowing down to his legs. He felt goose bumps rise on the top of his head, travel down his neck and cascade across his back. He lost all emotion in a void of darkness, letting go of the rage, frustration, and confusion he was feeling. He did nothing but breathe until it was gone. All that remained was absence.

But, in that absence, there was still *something* there—floating just close enough for him to sense but too far to grasp. For a moment he could feel it, then it was gone. Just as he was about to open his eyes and decide what to do next, it reappeared on the fringe. Whatever it was, it was toying with him. He felt irritation creep back into him, but he rejected it. Instead, he released his anger again and he felt a slight surge within.

It was warm and it vanished just as quickly as it had appeared. Dalinil opened his eyes and looked around. The forest greeted him. The birds still chirped happily and it—whatever it was—was still there. It was slightly closer now. He beckoned to it, reaching out with his emotions—anger this time—and felt it inching closer. *It's as if I am trying to remember something that I've never actually experienced. It's on the tip of my tongue but I can't get the words out.*

And it got even closer. There was no physical or visual representation of what "it" was, so Dalinil decided to assign it an image of sorts. He again closed his eyes, now imagining it as a tiny red sphere with swirling currents on its surface, glowing and pulsing. He visualized his hand reaching out to grab it. His hand was laughter, anger, love, hatred, and frustration. He reached out and touched the sphere.

It melted into him, and uncontrollable rage infected him. He felt strong and powerful, confident and secure—as if he could singlehandedly defeat 100 enemies at once. He *wanted* to defeat 100 enemies at once. He wanted to kill something and tear it limb from limb. His heart was thumping inside his chest and he balled his fists so tightly that his hands began to ache. He badly needed to hurt something.

Opening his eyes, he looked around, every muscle inside him throbbing and pulsing in unison. The world now appeared darker and everything was tinted slightly red. His gaze searched for an animal he could rip apart. Finding nothing, he became even more agitated, and he yelled out in anger. Several birds scattered from nearby trees as he continued to scream at the top of his lungs. He felt feral and savage.

And he liked it.

With no thought about what was happening to him he walked up to another tree and attacked it, punching it with his left hand until there was a hole in the trunk. He was exhilarated. He pulled back his fist and hit the tree twice more. It groaned and creaked before snapping in two and hitting the forest floor, sending more birds fleeing to the sky. Dalinil grabbed the fallen tree and, to his own surprise, hefted it above his head as if were a mere branch. He heaved it deeper into the forest where it hit a larger tree and broke in two.

He was unsure how long he stood in place, staring at what he'd done. He could feel anger and rage coursing through every part of his body, commanding him to attack something else. This time, though it was immensely difficult, he resisted. It took all of his concentration to refuse, but he ultimately won the struggle and slowly calmed himself. He inspected his hands and was surprised to see no marks—no scratches or cuts of any kind. He flexed his fingers and looked closer. *How did I do that? I knocked down a tree with my hand!*

Dalinil closed his eyes and instantly could feel it—the pulsing redness—hovering at the edge of his emotions. He was too scared to call upon it again. He needed to take time to figure out what it all meant. What frightened him the most was what could happen if he *couldn't* resist it? What happened if he couldn't come back? He had quickly come to terms with the ability itself—somehow he had known it was there all along—but the pure rage he felt... that was something else entirely. The first encounter with those beastly things in the woods near the pond had brought it to the surface. At the time he wasn't sure what it had all meant, but this unintended experiment had answered some of his questions. It had also presented many more.

His axe was missing. He frantically looked for it and after a moment, he found it lying in the underbrush. At first he hadn't remembered, but slowly everything came back to him. This concerned him greatly—his memory was clouded. He slipped it onto his belt and looked around, unsure of which direction to go. *I'm turned around now. Where was I headed?* It came back to him quickly—the frustration he had felt and the anger... the sheer rage that consumed him—turned on instantly like a torch being lit. He felt none of that now, but he knew he could tap into it if he wanted—and, more importantly, he knew *how*. And then he would do terrible things.

Well, it's not as if you actually had a destination picked out in the first place. So just start walking and see where it takes you. Whatever it was, it's either gone or it wasn't there in the first place. Disappointment and confusion replaced his frustration and he decided to give up chasing illusions.

He started walking. He knew not in which direction he traveled, nor did he care, except that it was deeper into the forest. He made camp that night among the trees, eating some berries he had found from a nearby bush. They were sour but he couldn't be picky, and they eventually filled him up even if they left his mouth raw and sore. It took him just a few minutes to drift off into a solid, dreamless sleep.

When morning came, Dalinil opened his eyes and sat upright, unsure of where he was. He remembered falling asleep the night before, surrounded by trees and crickets. What he awoke to was entirely different. He found himself beside a cobblestone road that led further into the forest toward a very faint, white glow. He could only catch a glimpse of it from here, but he was certain that *this* was what had beckoned to him in the first place. *The road* begins *here. How is that possible? It wasn't here last night.*

Both elated and confused, he got up, shouldered his rucksack, slipped his axe through the belt loop, and followed the road. He did not have to walk very far before he found himself standing outside the closed steel gates of a pristine, white stone wall. He looked both directions, but he could not see where the wall ended. It simply disappeared into the forest, obscured by the trees and bushes. The birds had fallen silent. In fact, there was not a sound to be heard at all.

Peering between the bars of the gates he could see the road continued on into what appeared to be a town. Every building was white. Even the road was white once it passed beyond the gates.

"What is this place?" He expected no answer and, not surprisingly, did not get one. "Where did it come from? Or, more appropriately, where in The Abyss am I?" He turned to look back from where he had traveled, but could only see a short distance before everything faded from view—shrouded in some kind of a mist.

He backtracked, afraid that the forest somehow didn't exist anymore. Each step he took brought more of the forest back into proper view. Turning around, he could barely make out the white wall through the trees. The birds sang again and the forest was alive as he arrived at the end—or the beginning—of the road. "Well," he mumbled to himself, "this *is* what you were looking for, isn't it? You seem to have found it—whatever *it* is." He turned back around, making out brief glimpses of what lay ahead. "This journey just keeps getting more confusing with every step, now doesn't it? But what else have you got to do? You know you're not going to pass this up."

Once he was back in front of the shiny gates again he was unsure what to do next. They remained closed and there was nobody on the other side that he could see. *Is it deserted? Where is everyone?* The wall was smooth and looked newly-constructed. It was at least 10-feet high, Dalinil figured. One thing was for sure, he wasn't climbing his way in. For a brief moment he considered attacking the wall as he had attacked the tree yesterday. He was still afraid of losing control of himself, however. Aside from that, he wasn't entirely sure he could do it again.

The sturdy gates remained closed to him. "Hello!" he called. His voice echoed as he waited for a response that never came. "Is anyone there?" He was met again with the absolute, stark silence. "Anyone?"

He stood outside the gates for several minutes, hoping for a response. When nothing happened, he felt anger building up inside him again. He was tempted to give into it and almost did. Instead, with significant effort, he calmed himself. When he realized his axe was in his left hand, he gasped. *When did I grab it? I don't remember doing that.* He returned it to his side and took a deep breath. *But the gates aren't even locked, are they?* They weren't, and he wasn't sure how he knew that.

He put his hand on one of the bars and, before he could push, it creaked and slowly opened. He jumped back with his hand on the axe at his side and waited.

Again, nothing happened. The gate stayed open, though nobody appeared. Dalinil was becoming more confident that this town was devoid of any people. He cautiously passed through the open gate to the other side of the wall and into what he thought was a silent, deserted town.

And everything suddenly changed.

The forest canopy gave way to a sunny, cloudless sky that cast beautiful light down upon the town. Birds chirped and squeaked while two squirrels chased each other in front of a building to the left. Up ahead, a fountain propelled a jet of water several feet into the air. As before, everything—the buildings, the road, even the fountain—was white. On this side of the gates, however, it was animated and cheerful.

"Hello!" Dalinil called again. As before, he was met with no response. The fountain was centered in a crossroads, or maybe a town square. But it was as empty as the rest of the town. For a moment, Dalinil considered making this his new home but he would first have to find out more about it. Towns that appeared out of nowhere and changed their appearances were not something to take lightly.

He moved past the fountain through rows of empty houses, periodically calling out for anyone who might hear him. Every time he was met with silence and stillness. After a little while it felt less peaceful and more eerie. His imagination began to wander and he started to feel as if he was being stalked by something. *There is absolutely no doubt that this city has not been idle for long. It's in pristine condition. None of the structures are even remotely crumbling, and none of the metal is rusted. The fountains are still flowing.*

The road curved to the right and started downhill. Dalinil followed it and looked ahead. There was another open area—this one with several fountains—and it was surrounded by larger buildings that didn't look like houses. None of them had a sign or indicator as to what their purpose was, however. He started down the gradual slope and noticed a figure standing by one of the fountains. As he got closer he could see the figure was a man dressed in white robes.

The man waved his hand, beckoning Dalinil closer. Dalinil paused briefly, considering this new situation and inspecting the man. His hand felt at his side just to make sure his axe was still there.

"You won't have need of any weapon here," the man called out. "There is nothing to fear, my friend. Please, come closer so that we may speak. There is no danger, here."

Dalinil hesitated a bit longer, surveying the area for possible exits or threats. Being back among buildings, he felt much more comfortable here, but a lot remained unknown. He made his way down the hill, still apprehensive.

The man appeared to be an older fellow—mayhaps of 50 summers. His brown hair had receded to the sides of his head and he hunched slightly. He was not imposing and, in fact, looked rather diminutive. As Dalinil drew near he saw the man smile and felt any apprehension leave his mind. There truly did not seem to be any danger here.

"Welcome," said the man. He extended his hand. Dalinil shook it. The man had a firm grasp. "My name is Arcturas. We have waited a *long* time, and we have been expecting you."

Chapter 18

"But, where am I?" Dalinil asked. "And who are you?" He sat in the simple, wooden chair, dropping his rucksack onto the ground next to him. "And how were you expecting me? And—"

"Slow down, Dalinil." Arcturas sat in the other, identical chair, facing the boy. This was all familiar to him. Arcturas had done this before, but he did not remember when or with whom, and that frustrated him a little. His mind was constantly trying to recall the past but, unfortunately, he came no closer than recalling vague feelings. There were certainly more pressing matters at the moment.

Arcturas had brought Dalinil to his house. There was much that needed to be discussed. It was truly an exciting time, but this boy had a long road ahead of him, and it was always the first two weeks that were the most difficult. They sat across from each other in the empty room—a room Arcturas had emptied on purpose. He did not need distractions or items that may be used as weapons. Simple was always better.

Dalinil sighed and grunted beneath his breath. His impatience was obvious, and that was one reason Arcturas decided to move even slower. On the walk to Arcturas's house, his student had been overflowing with exuberance. Some of that excitement had, eventually, turned to irritation. Arcturas knew that this was always a possibility, but never was it a good thing.

"I am not sure that I can answer every question you have—at least not yet. But I will tell you what I can." This didn't seem to sit well with Dalinil. Disappointment showed through on his face.

"Who are you?"

"We are *Ilathri*. This city in which you find yourself is us. We are it. Everything you see around you is *Ilathri*."

A puzzled look crossed Dalinil's face and lingered for quite some time.

"And *where* are we?"

"That... is a little bit more difficult to answer. You are in *Ilathri*. That is the easy answer. You are here because you have a gift. You are unique, and *Ilathri* sought you out. We appear to those individuals who have a unique quality about them."

If anything, the puzzled look on his face only grew.

"I thought I saw something in the forest and it is what drew me here. Was it this place that I saw?"

"Quite possibly." Arcturas laced his hands together in his lap, carefully considering how he should proceed. He had not done this in quite some time. It was never easy. "Sometimes they come to us; sometimes we go to them. Most often, it is a little of both."

"So you led me into the forest, for what purpose?"

"I am afraid it is more complex than that. Come outside with me for a moment." Arcturas stood and walked outside. Dalinil soon followed. "Look around you," he continued. "What do you see?" There was a pause. Dalinil looked as though he wasn't sure what the proper answer was supposed to be.

"Buildings," he finally said. "Buildings and the road. The sky, clouds, and a few trees. And everything is white."

"Correct." Arcturas remained silent in case the boy had more to say.

"I don't understand. Am I supposed to see something in particular?"

"No, Dalinil. But I would ask you this—when you approached the city gates, you were deep inside a forest, correct?"

"Aye, but I don't—"

"So tell me," Arcturas continued, "Do you see a forest now?"

"I... no, sir. But..." He trailed off, unable to finish his thought. Arcturas could tell that he was busy pondering the situation but was getting nowhere.

"The answer itself is understandably simple, though, not simply understood."

"What do you mean?"

Arcturas ushered him back into the house and, opting for the floor, sat down, legs crossed. Dalinil, apparently unsure of what to do, joined him. "We are no longer in the forest. The moment you stepped past *Ilathri's* walls, you left it behind."

"But I—"

"My advice is not to dwell on this particular quandary." Arcturas knew all too well that there were more important things they had to address and he was unsure of just how much time together they would have. "We have more pressing matters to discuss."

"Are there other... people? More of you?" He didn't even hesitate with his next question. Arcturas was a little surprised, thinking that Dalinil would keep inquiring about his situation.

"A very good question. Yes. I am not alone. We work together."

"Work together to do what, exactly?" Dalinil ran a hand through his hair and fidgeted, adjusting himself on the hard floor.

"To help you, of course. We have other duties that, for now, I should not get into. Talking about them would only confuse you more, and you are probably already confused enough." *This one is our hope for the future. I can sense enormous potential in him, and great ability. If his world is to come back into balance, he will need to lead it into its new age.* Even now, just sitting in the same room with him, Arcturas could feel the Threads bending to his new student's will—even if Dalinil himself did not know it was happening.

He was quite certain that, indeed, Dalinil was completely unaware of it. If he recalled correctly, they were always oblivious at first. If only he could recall *more*.

"It is my turn to ask a question," Arcturas continued. Dalinil nodded quietly, obviously still overwhelmed. *That probably won't change anytime soon.* "You've felt it, haven't you?"

"Felt what, sir?"

"That radiance in the darkness. The inexplicable warmth. The cold without a source. Fresh air and decay, or the smell of flowers where there are none. That feeling as if there is something out there waiting for you to seize it and command it. You know it's there."

Dalinil took a moment. Arcturas could, once again, see him trying to process everything all at once. There was certainly a lot to take in.

"Yes, sir. I think that I have—well, maybe."

"And you've *used* it, haven't you? You've bent it to your will and you've shaped it as a tool... do you understand to what I am referring?"

"I... I am not sure."

Arcturas leaned in until he was but a few inches from Dalinil's face. He stared into his student's eyes and saw not only confusion but power—raw, feral power. This boy had the potential to shape the world—or to lay waste to it. Arcturas could feel it in him.

"Oh, but you have," he whispered and leaned back into his chair. "Once an individual has touched power of this kind they are... forever changed."

"I don't understand."

"I wouldn't expect you to." Arcturas got up and started pacing about the room. He had to handle this very carefully from here on out. "Before we found you, in the woods, you did something. I don't know what it was, exactly. We sensed your connection a while ago and then we felt it again yesterday, and it is this connection that we are here to help you with."

"I don't understand. What connection?"

"Your connection to the Threads, my son." Arcturas turned to look at him. The boy stared back, completely dumbfounded. *Good. He hasn't gotten frustrated enough to completely shut down. He is curious and willing to try to understand. He has taken the first step. Now I must lead him onto the second.*

Dalinil remained silent. He looked as if he wanted to say something but nothing came out. He then stuttered some incomprehensible gibberish. Arcturas tried to contain his laughter but failed. Thankfully, Dalinil also found it funny.

"And... you're going to teach me how to use this, this connection?" Dalinil rose and approached the window. Leaning on the sill with both hands, he stared out at the town beyond, his back to Arcturas.

"Yes. We are."

"And what is this going to allow me to do?"

"Wonderful things, Dalinil. Wonderful things."

"When do we begin?"

Arcturas walked up beside him and, putting his hand on Dalinil's shoulder, looked out the window with him. It was a beautiful day.

"We already have."

Chapter 19

When Cor'il awoke, Kendra was already up. She was sitting on the ground, staring up at the sky, completely focused. She didn't seem to notice when Cor'il sat next to her, waiting for her to respond. The rest of the camp was starting to stir as well, but nobody else was actually up and moving yet.

Cor'il had not intended to bed down in a group last night but the travelers had insisted, and their hospitality had been both generous and greatly appreciated.

"What are you looking at?" he asked. She either didn't hear him or was ignoring him—neither one would've surprised him. She was good at both. Whether she did it on purpose, he wasn't sure, but he suspected she simply wanted to annoy him. She was good at that, too.

"Ooh, that one looks like a dog!" he joked after sitting in silence for a few moments. "And there is another dog!" He bumped her shoulder and pointed. When she still did not acknowledge him, he decided to increase the intensity. "Oh, look!" he said, pointing again. "That one looks like your face when you've eaten something sour. It's all puckered and funny-looking!"

But she still did not budge—not even so much as a grunt or a look of disapproval came from her. He sighed and waited in silence for her to snap out of it.

"What are you on about?" she finally asked, several moments later.

"I was—you know, never mind. It looks like everyone in the camp is finally waking up."

"Indeed it does," she replied, rather emotionless. "Are you about ready to go?"

"Are we not waiting for them?" Cor'il pointed over his shoulder to the camp.

"I'd rather not," she said, getting up and dusting herself off. "In fact, we should probably leave as soon as we can." She walked back to where they had been sleeping and started hastily gathering her things.

"Wait," he called and went after her. "Why? What's the hurry?"

"Because we need to be on our way. I would suggest you get your things."

"But we'll get to Elston quicker with the group. Traveling by wagon is faster than walking. I don't understand—"

"Listen, treeboy." She stood up, a stern look on her face, and stared into his eyes. "I am leaving in a few minutes. If you would like to stay, then I cannot force you to come with me, but I *strongly* urge you to come with me, and leave right now."

Cor'il had never seen her so serious. It frightened him a little and without a second thought, he began packing up what few belongings he had. Whatever had her spooked, it was no joke.

"Are you two heading out?" Orvaril, a storyweaver, approached them. He had been entertaining the merchants on their travels. The striking thing about this man was that the left half of his head was bald. Brown hair, brushed to the right, covered the rest of his head. It wasn't shaved. It was simply missing.

"We are," Kendra replied, not looking up from packing. "And, if you would like my advice, you will do the same."

Orvaril nodded and immediately left, which struck Cor'il as a bit odd. Within a couple of minutes, he had returned, completely packed. Cor'il and Kendra said quick goodbyes to the group and thanked the merchants for allowing them to travel in their group. Then, with Orvaril accompanying them, they headed down the road.

"We should be only a couple of days out from Elston," the storyweaver said. "I recognize this area. Legend has it that there is a large stash of treasure hidden around here somewhere. Many groups have tried to find it but all have failed."

Cor'il found Orvaril quite amusing and entertaining. He always enjoyed the tales that storyweavers told, but this man was like no other storyweaver he had encountered. Even Kendra had admitted that it felt like she had no choice but to like the man. In fact, it was he who had convinced the rest of the group to let Cor'il and Kendra travel with them, even though there was no room left in the wagon. Everyone had gone from "absolutely not" to "absolutely" in a matter of a few minutes, all because of him.

"So what are you going to do once we reach Elston? Cor'il asked him. Up until now he'd not had a chance to actually talk to Orvaril because he was always so busy entertaining. The man also slept a lot and, as Kendra had pointed out numerous times, he snored loudly.

"I plan on playing music for the Storm's End." He pointed to the lute slung over his shoulder. He'd played it nightly for the merchant group and was extraordinarily talented. "I bet I can make enough coin to set me up in the finest inn for months."

Cor'il could not profess to know this man inside and out, but he had a sneaking suspicion that, contrary to what Orvaril said, it was not the coin, but the attention and performances that he *really* relished. Cor'il figured the man would probably perform for free just to have the opportunity to show off.

"Besides," he continued, "It's the largest stage I will probably ever have!"

Cor'il grinned.

"And you shall own it, sir." Cor'il bowed, exaggerating greatly.

"Why thank you, kind sir! I shall be sure not to disappoint!" Orvaril laughed.

Through all of this, Kendra remained focused. She said not a word but kept walking at a brisk pace. She looked behind them occasionally, and only mumbled to herself under her breath. Cor'il suspected she thought he couldn't hear it.

"See that you don't disappoint," Cor'il continued. "Or you shall be mucking the stalls!"

"Hey now," Orvaril laughed. "I've done my share of stall-mucking. And it's not as bad as you'd think!"

"Oh?"

"Indeed. You see, farmers' daughters often take pity on you. They bring you water and food and... well, they're very kind." Orvaril grinned lecherously. "Of course," he continued, "there is obviously a lot of shit—that's the unpleasant part."

Cor'il laughed. Outlanders were a lot looser with their language and they swore more than he was used to. Most of the time it made him cringe a little, but Orvaril somehow made it charming. In fact, Cor'il suspected, he probably made stable-mucking charming. He'd go so far as to say that Orvaril could probably convince everyone within earshot that scooping manure was fun.

"So if you were given the opportunity to clean out a barn tomorrow, you'd jump at the chance?"

Orvaril laughed and slapped Cor'il on the back.

"Only if it is necessary to get what I want. If so, then it would be completely worth it. It's all a matter of what you're willing to do for something—and how badly you want it in the first place."

Cor'il was thankful that Orvaril had decided to come with them. He was able to lighten the mood. The journey didn't seem so long when he was around. Certainly, Kendra wasn't helping to cheer anyone up.

"The Storm's End is going to be quite the celebration. It's supposed to go on for a month straight. I hear that King Alzine is essentially throwing money around, and I do believe I would like to be a part of that."

"While we're on the subject," Cor'il continued, "Tell me more about The Storm."

Orvaril shot Cor'il a shocked look, his mouth agape. He was silent for a moment or two. Cor'il began to wonder if he had somehow offended him.

"You don't know about The Storm?" he asked, still surprised but now laughing. "What, are you from Kuranthas or something?"

"Well, actually, yes. I am from Kuranthas."

Orvaril's laughter stopped immediately.

"Oh," he said. "Sorry about that. I was… uh… so anyway, yeah." Cor'il couldn't help smiling—he'd not seen Orvaril thrown off his game before. The man who had always been charming and in control was speechless. He recovered just as quickly, however. "So the stories are true, then? Excellent!"

"Well, yes. I guess they are. Kuranthas does not concern ourselves with Outlander affairs so our knowledge of the world outside Kuranthas is limited."

"Outlanders?"

"Outsiders," Cor'il explained. "We use both terms to describe anyone not from Kuranthas."

This apparently gave Orvaril cause for contemplation. Cor'il was impressed that he knew something Orvaril did not.

"Well, just in case you didn't know, 200 years ago was when The Storm ended. Before that, Kuranthas was rumored to be less isolated."

"Really?"

"Well, that's what I've heard. I'm not 200 years old, though." Orvaril grinned. "I'm not sure I believe it, either. Much of our historical accounts were destroyed when the hordes crossed into the Realm and overran everything like a plague. I am no historian but I've certainly heard enough stories to arouse my curiosity. In my travels I have found precious few answers though, again, some of those answers are suspect. Most or all of 'em, probably."

"My people's history is in much the same state. We have no accurate accord of anything beyond 200 years ago."

Cor'il was surprised to learn that it was not just Kuranthian history that had been apparently destroyed during The Storm.

"Aye. I have never traveled to your homeland but I have often wondered just how much damage the savages had done. So even Kuranthas was a victim... but at least we beat them in the end, right? Supposedly, they raged for 20 years in our lands. 20 years! Can you imagine? Did they plunder other realms, too? We know so very little."

"Kendra," Cor'il called. She was a good 20 paces ahead of them. He wasn't sure why she was so impatient this morning, but she was in the biggest hurry he'd seen from her. She stopped and turned around, glaring at the two of them. "Is it alright if we stop for a moment?"

"Yes," she replied. "Yes we can. But not for long." Cor'il was shocked. He'd expected, given her mood, to be yelled at.

"As I was saying," Orvaril continued. He set down his rucksack and took the lute off his back, leaning against a tree. "Nobody is even sure where the barbarian hordes came from. Their leader, Gorag Thrashbone had supposedly united all of the various savage tribes and brought them to our lands. He was rumored to command powerful, well, powers—summoning fire and lightning and whatnot. Magic is what they called it. You know, all of that mystical stuff."

"Rubbish," Kendra interjected. "Magic—if it can be called that—is simply explaining what can't be explained." Cor'il wasn't sure, but he *thought* he saw her wink at him. He fidgeted a bit.

"I've also heard that he was such a good leader and warrior because the clouds supposedly talked to him—they even told him what he should do. Cloudsight I think they called it?"

"If the clouds are talking to me," Cor'il interrupted, "then all they are telling me is to feed the dog or gortog or blob." They all laughed.

"Then you, sir, are a Cloudseer!" Orvaril announced. "Tell us the future, sir!"

"Well, I don't even have a dog, or a gortog... or a blob."

"Then that makes you a *terrible* Cloudseer, Cor'il." Kendra threw a handful of grass at him. She still seemed somewhat agitated but he took this as a sign that her mood might be improving.

He brushed it out of his hair, grabbed some from the ground, and threw it back, missing her by a foot.

"You're also terrible at throwing things." Was that a tiny grin he saw? Whatever had been bothering Kendra seemed to be fading.

"It was a man named Sturm Ironhelm," Orvaril continued, "who is said to have rallied a formidable army and met Gorag on the battlefield where Elston now stands."

"Right," Cor'il agreed. "I've heard that before—that Elston is on the site of the final battle. Everyone seems to be able to agree on that, at least."

"It might be the only thing that is true," Kendra retorted. "I wasn't aware of much of this as well, but I never paid very close attention. I guess historians wouldn't have a lot to go on without a written account. I just never really thought about it, I suppose."

"Most of what we have is stories." Orvaril casually strummed his lute. "But I have found there to usually be a kernel of truth in each tale. You just have to know what is truth and what is garbage."

"But," Cor'il interrupted, "how do you know which is which?"

"That, my boy, is the trick now isn't it?" He strummed a few chords and tightened one of the strings slightly. "I've spent most of my life retelling stories and embellishing them with my own flare. There is no telling what the original tale was like when it first started. Often, I simply make things up so that the story is more interesting."

"But doesn't distorting history bother you?" Cor'il could feel his own frustration. He was not naïve enough to believe everything a storyweaver said, but he believed that purposely telling falsehoods seemed wrong.

"I am an entertainer, not a historian. Without written documents, the facts are whatever you say they are. Even *with* documents it is still very easy to distort the truth. It all depends on what people are willing to believe."

"So," Kendra added, "We could all be living lies, then?"

"Well, yes and no." Orvaril put down the lute, obviously dissatisfied with something about it. "But ask yourself this; how many people do you know who can command magic? How many orcs have you seen? Stories are sometimes just that—stories."

"But sometimes," Cor'il interrupted, "Stories have truth to them, no matter how much they are exaggerated." He paused, knowing full well what he and Kendra had encountered during these last few days. "So tell me, what would you do if you *did* see an orc?"

"Me?" Orvaril laughed. "Are you serious, Cor'il?" He laughed some more. "Well, I guess I would run away as fast as I could!" He wiped a tear from his left eye, struggling to hold back more laughter. Cor'il found himself laughing a little, but for a totally different reason. He was not about to try to convince the man that orcs were real. Anyway, he figured Orvaril would find out for himself soon enough—one way or the other.

"Sometimes," he mumbled under his breath, "stories have more than just a kernel of truth to them." He saw the serious look that Kendra gave him.

"We've probably taken enough of a rest," she finally said. "We should get moving."

"What *is* your hurry, milady?" Cor'il could tell Orvaril was half-joking while trying to include a decent amount of charm to stay on her good side.

"I am quite anxious to get to Elston," she replied.

"I thought you were not looking forward to returning to Elston?" Cor'il remembered her apprehension when they talked about it last. Something didn't make sense.

"I... do not believe that it is very safe to be on the road anymore," she confessed after hesitating. She stood up and, without even brushing the dirt and grass from her skirts, she began walking. "Cor'il." She stopped and turned her head back toward them. "You of all people should know what I mean."

He didn't need to give it a second thought. Cor'il got up, shouldered his satchel, and followed her.

"She's right," he called back to Orvaril who was gathering his things. "Many places aren't safe anymore."

"What do you mean?" Orvaril yelled back, hurriedly slinging his rucksack over his shoulder. He had to run to catch up.

"You don't really want to know what we mean," Kendra replied. Cor'il was actively concentrating on trying to keep up with her. She was fast!

After a moment, Cor'il stopped.

Screams and battle sounds rang out from behind them in the distance. Kendra and Orvaril, also paused, curious, until they, too, heard it. Shrill yells and beastly noises made all three of them look behind them, though they could see nothing.

"What the—" Orvaril's mouth hung open as he stared into the distance. "That doesn't sound like any battle I am familiar with."

"It's not," Cor'il responded. He grabbed Orvaril's tunic and pulled as he started in the other direction. "We should go—now!"

Kendra was mumbling something to herself, irritated. Cor'il couldn't make out any of what she was saying, but he wasn't entirely sure he wanted to know. The sounds from behind them continued, and Cor'il knew that it had to be orcs and goblins. He looked at Kendra who looked back at him with a sullen look. The caravan they had left behind was under attack.

She was right. The Realm is not safe. That could have been us. One quick glance at Orvaril told Cor'il that the storyweaver was thinking the same thing.

"Should we... should we go back and see if we can help?" Cor'il knew the answer, but the question still had to be asked. He'd feel like a horrible person if he didn't at least *suggest* it.

"No," Kendra responded tersely. "There is nothing we can do. If we go back, we will meet the same fate. It's better we get to safety and start spreading the word about this. Surely, by now, someone else has—"

"Excuse me," Orvaril interrupted. "Yes, excuse me but what is it that I am missing, here? What, exactly, are you planning on spreading the word about?"

"Remember those orcs that you said only reside in stories?" Kendra replied. Cor'il waited for Orvaril to explode in fits of laughter but it never happened. Instead, the group traveled quickly, and in solemn silence, hoping to escape without encountering any new foes this day.

After walking all day, as the sun began to set in the West, they camped in much the same silence as they had traveled. Cor'il could tell that Orvaril had quickly accepted Kendra's word as fact since his usual, jovial demeanor had wilted, leaving only pensive silence with a hint of quiet despair.

Chapter 20

Captain Jarel Forsch got to his hands and knees and tried to shake off the fog within his head. He wasn't sure what had hit him, but whatever it was, it was big. Thankfully, his armor had deflected most of the impact—if it hadn't he wouldn't be alive. He stood and looked at his surroundings through blurry vision and ducked behind a wall crenellation to catch his breath. He closed his eyes to try to calm himself, listening to the sounds of battle. All around him he could hear men barking orders to one another and the familiar twang of his men's longbows followed by the screams from the victims their arrows found.

After a moment his vision cleared. His helmet lay on the ground. A large dent marred the front. He scurried over long enough to grab it and returned to the safety of the wall. It was a tight fit when he slipped it back onto his head. *You have to get up and keep order. Your men are counting on you.*

"Sir!" It was one of his men—Garl. "Sir, are you alright?"

"Yes, soldier. Help me up." Garl took his hand and pulled him to his feet. "One of those... those brutes nearly got me with a rock." He pointed over the wall to where there was a towering humanoid creature throwing large chunks of dirt and rock like they were simple pebbles. There were at least two of them he'd seen—the gray-skinned giants—and they were surrounded by other savage creatures, the likes of which he had never seen. They fit the description of orcs and goblins but that was ridiculous. *It doesn't matter what they are as long as we defeat them. Sort it all out after we repel them.*

The attackers had come in the night and taken Sulbar by surprise. They had broken through the city's north gates before anyone knew what was happening. Much of the day had been spent pushing them back out of the city. His men fought tirelessly, and many had already died. They were vastly outnumbered, but they were much more disciplined, much better trained, and better equipped.

Only a tiny contingent of the town guard had fled. They would be dealt with after this attack was over and the city was secured. Forsch had expected some of his men to flee. Simple guards and watchmen were accustomed to basic duties like apprehending thieves or, at worst, killers. These creatures were something completely savage, frightening, and unexpected. *I even thought about running. Damned beasts caught us all by surprise. I'm not sure I can blame those who fled but, still we must all remain disciplined or we will all die.*

The invaders had eventually been pushed back and most of the fighting now raged outside the city's walls. They had built a hasty, ramshackle barricade to block the entrance where the gates once were. It was little more than debris haphazardly piled up but it was, thus far, effective. Since one of the larger brutes had pulled the gates completely out of their supports they'd had to improvise with what they had, and this barricade seemed to work. It didn't block off the entire gap but any savage that made it over the pile met with a swift end.

Sulbar's walls stood only about 10 feet high and were showing their age but, thus far, they seemed to be holding up against the onslaught. They had to be careful not to let any of the larger brutes get too close, however, since they could probably tear down the walls with their giant hands alone. Thankfully, none of the larger creatures had approached the walls, because Forsch wasn't sure they could do anything to stop them if they wanted to get into the city.

"We need more archers!" he yelled above the din of battle. Garl nodded, looked around, and then hurried off down some stairs into the city.

"Archers!" he yelled. "We need archers on the wall over here!"

This army—if it could even be called that—was only attacking at the north gates for some reason. These savages didn't seem very tactical. To Captain Forsch's surprise, one of the larger creatures quit attacking in mid swing. It turned to one of the much smaller, green-skinned beasts behind it and grabbed it in one hand. The beast shrieked and squealed but was quickly silenced when the larger one bit off its head and ate it.

Captain Forsch's men quickly moved in, poking and stabbing at it with their spears while it devoured over half of its supposed, unfortunate ally. Finally, one of his men's weapons found purchase in the creature's groin.

Enraged, the brute roared and used the rest of its lunch as a weapon, knocking three men back several feet. Two more started backing up slowly, still thrusting their spears.

Captain Forsch turned around to survey the city. There were still several fires yet to be put out but most appeared to have either been extinguished or had burned themselves out. *I hope we pushed them all out of the city. If we missed any, we could have a pretty gruesome few days yet to come.* He would have to organize a group to comb through the city once this horde was defeated. And it *would* be defeated.

Horde, he thought. *Was this the type of invasion we once had to defend against when the Barbarian Horde invaded Cygil? The Barbarians fought with axe and club. These... things fight with tooth and claw. The Barbarians supposedly had battering rams and these creatures have giants?*

He ducked as something flew overhead, easily nowhere near him, but he was still jumpy. As he looked behind him, he realized that the thrown object was one of his soldiers—still screaming. The poor man was silenced when he hit the solid ground below.

Four archers rushed up the stairs and spread out around Captain Forsch. They immediately began firing arrows into the fray, dropping several invaders instantly.

"Focus on one of the big ones!" he yelled. "See if you can't bring at least one of those bastards down!"

In unison, each of the four soldiers fired at the giant nearest them—a bald brute with part of its nose missing. All four arrows hit the giant square in the chest but bounced off harmlessly or shattered. The monster didn't even seem to notice.

"Shit!" he yelled. "That thing's skin must be some kind of armor!"

"I can kill it, sir!" the soldier next to him yelled. A crude, stone axe flew over the wall and felled one of the other archers but *this* man remained undaunted. He pulled back on his bow, squinting.

"What's your name, soldier?"

"Borstin, sir. Eric Borstin." The man seemed awfully sure of himself.

"Well, Eric Borstin." He clapped the man on the shoulder. "If you make this shot, I owe you an ale!"

The remaining two archers continued firing their shots into the throng of attackers, dropping some of the smaller ones further back who were not yet in the fray. Borstin stared stone-faced at his target, still squinting and not moving in the slightest.

Captain Forsch stopped to watch, his intense curiosity piqued. The man's hands were steady as he kept the bow pulled back, concentrating on his aim. Captain Forsch inspected the arrow closely—it was perfectly still. And then it was gone. He followed it in flight as it hit the beast and shattered like the others before it.

"Nice try, soldier," he said. "We still have to find a way—"

"With all due respect, sir," he replied, still staring out at the gray-skinned behemoth. "But I will collect that ale after this battle is done." Was that a smirk that crossed his lips?

Captain Forsch looked again, forgetting the chaos that raged around him. He watched the giant stagger backwards. It was then that he noticed the blood running out of its left eye socket as well as the back of its head. The arrow had indeed shattered, but only after it hit the back of the creature's skull!

The giant cried out in pain and crashed to the ground, crushing several of its allies beneath its considerable girth.

"I'll buy you as much ale as you can handle if we get out of this alive!"

"Sir, you've got a deal. Now—"

Borstin was hit by a tree as it sailed over the wall, taking him with it to the ground below.

"Damn it! Somebody take down the big ones! Sulbar will *not* fall to this horde of savages, do you hear me?"

Two more of the large ones had moved up from the rear. His troops seemed to be handling the rest of the smaller enemies at this point. These creatures weren't skilled but they were ferocious and brutal. In greater numbers they would have destroyed the city. *The Abyss, they almost destroyed the city with just* this *army.*

At any moment he expected the now dwindling horde to retreat but it did not. If anything, each savage fought more fiercely now than before. *We are going to have to kill every last one of these bastards. They aren't going to give up.* He had been holding out hope that these creatures might be reasoned with at some point, but it had become apparent that this was not an option. *Fine. Let's get this finished quickly.*

When he finally looked around, he noticed the remaining two archers had moved to a different part of the wall. Scattered weapons lay on the ramparts. Captain Forsch eschewed the bows, knowing full well he could not place an arrow in the eye of one of those things.

"Men!" he shouted. "Lead one of the big ones closer to the wall!" He wasn't sure anyone heard him so he barked the command repeatedly until someone acknowledged his orders. Several soldiers engaged one of the giants and started backing up slowly toward the city wall. The creature lumbered forward, trying to both swing at them with its fist and stomp on them. The soldiers, in turn, backed up, baiting the creature forward.

Captain Forsch picked up a spear from nearby. It was missing about a third of its haft but he saw no other suitable weapon for what he needed to do. He grabbed it with both hands and stepped up to the edge of the wall, waiting patiently. The men were leading the oversized foe right to him.

"Now get out of there!" he yelled to them. They seemed to hear him instantly this time. Most of them fled immediately, spreading out to confuse the creature. "This could be the absolute stupidest thing you've ever done," he muttered. "Even if it works, it's still foolish."

Taking a deep breath, he hefted the spear in one hand and, when the beast was almost beneath him, he leapt from the wall. Gripping the spear with both hands, he cried out and pointed the weapon downward. The gray-skinned brute looked up just as the spear hit it in the chest and drove straight through.

Captain Forsch tried to hang onto the spear but was knocked loose by the creature's violent, thrashing death throes. He landed on the ground and rolled out of range, coming to stand up against the wall. The creature bellowed out in rage and pain, blindly lashing out at anything nearby and spraying blood as it did so. Man and creature alike were knocked aside, some thrown high into the air, as it wildly swung its arms until, finally, it let out a sad moan and slumped to the ground. It lay motionless as blood oozed from both ends of the wound, collecting in a pool around its large body.

For a moment, everything fell into silence. Captain Forsch and his men stared at the fallen foe. Likewise, the remaining attackers stood, dumbfounded.

"Huzzah!" several soldiers shouted and they resumed combat with new confidence. Captain Forsch drew his sword and charged into battle, cutting down one of the smaller beasts as he moved to engage the next foe. He dodged the strike of one of the larger creatures and stuck it through the neck. Using his boot to push the corpse off his blade, he shouted to rally his men. The creature's body fell to the ground in front of him as several of its comrades looked on but this time did not advance.

Instead, three of them looked at each other and then ran. Several of his men gave chase but were unable to catch the creatures. Captain Forsch looked to his left and saw at least a dozen of his men mob the final giant. They poked it in the legs with their swords and spears, and several of them were climbing the creature itself.

It grabbed one of them and, with one hand, crushed the man's skull. After discarding the corpse, it moved onto another, but the men were too numerous. They overpowered the creature and managed to bring it to the ground where they stabbed at it furiously. Finally, it lay motionless. The soldiers, after looking around and seeing no more monsters to fight, cheered in victory.

Captain Forsch allowed himself a brief moment of respite to smile and enjoy what they had accomplished, but concern quickly crept back into his thoughts. He had many questions that would likely go unanswered. *Many questions indeed—starting with what in The Abyss were those damned things?*

What made things worse was that his forces were probably at less than half strength now—either killed or fled. He suspected more of the former than the latter. He didn't see many deserters at the beginning, and the ground was literally covered with his men. *The enemy fled only in the end, and only a few of them. The men under my command who fled, did so at the beginning.*

He walked over to the nearest green corpse and kicked it over on its back. It was not one of the giants, but it was bigger than some of the others. It had large, sharp teeth protruding from its lower jaw. *Tusks. Those teeth look like tusks. They've got to be at least two inches long.* Its skin was pale green and it had a tuft of hair on the top of its head. The creature's one remaining eye was solid green with a black pupil. This thing was not a human.

He inspected one of the smaller ones. It was half the size and also had green skin. This one had no fangs or tusks, but its crooked teeth were dull and worn.

"Men!" he yelled. Several soldiers hurried over and stood at attention. "We must tend to the wounded. Once that is taken care of we will gather up all of the bodies. We'll need to bury our own." He paused for a moment and took one last look at the field of dead.

They all nodded in unison.

"Whatever these things were, we were fortunate that they finally retreated, but we had to kill damn near every last one of them. Burn them all."

Captain Forsch turned and walked into the city. The Council was not going to like what he had to tell them.

Chapter 21

Cor'il let out a huge yawn as the three of them walked. His satchel felt heavier today, as did his feet. *Why did Kendra have to get us all up so early?* He knew the answer, but he still bellyached to himself about it. He was never one to sleep more than a few hours anyway, but he'd barely gotten *any* sleep last night.

No sooner had he closed his eyes last night than Kendra had woken him and Orvaril so that they could continue their journey. She hadn't been excited about it—she had been scared. Orvaril looked sleepy as well but, somehow, he cheered up a bit. Kendra wasn't speaking much.

They walked under a still dark sky, keeping to the road. That had been Kendra's idea. She said she felt safer close to the road where they might find help if they needed it. It was sound reasoning, but Cor'il wasn't sure how much good it would do if they encountered too many hostile creatures. Sure, they'd fought off a few at a time, but he suspected that they could travel in greater numbers. How could they fight that many? Kendra was anxious to get to Elston. He understood that much. He could see the growing agitation within her.

From what Kendra had said they should arrive at Elston just before noon if they kept up their current pace. Both she and Orvaril had been to Elston before so Cor'il assumed she was correct. Their proximity to the city did nothing, however, to improve her mood.

The three of them kept as quiet as they could, hoping the cover of darkness would help them remain hidden from anything dangerous. Orvaril kept himself subdued, especially after Kendra had smacked him and nearly broken his lute the first time he'd tried to play a song. Since then they had all whispered to each other and moved as quickly as possible without a light source. He still carried the instrument, however, fidgeting with it as if he would break into song at any moment.

Cor'il walked with his sword in his hand. Orvaril and Kendra had no weapons out, but as far as Kendra was concerned, Cor'il knew she could have one in her hand faster than he could blink. Orvaril was a different story. He didn't seem to have a weapon of any kind on his person. Cor'il was more than a little curious about this. They would *all* need to be able to fight if the situation arose.

"So," Cor'il whispered. Kendra shot a glance back at him as if to tell him to keep quiet. "What ever happened to Sturm Ironhelm after

The Storm was over?" He knew they needed to be quiet but he also preferred to keep his mind occupied.

"There are several theories," Orvaril whispered back. He looked around nervously as if he expected something to hear him and come charging out of the darkness. "Some say he oversaw the construction of Elston and, once he was satisfied, he simply walked away and was never seen again. Others say that he ruled the Realm for a brief time before being stricken by a deadly illness."

"So nobody knows for sure?"

"Ah, but I'm not finished," he continued. "There's more. You see, still others believe that Sturm himself possessed either immortality or was extremely long-lived. They believe that, after the war was finally won, that Sturm went into seclusion but returned later and walked amongst the people. They say that he is indeed still alive and lives among us today."

"But how would that be possible?"

"And, of course, still others believe that he was mortally wounded in battle and died soon after."

"Wait," Cor'il interrupted. "I don't understand."

"Don't understand what?"

"Well, how is it possible that we don't know what happened to the individual who was instrumental in defeating the barbarians—the worst threat our Realm has ever seen?"

"That," Orvaril said, "Is an excellent question." Kendra shot him an evil glare and he lowered his voice. "That is *the* question! How is it that nobody knows what happened to the hero who supposedly brought the Realm back from the brink of collapse? And, finally, why are there so many vastly different accounts of what could have happened?"

"So what does it all mean?"

Orvaril shrugged and remained silent for a while, looking straight ahead as he walked. He fidgeted with his lute briefly, not actually playing it but coming very close at times.

"That is what I would *love* to find out. Instead of simply telling fantastic stories, I could actually be retelling history. But the history is flawed. It doesn't add up, does it?"

"Do you think anyone knows the truth? Are there not historians?"

"I hope so. It is one of the reasons why I travel the Realm. Surely *someone* knows. I understand how much of our literature and historical accounts could be decimated by war, but I cannot comprehend how they could *all* be lost."

"That all does indeed sound rather suspicious."

"Exactly!" He immediately hushed as Kendra scowled at him again. "Exactly," he whispered. "And why is nobody else asking the same questions?"

Cor'il had to admit, now that he thought about it, that something seemed fishy about it all. He had not questioned it before but, then, he had known next to nothing about Outlander history and culture when he started this journey. He was intrigued to find out that, apparently, Outlanders themselves knew nothing about Outlander history!

They walked in silence for a while longer, still in the dark. It was difficult to see but Kendra and Orvaril seemed to have a more challenging time navigating than Cor'il. He briefly considered summoning a light but, as the goal was to not attract attention, he decided against it. Explaining it to Orvaril would also be awkward.

Orvaril began reciting humorous poetry and Cor'il stifled his laughter. The man had a knack for levity in even the worst situations.

"Would you two keep it down back there?" Kendra didn't even bother looking back this time. "If you keep talking like two chatty sisters, you'll give us all away to anything within 100 miles."

Cor'il and Orvaril both looked at each other and suppressed laughter like little children avoiding their parents' scrutiny. They both nearly ran into Kendra when she suddenly stopped in front of them.

Cor'il expected her to admonish them both for their behavior, but instead she stood in silence. She looked around slowly as if she saw something in the darkness. Cor'il did the same. They were stopped on a part of the road with sparse trees. To their left was a slight hill leading upward and it looked as though, to their right, there was an even steeper hill that descended further into darkness.

"What—"

"Shhh!" She held her hand up. "There's something following us," she whispered. Cor'il wasn't sure when she'd pulled a weapon, but she now held a dagger in her right hand. Cor'il gripped his sword. It always felt strange to hold it. Though he'd had plenty of practice with the blade, he still hadn't seen much *real* combat.

Orvaril still held his lute, looking about for a sign of any attackers. He looked a bit silly, gripping his instrument tightly.

"I hear it, too," Cor'il whispered. "Off to our left, I think." There was more than one and they weren't making human sounds. "Orcs and goblins again?"

"Aye," Kendra responded.

"So," Orvaril interjected. "I guess this pretty much confirms it, eh?"

"We have been calling them orcs and goblins," Kendra whispered, "because they fit the descriptions from old tales."

"They're not bears, dogs, or any animal we know," Cor'il agreed.

"But they definitely *act* like animals."

"Actually, not all of them." Cor'il had given up whispering. There was something out there and it already knew where they were. "I fought one that spoke to me. Granted, it was broken Common Tongue, but I would say they aren't completely mindless."

"Charming," Orvaril retorted. "So maybe they'll tell us a joke before they eat us?"

"I doubt it'd be a funny one," Kendra snorted.

A squat, green figure came running out of the darkness, squealing and swinging a crude hatchet. Cor'il immediately prepared to fight it and Kendra quickly did the same. Before the goblin got within 10 feet of them, a small arrow imbedded itself in the goblin's chest.

"And that, my friends," Orvaril exclaimed, "is how it is done. Please, don't get all gushy. You can thank me later!" He was holding his lute by the neck and had a small arrow in his right hand. "The bad thing is dead—problem solved. Shall we continue on our way?"

But there was no time to chat as three more charged down the hill to the left, screaming a raspy, sick battle cry of sorts. Without a word, Orvaril put the arrow to a string on the backside of the instrument and launched it at their foes. Cor'il didn't wait to see the result as one of the goblins was upon him, swinging and thrashing wildly. Another goblin joined in, both attacking him at the same time. He slowly backed up, parrying some blows and dodging others.

He soon saw his opportunity and took it. One of the goblins threw itself off balance with one of its swings, and Cor'il's blade tasted the creature's soft belly, spilling its guts out into the grass. It gurgled and collapsed forward. At the same time Kendra came from behind the other one and ran a dagger across its throat. It quietly fell in a heap onto the other goblin.

Cor'il looked around for more enemies but neither saw nor heard any. Kendra and Orvaril appeared to be doing the same thing.

The danger now over, they all three stood and looked at the scene. Cor'il, having encountered these beasts before, *still* did not know quite what to make of it all. He wasn't sure he would ever get used to them, let alone *killing* them. It left a bad taste in his mouth and his stomach was queasy. All three goblins were indeed dead—two lying together and one a few yards away. The other goblin—the first one that had been courageous enough to lead the charge—was still a bit further up the hill. It had not moved since Orvaril dropped it.

"Do you think there are any more of them?" Orvaril approached the goblin lying alone. He rolled it over and pulled his arrow out of the creature's neck.

"I don't hear any more of them," Cor'il replied. He focused intently, listening for more, but everything was quiet.

"Neither do I," added Kendra. She wiped her dagger on one of the dead goblins' rags, inspected it, and apparently decided wiping it on the grass was a better idea. "Nevertheless, we should not tarry."

"Agreed." Orvaril inspected the other goblin. "Blast it! This stupid brute broke my arrow."

"How rude," Kendra smirked.

"Indeed. It could have at least been considerate enough to fall backwards. The nerve!" Orvaril chuckled and pulled the arrow out anyway. After inspecting it he frowned and threw it aside.

"Should we do anything with the bodies?" Cor'il asked. He, too, wiped his blade in the grass. Once he was satisfied, he sheathed it.

"Do you mean loot the bodies?" Kendra asked.

"No!" Cor'il frowned but Kendra was already looking them over.

"Oh," she mumbled. "Well, they don't have anything good anyway. Just these shoddy, half-rusted blades—if you can even call them that." She had one in her hand, scrutinizing it. Cor'il looked at it. He wasn't sure it could even break the skin.

Where are you coming from? Why has nobody seen you before?

"So," Orvaril stepped next to Cor'il, also interested in the dagger, "goblins, eh?"

"Goblins," Kendra and Cor'il both replied in unison.

"I'm beginning to believe you two are right."

"And there are larger ones," Cor'il continued. He headed back to the road. The others followed. "Larger, but they don't look like the goblins. They're more muscular, more skilled, and more savage."

"Not to mention," Kendra added, "smarter."

"Orcs?" Orvaril slung his lute back over his shoulder.

"Indeed." Cor'il started walking. He preferred to get away from this scene in case there *were* others lurking about. "They're much more dangerous."

"They sound like scholars. Mayhaps we shall read a wonderful book someday written by orcs called 'The Great Works of Orcitude'!" Orvaril made himself laugh. Cor'il and Kendra both joined in. It was silly but it broke the tension which, Cor'il suspected, was the whole point.

"Oh yes," Kendra retorted. "I can imagine it would go something like 'grunt grunt, snort, grunt, howl,' wouldn't it?"

"Shouldn't we be a little quieter?" Cor'il whispered. "You know, in case there are more out there?"

"Mayhaps." Kendra didn't seem all too concerned. Nevertheless, she lowered her voice a bit. "I am not sure it matters. They heard us before, even when we were trying to be quiet. In any case, I think we are safe for now."

"How can you be sure?" Cor'il inquired.

"Because... I just am."

"All of this," Orvaril interjected, "makes me wonder exactly what we are going to encounter next."

"Sulbar was under siege, or so I heard." Kendra paused and looked around briefly. Cor'il wondered if she had heard something. "I was headed that way until I heard that news. But it's likely that the secret is out. If you are looking for something new and exciting, chances are Elston might offer that."

"Personally, I'd prefer old and boring at this point." Orvaril said that, but Cor'il wasn't sure he believed it. He was more and more intrigued by this man—as if there were some mysteries surrounding him. At some point, *his* secret was going to get out—Kendra already knew. But she was observant. Or nosey. Probably both. *How are people going to react if they see the things that I can do? The Abyss knows I don't even know everything I can do! What if I accidentally destroy an entire town instead of just a few trees?*

The questions were many and the answers scarce. Kendra hadn't seemed to care, but Cor'il surmised that most people would see him as a threat just as everyone at home had. Destroying trees was a crime in Kuranthas, with severe punishments involved. But there was more... wasn't there? He knew that there had been multiple incidents involving him and his abilities but he still felt as though he was forgetting something. *My friends would know! Lena, Alton, and Brand had been with me almost every time something happened. If only I could talk to them.*

Cor'il felt a tear run down his face. He missed his friends and he was most likely never going to see them again. They were gone. No—*they* were not gone. *He* was gone, never to return. But he still felt that, one day, he would return to his beloved home. Something felt... unfinished, as if there was something yet to resolve. At the very least, he had to reconnect with his friends.

No, you can't. It is not possible. It won't be easy, but you will come to terms with this eventually.

No, he was *sure* that he would return. He *felt* it. Just as he *felt* that The Densewood was where he was supposed to be. There was no explanation for it, only a feeling. But it was a strong feeling—something he could not dismiss.

The sky slowly got lighter as morning's first rays of sun painted the sky. The clouds had mostly dissipated and Cor'il could see the stars fading. The terrain slowly transformed and eventually the three of them were walking past small farms. In the distance, Cor'il could make out what appeared to be the walls of Elston further down the road.

"There it is," Orvaril piped up. "Elston. Now *that* is a sight for sore eyes."

"Indeed it is," Kendra agreed. Cor'il could detect the apprehension in her voice—as if she were glad to approach the safety of a city but, at the same time, she was cautious.

Cor'il put his hood down and took a deep breath, making sure his hair adequately covered his ears. He still didn't wish to draw attention to them, especially when he didn't even understand why they were misshapen.

The morning air was sweet and smelled of grass and animals. As they walked, Cor'il began to see people starting their daily farm chores. The sky got lighter and the previous night's encounter seemed to wash away like dirt in the rain.

"What a beautiful destination," Orvaril said. "We shall find solace inside its walls and, possibly, answers."

Cor'il hoped so but, deep down, he was not optimistic. He had a sneaking suspicion that their troubles had probably just begun.

Chapter 22

There was a line of people at the gates of Elston, waiting to get into the city. Travelers and merchants with carts and wagons were positioned, one behind the next, as the city guards inspected each group. Horses whinnied impatiently and children ran around freely, playing games like Catch the Gortog and Avoid the Orc.

Of course, "Avoid the Orc" was a child's game, but Kendra didn't find it all that amusing anymore. The act of pretending to be an orc and killing other children once seemed harmless. However, with the knowledge they now had, she doubted anyone in the group found it to be just a silly child's game anymore.

A little brown-haired boy chased several other children. He snorted and grunted as he ran after them, pretending to slash at them with an imaginary blade of some kind. They screamed and scattered in every direction, one of them nearly running into a guard. The man took it in stride and played along, pretending to scare away the orc.

"Do you really think that Elston is going to want our cloaks?" she heard one merchant ask. He was sifting through a wagon up ahead, just a few people in front of them.

"Of course they will," another replied. His face was covered with gray hair. Kendra wondered if he had simply chosen not to groom himself and if he knew just how furry and unkempt he looked. "Our cloaks are of the finest cloth—all the way from Lawdwin. As I said before, once the word gets out, we won't be able to keep up with the demand. Trust me."

She turned her attention to another group of merchants that had gathered behind them. They appeared to be transporting weapons and armor, however most of their wares were hidden from view. She tried to inspect what she could see of their goods but eventually got antsy and approached them.

"I'll be right back," she whispered to Orvaril and Cor'il as she walked toward the wagon.

There were two muscular men and one older man. Their wagon was loaded with three crates—and though they were not covered, only a couple of items were visible without closer scrutiny.

"Good morn, gentlemen," she called.

"Good morn," one of the burly men replied. He had very short, black hair and his tunic appeared to be a size too small. The other man paid no attention to her as he was busy talking with the older man.

"I noticed that your weapons are of exquisite quality and, I must admit, I am intrigued."

"Well now," he responded. "I must say, that surprises me a bit." He was handsome and spoke with a very low but quiet voice.

"And why is that?" She tucked her hair behind her left ear.

"Well," he continued, "why would a lady such as yourself be interested in weapons? What need of them have you?"

"Oh, sir is too kind." She flashed him a coy smile and fidgeted a bit. "But you know as well as I that a lady must have a means to defend herself. It's a dangerous world, I am sure you are aware." She looked back to see both Cor'il and Orvaril watching her. Orvaril seemed amused while Cor'il looked concerned.

"But," he continued, "a man should be around to defend the lady."

"While that may be true," she rebutted, "a lady should be able to rely on herself if a big, strong man is not around." Kendra ran her finger gently across the top of one of the crates. She wanted to vomit.

"I suppose you are correct. Would you like to see some of our fine blades? They are sturdy steel, smelted from the finest iron ore mined from the Worldsblood Peaks themselves."

"Duncan," the other young man piped up. "We are not ready to sell them yet—you know that." He had shaggy, brown hair. What Kendra found most intriguing was that his left eye was blue and his right was green. Despite this, he was just as handsome as the man whose name was apparently Duncan.

"Yes, brother, I am well aware of that fact."

"As such, we should wait—"

"Try to worry less, Lethos," Duncan interrupted. He turned to face his brother. "There is no harm in simply letting this fetching lady take a look at what we will later be selling. If she is interested, she can come by our shop once we are set up."

Kendra stopped paying attention as the two began to bicker. She peeked over the edge of the wagon at the nearest crate. The box was filled with daggers and short, squat swords. Most appeared to be of decent quality—she certainly was not an expert—but none looked as though they were anything special. *Drat. I should have liked to add another fine blade to my collection, but these all look mundane.* She looked up at the brothers who were paying her no mind but instead continued to argue. Most everyone else around them was also watching what was quickly turning into a spectacle. She dug a little deeper into the crate, searching for something that might catch her eye.

Something did.

Well, now, isn't this *interesting. But what are you guys doing at the bottom of a crate of weapons, and in the possession of the two imbeciles?* The answer was obvious. What she had uncovered would land these three men in the dungeons if discovered. Without hesitation, she quickly reached into the box, grabbed one, and hid it in one of the pockets in her skirts. Most were wrapped in leaves and tied shut but a couple had fallen free of their wrappings.

Not one cut on my hand. Not one scratch. Truly, those aren't even real blades. Not surprising. She smoothed out her dress a bit and returned to where she had been standing by the two brothers, who now appeared to be close to a fist fight. The older man—probably their father—was trying to calm them down.

"It's okay," she shouted. Both men stopped arguing for a moment. "I can wait until your shop is established."

Both men lowered their voices and appeared abashed. The older man sighed and went back to looking at a piece of parchment he held.

"Where will you be setting up shop?" she asked. It didn't matter to her what their answer was unless she wanted more of what she'd found. But, then, she suspected *that* particular cargo would be offloaded somewhere else.

"We are not sure yet," Lethos responded, obviously relieved that the fight was over. "Hopefully somewhere in the main market, but it will all depend on where we can find the space. The Storm's End is probably packing the city tightly."

"Very well," Kendra replied. "I may take a look later on, then. Have a wonderful day, sirs."

"And you as well," Duncan bowed slightly. Kendra slowly walked back to Cor'il and Orvaril who *both* now seemed amused.

"We made a bet," Orvaril laughed.

"Oh?"

"Indeed." Orvaril was holding a coin in his hand. "I bet Cor'il that you were going to steal something from them."

"Aye," Cor'il continued. "And I bet Orvaril that it would be someone's tunic right off their back."

They both laughed. Cor'il was also holding a coin.

"It appears as though we both lost." Orvaril put away his coin. Cor'il did the same.

"Aye," Kendra laughed. "You both lost." She felt the lump in her pocket. Once she had reassured herself, she began to question whether it had been wise for her to take one. She knew precisely who would be interested in it, but she had to make it past the guards at the gate first.

The line moved forward as a large group was allowed to pass through the gates. The children had stopped running around now and stuck close to their parents' wagon, looking as if they had been admonished for their behavior.

If this is what I think it is, things could change dramatically. I wonder if those men know exactly what it is they are smuggling into the city. Furthermore, I wonder to whom they are planning on selling them.

"Kendra!" Cor'il snapped.

"What?"

"Are you alright? You didn't hear a word I said, did you?"

"Oh," she quickly gathered herself from her thoughts. "My apologies."

"I was wondering where you wanted to go once we get into the city."

"Um," she was flustered. "Wherever you wish, I suppose."

"We should find an inn first," Orvaril piped up. "I fancy something for breakfast and mayhaps some mead. Of course, a comfortable bed is always welcome." He laughed and took the lute from his shoulder. He strummed it a few times, not happy with the sound. A couple of adjustments and a few strums later he was satisfied and began playing a tune. Kendra recognized it before Orvaril even started singing. The song was called "If I Had a Coin."

"A great idea, Orvaril," she replied. "Might I suggest The Panting Calf Inn? It's near the center of the city."

"Very convenient!" Orvaril proclaimed, stopping his song only briefly. "If I had a coin," he sang, "for every time I lied, I'd have a thousand coins or would I?"

"Indeed," Cor'il added. The line shifted closer to the gates. There were only a few groups ahead of them now. "I do not wish to stay in Elston long, however. I'd like to head on to The Densewood soon."

Kendra's thoughts returned to the object in her pocket. It felt slightly warm and she was a little bit worried about transporting it. She could fool the guards with little effort—certainly more easily than those buffoons and their poorly-packed crates could. But those brothers were probably going to bribe the guards anyway. Either that or they were even dafter than she had imagined.

But how did they get them? And there was at least a dozen!

Not only had she been shocked to see so many, but she was also shocked to see them in the first place. In light of recent discoveries, she found herself thinking more profoundly about the source of the items.

Dragonstones.

"It's not that I've lied to you," Orvaril continued singing, "because that, I'd never do."

They, like many other things, were mentioned in stories and songs. Until now, she'd never seen one or given any thought as to whether they were real. *Dragonstones are supposed to come from... the stomachs of dragons.*

By The Abyss, a dragon! *Just a couple of weeks ago I would not have known what to think. But, now, am I to believe in dragons? Even after what we've seen lately, that is difficult to accept.*

She shivered. Unsure of what to think—should she be afraid or excited? Regardless, in her pocket, was hidden an object that she was *absolutely sure* was a dragonstone. It was red and smooth—like a ruby. Unlike a ruby, however, it was warm to the touch and, at its core, sat a tiny purple sphere. It was the size of an eye or maybe her thumb. This was certainly no ordinary gem stone, but she would need a second opinion, if only to confirm what she already knew. Fortunately, there was someone she knew in Elston who could help.

"If I said you were beautiful then I meant what I said," Orvaril was still singing. "If you think that I lied to you, may The Abyss strike me dead!" Kendra noticed there were several coins strewn about him on the ground. A rather attractive woman approached and dropped another coin at his feet. He winked at her and Kendra swore she saw the woman swoon a bit.

Well, now, that is entertaining.

Cor'il looked lost. He stuck close to the group and kept darting his eyes around, as if he was looking for something in particular.

Not a tree in sight. I bet that's what he's looking for. He'll be hard pressed to find many here in Elston. She smirked but she also felt a bit sorry for him. She remembered what it had been like when her life had suddenly changed. It had been drastic and jarring, for sure. Fortunately, it hadn't taken her long to adjust. She wondered how long it would take Cor'il. Granted, his life had changed in possibly more drastic ways than hers and, she noted, *she* had been responsible for herself. Cor'il had no choice in the matter.

She gazed up at the sky for a while, watching some of the wispy clouds float by. It was a gorgeous day, but she could feel the summer heat coming on—it might not stay quite so nice. With the peak of summer almost upon them, the heat could be brutal. She wondered how hot Cor'il got when the hood of his cloak was up. She had, for a while, wondered why he constantly wore it up but, after catching sight of his ears, she figured they were the reason.

As if on cue, Cor'il nervously adjusted his hood over his head. They were pretty close to the gates now and he was fidgeting.

"Hey, treeboy," she whispered. "Don't be nervous. It's just the city guard, and they're only checking everything to make sure it's safe for the Storm's End Festival. They won't give two gortog craps about your ears."

Cor'il threw her a surprised look and adjusted the hood again. He fidgeted a bit more, looking uncomfortable.

"Don't worry." Kendra winked at Cor'il. "It's our secret."

"Thank you, ladies and gentlemen!" Orvaril finished his song and began picking up the coins that littered the ground. Several entranced women stood around, disappointed that the song was over.

"Please, do play another!" one of them shouted.

"My apologies, milady." Orvaril shouldered his instrument. He deposited his earnings in his coin pouch, visibly listening to the clinking sound they made. "But I do believe the guards would like us to keep moving as quickly as possible. And, seeing as we are at the gates, I must oblige them."

There were a few disappointed sighs from the crowd. Several children walked away, moping.

"But if you enjoyed that performance and want more, don't fret! I shall be in Elston for a while! I plan to perform at The Festival!"

Cheers rang out. Orvaril bowed and the three of them moved up to the city gates.

"What is your business here in Elston?"

"Hello, good sir!" Orvaril stepped up in front of Cor'il and Kendra. "I am Orvaril Swordsong at your service! My friends and I are here for the Storm's End Festival, of course! We hear it shall be grand! I shall be performing for the good citizens!"

"I perform sleight of hand tricks, sir." Kendra produced a playing card from her sleeve, turned it over in her hand, and then made it disappear. Quickly, she reached behind the guard's waist and produced the card once again."

"Impressive, young lady. And you?"

Cor'il had a blank stare.

"Well now," Orvaril started. "There isn't really a name for what the boy does, yet. For now, let's just call it *magic*!"

Kendra saw the irony and snickered. Cor'il didn't seem to think it was funny at all.

"Anything you'd like to declare—questionable items and the like?"

"Not a one," Orvaril replied. "Just my lute and a sword or two."

Kendra fidgeted a moment, feeling her pocket once more. *And a dragonstone.*

Chapter 23

Orvaril led Cor'il past the gate and further into the city. Cor'il followed closely, looking more nervous with every passing moment as he tried to navigate the busy city streets.

Orvaril wasn't sure exactly when it had happened, but Kendra, at some point, had split off from them and vanished. He had noticed that she had seemed a bit jumpy as they were waiting to get past the gate. Mayhaps she'd just needed to use the privies. He grinned, somewhat curious what she was up to. *No matter! Elston is a playground and I shall make it my own!*

They walked past the Gryphonwing Tavern and followed the street up a slight hill. Orvaril did not pay attention to the fact that he didn't actually know where this inn was. He'd been to Elston before but he usually visited the same areas. And he certainly didn't know every nook and cranny of such a large city. It was easier to earn your keep when people knew who you were, especially when those people had more coin than they knew what to do with.

Orvaril was also a bit lazy—a fact he readily admitted. Easy money was so preferable to hard work. *It's always easier to have someone give you a coin rather than pay you a coin.* Not that he was lazy enough to sit around and expect people to throw coins at him. No, he performed for money, and it was always fun, but he preferred to perform for as much money as he could get in one sitting. He certainly had other important things to do and important people to see… oh, and ale to drink, of course!

Orvaril had talent, charm, and charisma and he knew it. Best of all, he barely had to *try*—the only way it could be easier is if his lute would play itself!

"So, Cor'il," he started. "Do you know where this Panting Calf Inn is?"

"I do not. I've never been to Elston." The boy was looking around, still a bit nervous and distracted.

"Where are you from, again?"

"Kuranthas."

"Ah, well, that explains… well, basically *everything*." He chuckled. Cor'il smiled back briefly before his gaze darted around once more. "I've never been—always wanted to visit, but never made it that far East."

Orvaril had to admit that Elston was truly the largest jewel in Cygil's crown. Sure, there were other great cities in the Realm, but Elston was beyond compare. It didn't hurt that King Alzine resided here. In fact, his castle was supposed to have been built on the very spot where Gorag Thrashbone was killed by Sturm Ironhelm.

Alzine was wise and humble—in all respects, a good and able king. Though Orvaril had never actually met the man, he had seen him just as he had seen the castle. It was not an extravagant building by any means. Alzine had had it built from the ground up when he moved the throne from Ten Kings to Elston. Orvaril had heard the stories—the tale of how Alzine defeated the Mad King Darl Brownshield for the throne. That story in particular—a bloody tale—was not altogether well-known. The Mad King's spirit was rumored to still walk the halls of Highmount Castle back in Ten Kings.

"Yes," Orvaril snapped out of his introspection. "Elston is quite the city. You could spend your entire life within these walls and never want for anything."

"But it has no trees."

"Well, uh... it's not a forest, you know. It's a city. Besides, there *are* trees in Elston."

"I certainly don't see any."

"Well," Orvaril laughed, "you'd have to visit The Kingswood."

"What's that?"

"It's a small common area in the center of the city."

Orvaril stopped for a moment and looked around. If they continued north they would eventually reach King Alzine's castle, which was near the city's center. If this Panting Calf Inn was also somewhere near the center, then it would be prudent to continue on.

"What I hear," he continued, "is that there were several steelwood trees in the grove and nobody wanted to spend the time or money to try to chop them down. Giant weeds those things can be."

"I think they're wondrous." Cor'il looked slightly appalled at the idea of majestic steelwood trees being seen as common weeds.

"Oh, now don't get me wrong, my boy! They are indeed fantastic plant specimens! Unless, however, they happen to grow in an inconvenient place! At that point, they become a nuisance." *Wait, there is a song somewhere in there. "You're the steelwood in my heart"... hmm. I'll have to consider this.* "They are quite difficult to remove. Even their roots are tough."

"I suppose so," Cor'il replied. "We have had some issues with steelwood trees encroaching on houses in Kuranthas. We have a saying back home. "You can't fight steelwoods." If a steelwood caused problems for us, we simply moved. They are quite beautiful in autumn. But, I agree, if your goal is to remove them, they could be considered nuisances."

They walked for a while, weaving between people on foot and on horseback. Orvaril had to make sure that Cor'il didn't get lost in the crowd. The boy was having a tough time keeping up and concentrating on where he was going. After watching the boy try to navigate a city, it truly was not difficult to believe that he was from Kuranthas. He literally *dragged* Cor'il through several streets and alleys, finally stopping outside a tavern. The sign hanging above the door had a rather ugly-looking woman's head that sort of looked like a bird.

"Are we at the Panting Calf Inn?"

"No," Orvaril said, staring up at the sign. "No, we are not. I fancied a bit of a rest here at this… fine establishment. Mayhaps an ale or two to quench my thirst before we move onto our destination."

"I'm not so sure." Cor'il looked dubious.

"Well, it certainly doesn't *look* like much," Orvaril rebutted, "but I'm sure it's a quality tavern! I mean, look at the craftsmanship of the sign! It's exquisite!"

"It smells a bit funny—even out here."

"Well, uh… yes, it definitely does. And you have my apologies."

"For the smell?" Cor'il still looked puzzled.

"For dragging you inside because this is where we're going!" Orvaril laughed, grabbed Cor'il, and opened the door.

"What *is* that smell?" Orvaril waved his hand in front of his face as a wall of stench assaulted his nose. *Well, it's not quite what I was expecting. Maybe we shouldn't be here. No, that's silly. This feels absolutely right. I just hope we don't pass out from that pungent odor— whatever it is.*

"You got a problem with something?" a rather gravelly-sounding voice asked from somewhere to the right.

The room was rather dark and Orvaril's eyes hadn't yet adjusted. He could vaguely make out the lay of the room but not any details.

"Why, no," he replied. "In fact, just the opposite! It smells," he took a deep breath and fought back the urge to gag, "it smells absolutely spectacular. I was simply curious about what that lovely... aroma is."

"That's our signature dish, that is."

Orvaril could see relatively well, now. He realized he still held Cor'il's arm and let go. There was a rather large—no, that was being generous—rather *fat* man behind the bar to the right. The room itself was sparsely furnished with a few mismatched tables and chairs strewn haphazardly about. Several lamps shone dim, flickering light onto the wooden supports from which they hung.

"I'm rather thankful for the dim light," he whispered.

"Why do you say that?" Cor'il whispered back.

"Because I might panic if I were able to see all of the dirt and garbage that is probably all over the place." He walked toward the bar, stepping over the body of a patron—hopefully just passed out. "So, good sir," he spoke up, addressing the figure behind the bar. He was indeed quite large and much of his face was covered with dark, ratty hair. "What might your signature dish be?"

"The Harpy's Head's specialty—raccoon guts minced with garlic and onion."

"Oh," Orvaril wasn't sure what to say. He considered himself fortunate that he hadn't emptied his stomach already. "That sounds... delightful."

"It's quite tasty. We get a lot of compliments about it."

"Maybe we should be going," Cor'il whispered.

"What's *his* problem?" The man pointed a rather sausage-like finger at Cor'il.

"Oh him?" Orvaril cursed himself. *Why did it have to be here? Why? I am sure there are plenty of other, cleaner establishments I could waste time in.* "Well, he was in a hurry to come in here and find out what the wonderful scent was. He would really like to try some."

"Is that right?" The man behind the bar grinned widely. He was missing several teeth. "Aye, he can have a nice bowl full. Have a seat wherever, and I'll get the cooks to dish some up for ya."

"I do *not* wish to eat that!" Cor'il whispered. He shot Orvaril a look that was both irritated and worried. "It sounds absolutely disgusting. It *smells* absolutely disgusting!"

"Sorry, kid." Orvaril scanned the room for a place to sit. "I had to think on my toes. Besides, maybe it isn't so bad. If it is their specialty then that means *someone* likes it well enough, right?" He nudged Cor'il with his elbow and inspected the room further. Three tables were currently occupied. He couldn't determine much more about the patrons in the dim light. There were a couple of overturned tables and broken chairs lying about, as well as what looked like either garbage or rubble.

"Cozy," Cor'il muttered.

"Indeed," Orvaril laughed. "Well, I guess we can pretty much sit anywhere."

"I think I'd rather stand."

"I think I agree with you. That table over there looks like it might not be entirely dirty." Orvaril pointed to a table in the corner. Cor'il seemed dubious and Orvaril couldn't blame him. He really wasn't sure why they were here in the first place. He looked around, scanning for something—anything. He didn't know what it would be or how long it would take. Sometimes, it could be infuriating.

They both sat down at a small, circular, high table. The stools were uncomfortable and wobbly. Cor'il nearly fell off of his while trying to get comfortable which, of course, made Orvaril snicker—until he nearly fell off his own stool. They then sat in silence for a spell, each of them looking around the place. Orvaril half expected to be robbed by thugs from the shadows. Cor'il appeared to be thinking very much the same thing.

The smell of "The Special" lingered heavily in the air. Orvaril could almost feel it seeping into his tunic. He suspected he may just have to burn his clothes and start anew. *That would be a shame. I really like this tunic.*

After several minutes, the hairy man emerged from behind the bar carrying a large, steaming bowl which he set in the middle of the table. Two spoons stuck out of a grey-brown colored liquid in which floated dubious chunks of something.

"That's five coppers."

Orvaril looked at Cor'il who gazed back at him. Neither one immediately reached for his coin pouch.

"Ahem," the man interrupted. "You need to pay for your boy's meal or I'll throw you both out."

"Yes," Cor'il chimed in, "father. I won't eat it all—I promise I will save some for you."

Huh. The kid isn't half-bad. But I can't believe I'm about to pay five coppers for some raccoon guts. Orvaril produced five copper coins from his pouch and laid them on the table where they were promptly scooped up.

"Enjoy!" The man went over to one of the other occupied tables, leaving them to their "food." The staring match continued.

"I'll, uh, try it if you try it first." Cor'il grinned.

'You know what?' Orvaril grabbed one of the spoons and scooped it full of the muck from the bowl. The smell was intense! There was absolutely *nothing* appetizing about this slime, but he had already committed. He shoved the spoon in his mouth and swallowed hard. "Delicious!" he proclaimed, smacking his lips. He then put the spoon back in the bowl and looked at Cor'il.

"You've got to be kidding me."

"I would not kid you," he proclaimed again, this time using the fanciest voice he could muster. "It truly was quite delicious. It was a veritable cornucopia of greatness, bursting with flavor."

Cor'il grabbed the spoon and inspected the thick slurry before him. "Why don't I believe you?" he asked. Orvaril remained silent, quietly daring the boy to take a bite. Cor'il slowly raised the spoon to his nose and sniffed it.

His face puckered. He winced and slammed the spoon back into the bowl.

"It's disgusting! I am *not* eating that!"

"It *is* disgusting!" Orvaril laughed. He tried to keep it down so as not to attract the attention of anyone. "But at least I tried it! You were too cowardly!"

"I prefer to call it 'smart'!" Cor'il was laughing along with him. He seemed pretty proud of himself for seeing through the ruse. Orvaril had to admit that it wasn't a very good one. No matter how hard he'd tried to hide it, he was sure his face had given him away.

He couldn't believe that he'd actually *eaten* the stuff. And it really *was* horrid. The taste it left in his mouth was not going to go away easily, and the film on his tongue would probably be with him the rest of his life.

"It tasted worse than Scorovian hog juice!"

"I have, most unfortunately, tasted that."

"As have I. But only because I was attempting to trick someone else into trying it."

"Did it work then?"

"Sadly, no." Orvaril grinned. "To be honest, it rarely ever does."

He watched Cor'il slosh through the muck with a spoon. He looked intrigued by the mixture. Orvaril tried to occupy himself any way he could but his frustration was mounting.

Alright, I give up. Why did we come into this dump? It felt right when I first saw the place, but I'm starting to think it was a mistake.

It had always been something he couldn't explain, and he didn't remember when it had first happened. In fact, once it happened—when he received a spontaneous burst of inspiration—he usually forgot it happened at all. Every once in a while, he would feel compelled to do something impulsive. There was never a rhyme or reason to it and, oftentimes, it got him into trouble. He figured it was a love for mischief, and the results were always wildly unpredictable. However, at this point, he was just about fed up with this horrible, smelly pit of a tavern.

He had taken to calling them *flashes*.

"So," Cor'il started, "why are we here again?"

"I merely felt I needed a rest." *He'd think you're crazy if you told him "because mischief compelled us!"* "I thought it as good a place to relax as any. Mayhaps I was just a teensy bit wrong." He held out his thumb and index finger slightly apart, grinning.

"So what now?" Cor'il was still playing with his food, swirling the spoon around in the stinky sludge. His elbow was on the table and his head rested on his hand. He stared down, picking up a spoonful of goop and watching it drop back in the bowl with a wet plopping sound.

Orvaril tapped his fingers on the table impatiently. He desperately wanted to get up and leave but his curiosity compelled him to stay. He inspected the other people in the room. The hairy man had disappeared into the kitchen and the other patrons were all quietly eating, drinking, and talking.

"Well this isn't supposed to be in here," Cor'il muttered.

As Orvaril continued scrutinizing the room, the hairy man returned from the kitchen and began looking for something around the bar.

"Orvaril," Cor'il whispered. "Look what I found in the bowl!"

"What is—" Orvaril turned around to see Cor'il holding a ring in his hand. It was still covered in slime but there was no mistaking it. "Interesting. May I see it?"

Cor'il shook it off a bit and handed it to Orvaril. He hopped down from his stool and wiped the ring off on the clothes of one of the men who was passed out on the floor. He then sat back down and inspected the piece of jewelry in the dim light, squinting to see.

The ring was made of three gold bands braided together with a small, triangular blue gemstone set into it—a sapphire, perhaps. It still had a little bit of raccoon guts on it but, even so, it probably wouldn't fetch much if he were to try and pawn it. He tried it on anyway.

After slipping it onto the ring finger of his left hand he admired it in the flickering lamp light. He wondered if it looked any different in better conditions.

"You're going to keep it?" Cor'il whispered.

"I was thinking about it. But it's a little too simple for my—" As he put his hand down on the table, the ring slipped off and rolled away, settling in between them. It didn't fall over. Instead, it balanced on edge with the gem facing up. "Well now *that* is intriguing. See how it looks on you."

"I shouldn't. It's not mine."

"Not to worry, Cor'il," Orvaril reassured him. "If it belongs to someone, we'll just give it back."

Cor'il slowly picked up the ring—somewhat reluctantly—and held it up in front of his face.

"Are you sure about this?"

"Of course I'm sure about it. There is nothing to worry about, my friend. Have you not worn a ring before?" More than anything, Orvaril was simply egging him on because Cor'il was so hesitant. He made a bet with himself as to whether he would succeed, even though he was pretty sure he already knew the outcome.

"Well, actually—"

"Ah," Orvaril chuckled, "of course you haven't. How silly of me. Well, go on. See how it looks on you."

The boy gave Orvaril one last hesitant look, inspected the ring again, and slowly slipped it onto his left hand.

"Well, hold it up," he urged. "Let's see how it looks on you."

Just then, the hairy man appeared at their table with a rather panicked look on his face. He inspected the table, lifted up the bowl, and looked under it.

"Is there something we can—"

"I lost a ring," the man said. Orvaril could hear the worry in his voice. "Have either of you seen it?"

"Yes, sir," Cor'il spoke up. He started to hold up his left hand to show the man the ring they had fished out of the bowl. But, he hesitated and quickly pulled it back with a look of concern on his face. "Uh," he stammered nervously. "I mean, uh, I believe I saw something shiny on the floor somewhere. It very well could be the ring you're looking for, sir."

"Really? Oh thank you!" The man perked up instantly. He got onto his hands and knees and began crawling on the floor, inspecting every inch.

"It might help a bit if you had better light in here," Orvaril jibed. But it didn't appear that the man heard him. "Well," he muttered, "it would, you know."

"We should leave." Cor'il got up and shouldered his satchel. "I'm anxious to get to the inn."

At that moment, Orvaril recognized the familiar, satisfied feeling within him. He knew it was, indeed, time to go. He got up, put his rucksack on his back, did the same with his lute, and followed Cor'il out the door.

"Thank you, sir," he called as he left, "for the... tasty guts!" He didn't wait for a reply.

The sun was still high in the sky and shining bright. Both he and Cor'il had to squint and cover their eyes until they adjusted. The smell followed them outside but it wasn't nearly so strong.

"So you decided to keep the ring, then, eh?" He nudged Cor'il in the ribs as they resumed walking down the crowded street toward the center of town. Orvaril noted how, outside the Harpy's Head, there were very few people in comparison to the rest of the city. This didn't surprise Orvaril at all.

"I had no choice," the boy replied. He held up his finger and showed Orvaril a completely different ring from the one he'd put on.

"Wait, how did you... I don't understand."

The ring still appeared as three bands intertwined, but now they were leafy vines. And the triangular gem—the sapphire—had become an octagonal emerald.

"Precisely my thoughts," Cor'il replied. "And it doesn't come off. I tried removing it."

"Curious." Orvaril grabbed Cor'il's hand and inspected the ring more closely. "Very intriguing," he mumbled. They continued walking while Orvaril looked at the ring. Several times they very nearly toppled people over by running into them. Finally, he let go.

"So what do you think?" Cor'il asked.

"Why, I've no idea what to think!" Orvaril scratched his head, pondering. "Maybe it's some cursed ring?"

"Cursed?"

"I'm just joking, my boy!" He *was* joking but there was a part of him that was not going to dismiss the idea. In his travels, he'd heard—and retold—stories about items that supposedly brought the untimely demise of their owners. *But if it was cursed, then why didn't it act this way for me? Ha! I think I am actually a little envious!* He couldn't help but laugh. "So, either you will die a terrible death or the ring simply likes you better than me!"

"That's very reassuring."

"Well, in any case, there isn't a thing to be done about it now." He put on his most proper demeanor. "For now we shall avail to the Panting Calf Inn where we shall dine on something that *must* be better than what we just ate."

"You mean that *you* just ate."

"Yes, that."

Chapter 24

Kendra sat, alone, in the brightly-lit hall of the Bearded Goat Tavern, staring into a now empty glass. She toyed with it, rotating it between her fingers on the pocked table. It still smelled of wine and, she had to be honest, the wine had been quite to her liking. She may have downed it a little too fast though, so she stayed at the table pondering her next move.

She knew this had been a long shot. Cyril really wasn't one of the best choices for a first contact, but he was always easy to get in touch with. Mayhaps he just had too much time on his hands—never a good situation for someone who deals in "used items," as he put it. Kendra called him what he was—a dealer in stolen property. There was no need to sugar coat that fact.

She hadn't necessarily been interested in selling anything to him. More than anything, she had wanted to know whether he had come by any dragonstones. Before she had even spoken to him she had known what the answer was going to be. He hadn't disappointed her. He'd tried to lead her on, clumsily making up lies meant to make her think that he knew what he was talking about. She'd seen through them before he had even opened his mouth.

He'd simply laughed at her when she finally called his bluff. She didn't blame him—right up until she'd held one in her hand she, too, hadn't believed that dragonstones truly existed. In fact, she *still* had her doubts. *It could be a crafty replica for collectors or a facsimile to fool the rich. Or maybe it's just an ornament made to look like a dragonstone.* But, if any of those was true, then why would someone be trying to sneak them into the city? The whole situation was suspect, and it concerned her

As expected, Cyril had been just as worthless as usual—and just as smug too. What made it worse was that she'd had to buy him drinks! Of course, both his drinks and her wine had been actually paid for with *his* coin. He was unaware that she'd lightened his money pouch during the conversation. She'd had to get closer to him than she had wanted and she hadn't lifted much but, even so, she couldn't help but smirk a little. It was too bad that she couldn't spend the money on something more useful though. More wine, for example.

At least Cyril drank only the cheapest ale—even when someone else was paying. That's how smart the guy was. *His flame definitely doesn't burn the brightest.* Of course, she had not actually *shown* him the stone. He may be stupid, but he still would've tried to take it for himself. She would have.

She was alone in an empty tavern. Even the woman who had been standing at the bar had gone off somewhere. Her eyes darted around the room as she pretended to still be focusing on the wine glass. She had already closely examined her surroundings the moment she'd walked in. There were exactly 21 paces between her and the front door, one entrance to the kitchen ahead and to the right, and a doorway to the privy on the back wall behind her. Her back was to the wall and she could see the entire room before her. From here she could see out through the front windows as well.

Her thoughts turned back to the dragonstone and lingered there. Surely *someone* knew something. She knew Cyril had been a longshot but, the more she thought about it, the more she knew it had been a mistake and a waste of time to consider him in the first place. She stretched and yawned, testing her balance. The wine had only a minimal effect so she stood up and headed for the door.

She walked past the kitchen entrance, turned, and threw a punch at the face of the man who was standing behind the doorway. He dropped his sword when she kicked out his right knee and, as he collapsed, she hit him in the jaw with *her* knee. As he fell backward and collapsed in a heap, another man emerged from behind the bar and swung at her with two daggers.

Kendra ducked under his attacks, turned her back to him and elbowed him in the stomach. Then she turned and grabbed both of his hands, turning his own weapons on him. Without a sound, he slumped to the floor. She quickly walked over to the front door.

"Were I you," she shouted, not yet opening it, "I would run away and tell Raynar whatever lie you are going to tell him." She counted to two and then opened the door. Sure enough, a man was running down the street as if death itself was chasing him. "Oh," she mumbled, "I almost forgot." She walked back to the man she had felled just seconds before and inspected his two daggers.

They both looked of about the same quality—not bad but certainly not special. She randomly picked one and, finding a spot on the man's tunic that wasn't soaked in blood, used it to wipe the blade clean. Then she cracked open the door to the kitchen and peeked in. Three people—the woman she had seen before and two men she did not recognize—were cowering in a corner.

"I apologize for the mess," Kendra said. Then she walked back out into the fest hall. As she passed by the bar she grabbed a bottle of wine and slipped it into her satchel. Then she walked out the front door and into the sunlight outside.

She disappeared into the crowd, weaving down different streets and alleyways but remaining aware of everything around her. The wine interfered a little, so she had to concentrate more than normal. She darted her gaze upward occasionally in case Raynar's men were traveling by rooftop.

Kendra debated with herself as to her next move. There was *one* person she trusted enough to give her reliable information. If he said he knew nothing about dragonstones, then he knew nothing. He wouldn't lie to her or cheat her. He probably *would* try to kill her, but that was expected. Each time was always for a different reason, though. Sometimes she made a game of it—guessing why he wanted her dead.

Once she reached a secluded alley she climbed up one of the gutters to reach the rooftops. Only then did she relax.

As she knelt on the flat roof, looking out over the city, she felt slightly vulnerable. Not only was she in need of help, but also that help was going to come from *him. And what if he doesn't have the answers? What then? Who will you go to next?* She suspected she might have to deal with those two boneheaded brothers she lifted the dragonstone from, but it was doubtful that they would have any *real*, useful information.

A gentle breeze wisped past, blowing hair into her eyes. She tucked it behind her ear with her finger and squinted, scrutinizing several people on the streets below. Their bright, colorful garb nauseated her as they sauntered by, stopping in front of a crowd to entertain them with acrobatics and juggling. Kendra resisted the urge to throw a rock at them, but only because she couldn't find any.

She hoped Cor'il wasn't getting into any trouble. Certainly he was not suited for a city—at least not yet. Orvaril was with him and, as goofy as that man was, she was sure his demeanor belied his actual intelligence. He was one of the more knowledgeable storyweavers she had met and, though he suffered from a lack of seriousness, he was no fool. He was possibly the only one she'd met whom she didn't immediately wish to plant a knife in… at least, not yet.

She waited patiently, watching the city's inhabitants go through their daily routine. These days, everything seemed to involve the Storm's End. She didn't understand what all the fuss was about. Maybe it was because The Storm, in her mind, ended so long ago. 200 years was a long time to hang onto something and celebrate it in such a grandiose magnitude as far as she was concerned.

"You certainly took your sweet time," she finally said, not taking her eyes off the streets below.

"I had other... more pressing engagements to attend to," a man's voice replied from behind her. "I knew you'd wait patiently—you're very predictable, you know." He had a calm, soothing voice that, despite her better judgment, always put her at ease. It was a false sense of security, of course. She quickly checked her daggers for reassurance and then turned to face him.

He wore the brown fedora—the same as always—with strands of black hair peeking out from underneath. Since he often kept his head down, it obscured much of his face but Kendra could see his stubbly chin poking out. In his mouth was a lit cigar butt. As usual, every bit of his clothing besides the hat was black—his boots, his cloak, tunic, and breeches. All black.

"It's good to see you again, Blacksmoke," Kendra said sarcastically. She walked away from the edge of the roof and stood before him.

"Somehow, I doubt you're serious."

Kendra smiled. They knew each other quite well enough. They had played this game for a long time.

"Have you come to return what you took from me?"

"I merely *borrowed* the money and then... lost it... but I was fortunate enough to find a really nice necklace shortly thereafter. It's funny how fortune works."

"Yes," The Blacksmoke smirked, "quite hilarious, actually."

There was silence for a brief period. It wasn't tense. It was always like this.

"You know that Raynar is looking for you."

"Of course he is," Kendra chuckled.

"He says you have something of his and he wants it back."

"I have *several* somethings of his."

"He has asked me for help."

"Oh?" That was a bit worrisome. She could handle Raynar, but if The Blacksmoke was helping, then there was probably not a city in the Realm she could hide in. She wondered if Raynar had reached out to anyone else.

"Aye. I told him I would consider his offer. But I've got much more lucrative contracts that require my... immediate attention. He doesn't pay well, you know."

"He always was rather cheap," Kendra agreed.

"None too bright, too."

"Alas," Kendra continued, "I don't have anything for Raynar but I *do* have something that might interest you."

"Oh?" He lifted his head slightly. She always knew how to pique his interest. It was a subtle task—like strumming a harp. She couldn't be outright honest but she had to make sure he wasn't bored. It was yet another game they played. Information was probably not going to come cheap. She was beginning to wish she *did* still have his money... or the necklace. Or both.

They stared at each other for a moment while he chewed on his cigar. This would probably be the moment when he decided whether to try to kill her or not. Thankfully, he hadn't tried that for quite a while. Not since they'd given each other matching scars.

"Alright," he finally said. "I'll bite. What have you got, then?"

"Uh uh," she replied, shaking her head. "I also need information related to it."

"So, my dear," he grumbled. She could tell he was already curious. "Where do we go from here?"

"It's simple." She put her left hand into one of her pockets, clutching the dragonstone tightly. Its warmth was eerie, but reassuring that she might actually be right. "I'll show you what I've got. You tell me all you can about it and, if you cooperate, I will tell you where you can find more."

"Sounds risky," he snorted. "What if I don't give a rat's rotten ass about what you've got?"

"Well," she chuckled, "you'll simply have one more reason to want me dead."

"I already have too many to count."

"What?" she laughed. "Not enough fingers?"

To her surprise, The Blacksmoke laughed with her.

"I have the 10 that I need." He began pacing in silence.

"Alright," he finally said after several moments. "If it were anyone else I would have killed them already and taken what they had. Consider yourself fortunate."

"Always."

She slowly and carefully produced the dragonstone from her pocket and held it out to him. He looked at it and laughed.

"Costume jewelry?"

"I think not." She held it closer to him. "Take a closer look." She finally handed it to him and he turned it over in his palm, inspecting it closely. After a moment she saw it wash over his face—he recognized it.

"You're telling me you have—"

"A dragonstone, yes. Or, at least, I *think* I do. If it isn't a true dragonstone, it is a reasonable facsimile, aye?"

He kept pacing, scrutinizing the gem and mumbling to himself. Kendra had never seen him this intrigued. He'd certainly been *interested* in items before, but this was different.

"Aye," he finally replied. "Most anyone else, if they came to me with something like this, I'd call them a fool. But I know you, and you're no fool." He paced some more, still inspecting the stone. "Where did you find this? Wait, no, it's you. From whom did you *steal* this?"

"Not so fast," she countered. As he was holding the stone into the sun's light, she quickly grabbed it from his fingers and had it back in a pocket before he'd noticed. "I told you, I need information. I want to know where something like this—something out of myth—came from."

"Ah, yes, you certainly did. Unfortunately, on this particular item, I have none to give you."

Kendra was disappointed but not surprised. She had not honestly expected The Blacksmoke to have any useful information, but she *had* hoped.

"I know you have a vast network of contacts. You can most certainly *get* information. Surely *someone* knows something."

"That I can, my dear." He stepped in, closer to her. "It would truly help if I knew where it came from," he whispered. At that moment, she had no doubt he was serious. He wasn't just trying to double-cross her.

"I lifted it from a merchant family at the front gates. There were other dragonstones in their crate. They made sure to conceal them under a pile of weapons."

"They were wise to do so."

"They did a piss poor job, though."

"Then they either know not what they have or they are fools. Do they have a shop set up? What did they look like?"

"They didn't when I spoke to them, but they said they hoped to have one set up in the main marketplace. They were both well-muscled. One man had messy black hair and the other had short brown hair. They looked none too bright."

"They *are* fools," The Blacksmoke laughed. "*Everyone* wants a shop in the main market. If they're smart they will be looking for a more secluded spot. You can't do business with these items out in the open. And if these gems *are* genuine, then we'll have a bunch of fools walking around with pocket fireballs." She saw a look in his eye as if he'd just had an idea.

"No, Blacksmoke." She knew *exactly* what he wanted to do. "We are not going to test it. It could destroy half a city block, and I only have the one."

"You disappoint me, Kendra. But you're right—we don't need to draw attention to ourselves."

"So you will see if you can find out anything?"

"Aye, my dear. When I do, I will come find you."

"If you don't want a dagger in the ribs, I would recommend you use the front door."

The Blacksmoke grinned and began walking away.

"And," she added, "I've already told you to stop calling me that."

He stopped for a moment and, looking back at her, tipped his hat down, then he continued on his way.

"Yes, my dear."

Chapter 25

"Are you sure you don't wish to reconsider?" Kendra asked.

"I really don't feel I should stay," Cor'il replied as he loaded the book into his satchel. "I don't feel comfortable here in Elston. I'd much rather be among the trees of The Densewood." He could see the frustration on Kendra's face. It was impossible for him to describe to her the longing he felt. He was close now—close to finding his new place in the world—and he was eager to start his new life.

"And where is the storyweaver?"

Cor'il could now *hear* the frustration in her voice. She even sounded a little angry. When she had met them in their room at the Panting Calf Inn yesterday, she'd seemed fine... although Cor'il still wasn't sure why she had come in through the window and not the door. This morning she was quite obviously annoyed with him. He could only surmise it was because she did not want him to leave? She knew of his plans for quite some time now, so why was today any different?

"I woke up as he was leaving," Cor'il replied, checking his satchel to make sure he hadn't forgotten anything. "He said he had some people to talk to, and maybe some ale to drink."

"Does *he* know you're leaving?"

"I told him as much yesterday, yes." Cor'il shouldered his satchel and fastened his cloak. "You could come with me, you know," he added.

Kendra paused. It was obvious that she was considering it. He figured that it was only a slim possibility, but he had also heard her say numerous times that she did not consider Elston to be safe.

"I can't," she finally said. "Just as you feel your place is among the trees of The Densewood, I feel my place is in a city—apparently Elston for the time being. But I do understand how you feel, Cor'il." She moved in closer to him and took his left hand in hers. Then she gently kissed his cheek. "I know this is what you have to do," she whispered. "But I don't have to like it. I feel, in you, that I have made a good friend, and those are difficult to come by."

Cor'il was struck speechless. Until now he hadn't realized how close they had become in such a brief period. He *would* miss her. He would miss the storyweaver as well. They'd become friends in a brief time, and he'd been too caught up in everything to realize how strong the bond had become.

"This is where we part ways, Cor'il. You are my friend and you always shall be."

Cor'il felt tears well up in his eyes. This is how it had been when he'd left Kuranthas—and his friends—behind. Thinking about them made it even worse.

"Will we see each other again?" he asked.

"You'll be back," Kendra grinned.

Cor'il could see Kendra getting misty-eyed as well. They both turned away at the same time, laughing as they wiped their eyes.

"I should probably just go," he said. "There is no sense in making this more difficult than it has to be."

"Aye. I've got a busy schedule today, anyway, starting with breakfast with King Alzine, of course!" Kendra laughed, still drying her eyes.

Cor'il started to say something but ended up merely nodding as he left. He hurried through the hallway, down the stairs, and out the door of the inn. Unsure exactly where the nearest city gates were, he headed in the direction he thought was north, passing by King Alzine's castle. Orvaril had been right—it was a rather simple, unassuming structure—not at all what he expected for a king of the Realm. He would've liked to have taken more time for sightseeing, but thought it best to move as quickly as he could. *It's best to simply cut off the arm rather than let it fester itself to death.* His father used to say that. A hardened man, he was.

He reached the city's northern gates shortly after noontime. Leaving the city took much less time than entering, as the guards did not need to ask his business or search him. Once outside the gates, he took to the road and left Elston behind as quickly as he could. He was most certainly going to miss Kendra and Orvaril, but he also looked forward to what lay ahead. Mayhaps he could start his own Kuranthas amongst the trees of The Densewood. At this point, anything was possible.

As he camped that night he found it difficult to get to sleep. He was tired but his mind would not stop moving. It wasn't unusual for him to only sleep for a few hours anyway but, with all of the thoughts churning in his head tonight, he feared he wouldn't sleep at all. Instead of fighting it, he packed up his belongings and continued traveling in the darkness. The mote of light floating above his head helped his vision, but since he could already see well in dim conditions he did not create one that illuminated a large area.

• • •

Cor'il was two days north of Elston when he came upon the town of Listerville. He'd learned from merchants that The Densewood lay across the Landsblood River and further to the north. His excitement grew when he topped a hill and gazed upon the small town. Beyond the town was the river and, in the distance, he could see what he hoped was his destination. His heart pounded with anticipation and he wanted to run, suddenly filled with a new well of energy and excitement. He had to restrain himself from doing just that. Instead, he quickened his pace down the hill, whistling while he traveled.

As he entered the town he was greeted by several men who were farming a field of beans. They waved and yelled "hello" as he walked past. He crossed a small, stone bridge over a babbling creek and continued on into the town. The buildings here were simple stone structures. None of them was taller than two stories and the vast majority were only one story high. Cor'il stopped short, nearly falling backward, as a woman guided a mule in front of him, pulling a cart full of vegetables.

"Oh, sorry dear," she exclaimed, stopping what she was doing. Her pants and blouse were covered with mud. "I didn't see you there. Are ya okay?"

"Yes," he replied. "I was looking around and not paying attention to where I was going. My apologies."

"So was I!" she laughed. "Actually, this mule is a little difficult to work with sometimes. Something's drawn his attention. Probably a squirrel or a bitefly, I'd imagine. He's none too bright he is!"

Cor'il laughed.

"I'm Lynara." She wiped her hand on her blouse and held it out to him.

"My name is Cor'il." They shook hands.

"Are you planning to stay a while or just passing through?"

"The latter. I am headed across the river, but I could also use a good meal. It's been a couple of days since the last one."

The mule bucked its head and snorted, obviously not content with standing still. She patted it on the neck to calm it. It seemed to work a little, but the animal was still obviously wanting to move.

"Well, if it's food you want, I'd recommend The Spouting Fish. Ilyeg cooks up the best food in Listerville."

"Thank you."

"You're quite welcome. It's near the river—just keep walking down this street and turn right when you get to the fountain. You'll see it. You can't miss it."

Cor'il nodded and patted the mule on the side of the head. It whinnied and pulled its head away from Cor'il's hand.

"He's quite an opinionated creature. But he's strong, and very handsome, he is. Look at that face!" Lynara patted the mule's face. It didn't pull away from her, but it still appeared occupied as he gazed off to the West.

"Thank you again for your recommendation." Cor'il nodded to her and continued down the street.

"Oh!" he heard her shout from behind him. "The last ferry across the river departs at the sun's last rays! The first one tomorrow leaves at sunrise!"

Cor'il turned and waved at her, nodding again. He looked up at the sun. *I've got a good few hours left; it shouldn't be an issue. Hopefully The Spouting Fish has some decent food—the stuff in my satchel just doesn't sound appealing today.*

It wasn't long before he had reached the edge of town. Cor'il walked to the end of the road, curious to see the river. The town ended at a hill with steep stone steps leading down to a long, wooden dock. From here, Cor'il could see the other bank of the river and the ferry traversing the water, on its way back. He headed back into town and stopped when he found The Spouting Fish. It was a rather unassuming stone building and Cor'il wouldn't have paid any attention if it wasn't for the fountain.

On his left, was a large, stone fish in a pool of water. About every 10 seconds it would spit water through the air and into another pool of water that sat just outside the building. Cor'il stood in the street watching it for a while, fascinated. He inspected the stone fish and nearly got sprayed in the face, receiving several funny looks from some passersby.

"Don't worry," someone shouted. "It's magic!"

"Watch out!" someone else yelled. "You're going to get wet!"

Finally, Cor'il gave up trying to understand the fountain and opened the door to The Spouting Fish. Immediately, he was greeted by a colorful, brightly-lit dining hall that smelled of wonderful foods cooking. Most tables were full of patrons laughing, talking, and eating, and several of them greeted Cor'il as he stepped inside.

Each table was a different, vibrant color as were the chairs. The walls were adorned with colorful pieces of artwork—paintings and tapestries—and several sculptures were placed about the room. Every lamp had a different-colored shade and even the serving maids were dressed in vibrant clothing that seemed to come alive every time they moved. By merely looking around, Cor'il felt his mood lift. He couldn't help but smile.

Locating an empty table was difficult, but Cor'il finally found one near the center of the room by a wooden support beam. Just as he was getting comfortable, a serving maid approached him, her vibrant yellow and blue skirts flowing and shifting as she walked. She had curly brown hair and piercing green eyes. Cor'il found her quite fetching.

"Hello, sir!" She sounded very happy. "What can I get for you today?"

"I, uh, I've never been here before," Cor'il stammered. He hadn't expected to need to make a decision so quickly. "What do—"

"I can save you the trouble and just get you one of the oven-roasted pheasants. They're always quite tasty! Most people would say that they are the specialty here at The Spouting Fish." She turned and headed for the kitchen before Cor'il could even say anything in response.

"That would be wonderful," he said jokingly to nobody. "And might I have some Scorovian hog juice with that?" He laughed, having absolutely no idea what he would end up with. He was relaxed and happy—full of hope and ready to arrive at his new home. He was still a bit anxious to get there, but he was also conscious of his stomach. Besides, he was close now. There was no reason to hurry.

• • •

The sun was well on its way to setting when Cor'il stepped out of The Spouting Fish. He sighed happily, his hunger now just a memory, and looked toward the river. *It most certainly is time. I can leave all of the world's troubles behind and live my life in peace.* He headed for the river and traveled down the steep staircase to the dock. The ferry was making its way across as Cor'il walked to the end of the dock to meet it.

The ferry appeared large enough to transport at least one wagon. It looked like it was actually a piece of the dock that somehow detached and traveled across the river by the two men pulling on some kind of rope. It moved between pillars rising out of the water that were connected by ropes. Cor'il waited patiently, gazing past the river to the horizon on the other side.

The ferry pulled up to the dock and, to Cor'il's surprise, attached itself to the structure. Cor'il could no longer determine where the dock ended and the ferry began. He knelt down to look closer but still could not figure it out. He looked up to see two men staring down at him with confused looks on their faces.

"Are you my last trip for the day?" the man on the right asked. He wore a wide-brimmed hat and looked like he had seen many winters. He was tall and wiry but, at the same time, his muscles were well-defined.

Opposite him was a much younger, bald man. His tunic had no sleeves and Cor'il watched his arms bulge as he flexed his hands.

"I suppose I am," Cor'il replied.

"Step on," said the man on the left. He had a considerably deep voice. "The price for transport is four coppers."

Cor'il stepped onto the ferry, expecting it to sway under his weight, but it didn't move at all. He fished out four copper coins and handed them to the man on the left who immediately pocketed them.

"Everyone wonders their first time," the older man said. He didn't seem to have any teeth. "They wonder why the ferry doesn't move or get heavier with people on it and why it doesn't sink in the water."

"Well, yes, I—"

"This ferry is old," the man continued. "I've heard it was here before Listerville itself. I've traveled back and forth across this river countless times and even *I* don't know how it works. The wood probably should have rotted a long time ago. Even the pillars look the same as they did the first time I crossed the river. I wish I could explain it to you but I think this ferry is older than even me."

"Aye," Cor'il responded. "It is quite fascinating."

"Let's be off," said the younger man as he grabbed hold of one of the ropes.

Both men tugged on their respective ropes and the ferry began to move. The ride was smooth, and the ferry did not sway or bob as it glided across the river. There was something very unusual about it all. The river's current should have affected the ferry's direction, but it did not.

"The stone pillars on either side somehow keep the ferry aligned to the path between them." The older man kept his gaze ahead of them while he spoke. "At least, that's what I figure. We added the ropes as a way to better propel it."

Cor'il continued to marvel at the ferry. He closed his eyes and could only barely feel that he was moving. *Remarkable! If the people of Listerville did not build this ferry, then I wonder who did. And how long ago?*

"So where are you headed?" the older man asked. "Ten Kings?"

Cor'il nervously adjusted his hood, unsure of how to answer the question.

"Aye, Ten Kings." He hadn't wanted to lie but it was an easier answer than telling someone that he was headed to a deserted forest. He was not much in the mood to talk. "That's where I am headed."

"Great city, Ten Kings." The older man grunted as he pulled on the rope. The younger man seemed to have much less trouble doing his part. In fact, Cor'il thought he might be holding back a bit. "Dangerous, though."

"Dangerous? How do you mean?" Cor'il focused on the conversation.

"We've had several caravans come through here as of late." The younger man's voice really was rather unique. "Most of them have told stories of farmers and their families disappearing or livestock being slaughtered. I've also heard that there is unrest within the city itself. Something about a murder, and mayhaps a revolt."

"Aye," the older man agreed. "If you are headed to Ten Kings, I would use caution. I hear more terrible things every day."

"I thank you for your concern." Cor'il was all of a sudden very thankful that he was indeed *not* traveling to Ten Kings. "I will keep my eyes open for any brigands or—"

"Not brigands, fool." The deep-voiced man looked at Cor'il with a serious glare. "From what I've heard, this is something much more sinister. There is evil to the north. These are not common thieves about, stealing weapons or money. No, it is something much different... much more dangerous."

"You say *it*," Cor'il replied. He was extremely interested in what this man knew. *Mayhaps the orcs and goblins have made it as far north as Ten Kings? But, if so, where are they coming from? How did they make it this far into the Realm without word of their existence spreading?*

The older man laughed hard enough to send him into a coughing fit. He doubled over, hacking as if he was dying.

"Don't let Kaldaren scare you, son." He was still chuckling as he resumed pulling on the rope. To Cor'il's surprise, the ferry was traveling quickly over the river—they were already past the halfway point. "There have been some mighty strange tales riding along with these travelers, but I don't put stock in any of them."

"And why is that?" The young man, Kaldaren, was still very serious. He did not seem to find any humor in the older man's words.

"Because, whatever's happening up in Ten Kings, it can't be as bad as everyone is saying. It all sounds like stories to me—made up to scare people away. Or mayhaps some ruffians have become a little bit too theatrical. Local militias will get them in line."

"You would be wise," interrupted Kaldaren, "to look past your short sight, Zalovar. An ill wind blows this way. I can feel it approach."

"You always were a superstitious one, Kaldaren. In all my years, never have I heard such a load of horseshit from one person before."

They both stopped pulling on the rope while they stared at each other for a moment. Then, as if nothing were wrong, they resumed their labor.

"Maybe I am," Kaldaren responded, pulling on the rope again. "But I will never be surprised."

"But always disappointed?"

"Aye."

Cor'il found these two men to be rather peculiar, but they amused him. Between that and his fascination with the ferry itself, the journey across the river didn't seem to take long. Their pace was quicker than Cor'il had anticipated and, after only 15 minutes, they had reached to the dock on the other side. The ferry once again seamlessly attached itself to the structure. Cor'il stepped off and thanked the two men for their help as they pulled away. Then he took a deep breath, calmed his nerves a bit, and headed down the road until eventually, he left the road and turned toward The Densewood.

Finally, several hours after the sun had set in the West, Cor'il approached the forest. As he passed through the tree line, a calm, warm breeze drifted by. He was certain he heard a soothing susurrus in his ear and he knew that he was home.

"Yes," he said. "This will do nicely, I think."

Chapter 26

The Blacksmoke pulled his dagger out of his victim's body and dropped the corpse off the roof and into the alley. The man's glassy, empty eyes still stared up at him, a look of shock and fear lingering behind them. He immediately went to work concealing the body. This spot had been the perfect location—secluded and littered with garbage. Most advantageous of all, it was a dead end.

When he was done, there was not a clue left behind that could give away the corpse. It would begin to stink soon enough but for now, he could walk away and nobody would be the wiser. Of course he had already relieved the unfortunate man of all valuables.

He walked back down the alley until he was about halfway to the street. Then he jumped onto the wall to his left and, without hesitation, deftly scrambled up it to the A-frame roof. From there, he connected with another, taller building and did much the same until he was high above the city, looking out over the rooftops.

It had been an unintended encounter—the man in the alley. He wasn't a mark. He had been unfortunate enough to target The Blacksmoke as *his* next victim. When the man had tried to pickpocket him, The Blacksmoke had pretended to flee into the alley and, shortly after, he had made the attacker into the victim. He would've thought it was funny except that it was pathetic.

Well, maybe it's just a little funny.

Before he'd gotten sidetracked, he had been following a merchant he thought to be one of Kendra's dragonstone smugglers. He was irritated that he would now have to track him down again.

The Blacksmoke ran along the top of the roof and leapt to the next one, landing quietly. Then he peered down at the streets below and swore under his breath when he didn't see the man. He'd never gotten a description from Kendra, but he didn't need one. He had always been good at finding people.

But that didn't change the fact that The Blacksmoke had lost track of him. He stuck out from the crowd, too—with shaggy, unkempt brown hair and a tunic that looked like it was three sizes too small. This man should've been easy to find again. He certainly was easy enough the first time. *Where did you run off to?*

He eventually spotted the man again after he hopped across two more buildings, and he followed his target as the man made his way through several streets. He waited and watched while his target was picking up some items he had apparently spilled onto the street. *While this isn't usually my specialty, I think I can get everything I need from this oaf another way.*

The Blacksmoke looked around to get familiar with his surroundings, then he sprang into action. First, he jumped onto the slanted roof and slid down it. When he reached the end, he leapt into the air and over the street below and landed on another lower roof on the other side. He heard several gasps from the crowd beneath him so he made sure to disappear over the roof and hide on the other side.

He normally was not so brazen and careless, but time was limited. Once away from prying eyes, he crouched behind a protruding window. As soon as it was apparent that nobody on this side of the building noticed him he found the least conspicuous location to descend to the street below. After a small drop and some creative climbing, he was once again back on the ground. He quickly rounded the corner back to the previous street.

"Here," he said, "let me help you with that."

"Oh," the man replied, looking quite flustered. "Thank you, but I think I've got it."

"I insist." He started picking up whatever he could—most of what had spilled out were fancy-looking knives decorated with gold and jewels that were obviously fake. *Either he's an amateur or he is just merely stupid.* And, yet, people would probably fall for this pathetic ruse, so who was the *real* fool?

"Really, sir, it's okay. I've got almost everything loaded back in the crate."

"Are you sure? Because, really, I'd be happy—"

"I'm fine!" the man growled. He looked nervous as he recklessly grabbed for anything he could and carelessly threw it all back into the wooden crate.

The Blacksmoke resisted the urge to stab the man in the face right there. Then he remembered that *he* was actually swindling this man which nearly made him laugh. Though he still really wanted to kill this man. Restraint was painful, sometimes.

"Very well, sir," he said politely while bowing. "May you have a wonderful day." He turned and walked down a smaller street. Once he was out of sight, he pulled the leaf-wrapped package from his pocket and unwrapped it. Inside was a stone much like the one Kendra had shown him. He rolled it around between his thumb and forefinger. *Ruby red with a sapphire core. And it's slightly warm to the touch.*

This irregularly-shaped stone was about the size of a large marble and it shimmered as he held it up to the sun. He slipped it back into his pocket and peeked out into the street. The man had just finished loading the crate and was now carrying it again. The Blacksmoke tipped his hat down and, keeping his distance, resumed following him. It wasn't long before his target stopped in front of a house.

He knocked on the door and was soon ushered inside, but The Blacksmoke couldn't see by whom. *Let's have a look, shall we?*

He scurried up the wall to a deck with a door on the second floor. The lock was simple enough to pick and, after just a few seconds, he quietly slipped inside.

The floor creaked beneath his first footstep. He immediately stopped and listened for a few seconds and once he was sure nobody had heard him, he relaxed a bit.

Traversing this small room was going to take forever if he had to avoid a creaky floor. He stepped up onto the bed to his left, then to a chair and onto the top of a desk next to the door to the hall. He carefully tested the floor and once he deemed it safe, he deftly stepped down and made his way to a staircase.

"Just as if the floor were made of thorns," he muttered to himself and grinned.

Instead of using the stairs—which he was *sure* would make noise under his weight—he perched on the handrail and quietly walked down it until the wall on his left ended and he could adequately see into the room below. The handrail was sturdy, thankfully, but he knew it would probably not hold his weight for long.

"I had a little trouble on the way over here. I tripped and dropped the crate." The man he followed was sitting in a simple, wooden chair with his back to the stairs.

"You are a clumsy fool," said another man. The Blacksmoke recognized the voice and when its owner stepped into view, he confirmed the man's identity. *Raynar. Between him and that inept idiot, whatever plan they're hatching is sure to be doomed before they even get started.*

"Not to worry," the man continued, "Nothing was damaged. All of the gems are fine. We made sure to individually wrap each one."

"Well," Raynar replied, "The very fact that you're still alive is a testament to that." He was pacing the floor and did not sound the least bit happy.

"What do you mean?"

"Don't think about it too hard. I wouldn't want you to strain something." There was silence for a moment while Raynar looked in the crate. He then started hastily removing the shoddy blades until only the individually-wrapped gemstones remained.

"I told you," the man in the chair continued. He sounded perturbed. "They're all fine. My brother and I took good care of them just as you said."

Raynar unwrapped one and held it up to the light just as The Blacksmoke had done. He gasped and marveled at the gem.

"They're beautiful," he muttered.

"Yes," the man replied, "they are. We did everything you asked us to. And everything you asked was a pain in our asses. I trust you have our gold?"

"What? Oh, yes. Of course I have your gold." Raynar carefully put the gem back in the crate. "Take this satchel as my appreciation."

What are you planning, Raynar? No matter. I suspect we'll all know when it backfires. Though he wasn't overly concerned, The Blacksmoke had to wonder if Raynar actually knew what he might truly have in that crate. Mayhaps Raynar thought they were simply gems of peculiar origin and that he could sell them to the nobility. Of course, The Blacksmoke wasn't even sure what this gem actually was—if it was truly a dragonstone. *I know one way to find out.*

He quietly scurried up the bannister and leapt onto the bed, then out the door. *This one is going to be a little more difficult to cover up.*

Chapter 27

Several days had passed since Kendra and The Blacksmoke had spoken. She was beginning to wonder if he had no information for her or if he had simply decided to ignore her request. Maybe she was just being impatient, but she wouldn't put it past him to make her wait simply for his own satisfaction. After all, she'd do him the same courtesy if their roles were reversed.

She sat at a table in The Panting Calf's dining hall with all kinds of thoughts swirling around inside her head. She was unable to focus on any one in particular and it was getting on her last nerve. She even refused to drink any wine for fear that it would cloud her mind. Working through everything was already difficult enough.

Given the events of the previous weeks she could hardly ignore the idea that the old stories—at least some of them—might actually be true. And now, with the sudden unexplained appearance of dragonstones... well, dragonstones came from only one place—*dragons*. If The Blacksmoke returned to her with confirmation, well, that was nearly impossible to fathom. And then there were the hundreds of questions that came along with this information.

She held the dragonstone discreetly between her thumb and index finger, staring at it. It was beautiful. Beautiful, yes, but Kendra found herself despising the gem. She despised what it signified and its possible origins and, most of all, the change that it could bring about. People could die and whole towns could be decimated. And that was just the dragonstone. If there were dragons out there, it was all much worse. *You're putting the cart before the horse. Find out its origins first and worry about it later.*

For now, there was nothing to do but wait. Orvaril was generous enough. He told Kendra not to worry about paying for the room—that he'd taken care of it. This was quite a relief since she wasn't willing to part with her hard-earned coin. She'd have no problems finding somewhere secluded and abandoned to spend her nights, but a warm bed was far more preferable to musty hay.

She hadn't slept well last night. It had been difficult to get to sleep in the first place, and when she finally slept, she had woken up often. At one point, there had been a terrible crash or explosion somewhere in the city. When she had looked out the window for any sign of what happened she saw nothing but a faint glow in the distance. In her drowsy state, the first thing she thought was that maybe someone had tried to tinker with a clock.

Her thoughts turned to Cor'il every so often. Part of her still felt as though she should have gone with him, but she knew that would have been a mistake. Still, it didn't help her sleep at night. More than anything she hoped he was safe. *Sure, he's got an interesting ability, but creating a flame in one's hand is not a great defense against orcs... or worse. Hopefully he's got some other tricks up his sleeve.*

Then there were all of the other thoughts and fears running through her head: the sum which made it very difficult to relax or sleep.

Orvaril, when he was actually around, seemed to have no problems sleeping. In fact, he snored quite a bit—last night, for example. That obviously didn't help matters, either. At one point, Kendra had gotten out of her bed and kicked him as he slept on the floor. That only made him snore louder. If she hadn't known better, she would've thought he was awake and did it on purpose.

She found herself nodding off, snapping awake just before her head hit the table. She grabbed for the dragonstone but missed as it rolled off the table and landed on the floor. She quickly snatched it up and laid it on the table when it burned her hand. *Oh now that's not good.* She wasn't sure if she needed to wait around for The Blacksmoke any longer. She might already have her answer. If the stone hadn't erupted in a miasma of fire when it hit the ground, mayhaps it wasn't a dragonstone after all.

A group of people brushed past her table, nudging her chair and briefly interrupting her thoughts. Two of them were talking and laughing boisterously and, though she tried to ignore them, it was difficult. They eventually sat down at a table nearby, continuing their raucous conversation.

"Ale for the three of us!" one of them proclaimed. He was a bloated man with a prolific brown beard that covered his face. His head, however, was completely bald. "And something to eat!" He belched loudly and pounded a fist on the table—a fist that looked like it was made up of five sausages.

Several patrons looked up from their meals to see what was happening, but eventually returned to their own business. Kendra, however, was slightly amused and continued to observe the group. She even decided to name them.

The man who had just spoken, she dubbed "Beardy."

There was a rather thin, younger-looking man. He probably hadn't seen more than 20 winters. He had short, blond hair and wore baggy clothes that looked as though he could get lost in them. She named him "Stick."

The last individual was a woman, sitting quietly as Stick and Beardy carried on loudly. She looked strong—possibly strong enough to beat Beardy in a fight. Her black hair was in a ponytail and face was stone cold but, her eyes were warm and soft. Kendra didn't name her—she couldn't figure her out.

A serving maid promptly appeared at the table and soon after, disappeared into the kitchen after a quick stop by the bar to talk to the young man behind it. He began pouring ale out of a barrel.

A serious air befell the group as their laughter died down.

"So," Stick said in a hushed tone. Kendra could still hear him quite well despite his attempt to be quiet. She could also read his lips. "What exactly was it that we killed out there?"

"It doesn't matter, my boy!" Beardy clapped Stick on the back, laughing. "It's dead, we're not, and food is on the way!"

"It *does* matter, Loradon," the woman hissed. "And keep it down. The Abyss knows that we don't need everyone in this room hearing you."

The man emerged from behind the bar with three tankards. He set them down on the table as Beardy paid him. Loradon (Kendra had a difficult time calling him that now) drank deep before slamming the tankard back down on the table.

"Father, please," Stick pleaded, "let's keep this to ourselves."

"We're *heroes*, son! Everyone here should know it!"

Kendra slipped the dragonstone back into one of her pockets and, her curiosity piqued, approached their table.

"Hello," she said. "Might I sit for a moment?"

"Hello there, pretty one." Loradon's eyes locked onto her. Kendra resisted the urge to gag.

"I don't think now is—"

"Nonsense, Halari! Let's not be rude!" Loradon clumsily stood up, nearly falling out of his chair. "Of course you may share our table." He tried to do what Kendra could only assume was a bow. His gut spilled onto the table and kept him from being able to bend very far. She hoped her wince went unnoticed by the three of them. The woman—Halari—looked apprehensive.

"Thank you, kind sir." Kendra sat down at the empty side of the square table. Halari was to her left and Loradon to her right. She noticed Stick was also unable to take his eyes off her. "I couldn't help but overhear—"

"See, Loradon? I *told* you to be quiet!" Halari shot him a furious gaze, her lips pursed tightly.

"It's nothing to worry about, ma'am, but I *was* a slight bit curious." Kendra turned on the charm. At the same time, she inspected their possessions for anything valuable. "The lands around Elston have been calm for so long, I merely wondered what, or who, it was that encroached upon the land."

"The Abyss if I know," Loradon replied hastily. Halari, once again, glared at him. "Well, I mean, you wouldn't believe me if I told you."

"Was it green-skinned and savage?"

"Wait," Halari replied, leaning in. She looked very surprised. "How did you know?"

"Big teeth and not very bright?"

"Yes," Stick whispered.

"A little larger than a man?"

"No," Halari responded, now looking a little confused. She hesitated before continuing. "Much larger."

"It was *huge*!" Loradon roared. "I mean to tell you it was the biggest damned—"

"Wait," Halari interrupted. Her eyes hardened. "Are you saying that you've seen... other things?"

"Unfortunately, yes." Kendra refused to show it but she was just as surprised as Halari. Orcs and goblins were one thing, but something bigger... she already had a queasy feeling in her stomach just thinking about the dragonstone. This made it worse. "We call them orcs and goblins."

"Orcs and goblins!" Loradon laughed. "Preposterous!"

"Then how do you explain what we slew out there in that farmer's field?" Halari looked as though she would strangle Loradon, and Kendra suspected she could easily do it.

"This was neither orc nor goblin, at least not from any story I've heard." Stick piped up.

"I believe you," Kendra remained calm, "and that is worrisome. I am saying, however, that whatever you killed is not the only creature out there. I have no actual knowledge if what I've seen, and killed, truly can be called orc or goblin but they certainly fit the description. If children's stories of yore talk about orcs and goblins, then mayhaps this creature is in them as well."

"A troll!" Stick whispered. He seemed excited. Or afraid. Maybe a little of both. He fidgeted in his chair, unable to sit still as he grinned wildly.

For once, Loradon was subdued. Kendra could see the thoughts churning in Halari's head as she tried to make sense of it. Kendra had once been there. She knew it well.

"As preposterous as it sounds," Halari added, "it fits. It was not an easy kill by any means, and we even sneaked up on it—well, most of us, anyway." She shot an accusatory look at Loradon who didn't seem to notice.

"Tell me," Loradon whispered. He seemed to understand the magnitude of the situation at last. "If what we killed is indeed a troll, then what does it mean?"

"It means," Kendra retorted, "that things are changing. I don't know how or why but I've killed more orcs and goblins than I should have."

"Considering they are supposed to be fictional—fairy tales." Stick ran a finger nervously over the lip of his tankard, his mood having changed almost instantly. "It's impossible, isn't it?"

"Precisely." Kendra rose from the table just as the serving maid appeared with a large tray of food. "I bid you good day," she said. "This has been most productive."

She left the common room, stepping outside into the sunlight. She was done waiting for The Blacksmoke. She suspected she already had her answer, and it terrified her.

As if on cue, a man grabbed her by the arm.

"Keep walking, my dear," he whispered.

"Didn't I tell you not to—"

"Now's not the time for our usual pleasantries. We can go through all of that later. Right now, just act normal and walk with me."

"Get yourself in trouble again?" She smirked.

"Not really," he chuckled. "The city guard and I are playing a little game of Catch the Gortog, and I'm the gortog at the moment."

"I assume you have information for me, then?"

"Aye. And because you are currently doing me a favor, I will do you one and tell you what I know."

"You're too kind, mister gortog."

"Cute as always," he sneered. "It's one of the things I like about you. Mayhaps the *only* thing."

"Enough small talk, then."

They turned down a smaller street. Kendra quickly glanced behind them and noticed several city guards hurrying through the street, looking around, searching for something… or someone.

"Right," Blacksmoke continued. "So, the stone. It's real. It's as bloody real as you and me. I don't know where that simpleton got them but he does indeed have quite a few. He sold them to Raynar."

"Raynar." Kendra wasn't sure if she should be relieved or concerned by this information. Raynar was largely incompetent, yes, but he had, every once in a while, been able to pull off competent things. *Even a sightless razorbeast gets a kill every now and then.*

"If Raynar actually understands what these are then he's got quite an arsenal on his hands."

"So let me see if I understand," Kendra paused for a moment. She stopped walking but The Blacksmoke urged her on. "This *is* a dragonstone, then?"

"Aye."

"So, if it's actually a dragonstone—"

"Yes, they explode—powerfully. *Very* powerfully." The Blacksmoke looked down a street to the right but skipped past it and continued in his current direction.

"And you know this how?"

"Because." The smile on his face told her everything she needed to know before he opened his mouth again.

"You tested one?"

"Aye," he smirked, "last night. You've always been a light sleeper—one of your more… frustrating qualities. Surely you heard it?"

Kendra remembered the explosion last night.

"As a matter of fact, I believe I did. I wasn't aware that it was your handiwork." Kendra instinctively started to look behind her to see if they were still being followed.

"It was indeed," The Blacksmoke continued. "And there is no need to look back—there are still two guardsmen behind us." One of these days she would need to find out how he did that. "Listen," he said as they dodged around several groups of people. "This changes things. Where there are dragonstones—"

"There are dragons."

"Aye."

They turned down another street.

"But that assumes the old stories speak truth." She knew how pathetic that sounded. She was trying to convince herself of something that she herself knew better.

"Surely you know the truth, my dear. You've only been in Elston for a few of days." The Blacksmoke grinned. Kendra knew how he operated. Nobody entered or left the city without him knowing. It was eerie. "So you've obviously been traveling, and that leads me to believe that by now you've encountered... anomalies of a sort."

"Well, yes, but... dragons?"

"I can't say I fully believe it, either, but it looks more probable today than it did yesterday, does it not?"

"I can't disagree." Her head was swimming. She felt naïve trying to ignore the situation. The truth was, it *did* sound plausible. *Dragons... damn.*

"Sulbar was besieged many nights ago," he continued.

"Indeed. I heard. Otherwise, I would be there now."

"And do you know by what? I'm sure you can guess." It really was creepy how much this man knew—even about a city that was far away and about something that had happened so recently.

"Orcs? Goblins?"

"If that's what you wish to call them, then yes. You are correct. City guards are about to be the least of our worries. Thieves? Brigands? Those will be minor nuisances akin to biteflies in comparison."

"Maybe the guard will leave you alone, then," Kendra tried to laugh.

"Highly unlikely. They do love playing their games with me."

"You could just do away with the two guards following us, you know."

"One," he replied. "There is only one now. And, no. I've no need for senseless bloodshed. They're easy enough to shake when they get bored. Ironically, you're safer dealing with the likes of me than being outside a city anymore."

"I am not sure I'm convinced," Kendra smirked.

"This Realm is on the cusp of something—teetering on the edge. I'm not sure what and nobody else seems to know, either. The stories are coming true. I know how foolish that sounds so keep your sarcastic jab to yourself, my dear."

"And what do you suggest we do?"

"Weather the coming storm." He took a subtle look around him, then nodded. "This looks like as good a place as any. I'll see you around, my dear." The Blacksmoke turned left down a narrow space in between two buildings and, hopping from one wall to the next, climbed up to the roof and disappeared.

Kendra wasn't even sure what to do. She turned and slowly headed back to The Panting Calf Inn, unable to comprehend everything she had learned in the past hour. She passed the guard who continued hastily down the street, cluelessly looking for his target that he would never find. She giggled briefly as she approached him.

"Is there something I can help you find, sir?" she asked in a rather coy voice.

"No, ma'am," the guard replied politely. "But thank you for inquiring." He hurried past her and further down the street.

I do hope that treeboy hasn't gotten into any trouble. Trolls? Dragons? It's bloody madness.

Chapter 28

When Dalinil awoke and opened his eyes he immediately noticed something was wrong. Last night, he had fallen asleep in a comfortable bed within a small house in Ilathri. Now, however, he was beneath a canopy of leaves in the forest. He sat upright, looked around nervously, and saw only the trees around him. What once had been a stone road, houses, and fountains all of white, was now dirt, trees, and bushes of various green hues. Dumbfounded and disappointed, he sat in silence for several moments before finally deciding to get up.

Ilathri had afforded him protection and knowledge beyond anything he could've imagined. During the months he had dwelt within its walls he not only learned much about the world, but also about himself. He had learned to control the raging rivers within him and also—more importantly—to *command* them. Arcturas had never expressed any displeasure with him.

So why am I not still there? What happened? Did I disappoint Arcturas somehow?

Even though Arcturas had told Dalinil that there was not much else the Ilathri could teach him, Dalinil had not expected to simply be cast aside. A simple "goodbye" would have sufficed. Now, however, Dalinil was left wondering if he had done something wrong. He felt a tiny bit perturbed and with that, he could feel the familiar warmth welling up inside of him. Thankfully, he now knew what this feeling meant. He could now control it.

No, I did nothing wrong. It must just be time to move on. Mayhaps they've given up their search for me by now. After all, several months had passed. But then he remembered what Arcturas had told him. Ilathri was unique and, because of its qualities, it was not affected by the passage of time in the same way everywhere else was.

Arcturas had told him that time in Ilathri passed "appropriately." Dalinil still wasn't quite sure what that meant, but he had grown tired of asking Arcturas to repeat his explanation. He had simply pretended he finally understood. The truth was, there were a lot of things he didn't understand. Arcturas had not seemed to be concerned about this fact, however, even though it worried Dalinil.

But the one thing that stuck with him was how Arcturas repeatedly urged him to control his anger. Last night had been his first success and, though he had had many failures, Arcturas pointed out that they were just as important as success. *And what if I don't* want *to suppress it? Is that a bad thing?*

There was little light in the forest. Dalinil wasn't sure whether it was morning or still night. He was no longer tired, so he got up and, not knowing what else to do, started walking. If someone still sought to find him he would need to continue moving, even if he still did not know exactly toward what.

Eventually, rays of light made their way through the forest roof, dappling the leaves with warmth, and crickets and other noisy insects were quickly drowned out by the songs of birds. Dalinil pulled an apple from his rucksack and ate it while he walked, enjoying the feeling of relative safety. He found that his pace was more relaxed today than it had been in a long time. He still sought to avoid anyone who may be looking for him, but he no longer feared them—not anymore.

He had also decided that he needed to set things right, though he had to figure out how he was going to do that. He needed to make sure that he could eventually live his life without constantly having to look over his shoulder.

For the first time since he had fled Ten Kings, Dalinil felt a sense of direction—not so much a purpose but more of something to strive for. He felt safe. In fact, he'd nearly forgotten about everything that had happened—things he had seen and done. Unfortunately, Arcturas had been unable to answer any of his questions regarding the odd creatures he had encountered on his journey.

But he *had* been able to answer other questions—questions Dalinil wasn't aware he'd even had.

For a moment, he paused. He briefly felt the urge to turn and head back to Ten Kings, now confident that he could settle everything. He had killed no one and he needed to clear his name—to prove his innocence. The problem was, he didn't know who *had* killed Lord Emory or how to find out who did.

No, it would certainly be foolish to return home now, but the urge wouldn't go away. And, while he fully understood that returning to Ten Kings would only get him into trouble, he still *wanted* to. With what he'd learned, he could *make* them accept his truth and, if they opposed him, he could remove them. *But... no. That does nothing but make me a monster... and I will not prove them right.* That didn't mean that he had to let any trackers take him back, though, either.

Forcing himself to continue, he found he was walking slowly, hoping that mayhaps Ilathri would reappear nearby. He knew that this was wishful thinking, yet he continued his search just in case.

Instead of finding Ilathri he found something familiar. As he looked ahead of him he noticed, up in the trees, a building identical to the one in which he'd hid from the faceless monster some time ago. From where he was he could not see much detail but it was unmistakable—except that this one was easier to spot among the foliage, and it looked a bit misshapen. *Well, what else have you got to do?*

Confidently, Dalinil strode up to the tree in which the house was perched. He looked around but didn't see an easy way up. There were no low-lying branches he could climb that would hold his weight. *I guess it is time to test out what I've learned.*

He closed his eyes briefly and, when they reopened, he was able to see them—the shimmering lines that ran between everything. He lost his concentration and they nearly faded from view, but he regained control quickly. His heart pounded with excitement and he almost lost his concentration again. For a moment, he felt the warmth that was welling up inside him almost escape, but he caught it just in time.

With his finger, he plucked at the green line nearest to him. It flowed through this tree in particular, causing a few of its branches to shake. He tried it again with the same result. *So far so good. Time to try and exert control.*

He touched the line again, but this time let its energy flow into him. It filled him up with warmth and swirled within him. He took a moment to revel in the raw power he held as he was connected with this tree. He could feel the leaves sway in each breeze as he concentrated.

He prodded the tree with the line of energy, causing some of its branches to shake again. He poked deeper but received the same result. He could do nothing more than cause the tree to shiver. *Is the tree resisting me? I should be able to do more than merely jiggle branches.* He felt frustration and anger build up inside of him.

Dalinil released the green line and approached a different tree nearby. He grabbed one of the green lines emanating from it and concentrated. This time his efforts produced different results and he watched as one of the lower branches bent down to him. He grabbed it and, again using the green line, commanded the limb to raise him up to another, thicker branch. Once there, he stood, marveling at what he'd done. He relaxed for a moment but kept all of the lines in his sight. The lines—Arcturas had called them "Threads," hadn't he?

The structure was a good 20 feet above him still. *I could probably climb the rest of the way up but with this ability, why should I? The trees can lift me up the rest of the way.* He concentrated some more, and after a few moments, had reached the same level as the building. There was, however, a gap between the trees. Undaunted, Dalinil released his current Thread and grabbed one from the other tree. He felt it connect with him, the energy coursing through his body, and through it, he commanded the tree to create a bridge. He'd done it before—back when he'd first discovered the tree houses—but back then, he had no idea what he was doing.

The tree ahead lowered a branch toward him, about to bridge the gap. But there was resistance. Something was pushing back through the Thread and it overwhelmed Dalinil. He lost control of the Thread and instead of aiding him, the branch swatted at him, knocking him off of the branch on which he currently stood. He yelled as he fell and hit a branch below, knocking the wind out of him. He reached out to grasp for something—anything—to grab onto. He was too flustered, and he couldn't concentrate long enough to connect with a Thread. Every time he tried to grasp one he lost concentration. Or was the Thread yanked away from his grasp?

He was finally able to cling to a branch after falling onto it. He could barely breathe and he felt banged up, but at least for now he was alive.

His hands shook with fear and exertion as he looked around for a way out. Seeing a branch slightly below and behind him he stretched out his right leg and used it for support. He moved his left leg onto the branch and then pushed off with his arms, quickly grabbing the tree to steady his balance. He peered out from behind the trunk to see if he was going to be attacked again. Everything was still—as if he'd imagined it all.

Okay, take a moment to relax. What just happened? He brought the Threads back into view. They were countless, spanning out from every tree as well as the ground, rocks, and the sky—all different colors according to their source. He reached out for one of the brown Threads but it was quickly snatched away. It became rigid and unyielding. When he tried again with a white Thread. The same thing happened—at first, he was able to bring the Thread under his control but shortly thereafter, it turned stiff and colorless, and it refused to respond.

Dalinil grabbed a red Thread and felt it connect. Anger welled up inside him, slowly growing stronger. How dare the Threads ignore his commands! Though he felt his anger swell he remained calm. Rage would only cloud his judgment and there was certainly something dangerous nearby that he needed to contend with. He reached out for another green Thread, but once again, it would not bend to his will. This made him even angrier and he seethed with rage. He tried to grab for a branch but it swatted at him. He ducked and narrowly avoided the attack.

The fury within him grew, and at first he tried to suppress it. Ultimately, however, he gave into it, letting it wash over him like a wave of water. Instead of letting that wave carry him away, he rode it and shaped it to his will, and he felt *alive*!

He used the red Thread. By tapping into it, he created a jet of flame from his right hand, igniting the tree branch in a fury of fire. He sprayed fire at another branch, setting it ablaze as well. He felt his strength bolster and grabbed another limb, ripping it from the tree as his vision clouded and he began to feel lightheaded. He had experienced this before. Arcturas had said that it was caused by overexertion—by channeling too much energy at once through the Threads. Before Arcturas had taught him to control his anger, he had passed out several times during the lessons. He released the Threads and struggled just to keep from falling off the tree branch on which he stood.

He clumsily dodged several more attacking branches, hanging on to whatever he could reach. Soon enough, however, he found himself trapped and unable to even fall off the branch he was on. The tree limbs wove themselves around him and bound him to the tree itself.

"What do you want?" he yelled weakly, barely able to stay upright. *What am I doing wrong? Why won't the Threads respond to me?* "Why won't you work? What am I supposed to do?" He tore wildly at the prison the branches had created, destroying it in a matter of seconds. His fist connected with the trunk of a tree and completely punched through it, cutting his arm as he pulled it back out. But the trees reacted instantly, regenerating just as quickly as Dalinil could damage them.

His vision clouded more and he lost his balance. Vines and branches engulfed him, wrapping him up in a cocoon. He was too exhausted to fight anymore, and too full of anger to think straight. On the verge of unconsciousness, he was eventually able to calm himself enough to wait patiently. *If I'm not able to get out of here, I may as well see where this leads. If someone or something wants me dead, it probably would've happened by now. Just wait patiently and strike when you know who your enemy is.*

He felt himself being lifted higher, probably being passed from tree to tree. He couldn't see very easily out of his makeshift cell so he assumed his enemy couldn't see *in*. He carefully removed his axe from his belt and kept it ready, gripping it so tightly that his hand started to hurt.

Eventually, he stopped moving and the vines and branches parted. He squinted briefly as light poured in and he saw a figure standing in front of the tree house. Stepping precariously onto the branch he cautiously approached the hooded man, his axe still held in his hand.

"Who are you? Why did you attack me?" Dalinil did not raise his axe but he was ready to use it.

"I should apologize," the man said.

"Take down your hood so that I can see you better." Dalinil paused, wary that this was some sort of trap. He stood about 10 feet from his adversary, who did not move for quite a while. The two stared at each other until finally, the figure reached up and removed the hood of his cloak.

He appeared to be no older than Dalinil! The boy's brown hair hung to his chin, and his green eyes were piercing. What really drew the focus of Dalinil's observation was this boy's ears. They were oddly-shaped—almost pointed.

"I ask again," Dalinil continued, "Why did you attack me?"

"I did not mean to attack you," the boy said. He slowly approached with his hands outstretched. Dalinil still embraced his Thread. He noticed that most of them, now colorless, bent and surrounded this individual. He tried to grab them but it was like trying to push down a wall. They refused to yield to him. In fact, the one Thread Dalinil held now joined the others around this... boy.

"If you promise not to use them against me," the boy said, "I will release them." Did he know what Dalinil had been trying to do?

Dalinil nodded in compliance. Instantly, the Threads unraveled and their colors returned. Dalinil was becoming less cautious and more curious. Arcturas must not have told him everything—or he didn't *know* everything.

"Who are you?"

"Please put away your axe. You do not need it. As I said before, I did not mean to attack you."

"If it's all the same, I'd like to hold onto it."

"I apologize in advance, but I would rather you put it away."

The boy held out his palm and muttered something that sounded like gibberish. A red Thread briefly touched the boy, then wrapped itself around his axe which became burning hot to the touch.

"The Abyss! How—" Dalinil immediately dropped the axe which tumbled down through the various tree branches and out of sight. The red Thread returned to its normal state.

Dalinil reached out with a white Thread, and tapping into it, felt his axe on the ground. Using its force, he lifted it back into his hand within a matter of seconds.

"Very nice," the boy said.

"Are we enemies? Because I am confused." He slid the now cool axe into his belt loop.

"I do not believe so. In fact," the boy continued, "I think that we are to become strong allies. You can use the Threads as I can."

"What does it mean?"

"I am not sure. Again, you have my apologies. I felt someone using the Threads and moved to defend my home. The world has changed and one can never be too careful these days."

"I think I know what you mean. I've seen things lately that I'm not sure I understand. It's like they don't belong." Dalinil felt the anger drain out of him and he relaxed, though he was glad his axe was back at his side.

"Precisely. I, too, have seen things that I'd only read about or heard about from storyweavers. Today, I've learned that the Threads take commands from another." The boy turned briefly and waved his hand in front of the wall of the house. Immediately, green Threads attached to the house and a passage opened around them.

"I am as surprised as you are," Dalinil replied. "I was told that I was the only individual who had this ability." Dalinil slowly approached. He did not feel threatened anymore. This boy, at first glance appeared calm and in control, but Dalinil could see him fidget every once in a while.

"I've learned to not take anything at face value anymore," the boy said, heading into the house.

"Aye. I think I understand what you mean."

"Come inside if you wish. I've got some tea brewing, and it's not particularly safe out here."

"Dalinil Thruscar. My name is Dalinil Thruscar."

The boy turned and held out his hand. Dalinil shook it.

"It is nice to meet you, Dalinil Thruscar. I am Cor'il Silvermoon of Kuranthas.

Dalinil followed Cor'il into the tree house. The wall sealed up behind them.

Chapter 29

"So how did you create that house?" Dalinil asked Cor'il as they walked among the trees. Cor'il was torn—he very much wished to stay in the Densewood but he also felt drawn to his new friend who was most likely moving on. To find someone like him who could use the Threads was a boon, and Cor'il was excited to share his experiences with someone who understood. The pull of the Threads was stronger than the pull of the Densewood and it had taken Cor'il completely by surprise. He felt as if there were two places that he belonged—in the Densewood as well as with his new friend.

They had spent most of yesterday getting acquainted, and Cor'il was overjoyed to know that he had found someone else who could do the same things he could. They both were weary from their confrontation and Cor'il, who usually didn't sleep for more than a few hours each night, found himself trying to doze off shortly after the sun had set.

"I used green Threads. I looped them several times and slowly molded the tree." That was about the best way Cor'il felt he could explain it. But it was less "molding" of the tree and more "asking" the tree to take a different shape. Before they left, he made sure to remove the loop, allowing the tree to slowly resume its normal form. Within a few hours the house would be gone and the tree would be back to its normal shape.

During the past three weeks, the book had taught Cor'il much. He had, in fact, been able to finish it. While he still didn't fully understand *why* the Threads worked as they did, he understood how to manipulate them. He realized that he had been using them for a while in a much simpler form. Being able to tap into the Threads and control them was powerful, but using the power words, or spells, was also quicker and took less effort.

They walked in silence for a bit Cor'il listened to the birds and tried to make sense of recent events.

While Cor'il was able to use spells with ease, he often made serious mistakes when trying to control the Threads directly. He hoped that Dalinil could help him and, mayhaps, he could return the favor somehow.

Dalinil said he was headed south but he wasn't sure where. This struck Cor'il as peculiar, and when he had questioned Dalinil further, he had received no better answer. He decided to bring it up again today.

"As I said before, south." Dalinil muttered. Cor'il remained silent, hoping for more information. "Mayhaps to Scorovia."

"I am unfamiliar with that city."

"Scorovia is the Realm to the south," Dalinil chuckled. "I've not traveled very much and decided it was time to see the world. I've spent most of my life in the city of Ten Kings."

"I, as well, have not traveled much. Mayhaps I will one day see Scorovia. If you would prefer another city, you might like Elston—also south of here. I have friends there." Cor'il wrestled with his emotions, trying to make sense of things. Why did he want to leave the place he had once sought so adamantly? Was he *that* intrigued with someone else who could use the Threads?

"I'd prefer not to travel alone. This axe has seen more action than I would prefer."

"Indeed," Cor'il replied. "My sword has spilled blood as well— blood from unnatural... things."

"Aye. I have had the same experience."

"You have fought orcs? Goblins?" Cor'il was oddly relieved that someone else had seen these creatures. His relief was quickly replaced with concern. *How common are these creatures? Do they roam the entire Realm?*

"If that is what you wish to call them. I fought some smaller, green snotty creatures. I avoided fighting a much larger beast that was using a tree to attack some merchants. Then there was the monster without a face."

"Without a face? Surely you must be joking." Cor'il mustered a nervous chuckle, but deep within he knew that Dalinil probably was not joking. Cor'il remembered the skeletal creature he had encountered and a shiver ran down his back.

"I wish I were joking." Dalinil appeared to have lost some color in his face and he looked slightly scared. "It was terrifying. It had wings and it could be in one place one second, then be in another instantly— without walking. It simply disappeared and reappeared—"

"Just like storyweavers' tales?"

"Aye. I've laid eyes on things I never thought I would see. Before I started this journey I had never once had to use this axe for anything. When I crafted it, I made it with the strongest steel and the sharpest edge." Dalinil took the axe off of his belt and inspected it, picking at the blade. "I never wanted to test it, and I certainly never thought I would have to use it against the things I've seen."

Cor'il's concern grew. *So it doesn't stop with goblins and orcs. There are other things out there. Things that not even the stories spoke of.*

They proceeded down a steep hill, taking their time to manage the difficult terrain. Cor'il reached the bottom first and waited for Dalinil who soon stood next to him. The sun was shut out by a thick forest canopy, shunning the light in such a way that gave Cor'il pause. It was not difficult for Cor'il to see around the area but none of the sun's direct rays seemed to penetrate this part of the forest.

"We shouldn't be far from the end of the forest." Cor'il pointed ahead of them. "When I first came here I couldn't have walked more than a day's distance in."

"Why is it so dark down here? Maybe the forest is thicker here?"

"I'm not sure," Cor'il muttered, looking around. This part of the forest looked no different than any other area. Cor'il brushed it off at first but as they walked further, he also noticed that he began to feel cold. Ben Falhar's words lingered in his mind. *"There are places out there that exude unnatural darkness and cold. You would be wise to avoid them."*

It was then that he noticed how quiet it was.

"Do you feel that—that cold air?" he asked, his breath fogging up in front of him.

"Aye." Dalinil looked concerned. "Does this seem normal to you?"

"No." Cor'il rested a hand on his sword and looked around cautiously. "I think we should hurry."

"Why do you say that?"

"This—the cold, the darkness—this is unnatural." Cor'il tightened his grip on his sword.

"Is it possible that a nearby cave is emanating this cold air? Combined with the trees blocking the sun—"

"In most cases," Cor'il replied, "I would probably agree with you." He embraced the Threads and his sight changed. His surroundings became dull and slightly blurry. But the Threads shined brightly, like beacons in the darkest night. They were a gleaming latticework of radiance and each one pulsed with the energy contained within. He noted mostly green and red Threads creating a web between trees and rocks. Hiding among them were a few white Threads and one or two silver Threads.

But the particular color that outnumbered them all was black. By far there were more black Threads than all other colors combined. *Well now, those are new.*

"Dalinil," Cor'il whispered. He'd stopped walking but Dalinil hadn't noticed.

"What? Why are we whispering?" He stood by Cor'il, obviously a bit confused.

"Look at the Threads."

Dalinil paused. Even through his slightly blurred vision he could tell Dalinil was concentrating much harder than he should have had to.

"Black Threads?" he finally asked.

"Aye. Have you ever seen *black* Threads before?"

"No." Dalinil looked around a bit. "Have you?"

"No."

"There certainly are a lot of them, though."

Cor'il carefully and hesitantly tested one, tapping into a minute amount of its power. Immediately he felt its energy fill him up and, with it, a chilling, nauseating cold. He shivered and let it go instantly, feeling its oily slime wash off of him.

"I am guessing that wasn't pleasant?" Dalinil asked. "You had quite a contorted look on your face."

"No," Cor'il muttered. "Not pleasant at all." His mind was slightly cloudy, as if he had not been awake very long, and he felt sick to his stomach.

Cor'il saw movement and he began to shiver.

"You," he whispered. A chill ran through his body and he felt his muscles stiffen. He turned to flee but he couldn't move. For there in the distance, was a floating, cloaked, skeletal figure approaching from behind some tall bushes. It weaved between the trees, floating calmly toward them. "Dalinil," he said through labored speech. "Do you see that?" Cor'il struggled to control his arm enough to point in the creature's direction. He barely was able to move.

"What in The Abyss is *that?*"

"Run. Now."

Cor'il had to force his muscles to move. Dalinil appeared to have the same problem. Eventually they were both able to clumsily run but the creature pursued them.

He stopped and channeled a red Thread. Using its energy, he sent a flame at the creature which was undeterred as the fire merely washed over it. He let go of the red and found a white Thread. Using its power, he conjured a strong wind but it, too, did nothing. He then used it to hurl sticks and rocks but the creature easily dodged them. With great difficulty, he drew his sword. The closer the creature came, the more difficult it was for Cor'il to move. He lost contact with the white Thread and was unable to tap into it again. He could feel his body freezing with raw fear—now unable to even speak as the creature drew to within feet of him.

It stared at Cor'il with empty eye sockets, hovering before him. Its head tilted slightly, apparently scrutinizing Cor'il, but it made no move to attack.

"Cor'il!"

Cor'il heard his name. He heard Dalinil but his voice seemed muffled and distant. Then he felt a hand on his shoulder which yanked him away from the creature.

"Release the Threads! Cor'il! Release the Threads, damn it!"

As he was jerked backward he lost his balance and, with it, his concentration. His vision returned to normal and he tumbled to the ground, instantly scurrying back to his feet and gasping for breath. He still felt the chill and the forest wasn't any brighter, but the creature had vanished. He gasped for air and darted his gaze around, looking for more of those things. But it was just the two of them now.

"What was that?" Dalinil asked, helping Cor'il up from the ground.

"I don't know." Cor'il sheathed his sword and brushed the leaves off of him. He was still breathing quite heavily and was shivering both from the cold and fear. "I've seen one once before. Thankfully, it's gone now."

"I don't think it's gone."

"What do you mean?"

"The moment I dropped the Threads, I felt normal again. But you were in trouble. It could be here still, watching us, but unable to affect us because we can't see or touch it."

"Either way," Cor'il continued, "let's get moving. We should leave as quickly as possible." He heard a feral scream in the distance.

"Agreed."

"Nothing I did seemed to affect it." Cor'il ran alongside Dalinil, jogging at a decent pace. "I threw fire at it and that creature just shrugged it off."

"How are we supposed to fight something like that?"

"I'm not sure we *do* fight something like that." Cor'il slowed his pace a bit. He noticed that the sun was now shining through the trees, and the temperature had risen. "I think we're safe now... if there *is* a safe area anymore." Cor'il contacted the Threads and embraced them once again. Instantly the energy surged through him and everything around him distorted in a slight blur. He looked around, ready to release the power should he encounter one of those skeletal monsters again.

To his relief, he saw nothing. He exhaled, only now realizing that he had been holding his breath. He thought he could feel it somewhere in the distance, beckoning to him and searching for him. He released the Threads.

"Nothing?" Dalinil asked.

"Aye. It looks like we are safe. We're not far from Listerville. We can stay there tomorrow night before heading to Elston. It seemed a nice little town." Cor'il stepped over a fallen log and around a tree. With each step, he kept vigilance, and Dalinil appeared to be doing the same. Though the forest appeared placid enough, Cor'il knew full well that it could be misleading.

The sun had just about set when the trees finally gave way to grassy hills. Cor'il stretched his back and relaxed a bit. He was looking forward to arriving in Listerville, but the ferry would not be running until first light. A soft bed would be most welcome. But for now they needed shelter of some kind.

"If you'd like to gather some firewood I can work on a shelter for the night. It won't be anything fancy—that house took me the better half of a day to create and, even then, it was less than perfect." *And I nearly destroyed the entire tree by accident while I was trying to shape it.*

"Alright." Dalinil began looking around for sticks and fallen trees which he then cut into pieces with his axe. He was definitely strong without using the Threads but, in this case, Cor'il could see that he was connected to both silver and red Threads. Dalinil was chopping through sizeable logs as if they were twigs.

Cor'il brought as many green Threads to him as he could handle and beckoned the nearby plants to form a hut of sorts. Every time he used the Threads he couldn't help but be amazed. Sometimes he wanted to laugh, he got so excited. Whenever he embraced them, they filled him up with a radiant glow and a mix of emotions. They made him feel alive, as if he was one with everything around him—even the sickening black

Threads. *I will have to explore the black Threads at some point. I wonder why I've not encountered them before today.*

Whenever he thought about it, Cor'il was always surprised by how much he'd learned. He'd finished the rest of the book during his two weeks' time in The Densewood, sometimes breezing through 50 pages or more a day. He still carried it with him, but the pages were once more illegible gibberish and of no use. It was remarkable how he had learned it all so quickly.

The hut was crude but Cor'il finished shaping the shelter by looping some of the green Threads around it. He'd basically made a simple, if not sloppy, weave of branches and vines under which they could sleep.

Dalinil soon returned with an armload of firewood, and before long the two shared small talk around a fire, eating whatever they had brought with them.

"Hopefully Elston will be safer than out here," Dalinil said, still chewing on some dried meat. "At least it has city walls, right?"

"It does have walls," Cor'il replied. "But I'm unsure how much protection walls can offer. Certainly more than camping out in the wilderness, though."

"It certainly can't be any worse." Dalinil picked up a stick and poked at the ground.

"I'm not all that worried. I think we're pretty safe, though I admit, I'd rather be up in the trees."

Dalinil dug up some dirt with the stick and flicked it into the air. The dirt hovered above the fire and rotated as Dalinil held out his hand, manipulating the clump. But it suddenly fell into the fire as Dalinil swore under his breath. He then tossed the stick into the fire and yawned.

"Agreed," Cor'il yawned. "I'm pretty tired, too. It's probably best we got some sleep. I suspect tomorrow will be a busy day."

Chapter 30

The sun had already risen by the time Cor'il awoke. He was surprised to discover that he had slept as long as he had. He'd had a tough time getting to sleep, but must have slept solidly once he had finally nodded off. Instinctively, as he so often did, Cor'il opened the book and tried to read it.

He wasn't sure why he still did this. After all, he'd already gone through the entire tome. What made him curious was the fact that he could no longer understand the writing. This made him more determined to try.

He slipped the book back into his satchel, disappointed. What he had learned so far was immense, but he'd hoped to somehow glean more information. He still had so many question. Who knew what else was possible?

And now that he understood what had happened back in Kuranthas before he was exiled, mayhaps he could return! While his handling of the Threads was not flawless, he was positive that there would be no more accidents now that he understood the Threads and was working on controlling them. He wondered if his homeland was under attack by orcs. It pained him to think that his friends and family could be fighting for their lives and he could not help them. *I need to go back and make sure everyone is alright. Maybe Kendra and Orvaril could come with me. I am sure that I could convince them.*

"Are we ready to get going?" Dalinil got up and stretched. Then he put his axe through his belt and shouldered his rucksack. "I don't know about you, but I'm ready to sleep in a bed. This Listerville sounds quite appealing."

"The folk in Listerville seemed a happy bunch. I should have liked to stay longer. You may like Elston, too." Cor'il unraveled the Threads for his shelter and the plants all quickly returned to their natural states. He started walking with Dalinil beside him, following the road shortly after they exited the forest. Cor'il instinctively reached to pull his hood up but hesitated and decided not to, as his newfound confidence took over.

"So," Dalinil said, "are you going to stay in Elston?"

"I'm not sure." Cor'il kicked a small rock. It skipped down the road a bit before angling off into a small pond. "I have some friends in Elston, so I am going there first. After that, I suppose I will see where things take me. I'd really like to see my friends and family back home. Lately, however, nothing has gone as planned."

Cor'il wrestled with his feelings. He felt as though he was being torn in three different directions—home, The Densewood, and Elston. It would have been easy to stay within the forest and make his home—and he *would* return—but, for now, this felt right.

Dalinil laughed.

"It's good to know that I am not the only one who feels that way. I was beginning to think I had the worst luck."

"I am not certain it has much to do with luck. My father used to tell me that there was no such thing as luck, there was only fortune. And you have to make your own fortune."

"You and I," Dalinil responded, pointing first to Cor'il and then to himself, "we *can* make our own fortune."

"I don't understand."

"You and I have... abilities—skills, if you will—that nobody else has. We have the power to shape the world. We can *make* our own fortune and *create* our own path. We have the ability to strike down our enemies and help our friends—the power to control our futures."

"Mayhaps." Cor'il was unsure. He felt dubious about how he should use the Threads. They could be weapons or tools, life savers or destruction. Or, possibly, there was a purpose he had not yet considered—something hidden to him. He did not know. After all, he had just recently begun to realize a fraction of his potential. He thought Dalinil was in much the same situation, but his newfound friend seemed more headstrong—not as knowledgeable, but he possibly had more experience than Cor'il.

Mayhaps I am limiting myself. What Dalinil had said was worth considering. The abilities they had—the potential power they could wield—really *might* be able to shape the world. Cor'il hadn't before thought about it in that grand of a scale. *What are the limits of the Threads, if any?* Cor'il felt excitement welling up inside. Grandiose visions of him building elaborate cities with the wave of his hand played through his mind. He imagined himself curing disease, famine, and preventing natural disasters. He could be a hero for the ages!

But then he had thoughts of losing control and accidentally harming his homeland and a chill ran down his back. He put all such thoughts out of his mind for now. *It's best not to get ahead of yourself. Nobody can move mountains.*

At this point he'd stopped caring about hiding his ears. Given the strange creatures that roamed about, he decided that misshapen ears would probably go largely unnoticed. After all, they weren't that different. They were merely a bit longer and slenderer. Besides, it always seemed that telling someone he was from Kuranthas apparently excused any weird behavior or idiosyncrasies. Mayhaps it would also work for something physical. He hadn't decided whether he was more comfortable or whether he simply didn't care anymore.

The world outside of Kuranthas was still largely foreign to him, but he began to realize that his fear was being replaced by curiosity. He hadn't noticed this until recently and it felt wonderful.

"Cor'il!" Dalinil shouted.

"What?" Cor'il snapped out of his daze and stared at a seemingly annoyed Dalinil.

"You've not heard a word I've said, have you?"

"My apologies," Cor'il replied.

"I was saying that, no matter what we can do with our abilities, that I am certainly glad I can handle the orcs and goblins out there."

"I would prefer that we didn't have to deal with them at all." Cor'il had to admit that Dalinil's words were accurate. It truly *was* nice to know that the Threads could keep them safe from their newfound threats.

They walked largely in silence for a while, following the road that would eventually lead them to the ferry. Cor'il was unsure how exactly they were to signal Zalovar and Kaldaren to get back across the river, and for a brief moment, he pondered how he could use the Threads to get across the river without the ferry. He thought of several ideas and kept them in mind just in case.

His thoughts turned to Kuranthas once more. Not only could he now show them that he was harmless, but he could *help*. He could rebuild or fix things. Most importantly, he could defend his home if need be. He suddenly felt an urge to return to Kuranthas and skip Elston altogether.

But is it really home anymore?

No, he would meet up with Kendra and Orvaril in Elston, first. He missed them both more than he thought that he would, though he missed his friends and his homeland more.

Then there was his father. While he *did* miss his father—he sometimes tried to convince himself that he did not—he wasn't really longing to see him all that much. His father had never been the loving sort. He never gave Cor'il compliments, nor had he really ever seemed to care much for him. In fact, many others in Kuranthas treated Cor'il more like a son than his own father had. Even now, however, Cor'il *did* still wish to see his father again. He found that he had to think about that for a moment—to consider exactly *how* he felt about that situation. It was a bit more than "just uncomfortable," but he was family, and you couldn't just turn away from the only family you had.

• • •

The sun was setting in the West when Cor'il spotted the river. They hurried to the bank, hoping it would not be too late to catch the last ride before dark. When they got there, the ferry was nowhere to be seen and Cor'il immediately became worried that they would not be able to cross tonight. A misty fog now hovered above the water, and Cor'il was unable to see to the other side. They walked to the end of the dock and peered out over the dark, foggy river water, trying to catch even a glimpse of the other bank. The water lapped at the dock as it slowly flowed downriver, rhythmically beating against the wood. It was both peaceful and eerie, especially since no other sound could be heard.

Cor'il looked around, hoping to see some sort of mechanism that might bring the ferry to them, but all he saw were the two ropes that stretched out into the river and disappeared into the fog. He could see the first stone pillar before the rope was obscured from view.

"So how do you suggest we get across?" Dalinil was anxiously looking around for a sign of passage as well. "Hello!" he yelled. "Is anyone there?"

There was no response.

"There is a ferry here but they stop operating it after dark. It appears we're too late."

From across the river, Cor'il heard several screams. Some sounded human. Others did not. He and Dalinil both looked at each other, realizing the severity of the situation, and resumed looking for a way across the river.

"I doubt it is wise to camp out here," Dalinil said, only half paying attention. "But I'm wondering how safe it is on the other side. Those screams…"

"I tend to agree." Cor'il tugged on one of the ropes, hoping that it might do something. "We either need to get to town or find somewhere safe to camp."

"If there *is* somewhere safe to camp."

"I think I have an idea, though I don't know how well it will work."

"Very encouraging, Cor'il."

"You'll have to excuse me, sir," Cor'il replied as sarcastically as possible, "but I'm still relatively new at this. *D'rosoco!*"

A mote of white light blinked into existence above Cor'il's head. He faintly heard Dalinil gasp but paid him no attention as he concentrated on the light, commanding it forward and out, over the water. It floated smoothly into the fog, which almost seemed to slightly withdraw from the illuminated area only to return once the light had passed.

"How did—" Dalinil trailed off. Cor'il could almost feel his stare following the light as it hovered out over the water. They both watched in silence as it finally came to a stop, mostly obscured by fog. "Why has it stopped?"

"That is as far as I can move it." His curiosity piqued, Cor'il concentrated and the Threads appeared. He noted a white Thread intertwined with a gold Thread. Together, they produced the light that Cor'il had created.

"Do you see anything?" Dalinil asked. "All I can see is a foggy river." He appeared to be trying to create a light of his own but was having difficulty. With some effort he clumsily tapped into another white Thread but was unable to find a gold Thread. Cor'il looked around and could not find another one either. At one point, Dalinil tried to tap into the gold Thread tied to the light but failed.

I wonder if that is possible—splitting a Thread to use some of its energy for another purpose. He would have to experiment with that at some point. Right now, however, he was much more concerned with getting across the river.

"I think I see something," Cor'il muttered. "I'm not sure." He squinted a little and tried to push the light further forward but it would not budge. Beyond the light, just at its far edge of illumination, he thought he saw what might be the ferry.

There were plenty of green Threads around—some of them even emanating from the water itself. Cor'il tapped into several of them and after twisting them together like a rope, redirected them out over the water. They snaked along the surface until he sensed them bump into something. He didn't know what it was but it was solid and unmoving. He closed his eyes and concentrated, winding the Threads around the object, beckoning them to pull it. He wasn't sure it would work but it was worth a try.

Cor'il opened his eyes and continued concentrating on the rope of green Threads. He watched as pulses of bright green energy traveled from him down each Thread and disappeared into the fog. They did not provide illumination, however, which would have been quite useful.

Dalinil stood beside him, and with significant effort, weaved his own rope of green Threads. Though sloppy and unstable, they spanned out over the water and, soon, Cor'il sensed them working together with his own weave. The object was moving much quicker now and, when it came into view, Cor'il was relieved to see that it was indeed the ferry that approached.

"Is that—" Dalinil started.

"I hope not." Cor'il had a bad feeling in the pit of his stomach.

As the ferry bumped up against the dock they could both see the body more clearly—what was left of it. Cor'il released the green Threads and summoned the beacon of light back to him. The body looked to be that of Zalovar—the older ferry man. He was horribly mangled and mutilated—barely recognizable except for the blood soaked wide-brimmed hat which he still wore. It looked as if parts of the man were *missing*.

"I have a really bad feeling about this," Cor'il whispered, letting go of his weave. "I wonder if we should wait until tomorrow."

"I am not sure anything is going to be safer tomorrow," Dalinil replied, also letting go of his weave. "Besides, I'd rather sleep within the safety of four walls than outside." Using his foot, Dalinil nudged the remains of the ferry man into the water. "My apologies, sir, but we need this ferry."

Cor'il wanted to say something about respect for the dead but he wasn't sure if it mattered anymore. The old man was already gone and, while it didn't seem right, he really would rather not make the trip with a body on the ferry.

"So how does this thing work?" Dalinil asked, seemingly having already forgotten about Zalovar's body. He was looking around, trying to figure it out for himself.

"We each pull on one of these ropes and the ferry moves across the water. The stone pillars somehow keep the ferry from drifting."

Dalinil grabbed the closest rope and, after testing it a moment, pulled on it. The ferry lurched forward. Dalinil pulled some more and the ferry moved more quickly. He was surprisingly strong! Both

Kaldaren and Zalovar, working together, had more difficulty on Cor'il's first trip across the river than Dalinil was having now. Cor'il felt a twinge of sadness for Zalovar and hoped that at least Kaldaren was alright. He beckoned the floating light and it came to rest above his head, following their movement across the water.

Dalinil grunted a few times, but they were moving across the water with ease. Cor'il thought about helping Dalinil by pulling his own rope but he suspected it would most likely only slow them down. Instead he kept an eye out for any potential danger. He was not only shaken from the screams they had heard but he was also concerned about whatever had killed Zalovar.

The fog was thicker than Cor'il had first thought. As they got further out into the river, their visibility decreased. Even Cor'il's hovering light seemed to eventually be swallowed up by the mists until it was merely a faint, stifled glow several feet above him. Dalinil tirelessly pulled on the rope, keeping them moving steadily forward as Cor'il continued looking for the opposite dock. *If this fog is normal, I guess I understand why they don't operate the ferry after sunset.*

"How long do you think it's been?" Even Cor'il's voice seemed to almost be swallowed up by the fog. Everything around them was muffled—not that there was much of anything to hear in the first place.

"What?"

"How long—since Zalovar died. How long do you think it's been?"

"I don't know." Dalinil sounded annoyed. "I didn't pause to ask him. But the blood on this raft, or ferry, or whatever you call it is dry." He grunted, pulled the rope harder, and the ferry moved forward with a jolt. "Now, if you'll excuse me, I am trying to get us across this river."

Cor'il was certain that they must be getting close to the other side, and he was both anxious and worried. He kept his right hand close to his sword just in case. *It seems as though I've been doing that a lot lately—making certain that my sword is ready "just in case." I should probably learn to use it better.*

"How wide is this river, Cor'il?"

"It shouldn't be too much longer." The moment the words left his mouth, he began to see the other shore. Shrouded in fog, it was difficult for him to make out much of anything at first but, once they had pulled a little closer, he was certain he saw people moving about. "I think I see the town. We're close."

Cor'il fidgeted, trying to occupy himself. He straightened his cloak and checked his sword multiple times. He was now most certain that he could see people slowly milling about the town but he couldn't determine what they were doing. They were quickly approaching the dock. Dalinil certainly had them moving quickly!

"Ah," Dalinil said. "I can see better now." He squinted and looked puzzled. "Why are there no lamps lit? Or, at the very least, torches. There is no light."

It was then that a wave of deep, frigid cold washed over him. Cor'il shivered, knowing full well what it meant. He had felt it before—most recently in The Densewood. As they approached the dock the town came fully into view. What once was a vivacious, active town now was dark, ominous, and eerily quiet. He quickly embraced the Threads. A surge of energy washed over him and his whole body tingled, but with that familiar feeling came nausea and disgust that sat in his stomach like a brick. *All black. All of the Threads here are black. There's not one of another color.* The black lines formed a web throughout the town, connecting buildings, dead trees, the ground and... the villagers. *They're connected to the black Threads? What does that mean?* He quickly let go and the world returned to its normal hues.

"This is not good," he mumbled. He now noticed that, though he could see the villagers still moving, their motions were very unnatural. Their gait was slow and labored as if moving was difficult. They appeared to be stumbling, limping, and lumbering about with no real purpose. His ears picked up moans and growls and he began to smell something rotting.

"Dalinil," he whispered, "we should turn back."

"Turn back?" Dalinil shot Cor'il a frustrated stare. "We're almost there! Why would we turn back?"

"Something's not right. You were correct—there are no lanterns or torches. And the people..."

"What about them? What do you mean?"

"Something has happened to them, I think." Cor'il couldn't explain, except that he knew something was wrong—the overabundance of black Threads and the fact that the villagers all seemed to be directly connected to them. "We are in serious danger."

Dalinil took another powerful pull on the rope and looked toward the town. Before long, his face drooped and his eyes widened. He muttered something that Cor'il couldn't hear well enough to understand.

"They all look... injured," he muttered, still staring up the hill.

"Maybe we can help them. I fear what will happen if whatever attacked them is still around."

"If they... or *it* is still around, they probably wouldn't still be alive." Dalinil tugged on the rope again. The ferry cut through the water with ease, and he let its momentum take them all the way to the dock. Once it gently bumped into the dock and stopped, they stepped off hesitantly. "Hello!" he called and waved his arms.

"I'm not sure that's a good idea," Cor'il whispered.

"Why not?"

"Doesn't something feel... wrong to you?"

"I think you might be a little jumpy, Cor'il." Dalinil shrugged, seemingly unfazed by whatever Cor'il was feeling. He began walking up the stone stairs set into the hill. He fingered the axe at his side however, and Cor'il knew what that meant.

The fog appeared to thin out a bit up the hill. Cor'il sent his hovering light ahead while he stood on the dock, waiting, and watching Dalinil. He slowly drew his sword and held it at his side, trying to keep calm. Dalinil continued ascending the hill but seemed to have slowed his pace.

The floating light reached the top of the hill and stopped when it reached its limit. Cor'il slowly moved forward, climbing the stairs behind Dalinil. Dalinil stopped once he reached the top of the hill, soon followed by Cor'il.

The townsfolk continued moving about, paying no attention to either the light or the two of them. Dalinil seemed puzzled as he looked to Cor'il for their next move. He shivered momentarily so Cor'il knew he at least felt the unnatural cold. Unlike Cor'il, however, he didn't seem to be concerned with it, but his hand rested on his axe, now.

Several figures staggered around at the edge of town. Cor'il's light did not reach far enough to make out fine details, however. Even the wispy fog here seemed to suppress the light and shroud the landscape in shadow.

Against his better judgment, he sent the light forward to the nearest person and hovered it above their head. He could see the man, now illuminated clearly, with his back to Cor'il. There was no reaction from him.

"Hail!" Cor'il exclaimed as he walked a few steps forward, making sure to keep his sword lowered. He raised his hand and waved, trying to get the man's attention. For a moment he didn't think the man heard him, but he soon turned around.

Cor'il froze. The man was... rotting! His face was covered with maggots and part of his head was completely gone. He made a sound that started out as a moan but ended up as a primal growl and then the man—the *creature*—moved toward them. Cor'il gripped his sword but he was struck with fear and confusion, not ready to attack another person.

"Okay," Dalinil said. He sounded nervous. "You were right. Now, what... what do we do?"

"I... don't know, "Cor'il stammered. "What is it?"

"Whatever it is, it's coming after us."

The creature shambled faster, growling and spitting a dark liquid from its mouth. Its clumsy movements belied its speed as it continued its advance. Cor'il could do nothing but watch. *Move! Attack it! It's not still alive, is it? Do something!*

When the creature got close, Dalinil lashed out with his axe, catching it in the side. He kicked it back and pulled his axe free, expecting to hear a scream. Instead, however, the creature hissed and, continuing its advance, lunged at them.

Dalinil swung again, burying his weapon deep into its chest, and knocked it down. Cor'il stepped back, trying desperately to make sense of what just happened.

The creature continued moving, convulsing on the ground. *By The Abyss, it's trying to get back up.* Dalinil obviously noticed the same thing and hit it three more times with his axe until it finally stopped. Cor'il, who had been standing away from the fray, cautiously approached Dalinil while keeping his eye on the other figures shambling about.

"Don't ask me what that was," Dalinil whispered. "It wasn't... it wasn't a person anymore. "They're rather difficult to take down." Dalinil swung his axe into the corpse's face one last time, caving it in completely. Chunky, black ichor spattered outward like an overly full water skin that had just been punctured. "It was not human."

"I would guess," Cor'il said, feeling sorrow in his heart, "That neither are *they*." He pointed to the crowd of fog-shrouded, shambling figures meandering about. He could feel fear trying to overtake him, but he knew that he had to suppress it.

"Aye. But what *are* they? And what happened to them?" Dalinil sounded calm now, as if he had just finished splitting firewood.

"We need to either get out of here or hide." Cor'il pointed around them. "It appears that we have attracted some of the others' attention." Several of the walking corpses began lumbering toward them. Cor'il felt a lump form in his throat. There were a lot of them.

"We could probably run past them," Dalinil said, moving closer to Cor'il. "They're not very fast."

"Except for *those*." Cor'il pointed to three of the corpses that now sprinted toward the two of them from about 30 feet away, emitting a shrill scream and waving their arms wildly.

"The Abyss... you know how to use that sword, right?"

"More or less."

"At one point, during my travels, I fought an orc who swore that he could cast a spell! 'Axe,' he called it. It wasn't a very good spell, I must say."
—Darian, *Out and Beyond*

Chapter 31

Dalinil's axe tore through the creature's chest, spewing gore in every direction. He followed up with another strike, cutting through its arm and removing its head. The body collapsed to the ground and Dalinil immediately moved on to the next one. He ripped it open and kicked it backwards into several other attackers.

To his left, Cor'il was barely holding his own. He was much more conservative with his sword, mostly just repelling the creatures by kicking them or hitting them with the flat of his blade. They took the blows and fell back, but they instantly recovered and resumed their attacks. Cor'il was going to be quickly overwhelmed.

"You have to slay them, Cor'il!" Dalinil shouted, burying his axe in another creature's shoulder, nearly splitting it in two. He planted his foot on its chest and pulled out his weapon, knocking the creature backward. "They stop attacking if you cut off their head! Otherwise you just have to chop them up!" They weren't going to get through Listerville unless Cor'il could hold his own.

"Are you *enjoying* this?" Cor'il dodged under an attack and jumped backward. He parried another swipe with his sword and then cut off the creature's hand at the wrist. "We've no need to kill them all. We simply need to get out of here!"

"I think I am!" Dalinil laughed. He felt the fire within him and embraced it. It was as if a floodgate had opened, filling his entire being with excitement and bloodlust. He could feel his heart pounding in his head and his vision pulsed with the same rhythm. He felt alive and unstoppable! His laughter amplified and he charged into battle with several of the slower beasts.

His axe dug deep into his next target, tearing it apart. With the same swing he connected with another creature, cutting it in two just below the arms. He kicked yet another, knocking it backward several feet through the air. He roared and moved onto the next closest enemy, separating its head from its shoulders without even stopping. He spun around and with several quick but powerful strikes, dropped another one.

One of the faster creatures charged at him from his right. He ran headlong into his enemy, knocking it to the ground with his forearm and then he dropped his axe so forcefully that it bit through the creature and into the dirt. He didn't bother cutting its head off. Instead he continued savagely chopping at it until it was a pulpy mess.

He heard something behind him turned around, swinging his axe. Cor'il ducked back out of range, his palms out in front of him. He was saying something but it sounded like gibberish. Dalinil couldn't hear anything over the pounding in his ears. It sounded as if he was underwater. He stood for a moment, trying to understand what Cor'il was trying to say, the urge to fight rising further within him.

Finally, Cor'il pointed ahead. Dalinil shifted his gaze and saw the oncoming horde—the streets were choked with a throng of walking dead bodies! *Slay them! Slay them all! You can destroy them!* He turned back to Cor'il who was still talking and pointing.

Dalinil shook his head and tried to clear his mind. He fought the urge to charge at the crowd of corpses. He only wanted to wade into battle and decimate them with his axe! His rage nearly got the best of him. He started to move toward them but stopped himself. His head began to clear and he could hear Cor'il.

"…many of them! Dalinil! What is wrong with you? Are you alright?"

"I'm… I'm fine. We, uh," he was overwhelmed. His thoughts were racing every which way and he couldn't concentrate. "We need to either hide or flee back across the river! We can't defeat that many." *Or maybe I can... but you will slow me down.*

"Agreed." Cor'il seemed to be scanning the area for a safe haven. "Let's make for the Spouting Fish!" Cor'il pointed to a large, stone building near the edge of town. "Come, we need to hurry!" He took off running down the road, passing several walking corpses that were too slow and clumsy to catch him.

Dalinil sprinted and easily caught up to him. He felt a brilliant energy in his legs, as if they were much stronger now. He easily passed Cor'il and reached the Spouting Fish first. Several of the corpses took notice and shambled toward him. He opened the door just as Cor'il arrived and they slipped inside the building. The fog seemed to try to follow them inside as Dalinil slammed the door shut.

"Bar the door," Dalinil commanded. He looked out over the common room, at the lumbering corpses within. They all seemed to notice him at the same time. "I will handle this."

One of them leapt into the air, arms outstretched. Its hiss was cut short by Dalinil's axe. He moved onto the next one, then the next, easily cutting each enemy down like it was a fragile twig. One by one they fell before him as he plowed through the room. *Die! Die, all of you abominations! I will destroy you all!*

When there was nothing left to fight, he turned back to Cor'il, but instead found that another walking corpse had sneaked up behind him. It reached out to grab him but stopped short, a blade protruding from its eye socket. The blade pulled back and the creature hit the ground. Cor'il lowered his sword, now dripping with thick, black goo.

"So you *do* apparently know which end goes where," Dalinil whispered. Cor'il did not appear amused.

"That door will hopefully hold them," Cor'il replied. "They don't appear particularly strong and, if we remain quiet, they may forget we're here."

Dalinil nodded. The common room had become a slaughterhouse, defiled with the blood of these creatures. The bodies were one thing but the stench that hung thick in the air made him gag. His tunic and breeches were covered in blood and gore.

"We should investigate the rest of this building," Dalinil whispered. "We need to make sure there are no unforeseen... surprises."

Cor'il nodded and disappeared through a door behind a counter. Dalinil headed toward what appeared to be the jakes. It didn't take him long to make sure the area was clear. Cor'il quickly emerged and held up two fingers.

"The kitchen is safe... now."

Dalinil looked around. He moved to pull the brightly-colored curtains over the windows. The entire room was splashed with vibrant colors and fancy decorations, some walls now marred with the blood of these... things. It was quite a contrast to the corpses that now littered the floor, lying in pools of chunky, black slime.

"Do you think they'll be gone by morning?" Dalinil peeked out the window. The fog appeared to be creeping in from the river, overtaking Listerville. The sliver of a moon in the sky was a hazy nimbus that didn't provide much in the way of light, but instead played tricks on Dalinil's eyes. Shapes and figures moved about in the fog, their unnatural, jerky motions now very obvious. They seemed to ignore each other, wandering aimlessly, and clumsily staggering about with no real purpose. "I think the whole town is out there."

Dalinil balled his fists, but relaxed them. He fought the desperate urge to leave the safety of the common room and kill more of them. They weren't difficult opponents and he thought, given enough time, he could eliminate enough of them to provide a proper escape route. Besides, they were abominations and they deserved nothing less than total destruction. He had no qualms about it, and slaughtering them all would be enjoyable.

These weren't just mere orcs. These monsters were not natural.

Cor'il, though, he would just get himself into trouble. *If I go back out there and fight them he will feel compelled to go with me, and I cannot keep him safe. The Abyss damn it! Hiding like children is cowardly! These things won't stop me!*

"Are you alright?" Cor'il asked.

"What?"

"Are you alright?" he asked again.

"What do you mean? Of course I am alright."

"It's just," Cor'il paused for a moment, staring at Dalinil's hands.

Dalinil looked down. He hadn't been paying attention to what he was doing. To his surprise, he found that he had dug his axe into the wall several times. There was now a decent-sized hole in it.

"Bah!" He waved a dismissive hand at it, stepped on several corpses and sat down at a nearby table, pounding a fist on it and rattling several plates and tankards. "This Realm is sinking into The Abyss, that's what is happening. It will claim our land and we will all suffer until we die."

He wasn't sure he actually believed that. It sounded feasible, given everything he had encountered as of late. His sour attitude was fueled by frustration—that much he knew. He watched Cor'il move a table over to the wall and tip it over to cover the hole.

"It won't really keep anything out," he said when he'd finished, "but we certainly don't need to provide them with an easier way to discover us."

"We should be out there destroying those things instead of hiding in here like children." Dalinil really was not sure where all of his newfound confidence had come from. Arcturas had told him that he might be guided by the Threads at times. Was this one of those times?

Arcturas had never been clear about this. That man was so infuriating! He always answered questions with yet more questions!

"You and I," he continued, "have the abilities to send these creatures to The Abyss where they belong. We should do just that."

Dalinil remembered many days spent with Arcturas, trying to calm his emotions and concentrate. *You must learn to embrace the fire within but, also, you must separate it from the anger and rage that roils inside of you*, he'd said. And Dalinil now had some modicum of control over the wealth of emotion inside him. He found, when he let it flow, that he could do amazing things. He felt alive and, oddly, at peace, and it was just easier and more natural to *use* his rage instead of suppressing it. It was a tool just like the Threads—just like his axe. A tool was meant to be used, not left in a cabinet to rust out.

He gritted his teeth. Despite what he *wanted* to do, he resolved to stay put. They would wait it out through the night and hopefully have an easy escape tomorrow. *Maybe they'll wander off somewhere. What awful thing happened to these people to cause this? And what are we going to discover* next? Every day, since leaving Ilathri, it seemed something new and terrible happened.

"So," he said, keeping his voice low. "Do we have any kind of a plan for tomorrow?" He looked out the window again, longing to, at the very least, leave this place. At the very most, he still had the urge to slaughter everything outside. "I don't relish the thought of spending more than one night here."

It took Cor'il a moment to respond to him. He seemed to be in a trance, concentrating intently. He was moving his hands around, manipulating something Dalinil couldn't see.

Dalinil concentrated and, after some difficulty, the Threads came into view—all of them black. But Cor'il was manipulating two greens and a red—which seemed to come from nowhere. They simply appeared out of thin air—immaterial at first but quickly becoming solid, as if they were emerging from mist.

"Mayhaps," he said, letting go of the Threads and sitting down at the table with Dalinil who let go as well. The warmth and the rush of radiant energy quickly disappeared and the world around him became sharper once again. It was never difficult to let go of the Threads, but it was always disappointing. To part with such power was almost depressing.

He wasn't sure what Cor'il had been weaving just a moment ago. Even if he had asked him he wasn't sure he would have understood

Cor'il's explanation. His newfound friend was talented in the art, and he hoped to have Cor'il teach him eventually. For now, however, it was prudent to focus on how they were going to survive the night and escape in the morning.

"So what do you suppose those things out there are?" Dalinil knew that he really didn't need to ask. He suspected he already knew what Cor'il was going to say.

"Have you ever read the book *Out and Beyond*?" Cor'il rested his satchel on the table before getting up and looking around some more. He seemed uneasy—nervous.

"Not all of it. Well, actually just bits and pieces." Dalinil chuckled. He had indeed tried reading it several times but always got distracted and bored. "I never could really get very interested in it. I always wanted to *live* an adventure instead of reading about someone else's."

"It is my favorite book. I've read it probably half a dozen times at least." Cor'il rummaged around behind the counter next to the kitchen door and produced two tankards that he filled with water. "In one of the chapters, Darian talks of creatures that are neither alive nor fully dead. He called them—"

"Restless." Dalinil was right. He knew Cor'il was going to say that. It was eerie how this had become commonplace—naming these creatures after those that, before, existed only in stories.

Cor'il returned to the table and sat the tankards down. He took a long drink from his and wiped his mouth. They sat in silence for a spell. Dalinil slowly spun his mug around the table staring at it.

"Ghouls," he heard Cor'il whisper.

"What?"

"I think these... things that used to be people are what Darian, the author, called ghouls." Cor'il took another drink from his mug. Dalinil did the same. It was a sobering situation to ponder. Dalinil could tell that Cor'il was giving it a turn in his head, trying to puzzle things out.

"Does the book ever mention *how* ghouls are made or born or whatever?"

"Unfortunately, no. Darian wrote about his encounter with them and how he managed to evade them. I really wish I had a copy of the book with me." Cor'il ran a hand through his hair. He looked a bit worn.

"It's funny," Dalinil chuckled. He took a drink from his tankard and watched Cor'il for a reaction.

"What is?"

"You're using a book of fictional children's tales as a guide." When Dalinil said it like that, it really *did* sound preposterous. History books were more appropriate.

They both had a good laugh for a moment. The irony was lost on neither of them, but their mood quickly darkened again. Dalinil wanted to ask what other creatures were in *Out and Beyond,* but he was afraid of what the answer might be. Besides, he'd heard the tales. He knew the possibilities. He simply would rather not think about them.

Outside, he heard a growl and a banging sound. His hand instinctively went to his axe on the table but he eased back, trying not to be too hasty. The last thing they needed was another hole in the wall.

"Do you think one of them knows we're in here?" Cor'il asked. Dalinil could see fear creep into his friend's eyes.

"I think there is a good possibility of that. Do you think it heard us in here?"

"Or smells us. Or mayhaps it's just walking into the wall." Cor'il laughed nervously.

"These things seem relatively mindless. If they can't think then it's safe to assume that they act on instinct alone. And if this one is hungry... I don't suppose *Out and Beyond* goes into any great detail about that does it?"

"Not that I remember." Cor'il's hand was resting on the sword at his side. Dalinil felt a little relieved to know that he was not the only one who was a bit jumpy. But, given the circumstances, how could anyone *not* be nervous? "I saw a game of Capture back behind the counter."

"Ah," Dalinil laughed, "I haven't played that in quite a while. Let's play."

Cor'il got up and quickly returned with the game board and pieces. Dalinil soon found out that the rules Cor'il played by were slightly different than his. Nevertheless, he handily won the first game.

The ghoul outside banged on the wall until they were halfway through the second game. Dalinil felt better once the noise had ceased but he also wondered where the creature had gone. *Hearing your enemy is often better than the alternative. If the ghoul is no longer out there, is it possible that it actually made it inside somewhere? Surely it wandered off.*

Dalinil knew full well that he was being paranoid, but it never hurt to be cautious. He made a circuit of all of the rooms, looking for any danger. Fortunately, he found none. He peeked out the window, careful not to alert any of the ghouls outside. They still wandered about the town, the fog now shrouding them in a cloak of concealing haze. Some were faster than others, and more agile while others clumsily bumped into things but didn't seem to care.

As he watched, he was surprised to see two ghouls start attacking each other. He couldn't determine what set them off but they tore into each other with vicious savagery until only one remained. It, however, had significant trouble walking after the fight. *If you could call that walking in the first place. Why those two? Why are they not all attacking each other?*

The night wore on and soon Dalinil found himself dozing off. Cor'il obviously took notice of this and packed up the game. Why wasn't he tired, too?

"Feel free to sleep," he said, putting the pieces back into the box. One of them rolled off the table but he caught it quickly before it fell. "I'm not really very tired so I can stay up and keep a watch of sorts, though I think we're relatively safe. If they knew we were in here, they probably would be beating down the walls."

"You're probably right," Dalinil replied in the midst of yawning. "I think I will try to get some sleep." He looked around for a place that wasn't covered in blood or the corpses themselves. He spotted an area at the far end that appeared relatively clean. He moved aside a table and some chairs, laid his head down on his rucksack and shut his heavy eyelids. "Wake me if you need me," he mumbled, already drifting off to sleep.

Chapter 32

Cor'il had spent most of the night listening for any for any potential danger. He was thankful when the first rays of sun gleamed through the windows but, unfortunately, the ghouls still roamed about outside. *So sunlight does not bother them. I was hoping that maybe it would.* He had, in fact, been *counting on it*. Now he needed to come up with a different plan.

While keeping an eye on the ghouls outside, he had passed the hours last night by experimenting with the black Threads. He definitely did not like them. Every time he embraced them, he felt ill—as if he was going to vomit. The black Threads were cold and oily and smelled putrid! They had a smell! But, oh, there was so much potential within them.

When he started his experiments last night he had been able to use some green, red, and white Threads. There were certainly no Threads of those colors available, so the fact that he could summon a few of them surprised him. Unfortunately, calling Threads to him was exhausting and it quickly took its toll. He had only been able to call on them twice before his concentration floundered and he nearly lost control. He was careful not to overexert himself, lest something terrible happen.

In this case, Cor'il was fortunate not to need much sleep on a regular basis. True, he would have liked to have slept for more than an hour or two but he would hopefully catch up tonight. *That assumes that we won't be stuck in some other kind of danger. And we need to get out of here first.* Cor'il found it sad just how true that was. If he had felt that the world was a dangerous place when he first started this journey, it appeared more so. *The Abyss, is anywhere safe anymore?*

He watched two flies circle each other a few feet away. He briefly wondered if flies played or fought, or if they were just mindless insects operating on instinct alone. *Like the ghouls outside. Are they any different from these flies here? Well, except for the "wanting to kill us" part.* Cor'il had to admit that he was slightly intrigued. It was a morbid thought, though—to wonder so whimsically about the creatures out there... creatures that had once been human. He wondered if the serving maid he'd met was among them. She was once bubbly, happy, and vivacious, and now had possibly been reduced to a mindless monster.

Dalinil stirred and slowly sat up. He looked as though he could use several more hours of sleep. He leaned back on his elbows and looked around, bleary-eyed and probably not completely awake yet.

"The good news," Cor'il started, "is that we've made it through the night."

"And the bad news?" Dalinil yawned. He'd slept with his axe tightly clutched in one hand. Cor'il wondered if he'd ever cut himself in the middle of the night.

"The bad news," he continued, "is that we now have to make it through today."

"They're all still out there?" Dalinil slowly rose, rubbing his eyes, and headed to one of the windows.

"The last time I checked, aye, they're still out there. I don't think they have anywhere they need to be."

They both laughed nervously. It seemed that nervous laughter was about the only kind of joy Cor'il got to experience these days. But it was better than nothing.

"Wow," Dalinil muttered, still peering out the window. "Now that I can get a better look at them, I sort of wish I hadn't."

"Indeed," Cor'il agreed.

"The ghouls we killed in here looked somewhat like normal people," he continued. "But the ghouls outside, most of them are hideous—either half-rotted or half-eaten. And they appear to have *claws*. The Abyss! What could do this?"

"Even if we knew, there isn't anything we can do about it."

Dalinil skittishly jumped back from the window, nearly falling backwards into a table. He staggered for a moment before quickly regaining his balance.

"I think it saw me." His axe, which had never left his hand, was raised at his side. "There is one out there, right outside the window—and it looked straight at me."

They stood in silence, staring at each other. Cor'il held his breath.

Something began pounding on the wall by the window. Both of them stood absolutely motionless, still trying not to make any noise. Several moments passed but the pounding did not subside. They heard growling which soon turned into an earsplitting shriek. Cor'il looked at Dalinil who had the same concern on his face.

The one shriek became two. Then three. The pounding became louder and was accompanied by scratching sounds. Cor'il instinctively drew his sword. He had dispatched several of the ghouls last night but not nearly as many as Dalinil. His friend had completely obliterated at least 20 in the time it had taken Cor'il to down five or so, but he had appeared to lose himself in combat, attacking anything that moved. Cor'il feared that he might accidentally attack an ally while in the heat of battle.

Cor'il moved to the door. It was still securely barred and none of the ghouls was trying to beat it down... yet. He carefully lifted the bar and set it on a nearby table.

"What are you doing?" Dalinil rather whispered.

"We need to see if we can escape this way," he whispered back.

"Just don't let any of those *things* in here!"

Cor'il pushed gently on the door, opening it just a crack. There were more ghouls outside than he remembered seeing last night but, fortunately, none of them had wandered too close to the front door. The street was teeming with the restless and there was no way they would be able to simply avoid the throng of ghouls outside unless they kept close to the buildings.

"I think I have an idea," Cor'il said, quietly shutting the door and replacing the bar across it. It really would have helped to know what these things were capable of. They weren't even sure if the ghouls currently trying to get in had seen, heard, or smelled them—or maybe all of those.

"So what is our plan, then?" Dalinil asked as he briefly looked out the window again, then backed away and approached Cor'il. "Because there are about 20 ghouls out there piling up against the wall trying to get in."

The beating on the wall had grown to a cacophony with the groans, growls, and shrieks. There was no question—it was time to leave.

"Well," Cor'il stammered a bit, "we run."

"That's it? That is your plan?"

"Aye."

"Forgive me for being skeptical but that doesn't sound like much of a plan to me."

"Well, that's not all of it. There's more."

"Oh," Dalinil said. Cor'il could sense the sarcasm. "Please, genius, do tell!"

"We keep close to the buildings. You cut down anything that attacks us. It'll mostly be the quicker ghouls."

"You're still not filling me with a lot of confidence, Cor'il."

"The rest—well, you're going to have to trust me."

Dalinil looked frustrated. Cor'il didn't blame him. He was essentially building the bridge in front of them *while* they were crossing the stream. It was not the best way to do things, but they were running out of time. Cor'il wasn't sure if Dalinil had noticed the splinters of wood falling onto the floor where the ghouls were pushing their way in. Tiny beams of sunlight began to shine through the cracks in the wall.

Cor'il knew full well that Dalinil would rather wade through the crowd, cutting down everything in his path. *He might get his wish.*

"Alright," Dalinil finally acquiesced. "But if one of those things out there kills me I am going to haunt you forever."

Cor'il ignored the morbid humor as Dalinil moved to the door, ready to remove the bar.

"Oh," Cor'il started, "We're not leaving through the door."

"We're not?"

"No, we're not. The streets are clogged with them. There are more of them over there. I don't think we could evade them." Cor'il walked over to the wall that was slowly caving in. Dalinil followed suit shortly after, his axe held out in front of him. He looked confused. "The ghouls over here are all grouped together and more vulnerable." Cor'il paused, inspecting the wall. "I would suggest you stand behind me," he said. Dalinil obliged without question. "When it is time to run, we run."

"How am I going to know?"

"Trust me," Cor'il said, closing his eyes, "you'll know. It would be very wise to stay together. Once we get out of the town we will follow the road."

Cor'il embraced the Threads. He had little to work with since there was nothing but black Threads in the area. Unlike all of the others, the black Threads did not have brilliant shimmers of energy pulsing through them. There was energy but its radiance was very dull and lackluster. He braced himself for overwhelming nausea and tapped into them.

Immediately he felt cold enter his body and he started shivering. His stomach turned and a revolting taste entered his mouth—as if he had just drunk milk that had spoiled a month ago. He gathered up as many black Threads as he could as the sickness within him grew stronger. Then he called out to a red Thread, reached in, and grabbed hold of it. He had hoped for more, but he was happy just to have any at all. When he tapped into it, he felt it burning inside of him like a tiny candle trying to cast light in an immense, dark room.

Time seemed to slow as he weaved the black Threads into a thick rope. Then he carefully added the red Thread into the rope, striating it down the entire length. He manipulated the rope, expanding it into more of a wall, weaving the red Thread in and out as much as it would allow. He nearly lost control of it, causing his construct to lose shape briefly and emit sparks. He held his breath and increased his concentration.

Cor'il shrunk his creation and held it in his hands. He inspected it quickly to make sure he had built it correctly but, since he had never done this before, he couldn't be sure. He was using black Threads for something that was not their main purpose so the effect may not be nearly as powerful as they needed. *Thank The Goodness for that red Thread.*

He threw his hands out before him, launching his woven creation into the wall in front of him. For a brief moment, the wall shimmered and buckled inward as if it was being sucked into his hands. Cor'il wasn't sure if he had done something wrong—this was not the effect he had expected!

Just as he thought he should try again with another weave, the wall violently exploded outward in a fireball, sending wood, glass, and ghouls flying in every direction. His ears rung and his vision blurred briefly.

Dalinil immediately took off running and headed for the next building. Cor'il tried to move but instead, emptied his stomach onto the floor. His head spun and his vision was dim. He shivered uncontrollably and dropped to one knee, still retching. *Get up! Get up and run, you fool! You have to go now!*

He took a deep breath and forced himself upright. On wobbly legs he darted out of the fest hall and into the sunlight. He released most of the Threads and instantly felt most of the sickness subside as hurried to catch up to Dalinil.

However, Dalinil not only had a head start, but he was also much faster. Cor'il could see numerous black Threads connected to Dalinil and, when he had released his, they had immediately been drawn to Dalinil like a nail to a magnet. He tried to inspect Dalinil's weave but things were moving too quickly. He darted behind the nearest building to catch his breath. Fortunately, there were no ghouls nearby.

Cor'il only tarried for a moment before he darted to the next building. He easily dispatched two ghouls near the front door but, when he did so, he attracted the attention of several others. Suddenly, the creatures let out a shriek that alerted even more ghouls to his presence. Before he knew it, Cor'il had a pack of the creatures following him—several of them clothed in colorful garb, now tattered and stained with blood.

He fled, running as fast as he could and hoping he could either find a place to hide or figure out how to fight 10 or so of the creatures at the same time. Fear filled his mind and kept him from concentrating properly. It was all he could do to hold onto the Threads, much less actually use them.

The ghouls were closing the gap. *The Abyss some of them are fast!* He could no longer see Dalinil anywhere. He hoped that his friend was alright, but something told him that Dalinil was faring better than he was. He nearly tripped over a body lying on the ground but caught himself just in time. He had lost ground and the ghouls were getting closer.

Cor'il's lungs burned and his legs ached. He could not keep up this pace. He concentrated on the Threads, trying to calm himself. *If I can just get control, I can hopefully figure something out.* But the fear was strong. He fought it back, knowing full well that he *had* to. He was not going to outrun these things, and he could not fight them all.

More ghouls had joined the pursuit—most of them slow-moving, lumbering husks. In the distance, Cor'il could see the creek at the entrance to Listerville. His thoughts briefly turned to the first person he had met—Lynara. He felt a pang of sadness—that wasn't very long ago! Tears welled up in his eyes but he battled them back. It was enough to distract him from his fear, however. He grabbed the few Threads that he could get and began to weave them without knowing quite what he wanted to do with them.

He fumbled with the Threads at first, clumsily trying to throw them together like a child first learning how to lace a boot. He ignored the nausea and pain, focusing only on weaving something—anything. The ghouls were only a few short feet behind him, snarling and growling, and there were more up ahead. He could smell them. Their mouths oozed some foul liquid, the mere sight of which made Cor'il want to gag. *I'm out of time! I hope this works.*

He finished the weave. He stopped and turned, his hands outstretched. The ghouls were upon him as he released the power from within the Threads. One of the ghouls knocked his hands away and Cor'il released the weave's full force at the ground. Instead of knocking the ghouls backward, Cor'il was hurled high into the air.

He screamed as he was launched up and over a building, crashing down on the roof of another. He landed hard on his shoulder and nearly rolled off of the roof but managed to stop himself just in time. He scrambled away from the edge, desperately looking around to make sure he was safe. Then he collapsed, lying on his back and staring up at a cloudy sky, trying to catch his breath.

His left shoulder throbbed. It was badly scraped and bleeding. He clutched his shoulder and moved his arm around to make sure that nothing was broken. It certainly hurt badly enough, but did not seem serious. He cupped his hand over the wound and pressed his tunic's sleeve against it, trying to regain his breath.

He sat up and, looking out over the town, could see Dalinil—he'd made it across the creek already and was fighting off a pack of ghouls. At first, Cor'il was worried for him, but he watched his friend quickly drop several of the monsters without effort. Was he... laughing?

Without having to worry about Dalinil, Cor'il could focus on his own situation. There were several rooftops and the open ground between him and the creek. He looked beneath him. All but three of the ghouls had lost interest. Those three, however, mindlessly clawed at the wall, trying to climb up to get him. They snarled and gnashed their crooked, rotting teeth as their persistence continued.

He inspected the Threads he held. His weave had collapsed and he saw fewer Threads at his command. Several of them were missing! He frantically searched those which he held and quickly found them. They weren't missing. Instead, they were rigid and unresponsive. They no longer pulsed with energy. He tried to connect with them but they resisted—no, they were *dead*.

He didn't have the time to try to puzzle it out. He still needed to get to Dalinil and leave this place. Most of the buildings were relatively close together and it wasn't far to the next rooftop. It was too far to jump, however, but Cor'il now had a new trick! He only hoped he could exhibit more control this time.

He recreated his last weave, this time, without the dead Threads. He took the time to inspect it—poking and prodding it to test the energy it held, and he examined it much more closely. As a test, he released a tiny bit of its energy against the roof and felt himself propelled into the air a few inches. *It doesn't take much, now, does it? I used way too much last time. I am surprised I survived. Well, I suppose it's time to try this.*

Cor'il stood up and walked over to the edge of the roof. His shoulder had stopped bleeding for the most part, so he was able to concentrate, even though the sickness was still there. Right now, it only nagged at him instead of the overwhelming barrage he'd experienced earlier.

The three ghouls were still trying, quite unsuccessfully, to scale the wall. *These things do not give up. I wonder why the others did. Or mayhaps they didn't give up. Mayhaps they are simply more patient. Could it be a sign of lingering intelligence?*

Mindless or no, they were still frightful creatures. And, while Cor'il was curious about them, he much preferred to ponder them in safety when there was none of them nearby. He focused his thoughts on the task at hand, holding his hands out before him and angling them down at the ground. *Okay, Cor'il. Let's be gentle with this.*

He released some of the energy from his weave and was catapulted straight up into the air a few feet. He waved his limbs wildly, trying to stay upright, and landed back on the roof. *So this is a little bit more complex than I thought. I have to angle the flow a bit. But how much?*

He looked down again. One of the ghouls had fallen down and was getting back up, shrieking. Or had Cor'il *pushed* it down? He couldn't help but grin a little. The applications of this particular weave had numerous possibilities.

He held his hands out again, pointing them not only toward the ghouls but also slightly angling them at the wall against which the ghouls pressed themselves. He guessed that the next rooftop was about 10 feet away. It was large enough that he had some room for error, so long as he didn't shoot himself too high.

He took a deep breath and exhaled. He focused on his weave, feeling every Thread within. Then he let energy flow out of it, careful not to draw on too much power and miss his target. He felt the force push against both the ghouls and the wall and it launched him into the air. He wriggled and flailed as he flew, but he landed safely on the other roof, sliding to a halt.

"Alright!" he cheered, laughing. His hands shook from the excitement of it all and the rush of power. "You'll not get me today after all! So go back to The Abyss where you came from!"

Two of the three ghouls lay motionless on the ground, crushed and distorted. *Now that I know how to do this, it shouldn't be too difficult.* While he believed this to be true, he could also feel fatigue setting in. The nausea was getting worse and it was more difficult to concentrate.

Traveling to the next two buildings, while not anywhere close to being effortless, was relatively simple. The last two, however, were much more difficult to reach and Cor'il almost came up short on the last one. He landed at the edge of the roof, having to grab on and pull himself up. The ghouls had lost his trail and he was able to drop off the edge of the roof to safety. He made his way to the creek and crossed the little bridge. On the other side, Dalinil was waiting for him with a grin on his face. He was inspecting his handiwork with his axe resting over his shoulder.

There were at least two dozen corpses littering the ground. Dalinil seemed pleased as he looked them over, smiling. Cor'il noticed he had a couple of cuts on his arms but, other than that, he appeared to be in much better shape than Cor'il himself did.

"I saw what you were doing back there," he said, turning to the road. He began walking. Cor'il followed. "It was quite impressive."

"I improvised." Never mind the fact that Cor'il had discovered it by purely by accident—an accident that could have ended up much worse. Cor'il would have to be more careful in the future.

Dalinil chuckled.

"You also seemed to be doing well back there."

"They're not very formidable foes," Dalinil replied. "They have numbers and persistence but that's about all. They are mindless, which works to our advantage. If I had my way, we would march right back into Listerville and put them all down."

"For now, let's just focus on getting to safety. Elston should adequately provide that."

"Aye. Let's hope so."

They left Listerville behind. Cor'il couldn't help but feel sadness as the town disappeared in the distance. Worse yet, he feared what they would encounter next.

Chapter 33

The clouds in the sky looked angry. There was no wind—not even the slightest breeze passed through the leaves and bushes—yet, high above in the sky, the clouds raced past as if they had somewhere important to go. They weren't dark or foreboding clouds and they didn't threaten rain, but they swirled above her, constantly shifting and changing shape.

Itania Brightmoon brushed long strands of blond hair from her face as she gazed up into the sky. *I must have done a lousy job with my braid this morning.* She grabbed her ponytail and inspected the end. No hair seemed to be coming loose. *No matter. I'm not fixing it now.*

She planted the head of her shovel in the ground and, leaning against it, wiped sweat from her brow. She was no Cloudseer—not that they actually existed—but she knew enough to recognize that a storm was brewing. Though there was nothing visible on the horizon, she felt uneasy. No one else seemed concerned, and as she looked around her, she saw her fellow townsfolk working their gardens or leading their livestock just as they did any other day.

Storms were nothing new. Harvest Town had seen its share of bad weather over the years. She could remember when violent winds ripped through their village and destroyed over 10 homes. Several people had died that day. It still made her sad thinking about it. At the time, she had seen 20 winters. Five years had passed, but she now felt the same sick feeling in her stomach.

You're overreacting. You need to calm down and get this hole dug for the fence. You can't keep the goats in that small yard forever. Truth be told, her front yard wasn't much larger than the back yard. She had only four goats but they had eaten and trampled the back yard to where there was little grass left. She kept telling herself that she needed to move further out where more land was available if she wanted more livestock. That begged the question of whether she *needed* more animals. The four goats, two pigs, and one horse were about all she could handle by herself. Her garden was modest, but it kept her fed and, along with everything else, it kept her quite busy.

She often looked at her neighbors' houses and their larger plots of land with envy. They also had families to provide for. A family meant a spouse and children, which meant more hands to help till, milk, or feed. Itania felt that she did pretty well on her own. Her life was busy but not complicated. *It's also rather lonely.* She sighed, gazing up at the sky again. *Mayhaps it's time to move somewhere else. A farm outside of Sulbar sounds appealing. At least there I'd have the opportunity to meet more people.*

But, no matter how much she dreamed about it, she had a difficult time seeing herself anywhere else. Harvest Town had a variety of appealing qualities. The land was fertile and easy to work, her house was sturdy, and the town itself, while not very large, was full of helpful people. When she thought about them, she always managed to convince herself that she should stay—even though several of her neighbors had encouraged her to seek her future elsewhere. They'd tell her she was meant for greater things or that none of the men in Harvest Town were good enough for her.

She left her shovel where it was and after picking up a bucket, walked the short distance to the well near the center of town. She wiped some of the dirt from her hands on her breeches as she got in line behind a few others.

"Good morning, Itania." She turned to see Mistress Fontaine behind her.

"Good morning, Maria," Itania replied. She nearly hit her with the bucket when she swung around. "I heard about your dog. Is he feeling better?"

"Oh, Ripper? Yes, I believe he is. We think he ate something he shouldn't have."

"Oh, well, that's fantastic. I am glad to hear he is on the mend. What do you think he ate?" Itania moved ahead in the line. She was behind only two others.

"What *doesn't* he eat?" Maria laughed. "That little puppy eats everything in sight."

"Oh?" Itania was really not fond of small talk. She rarely ever paid attention to inane conversations and usually just nodded and said the occasional "yes." She figured this probably had led to confusion in the past. The truth was, she was too busy to keep in mind everyone's petty problems. The *real* problems were important. A dog that got sick, while sad, was not something she wished to put energy into.

The person in front of her stepped up to the well and began lowering his bucket.

"Damned anything and everything." Maria laughed again. "He's so fat he can barely walk. Pathetic, really." She paused briefly but started back up soon after. "Of course we aren't feeding him that much.

He noses around neighbors' houses or in garbage. Sometimes he finds something dead on the ground."

"Sounds... just like a dog, doesn't it?" Itania forced a giggle. The person in front of her had just raised his bucket and was unhooking it. Itania stepped up, hooked her bucket onto the rope and lowered it.

"That's what *I* say! He's always been this way. He smells bad, too. I'm not even sure why we keep him around, honestly."

"Indeed." Itania turned the crank and the rope started rising. She thought, after her chores were done, she might take a nap. If a storm was coming in, she would much prefer to sleep through it.

"Well," she said, unhooking her bucket, "I am glad he is feeling better. Take care, Maria!" Itania hurried off as quickly as she could without sloshing half of the water out of the bucket.

She set the bucket on the table in the kitchen and then reclined in the plush chair in the main room. Closing her eyes, she tried to relax while going through her list of chores in her head.

A loud clap of thunder jolted Itania awake, and she opened her eyes to a dark room. The rain pounded relentlessly against the roof, drowning out all other sound. She ran a hand through her hair and yawned. From where she sat, she could see out the window, and when she realized how dark it was, she got out of the chair and stood by the window. She could see neither the moon nor the stars. A flash of lightning lit up the night sky, but all she could see was heavy rain. She could barely see the tree that was only a few feet from the side of the house.

Another bolt of lightning illuminated everything briefly, and a great thundering boom followed shortly thereafter. *How long was I asleep? Surely it couldn't have been too long. In any case, it looks as though my chores outside are done for the day. But I at least still need to feed the horse.* The pigs and goats had access to the barn and, hopefully, were smart enough to take advantage of it.

As much as she would rather have stayed dry inside, she knew that she would have to check on the animals. She opened the front door and stepped outside, under the shelter of the porch. She gazed out into the rain, unable to see so far as the house next to hers. She could barely make out the road from here. Up above, the sky continued dropping rain at a rate that Itania wasn't sure she had ever seen before.

She walked to the right side of the porch and looked out and around toward the back yard. Though she could only see a shadowy blob that she *thought* was the barn, she couldn't see any of the goats or pigs out in the yard. *I am still probably going to need to check on them*, she thought, sighing hopelessly. There was no way she could avoid getting wet.

Lightning flashed again, casting a brief light down upon Itania and her surroundings. As she turned to go back into the house she hesitated a moment. *Did I see something out there? Or is my vision merely playing a trick on me?*

For a moment she thought she had actually seen someone out in the street, but there were also trees that could have resembled a person—the small trees, anyway. *Why would someone be out in this weather? Do they need help?* Itania watched carefully, waiting for another bolt of lightning to strike the sky so that she could get a better look.

Past the din of the rain she thought she heard something. Was it a scream? She couldn't be sure. But when the next bolt of lightning flashed across the sky she knew something was dreadfully wrong. In that brief moment of illumination, she saw what she needed to see. But not what she *expected* to see.

In that fleeting moment she saw the shadowy outline of a person holding another in the air—it looked as if it was by the neck—only one of them was too big to be a man. She froze, unsure of what she had just seen. The lightning flashed again and she saw the larger figure only. And it was holding an axe.

Itania started to scream but quickly stopped herself and ducked down behind the porch's railing, peering out between the slats. She waited, both morbidly curious and filled with paralyzing fear. She watched the figure slowly step out of the darkness, still mostly obscured. It was big and it was indeed carrying a large axe. She suppressed another scream, trying to figure out what to do. Her mind was scrambled and she couldn't think straight. Whatever it was appeared to be slowly moving toward her.

Remaining crouched behind the railing, Itania started backing up, not taking her eyes off of the figure ahead. Lightning lit up the sky again. There were more of them—lots more—and they weren't human! She screamed and fell backward, but scrambled to her feet, still screaming. Without looking back, she darted inside the house, locking the door behind her and leaning against it.

"What were those? Who were they?" She cowered behind the plush chair, her head buried in her hands. She was afraid to look at anything for fear of seeing them again. "You can't stay here. You've got to leave!"

After a moment, she forced herself to run through the house and hesitated at the back door. The barn was only 30 or 40 feet from the house. If she could get there, she might be able to ride her horse to safety. The rain would make it difficult, but it was the only option she could think of. She closed her eyes to gather her courage and calm herself. *Hopefully, whatever these monsters are haven't made their way to the back yard. If I can get to the horse, I can possibly get out of here.*

Her thoughts briefly turned to her neighbors. She wondered who, if any of them, had survived. There were *at least* 10 of those creatures out there. *Probably more than 10. But I'm not sticking around to find out. Alright, it's time to go.*

As if to punctuate her notion, Itania heard a loud crash from the front of the house—they were coming for her!

She fumbled in her pocket to grab the key. She pulled it out of her breeches but it snagged on her pocket and clattered to the ground, bouncing twice on the floor. She quickly bent down to grab it. When she stood up she saw one of the brutes standing in the hallway, staring at her. The furs it wore on its green body dripped with water as did its horned helmet.

"Shit!" Itania pressed herself against the back door as the creature stepped inside the room. She started to cry, too afraid to move as the creature snarled and raised its axe above its head.

Chapter 34

Kendra muttered a curse under her breath as she gazed out over the city. She watched as everyone below went about their daily routines, probably perfectly happy and content with their lives. Or not. It was of no consequence to her. At least they knew what they were doing and where they would go next. Kendra was listlessly spending her days in the inn, listening to Orvaril go on about how grandiose the Storm's End Festival was.

Sure, she'd ventured out into the crowded streets a few times to get a sampling of the spectacle, but she had found it largely unappealing. For the most part, she stayed in their room in the Panting Calf Inn, listlessly observing everything from above. Kendra now found herself absentmindedly turning the dragonstone over in her hands. She wondered what would happen if she accidentally dropped it.

She slipped the dragonstone into one of her many pockets and walked to the open window. Below was a flurry of activity as people clogged the streets, lining up to purchase baubles or to talk with one another. It seemed as though the festival reached to every corner of the city, causing chaos everywhere. Above her, the clouds serenely floated past, unconcerned with festivals or orcs. She gazed up at them and squinted, but she had a difficult time understanding them.

It was never easy—reading the clouds—and it was a rare talent. Most people thought of Cloudsight as a myth. Sure, everyone saw shapes in the clouds—a dog or a house or a face—but Cloudseers saw portents, warnings, and boons. Her boredom turned to frustration.

Something was about to happen—she could feel it. She didn't know exactly what, only that it was close. She cursed the sky and then herself for not knowing how to read the clouds properly. What good was it to have a gift if you couldn't use it correctly? But, as frustrated as she was with herself, she suspected that she *was* reading the clouds correctly and that they were simply ambiguous. After many years of using her talent she still wasn't quite sure how it was supposed to work—or even if there was more to it at all.

Of course, she'd looked to the skies earlier this morning but they had said nothing to her. She had received the portent of danger a few days ago and it had been extremely vague. She knew one thing, however—Elston was the center of it. That was enough of a reason for her to leave. If there was going to be trouble, she did not want any part of it. But there was a voice inside that beckoned her to stay... and mayhaps to help should something terrible happen. King Alzine was supposed to be making his grand speech today. Kendra was tempted to attend, if only to hear what he had to say. *Because, of course, whatever dangerous thing is going to happen most certainly wouldn't happen at the center of the city, near the king, now would it? That sounds like a fantastic idea!*

Kendra laughed at herself. Sometimes she could be so damned foolish! She often let a thirst for adventure override her rational thought and, on occasion, it resulted in rather unsavory circumstances. Though she explained this phenomenon with the fact that it added excitement.

"Fine," she said. She was alone, of course. Orvaril had risen early to perform for the crowds. From what he had told her, he was quite popular. Certainly he must be, since he returned every evening with quite a bit of coin. So, unless he was stealing said coins from people—and she wouldn't think less of him if he did—he was indeed as successful a performer as he had pointed out at every opportunity.

"I need to get out and about anyway. There is no sense sitting in this room every day, hoping to avoid something when you're not even sure what it is." *And now you're talking to yourself.* She knew full well that the results would be disastrous. At this point, she simply didn't care. *Mayhaps I should go live among the forest like treeboy. He's probably overjoyed living amongst the trees, enjoying peace and quiet and not having any responsibilities.* "Actually, that sounds rather appealing right now," she mumbled. "And, again, I'm talking to myself..."

Kendra slipped out of the room and climbed up to the roof. The new purple skirts she'd recently bought were more comfortable than her previous garb. They were easier to move around in and weren't as warm. She hadn't tried climbing until now, and she was pleased. She made it easily to the roof and cautiously walked along its length until she had to cross an alley. The Panting Calf Inn was not far from King Alzine's castle, and the streets were already packed to capacity with people waiting to hear him speak.

I guess it's a good thing I like to travel by rooftop. I get the best view. She slid down the angled roof and when she reached the end, leapt over the alley, landing gracefully on a flat roof on the other side. She walked to the edge and looked out over The Storm Citadel.

Kendra had always wondered why the castle itself was not more grandiose. She had never been inside it, but from the outside, it looked rather small and underwhelming. It was a simple, gray fieldstone structure with a square tower at either front corner. A simple portcullis, currently raised, normally closed off the two heavy wooden doors of the entryway. The main building, the keep, wasn't much higher than the roof on which Kendra currently stood.

From her vantage point, Kendra could see into the courtyard. There was a crowd of people filling the area—guards and important officials, mayhaps family and some friends as well. Kendra watched them mill about, stuck in a too-small space, probably trying to keep cool. She couldn't make out a whole lot of detail from here, but she guessed that it was probably uncomfortable.

The open marketplace around the castle wall was packed with people. They spilled out into side streets, main streets, alleyways, and onto the front stoops of various buildings. The cacophony of the crowd was formidable but, at least on the roof three stories up, it wasn't overwhelming.

Kendra patiently waited on the roof, keeping low and out of sight. She felt around in her satchel for the watch and checked the time. Two hours passed and she began to wonder if King Alzine was actually going to make an appearance. She found herself yawning and trying not do nod off.

"Lovely day for a speech, my dear."

Kendra whirled around and had a dagger in her hand instantly. The Blacksmoke knelt on the edge of the roof right next to her and she hadn't even heard him approach! She nearly lost her balance and fell off of the building but quickly recovered.

"Relax," he laughed. "If I had—"

"Wanted to kill me I'd already be dead."

"Exactly. You know me all too well, my dear."

Kendra thought once again about demanding he stop calling her that, but it hadn't done any good so far. It would be easier for her to stop getting irritated whenever he said it. Easier, but not *easy*. She clenched her jaw in frustration.

"You've come to hear King Alzine speak?" She made sure the sarcasm was heavy. She knew The Blacksmoke had no interest in something as mundane as a speech to celebrate a war that happened 200 years ago. He was planning something. He was *always* planning something.

"No," he replied, still looking out over the crowd. "But I knew you would."

"Oh, how very creepy of you."

"While I do like to keep a watchful eye over my city," he got up, slowly pacing, "that's not why I am here."

"Somehow, I'm not convinced." Kendra got up and leaned against a chimney, slipping the black dagger back into her sleeve. It had quickly become her favorite weapon. The Blacksmoke had a point—he was very good at sneaking up on even her. "But, please, go on, I am intrigued."

"Oh, well, don't let me *bore* you," he chuckled. "But since you asked nicely… my eyes and ears reported seeing a large army coming this way. If it is marching on Elston, it will arrive outside the gates soon."

"How soon?"

"*Soon.*"

"What are we to do? Should we flee the city?" *Is this what the clouds were trying to tell me?*

"I would not recommend it." The Blacksmoke stopped pacing and gazed out over the city once more. "You most likely wouldn't get far."

"What kind of army is it? Surely Ten Kings wouldn't start up another dispute with Elston, and I haven't heard of any discord from other Realms."

"I think you can probably guess what kind of army it is."

"Damn." If there were parts of the Realm that were unaware of recent events, they would not be left in the dark for much longer. If Elston was besieged by orcs and goblins, the Realm would hear about it. *Every* Realm would hear about it. "We should warn someone."

"Warn who? About what?" The Blacksmoke laughed, and he had good reason. Who would believe the story they had to tell? "You'd get thrown in the dungeons if you tried to tell anyone. No, this has to be *seen* to be believed."

"So we sit by and watch Elston fall? Kendra felt as if she was going to be sick. She had always lived in safety under King Alzine's rule. Sure, there were various disputes between different cities or Realms, but she had never considered an outright invasion before. She had certainly never considered *losing* to an invading army. But then again, lately, she felt uncertain about *everything*.

"I didn't say that." The Blacksmoke smirked and tipped his hat up a bit. He ran two fingers over the stubble on his chin, obviously pondering something. Traditionally, when he got this quiet, she got concerned. "But wasn't your first idea to flee the city?"

"Well," she stammered, "yes. I'm no warrior and neither are you. This is not our arena. But if we could warn someone we might be able to help."

"A noble thought for sure, my dear, but you know as well as I that the city guard are not friends to us. That is the path we've chosen. Nor would they believe us. Oh, but King Alzine is going to speak." He pointed down toward the castle as the two heavy doors slowly swung open and, along with his entourage, King Alzine emerged to fanfare and cheers from the crowd.

He was a handsome man. His salt and pepper hair and gray beard made him look all the more distinguished and his simple clothes, though of the utmost quality, were not common to royalty. He still looked very much the warrior that stories insisted he had been.

The Queen accompanied him, beautiful as ever. Her gown appeared more ornate than his garb but, certainly, wasn't lavish. Of course, from up on the roof at the edge of the market, it was difficult to discern many details about anything. When King Alzine began speaking, in fact, Kendra could not hear anything other than a quiet, low rumbling. Every so often the crowd would cheer for several minutes before quieting down again.

"I'm sure he's not telling them anything they've not heard before," The Blacksmoke said.

"Most likely," Kendra replied, "he's recounting the final battle between Sturm Ironhelm and Gorag Thrashbone. That always seems to fill everyone with pride." Upon closer scrutiny Kendra could see two armored individuals engaged in a theatrical battle of sorts.

"Ah, yes," The Blacksmoke confirmed, "that appears to be correct."

Kendra swiftly drew her black dagger and held it to The Blacksmoke's throat, grinning. At that very moment, she noticed that he had done the same to her. They both stared at each other, locked in a stalemate. Finally, they both eased back and slowly put away their weapons.

"After all this time," he said, "you still wish to kill me?"

"Aye," Kendra sneered. "Always. I feel the need to remind you."

"That's a fancy little blade you've got there."

"It is, indeed. I've grown quite fond of it, especially because Raynar wanted it."

The Blacksmoke chuckled.

Down below, the actor portraying Sturm Ironhelm had the other man on the ground, sword raised high in the air.

"It makes you wonder, doesn't it?" Kendra watched the two actors struggle some more, both of them now fighting on the ground. They almost looked like two children struggling over a sugary treat.

"Wonder what?"

"Well, a lot of things, I suppose. But, more specifically, I'm skeptical that this is how the Barbarian hordes were defeated." She watched the staged fight continue. The hushed crowd was enthralled.

"As well you should be... in light of recent events."

Sturm Ironhelm plunged his great two-handed sword down into Gorag Thrashbone who screamed loudly enough for Kendra to hear. The audience roared its approval and the King and Queen both clapped. But, beyond the din of the crowd, there was another sound—a sickening crash in the distance.

Kendra and The Blacksmoke looked at each other. She supposed her face had the same look that his did. At first, the crowd below did not seem to notice anything. But when the second crash sounded they began to quiet down. From here it looked as though King Alzine also noticed something was amiss.

"I believe, my dear," The Blacksmoke, seemingly unsurprised, took off running, "it's time to go see what all the fuss is about." He sounded almost... amused? Elston had an army knocking on its doors and The Blacksmoke treated it like a common tavern brawl!

Kendra followed, her heart racing. The two of them leapt across the rooftops, many of which had specially-crafted extensions or bridges put in place by The Blacksmoke for this very type of occasion. Most were well-hidden or blended in with the natural architecture so as to be nearly undetectable. You simply had to know where they were, but if you did, you could get around the city quite easily. It was one of his better ideas, she had to admit, and he had *many* good ideas. When he boasted that he "owned" Elston, he was not joking.

Kendra felt sick. She knew full well what was about to happen—what had already happened—and she could do nothing but sit by and watch. She wanted to help, to fight off the invaders. *Where did this newfound sense of responsibility come from?*

As they got closer to the city's north gates she could hear the distinct sounds of battle. People in the streets had begun to panic and were running every which way, clogging every avenue and trampling one another.

"What exactly are we going to do when we get there?" Kendra leapt from the platform on one roof to an outcropped window on an opposite building. The Blacksmoke effortlessly landed nearby, only a little higher up on the slanted roof. They both paused a moment to catch their breath.

"I reserve the right to do whatever I choose once I see the situation." He was always so nonchalant, portraying an air of extraordinary placidity even under extreme duress. In fact, she could only remember a couple of times he had lost his temper. She had made sure to quickly remove herself from the area when that happened.

Kendra nodded as he opened the window and began to climb inside the building.

"What are you doing?"

"I've got a more covert path to our destination." He slipped inside. Kendra was close behind. They were in a sparsely-furnished bedroom, with only a simple bed and a chair. Kendra followed The Blacksmoke through the door, down the hallway and then down a staircase. She followed him as they hurried through an empty room, turned a corner and then continued down another set of stairs into a cellar. The Blacksmoke suddenly stopped and looked around.

"What are we looking for?" Kendra glanced around, too. The filthy cellar was a relatively small, dilapidated room with only two stone pillars and a round table. Kendra tried as best she could not to come into contact with *anything*.

The Blacksmoke pursed his lips and once again played with the stubble on his chin. He was either thinking, pretending to think, or about to stab her. She kept her hand close to her weapon.

"I'm trying to remember where it is... it's around here somewhere."

"Where are we anyway? Who keeps an empty house in Elston?"

"I do, of course. I have several, in fact."

"You certainly don't live here." Kendra found herself surprised. The Blacksmoke was very thorough.

"Goodness, certainly not, my dear."

"And I'd be naïve to assume you have the funds to pay for multiple domiciles."

"That would be none of your concern." The Blacksmoke smiled briefly at Kendra. He then approached one of the walls and began inspecting it closer. "I have a... colleague who deals in housing."

"Makes sense. I assume he comes in handy."

"*She* does, yes." He stared at the wall again, ignoring Kendra as if he had forgotten her. "Ah, now I remember!" He approached the wall to his left and then pushed on a brick. It slid inward slightly. Then he pushed it to the left and it disappeared inside another brick, revealing a hole in the wall.

"Now what?" Kendra asked.

"Now," The Blacksmoke paused, smirking, "you help me push this door open." He put his hand in the hole and pushed on the brick to its left. To Kendra's surprise, a section of the wall slid slightly inward! "Help me push this back, please."

Kendra pressed against the other side and pushed with him. The door slid back further until it was about two feet from the wall itself. She marveled at all of it, amazed by how undetectable it had been—concealed enough to cause even its owner to pause and search for it.

"Do you also have a friend who deals in doors?" she quipped.

"Several. Follow me, through here."

Kendra followed him through the gap in the wall into a pitch dark room, nearly tripping over something on the ground. She bumped into The Blacksmoke, who had apparently stopped.

"Hold up," he grunted, irritated. Soon enough, light illuminated a passageway wide enough for three people to walk side-by-side. The Blacksmoke put his flint and steel away and handed Kendra the torch he had just lit. "I need to seal this back up."

"How exactly did you manage all of this?" Kendra marveled at the tunnel. "Surely somebody would have noticed."

The part of the door that slid back was perched on a small but sturdy set of wheels, Kendra noticed. The Blacksmoke had a slightly more difficult time pushing it back into place. Finally, he slid the brick back into its original position and was finished.

"I have another colleague who is an architect." He grinned and took the torch from Kendra. "The sliding brick is a locking mechanism. It was his idea." He started trotting down the hallway. "Keep up, now."

"I don't suppose you have a colleague who deals in repelling invading armies, do you?"

"I do not," The Blacksmoke replied. "But I've heard word that *you* might."

Chapter 35

When Kendra and The Blacksmoke finally topped the roof of another building, what they saw left them speechless. They watched as everything around them burned while hordes of invading orcs, goblins and... other, larger brutes stormed over the broken walls and clashed with horribly outmatched city guardsmen. Soldiers were pouring in from all directions to stave off the flow of invaders in the streets.

"Well," Kendra started, but she didn't have anything to follow it.

"Surprise."

Down below, men barked orders as soldiers tried to organize and form some kind of strategy to stem the chaos. Kendra watched as one of the larger creatures—*trolls... just say it. They are bloody* trolls—hurled a chunk of the wall into the crowd of soldiers, crushing at least five of men. Several other soldiers saw what happened and shamelessly fled in the opposite direction, pushing others out of their way in their panic.

A shower of rocks sailed over the army, striking orc and man alike. Kendra fought the urge to duck from the debris close to their perch, falling just short of where they stood. The Blacksmoke, however, did not move. She could see something behind his usually calm demeanor. *He's irritated! Or he might be angry. With him, it's difficult to be sure either way. Hopefully he's got a plan because I've no idea what to do.*

The Blacksmoke stared stoically out over the unfolding battle, as still as stone. Were he anyone else she would be sure that he was too frightened to move, but she knew him better than that. *He's planning something. I know that look.* She failed to see how just the two of them could enact any kind of significant plan, but The Blacksmoke was always good at surprising her. He was more resourceful than anyone else she knew—including herself.

Bodies fell—both beast and man, but man was losing. It was apparent that Elston's chances of survival were not very good. It wasn't just that the invaders were obviously more numerous or more powerful, but that Elston was ill-prepared for a battle of this magnitude. This army had taken them completely by surprise and was like no other force ever seen. How could you fight effectively against a foe that wasn't supposed to even exist? Most of the orcs weren't wearing anything but furs and the goblins wore even less and they were undisciplined combatants, but they were brutal and numerous.

Elston's foes fought with such feral savagery and chaos, such raw anger of purpose. In many cases it took several soldiers to take down *one* orc! She watched one brute take three stabs to the chest with a sword before it fell, and it took two men with it!

The Blacksmoke also winced when he saw it.

"Come on," he said, motioning for Kendra to follow.

"Are we leaving?" Kendra leapt across the rooftops, following his lead. It was difficult to keep up. How did he make it look so effortless?

"Hardly."

They crossed high over several battles that had broken out in the streets, pushed back from the original clash at the city gates. The combat was raging deeper into the city with the seemingly endless invaders continuing to pour in.

Several arrows shot past them, nearly hitting Kendra's leg. Glancing to her left she saw a group of archers perched on the rooftops, nervously firing arrows in their direction. Had the archers recognized her or were they just that bad?

She followed The Blacksmoke onto another rooftop where they stopped behind a chimney. *At least, for now, those bloody archers can't accidentally hit us here!* She indeed was still not entirely sure the archers weren't actually trying to hit them.

"So, now what do you suggest?" she asked.

"Do you see those poor bastards below us?" The Blacksmoke pointed down as if it wasn't obvious.

"Are you referring to the orcs down there or the soldiers?" Kendra looked over the edge. Two stories below, on the street, several soldiers had formed a wall with their shields while others behind them used long spears to keep the orcs at bay. It seemed to be working relatively well for the moment as several orcs lay dead, creating a partial blockage of the street.

"Yes."

She glared at him. He *was* joking. Wasn't he?

"This plan isn't exactly a well-aimed strike. I can't guarantee we won't hit the soldiers."

"Fine," she acquiesced. She would do whatever she could to keep the soldiers alive. She had no love for the town guard but they were essential to the city's defense. "What exactly is it you had in mind?"

"This chimney," The Blacksmoke lightly pounded his fist against the large, brick chimney, "is surprisingly unstable, don't you agree?"

Kendra pushed lightly on the chimney. It gave a little against her touch. And it was directly over the fight going on below.

"I am no builder," The Blacksmoke continued, "but I do believe that this is a hazard and should probably be demolished before someone gets hurt, yes?" He had that familiar grin on his face. He was most certainly very proud of himself.

"How did—"

"Elston is *my* city, remember? And I know *everything* about it." He paused briefly. Kendra was skeptical. As well-informed and crafty as The Blacksmoke was, there had to be something else going on, here. He looked quite proud of himself, though.

"That's a pile of gortog shit."

"Well," he replied, still grinning but apparently taken aback, "sometimes you have to make your own fortune. But we have a schedule to keep. So if you don't mind stepping out of the way, I can tend to the business at hand, my dear."

"Falling bricks!" she yelled to the soldiers below and then Kendra, without waiting for The Blacksmoke, heaved her right shoulder squarely into the chimney. She grunted as pain shot up and down her arm and she lost her balance as the large chunks of debris fell. After a brief struggle, she regained her balance and jumped back from the edge of the roof.

"Bloody Hell!" she heard one of the men yell. Looking over the edge, she watched as the soldiers handily finished off the remaining two orcs.

"I told you," she turned and glared at The Blacksmoke, "to *stop calling me that!*"

He smirked.

"And now, my... Kendra, we have other things to deal with, I'm afraid."

"Thank you," she growled.

"Don't get used to it." He was still grinning as he ran and leapt to another roof. Kendra followed. When she got there, he was crouched on the dormer of a window, looking down. Two orcs were fighting one man in the street below. Surprisingly, the man appeared skilled and was doing a decent job of staying alive but it was evident that he was not going to win the fight.

The Blacksmoke pointed to himself and then to her, then he made a jumping motion with his fingers followed by a stabbing motion. If Kendra understood correctly, this would either be the single most fun thing she'd done in days... or they would die horribly. She nodded.

She perched on the edge of the roof. It was about a 10-foot drop, but the orc was probably over six feet tall. *Not a problem at all... if you land it right.*

Without another thought she leapt off the rooftop and landed on top of the orc. It shouldered her weight easily but staggered as it lost its balance. She drew a dagger in each hand and drove them deep into either side of its neck. As it fell to the ground, wailing, she leapt off and landed behind its corpse. The other orc took notice but it was slow to react. Kendra charged the brute and buried her black blade deep in its chest.

The orc growled but did not fall. Kendra pushed the blade in deeper and then followed with her left hand, stabbing the orc in the side. For a moment, she thought that it wasn't going to stop, but it eventually dropped its weapon and fell in a heap.

"Uh," the soldier stammered, "thank you, ma'am!" He nodded to her and immediately ran off to join another fight. Though she couldn't see his face through the helmet, his voice sounded very young.

"Yes, well done, *ma'am*."

Kendra turned around and there was The Blacksmoke. He tipped his hat to her.

"Would it have been too much for you to help out?" She stepped on one of the orc corpses, walking over it. "Or was that not in your original plan?"

"Probably," he smirked. "But you handled it just fine." He walked with her, both of them strolling at a casual pace, now, as Kendra caught her breath. "Besides, the city guard and I... we don't usually see eye-to-eye, you know."

"Of course not," she agreed. "We're not the best of friends, either."

An explosion rang out and the ground shook. Before either could say anything, Kendra was already halfway up the nearest building to get a better view. There was another explosion—one that rocked the buildings and nearly threw her off the roof just as she had finished scaling the wall. The Blacksmoke arrived right behind her.

She looked toward the city gates. They were just a few blocks from the wall, and from here she could see that large chunks of it were completely gone. Rubble was strewn everywhere and the soldiers still fought the invading hordes, but there seemed far fewer of them now. Several trolls—a couple looking a bit different than the rest—savagely attacked the wall, buildings, men, and whatever else they could find.

"If the explosions happened inside the city," she said, "I don't know where."

"Indeed. I see no damage, nothing on fire. I wonder—"

Another explosion rocked the city but, this time, Kendra could see that it was outside the city walls. Bodies of orcs and goblins were propelled away from the blast, flying high into the air to land on their comrades.

Suddenly, a portion of the invading army turned its attention away from the city to something outside the wall. *Curious. I wonder what has them all in such a stir. Mayhaps someone has sent help?*

"We need a closer look."

"Precisely what I was thinking, my dear."

"That didn't last long, did it?" Kendra wasn't even looking at him but she could *feel* him grinning.

"Apparently not. Force of habit, I suppose."

Neither Kendra nor The Blacksmoke hurried. As they neared the crux of combat, they were careful to remain unseen. Fighting spilled over into most of the northern part of the city. Much of the invading army was already within Elston's walls, destroying whatever stood in its path. *There are so many of them!*

The air was thick with the sounds of weapons, shouts, and screams of the dying. Buildings and men alike crumpled beneath the wave of invaders. At some point, Kendra found that she had stopped moving toward the battle. She instead stood and watched, sadness growing heavy in her heart as Elston fell. She had called this city her home since she had fled Alarantha years ago. Although she hadn't spent *all* of her time since then in Elston, she held it dearly in her heart. *And, now, it is going to be overrun with these... beasts!*

The Blacksmoke looked as though he was feeling the same thing. He held a wicked, slightly curved dagger in a shaky right hand, and a scowl marred his face. Kendra had never seen him shaken like this. She knew that the two of them could fight as many orcs as they pleased, but they could not turn the tide of the battle by themselves.

Suddenly, a large group of orcs and goblins was launched high into the air. They swirled around in a whirlwind, screaming, before being violently thrown in all directions. Several of them landed just a couple of blocks away from where she and The Blacksmoke stood. At that same moment, one of the trolls began flailing wildly, grasping at its neck for some reason. It collapsed to the ground, crushing several of its allies.

"Well, that's one less troll." Under any other circumstances, Kendra would have laughed. At the same time, she was intensely curious about what was behind the counterattack.

"I believe, my dear," The Blacksmoke responded, "that was an ogre."

"Troll... ogre... they're both ugly, and that one is ugly *and* dead." Kendra found herself moving closer again. Several arrows flitted over her head and disappeared in the chaos below. She leapt over an alley to another rooftop with The Blacksmoke right behind her. Below she saw two soldiers get absolutely mauled, then buried by a group of goblins. Several of the attackers threw rocks and crude weapons up at her but, not only did she avoid them, she caught one of the blades and sent it back, burying it deep into one of the goblins.

"Is there another loose chimney nearby that we can push over onto these goblins?" she asked, stopping to see if there was anything they could do to help.

"No." The Blacksmoke didn't even stop moving. "Not over here. Come on. If someone has sent reinforcements, then we might be able to help them."

"Aye." Kendra followed.

"And if I help get Elston out of this mess they are going to owe me."

"Oh, sure," Kendra retorted, "They'll throw a party in your honor."

They picked up the pace. The battle was much more spread out than Kendra had thought. She could see that the invading army wasn't being slowed down much by defending soldiers. Rather, the army was destroying everything in its path. She also noticed that some of the attackers had broken off and moved back outside the shattered wall. *Whatever is out there has them worried.*

There was another explosion outside the walls, quickly followed by two more. Each one sent bodies—or parts of bodies—sailing into the air in all directions. Kendra could see the few remaining archers dodge the living debris as it rained down.

Suddenly, a troll burst into a column of flame. Kendra could feel the instant wave of heat from where she stood! It roared out and began flailing wildly, striking its allies and setting ablaze everything it touched. At the same time, several balls of fire launched into the air, arcing high and then exploding upon impact with the ground. *What is all of this? The only time I've seen anything like it was when—wait, no.* The troll's fiery corpse hit the ground hard, destroying yet more of the wall.

"Try and keep up." Kendra bolted across the rooftops with new purpose, hoping to make her way to part of the wall that was still intact. She should be able to see everything from there.

The Blacksmoke was indeed keeping up and, seemingly aware of her direction, he hurried out in front of her as if the whole thing were a race. She found herself working to keep up with *him*. Several times they had to travel through the streets because of destruction. They deftly avoided most of the combat, only stopping to dispatch enemies from which there was no escape.

When they got to the wall they wasted no time ascending. One soldier—an older man who was barking orders at everyone around him—tried to tell them to turn back but they brushed past him as if he wasn't there. Kendra rushed up the stone stairs and, once at the top, gazed out over the battlefield.

Man and beast were locked in savage battle all around her. Though better equipped, Elston's soldiers were still outnumbered and outmatched. Kendra desperately scanned the battlefield but stopped when she saw what she was looking for. *The Abyss take me, there he is!*

Cor'il stood in the midst of the fight, his hood down and his sword drawn. With him was a small number of soldiers and another boy who wielded an axe with lethal skill. Within seconds he had effortlessly felled three goblins and an orc.

Though Cor'il was not nearly as efficient, he managed to drop an orc in that same amount of time, running it through with his blade. Then he stood in place for a couple of seconds and, moving his hands in the air before him, he produced a jet of flame that seared everything he pointed to.

Kendra gasped. She looked at The Blacksmoke who, for the first time ever, had a look of utter shock on his face. *Well now, treeboy. You've acquired some new skills since we last talked. You're just full of surprises, aren't you?*

The blond-haired boy with the axe continued to chop through the enemies with more savagery than they themselves had exhibited. They almost seemed afraid of him! They certainly *were* afraid of Cor'il. The few orcs who were brave enough—or foolish enough—to get close to him quickly died in terrible ways.

"We have to help them," she said.

"I'm not entirely certain that they need our help."

Cor'il advanced closer to the wall, unleashing devastating attacks with fire or, sometimes, the ground itself. The invaders stubbornly continued to stand in his way.

"Cor'il!" Kendra called, waving her arms. She knew it was possibly the stupidest thing she could have done. The Blacksmoke shot her a disapproving glance, but was still largely dumbfounded by what he had just witnessed. Kendra looked on as Cor'il thrust his hands outward and brought part of the crumbling wall down on a group of orcs, crushing them.

Upon closer inspection, Kendra realized that the soldiers with Cor'il weren't soldiers at all. They were dressed in common clothes and wielded simple weapons—crude spears and farming implements. Very few of them had a sword and none of them looked as if they had seen battle before. They largely hung back behind Cor'il, probably trying to keep any determined orcs from flanking him.

Cor'il glanced up at the wall. *Did he see me? Does he need my help?* He stopped a minute, looking as if he was concentrating. Then he somehow launched himself high into the air and landed precariously on the wall next to Kendra.

"Hello again," he said, regaining his balance and breathing heavily. "I brought an army—sort of. They're from Harvest Town which was unfortunately destroyed by orcs."

"It would appear that *you* are an army—the two of you," The Blacksmoke interjected.

Cor'il looked quizzically at The Blacksmoke.

"Oh," Kendra responded, "this is The Blacksmoke. He's a… friend, I think?"

"It is nice to meet you, uh, Mister Smoke." Cor'il grinned briefly. "I apologize, but I am in a bit of a hurry."

"Oh?" Kendra couldn't put her finger on it, but Cor'il seemed… different. Had he matured? In just a few weeks? "What are you planning? And when did you learn to do *that*?"

"My friend, Dalinil, and I—we have to get inside King Alzine's castle."

"Oh really?" Kendra chuckled. "And why is that?"

"There's something in the castle. Well, *beneath* it, actually. Whatever it is, it's been calling to us. I think it might put an end to this." He pointed out to the battlefield. He looked tired and was still trying to catch his breath.

"Are you alright, Cor'il?"

"I should be." He paused another moment. "I may have overexerted myself a bit back there."

Kendra knew that she had a puzzled look on her face. She really didn't understand how he had gone from summoning a tiny flame in his hand to... this. She tried to ask questions but couldn't think of anything to say.

"I'll explain it to you later."

The other boy—Dalinil—had climbed the back of a nearby ogre and, after burying his axe in its neck, he leapt onto the wall as it tumbled, lifeless, to the ground. He looked winded as well.

"Do you think the city guard can handle it from here, Cor'il?"

"I've no idea. We should probably hurry to the castle. We have yet to figure out how we're going to get inside."

"I think," The Blacksmoke piped in, "I can probably help you with that."

"Hope shines brightest when the world is darkest" –Source Unknown

Chapter 36

The passageway through which Cor'il walked was both dark and damp. Water dripped from the ceiling and ran down the walls in tiny rivulets, but disappeared through porous stone in the floor. The only light source the group had was Cor'il's sword, which he illuminated with a simple weave of the Threads. The Blacksmoke led the way through the crude tunnel which occasionally branched off in other directions. At every crossroads he had to stop and think about which way to go. Cor'il felt doubt creeping into him—doubt as to whether this man actually knew where they were headed.

"Mayhaps you should install some signs or indicators?" Kendra asked sarcastically. "After all, you should know your own tunnels, right?"

"Funny," The Blacksmoke replied. "But I've better things to do with my time than make fancy signs with arrows and descriptions. Besides, I don't normally have guests."

"I don't mean to rush you," Cor'il interjected, "but time is growing short." He was careful to be polite since this man was giving them his help, but he found himself growing frustrated and anxious. Dalinil seemed to be exhibiting the same feelings behind them. Cor'il could hear him muttering under his breath, and he sounded annoyed.

"Listen, boy," The Blacksmoke growled. He turned to face Cor'il with a not-so-pleasant look about him—perfectly clear even in the dim light. "I indeed know where I am going, but unless you wish to resurface in the middle of a pack of orcs or up the ass of a troll I would suggest you let me figure the best route!" He paused for a moment, his scowl turning to a look of concentration. "Do you hear that?"

Everyone stopped and listened for a moment. The only thing Cor'il could hear, besides their collective breathing and Dalinil's annoyed grunts, was the sound of water dripping in the tunnel.

"I hear nothing," Kendra finally piped up.

"Exactly." The Blacksmoke resumed leading them down the tunnel. "The fact that you hear nothing means that there is no fighting going on above us. That's most likely a good sign because, if we have to surface for some reason, we should be safe.

From that point on, everyone stayed quiet. They walked in silence for what seemed like miles, snaking their way underneath Elston and occasionally backtracking.

"You must come to the castle. You must seek me out and create a new balance that shall restore order."

It was a woman's voice. It was *always* a woman's voice. Cor'il had begun hearing it soon after Dalinil and he had left Listerville. It quickly became apparent that Dalinil heard it, too. Cor'il wasn't sure how long the voice had been speaking to his new friend but he was glad it was not something that only Cor'il could hear. At first he had been worried.

In the beginning, Cor'il had tried to ignore it, but when the voice replied to a question he asked he could no longer dismiss the phenomenon. Neither he nor Dalinil understood the situation, but they both felt the pull toward Elston and decided to follow the voice's advice. She had led them here.

"Well," The Blacksmoke whispered, "here we are."

They stopped at a wall.

Cor'il could once again hear the muffled sounds of battle raging above them. He wished there was a way he could see onto the streets to get a view of the fight.

"You are close, now. I can sense you. I need your help. You can end this!"

The Blacksmoke pushed on the stone wall and it gave way. With the sounds of grinding gears, it slid back slightly and then opened like a door.

"Through that tunnel is a staircase that will lead you to another concealed door. Beyond it is a room in the castle's lower level." The Blacksmoke stepped aside. "I hope you find what you seek. Moreover, I hope it can save my city."

"Let's go, Cor'il," Kendra urged. She started through the tunnel but The Blacksmoke stopped her.

"You and I have... other things to attend to, my dear. And I'd rather not get caught lurking around the castle's basement."

Kendra looked annoyed and started to argue, but she eventually stepped aside as Cor'il and Dalinil passed them.

"Good luck, treeboy!" She smiled, but her words hid a hint of sadness behind them.

"I have no need of luck," he replied. "I shall make my own fortune."

"I can feel you drawing near. Come to me and this can all be over! Yes, this shall end and the world shall be as it should—in balance!"

The door slid shut behind them and it immediately became apparent that they were alone. Cor'il could still hear the muted, muffled noise of combat above them, but the sounds of dripping water had ceased. This tunnel was much drier than the others—it looked newer and much more meticulously constructed.

Cor'il paused a moment to gather himself. His command of the Threads was becoming easier with every day that passed, but it still fatigued him, and he was a bit wary from the battle outside the gates. Judging from Dalinil's face, he was feeling the same.

"Well," Dalinil said, "This could get interesting really quickly."

"Aye."

"Do we have any idea what to expect? Any notion of what we're looking for?"

"A woman, I think?" Cor'il really didn't have a solid answer. It was a woman's voice in their heads but that didn't necessarily mean anything. Were they looking for a person or an object? At this point, he assumed nothing.

They both walked in pensive silence. Cor'il had a bevy of questions nagging him but he kept them to himself. Hopefully they would be answered soon enough. However, in case they found something dangerous, Cor'il had his sword out for its light, but also for defense. Dalinil still had his axe in hand as well—he was on edge, almost as if he was spooked.

Cor'il noticed Dalinil's gaze darting around them, as if he was expecting danger at every step. Cor'il couldn't blame him, really. There were surprises waiting around every corner and behind every door. He felt much the same way, but somehow he kept most of his jitters under control. Dalinil, on the other hand, looked ready to attack anything that moved.

Fortunately, there was nothing but the two of them, alone in the darkness. The tunnel was straight and relatively short. A few minutes after they had left Kendra, Dalinil and Cor'il found themselves standing in front of four stairs leading up to a brick wall. Cor'il climbed the stairs and holding out his glowing sword, inspected the wall. He knew there was a door here somewhere; he just had to find it.

"It's too bad that guy—The Blacksmoke—didn't come with us," he chuckled. "This would probably take a lot less time—if he could remember how to open his own door, that is."

"Indeed. Mayhaps we could bust our way through?" Dalinil lifted his axe a bit, grinning. Cor'il must have given him a stern look because he shrugged sheepishly and lowered his weapon.

Cor'il searched carefully, running his fingers over each brick and inspecting the wall in the pale, blue glow. He felt his frustration increasing as he looked over the same bricks repeatedly, coming no closer to finding any kind of a door. To his surprise, the wall suddenly began to glow.

"I was about to let you use your axe," he whispered, backing away from the wall.

"What did you do?" Dalinil asked. Cor'il remained silent, trying to figure out what to do next.

The radiant, white light quickly eclipsed that from his sword. A shimmering line drew itself in the wall and illuminated the shape of a door.

Cor'il found the edges of the door with his fingers and pulled. The heavy door slowly slid open, grinding against the top stair.

"That was quite handy," Dalinil remarked, walking through the now open door. "How did you pull that one off?"

"I didn't. I'm not sure what happened." Cor'il stepped inside, and using an amazingly sturdy shelf attached to the other side, pulled the door shut. The room they were in held a variety of chairs, cooking implements, and linens. Once again, the only available light was Cor'il's sword. To their right lay another set of four stairs leading up and ending in a wooden door.

"Well," Dalinil whispered, "we're in. Now we need only figure out where—"

"You are so close. Oh, but there are two of you—I sense that now. Intriguing. I was expecting only one. This creates all kinds of new and exciting... possibilities. But I digress. You cannot get to me without my help." The voice sounded... excited?

Cor'il couldn't help but worry. He felt as though they were walking into a trap, but set by whom? The two of them had been following this voice's guidance for only a couple of days and, at the outset, they had both been suspicious. "Voices in your head aren't a normal occurrence," Dalinil had said. And Cor'il had to agree with that sentiment.

The communication so far had been largely one-way. They had tried asking questions of the voice but had never received any kind of response—except for the one relatively worthless response Cor'il got from a minor query. So, with no other ideas, they had both agreed to follow the voice.

"I am in an old, forgotten chamber beneath you. I have been here for countless years, trying to keep the balance. It is failing and I need your help. But, first, let me help you."

At the base of the stairs leading up, the stone floor receded, disappearing into nothing and revealing a passageway below into which another set of stairs descended. Cor'il approached and used his sword's light to peer down, but the light was quickly swallowed up by the darkness just a few stairs past the entrance.

"Are we going down there?" Dalinil looked dubious.

"It would appear so."

Cor'il went first, using his light to guide their way, but once they had descended a few stairs, a light appeared in the form of a small globe that sprang to life on the head of a torch sconce on the wall. Cor'il could now see that the stairs spiraled downward to the right, further than he had at first expected. Once they had passed the first orb of light, a second torch flared with light just ahead of them. He removed the weave on his sword and let its light die out.

The large, gray bricks soon gave way to more ornate walls with patterns carved into them. As they descended, more of the glowing orbs lit up, revealing increasingly delicate-looking designs to their left. The wall to their right became smooth and seamless as if it was one solid chunk of white marble, while the wall on their left was a light blue stone. The designs pulsed with a faint energy that changed colors with each burst.

"This chamber was here long before my time. I suspect it still holds many secrets yet to be discovered, but don't tarry. They will not be uncovered this day."

Dalinil cautiously followed Cor'il down the spiral stairs, his axe drawn as he looked about him. *Ready for something dangerous, I assume. But I should like to know what this place is. I've not seen anything like it.*

They continued their descent, their footfalls echoing through the stairwell. After several moments, the stairs gave way to a circular chamber. Cor'il stood in awe, staring into the room before him.

The room was about the size of a small tavern common room, but it was largely empty. Every surface was smooth and dull white with more detailed, pulsing designs. In the center of the room was a figure in black breeches and a white tunic, hunched over what looked like a very small well with blue puffs of smoke rising from it. Above the well floated two small crystals—one black and the other white.

After a moment, the figure rose slowly and turned to face them. Her radiant beauty was marred by a look of extreme exhaustion. Piercing green eyes peered out from behind brown hair that spilled just past her shoulders.

But what Cor'il noticed above all else were her ears. They looked very much like his own, but were longer and more pointed at the top.

She motioned them forward.

"My elation is boundless," she said. Her voice was soft and melodious, just as it had been in Cor'il's thoughts. "I am very happy to see you—*both* of you. It has been quite a long time since I have been in the presence of others."

"I am Cor'il, and this is my friend Dalinil."

"I am pleased to meet you both. Please, come closer."

Cor'il looked at Dalinil who looked back at him, and then he slowly walked forward. His blade remained in its scabbard. Dalinil must have thought that was a good idea, as Cor'il saw him slide his axe through the loop on his belt. They walked forward together but neither was in a hurry.

"You need not be afraid," she continued. "I have waited a very long time to meet you—much longer than I had anticipated."

"You've been expecting us?" Dalinil, judging from the look on his face, was very perplexed. "I don't understand."

"I, as well, am confused," Cor'il added.

"As well you should be." She held her hands out and raised her arms slightly. Two beautifully decorated stone benches rose out of the floor. "I shall explain. Please, sit."

Cor'il and Dalinil once again shared confused looks. Cor'il was the first to sit down, followed by Dalinil. The bench was oddly comfortable and contoured a bit. The smooth, seamless stone itself looked like ivory.

"My name," she said, sitting on her own bench, "is Antina Delovine." She gestured behind her to the white and the black crystals hovering in the blue mist. "I am their custodian." Each was about the size of Cor'il's fist.

"What are they?" Cor'il asked. He had probably a million questions and that was the only place he could think of to begin.

"Simply put," she continued, "Order and Chaos. For nearly 200 years they have remained in balance, floating in harmony above this well of souls. The well feeds them and keeps them aloft but, it also damages them if they get too close.

Cor'il could see that the black crystal was floating closer to the well than the white crystal. It appeared heavier, if that was possible. The blue mist spurted upwards like a flame, licking at both crystals.

"As you can see," she said, "The Chaos Stone is lower than the Order Stone."

"What are these stones for?" Dalinil asked. "What do they do?"

"A good question." Antina stopped and sighed for a moment. Her weary eyes drooped and her face looked tired. "Almost 200 years ago the world was very different from what it is today."

"Orcs," Cor'il mumbled.

"Aye," Antina replied. "And the differences reach far beyond just mere orcs or trolls. The Chaos Crystal is sinking ever lower into the well. And, while the Order Crystal is also sinking, it is doing so at a much slower pace. Every crack you see, every imperfection, is a rift between Chaos and our world. And every rift that opens allows those beings of Chaos to slip back through to our realm." Antina paused and stared past Cor'il. The black crystal rose slightly.

"The Chaos Crystal has many cracks in it," she continued.

Antina paused and inspected the crystals for a moment. When she turned her attention back to them, she seemed sadder.

"What about the Order Crystal?" Dalinil asked.

"Just as the Chaos Crystal bridges our world with Chaos, the Order Crystal does the same for the beings of Order."

Cor'il looked closely at the white stone but it appeared flawless.

"It doesn't have any cracks in it, then?" he asked.

"It does," she responded. "It has one very minute crack that is almost impossible to see. "I remember the day that crack appeared. It was many winters ago. 30 winters, if memory serves me properly."

"If the Chaos Crystal allows orcs, goblins, trolls, and other creatures into The Realm then what does the Order Crystal do?" Cor'il rose from his bench and started pacing. He was growing frustrated but, at the same time, he thought that he was beginning to understand. *Each question we ask gets us an answer but presents 10 more questions!*

"When that tiny crack appeared in the Order Crystal, one individual was born into this world—one being of Order."

"Who or what was it?" Cor'il had a sick feeling in his stomach. He wanted to throw up.

"I think you know."

"I don't think I do. What—"

"Can you think of no one?" Antina stood abruptly. Dalinil rose as well, ready for trouble. "The day that crack appeared in the Order Stone is the day, I suspect, that *you* were born, half-elf."

"That's a lie. It's not possible!"

"You know that I am telling the truth. Your ears give it away." She pointed to Cor'il who instinctively touched his ears. "You've had a rather long life already, haven't you? You're older than everyone you grew up with but yet, you do not seem to have aged as quickly as they have. Elves don't require much sleep. Do you?" She sounded angry.

"I have seen only 18 winters—."

"You have seen more than that, I suspect." Antina approached Cor'il who backed up, stumbling on the bench behind him. "I believe you are older than you remember."

Cor'il was speechless. He wanted to be angry with her, to shout at her and tell her she was wrong. But what she said began to make sense. He had always known he was different on some level. He simply wasn't sure *how* until now.

"It's not a bad thing, Cor'il. Do *not* be ashamed. You've no doubt noticed my ears—these are the ears of an elf."

"I am thoroughly confused now," Dalinil sighed. He sat back down on his bench, staring at the stones hovering above the well.

"In the past," Antina continued, "elves, ogres, gnomes, orcs, and many other creatures roamed these realms freely alongside humans. There was a constant struggle for survival as the creatures of Chaos waged war nonstop on the rest of the world. Superior numbers and uncontrolled savagery slowly overpowered discipline and knowledge to the point where we were all in danger of extinction."

Antina paused, turning her attention to the crystals again. She strained for a moment and then turned back to Cor'il and Dalinil.

"A great battle was fought right above where we are now—a last stand for Order. But the battle was merely a distraction that only I knew about—that I had carefully orchestrated for many years."

Cor'il took an opportunity to embrace the Threads. He was nearly blinded by the brilliance radiating from the countless strands that crisscrossed this room—Threads that all converged on Antina. Both crystals also gleamed so brightly that he wanted to shield his eyes.

You are beginning to understand, aren't you, Cor'il Half-Elven?

When he heard her voice in his head he let go of the Threads and the room's normal colors returned.

"The land above was a city. Not the city that we are accustomed to, though—not like the city that currently sits on the surface. The city of which I speak predates man and elf—built by a civilization long dead, I am afraid. This chamber shares a similar history."

"Nonsense!" Dalinil interrupted, leaping to his feet. "I've come to terms with orcs and goblins, but you are trying to convince me that there is some other..." He trailed off, apparently not sure of what to say next. He then sat back down and ran a hand through his hair, frustrated and grumbling to himself.

"While the battle raged on above me I was down here, in this room. You two are both Threadweavers, as am I. After I learned of the power held within these two crystals, I spent years developing a particular tapestry of Threads that I hoped would not just bring balance to the world, but would also allow us to live without the threat of Chaos altogether. Man and elf, dwarf and gnome—we all needed time to rebuild. Both our cities and our numbers had been demolished."

"And it worked?" Cor'il asked.

"Aye. I placed the gems over the well and wove the Threads to keep them aloft. As long as they remained above this vessel in balance, the Chaos world and ours—a world of Order—would remain separate."

"But your weave is failing," Dalinil said, "isn't it?" Cor'il could detect anger in his voice. "With your abilities you could have made a difference and probably turned the tide against Chaos. You could have commanded great forces to push back the Chaos in battle. Instead, you chose to hide down here like a coward."

"You misunderstand, child. You've no idea the danger of the orcish hordes. One person—even if that person is a learned Threadweaver—is but a drop of water in a large, dry lake. This was my only hope of salvaging this world. And it worked. For 200 years it worked."

She paused a moment and winced in pain.

"Once I wove the pattern, I immediately recognized the flaw. It was only a matter of time until the weave would eventually fail. I should have seen that beforehand, but I was blinded by my own hubris. With the weave firmly in place, I returned to the surface and slew the orc's leader in combat."

"Gorag Thrashbone," Cor'il whispered.

"Aye. Gorag Thrashbone."

"So that makes you—" Dalinil jumped up, pointing.

"Sturm Ironhelm, yes. I know well the history. I crafted it, after all." She paused again, then continued. "But now the Chaos crystal sinks lower. It needs to be lifted back up, but I fear I no longer have the strength for it. My weave was flawed from the beginning and, though it took a long time to happen, it has deteriorated. Even now, it takes most of my concentration to keep the crystals above the well."

"What happens if the Chaos crystal reaches the well?" Dalinil asked.

"It will shatter and the Chaos will return to our realm, letting loose everything I have worked so hard to purge from this world."

"And if the Order crystal reaches the well?" Dalinil continued.

"Then the races of Order will return to our realm."

Cor'il was still trying to think through everything he had just heard. Even if he'd had more time, he wasn't sure that he could fully grasp everything Antina had told them.

He had known, in some capacity, that he was different. It was well-known in Kuranthas that he was older than his peers. *Am I somehow a part of our distorted history?*

Then there was his father. The man had never treated Cor'il much like a son, but instead he had been treated more as a burden. He never had understood why, and this new information raised some new questions. *When I return to Kuranthas I will have a talk with him.*

"And if *both* crystals were to fall into the well?" Cor'il asked.

"Essentially, our Realms become a battlefield with humans caught in the middle once again."

"Why don't you let the white one fall into the well," Dalinil continued, "and keep the black one out of it? It seems that would be the best solution."

"The weave of Threads I have created cannot affect only one stone. I am using all of my power to keep the weave alive, but my command of the Threads is waning. I feel my power over them slipping."

"What are you suggesting?" Cor'il once again embraced the Threads. Immense power rushed through him, filling him up with warmth. He inspected Antina's weave, picking through it one Thread at a time. It was complex—beyond anything he'd ever seen or attempted. While he understood much of it, there was something in it that eluded him—something unique that he had never before seen. He took a closer look, but he became lost in the intricate machinations of the construct she had built.

"You are both quite strong with the Threads. There was only supposed to be *one* new Threadweaver—I was told that only *one* Threadweaver at a time may walk the land—but we have been handed a gift. *Two* Threadweavers! As far as I know this is the first time that has ever happened. It might be a portent that this conflict between Chaos and Order is coming to an end! You two have both come to me so that this can be finished once and for all."

Cor'il continued inspecting the weave. Just by looking at it, he was able to glean information about its very nature and that of the Threads themselves. He nearly lost himself in the weave but snapped back and let the Threads go.

"I don't understand," Cor'il said.

"I need someone to take my place—someone who is powerful and skilled with the Threads. Just one of you could take my place but *both* of you would ensure a final, permanent peace."

"Wait," Dalinil interrupted, "You want us to take your place down here in this... this prison?"

"That is," Antina replied, "the unfortunate price to be paid. But is it not worth the sacrifice for lasting peace throughout all of the Realms?"

"No." Dalinil did not sound happy. Cor'il saw his hand slowly moving toward his axe. This was quickly going to get out of hand.

"Those can't be the only two options." Cor'il slowly walked over to Dalinil, hoping to interpose himself between them. "There must be another way."

"Why do you resist? If you wish to keep things in balance then—"

"There *is* no balance!" Cor'il shouted. "Nothing is balanced!" He took a deep breath, trying to calm himself. "Orcs overrun our lands and invade our cities, and we can do nothing to stop them. Up above, they are destroying Elston right now. There *has* to be another option."

"There is!" Cor'il was easily pushed aside as Dalinil, gripping his axe, stepped between him and Antina. "I cannot speak for Cor'il," he continued, "but I'm not planning on spending eternity down here, waiting for failure. If we kill her, *both* crystals will fall into the well!"

"No!" she pleaded. "You can't! You will drown the whole world in strife and despair! If you kill me, the Chaos will overrun the land just as it did 200 years ago! At least, by tending the crystals, you give everyone a *chance*!"

Cor'il embraced the Threads again as Dalinil was bringing his axe to bear. He watched as Antina tried to manipulate the Threads, but they would not answer to her. He could see confusion and fear in her eyes.

With furious speed and precision Cor'il began unraveling her construct. He worked quickly and diligently as time seemed to slow to a crawl around him. One by one the Threads sprang out of the mesh, once again taut and bristling with energy, eager to be commanded.

Cor'il had the weave halfway unraveled when he gave pause. The anomaly he had encountered earlier—he saw it now. He gasped in surprise when he realized that it was Antina. She had woven her very *life* into her weave! It made sense now—why she was trapped here. She couldn't leave, lest her construct fail. *But it is failing anyway—it is failing with her age. As she gets older so does the power that keeps the crystals aloft! The Threads no longer answer to her. They answer to... to me.*

There was no time for a debate. Though he did not know for sure what the outcome would be, he continued disassembling what she had so intricately constructed.

"Now you see, don't you Cor'il?" She sounded almost sad, maybe even remorseful. "You understand." She paused a moment with a blank stare on her face. "But I feel as if I am forgetting something important. This troubles me."

Cor'il continued his work. He was almost finished.

"I see what you are doing. I cannot stop you, nor will I try. You have made your decision. Let us all hope that the world has matured enough to weather the coming storm."

The only part of the weave left to destroy was Antina herself. She and the construct were one in the same, and neither could exist without the other. He knew what he had to do, but he didn't have to like it.

"I am sorry, Antina," he said. "But we will find another way to restore harmony."

She only nodded in sullen response, ready for her fate. Cor'il removed the last Thread from her construct and, in a chain reaction, the rest rapidly unraveled by itself. He let go of the Threads and saw his vision return to normal at the very moment that Dalinil's axe fell, and Antina vanished in a burst of white light.

The two crystals plunged into the well's blue aura and disappeared. Both Cor'il and Dalinil braced themselves for some kind of explosion or quake but nothing came—only silence. The blue misty aura that emanated from the well died, leaving nothing behind.

"I think," said Dalinil, "that it's time to leave."

"What exactly did we just do?"

"Restoration?"

"For better? Or for worse?" Cor'il started toward the spiral stairs leading up. He found his curiosity mixed with sadness and hesitation. "What do you think we'll find up above?"

"A changed world. Mayhaps new allies and new enemies."

They slowly ascended the stairs, each torch extinguishing itself as they left. Cor'il felt sadness and confusion, but with a twinge of curiosity. He didn't know what it meant to be a half-elf, nor did he comprehend everything that had happened. But there was no turning back now.

"What do *you* think we'll find, Cor'il?"

Cor'il stopped on the stairs and turned to Dalinil. There were all kinds of possibilities as to what they would find when they returned to the surface. But he could only think of one thing for certain.

"We'll find unpleasant things, danger, and uncertainty," he said. "I only know of one other thing that we'll find up there."

"And what is that?"

"We'll find our friends."

THANK YOU

I thank you for taking a chance on this book, and for taking the time to read "The Call of Chaos." If you enjoyed it, and you know someone else who might enjoy it, please spread the word and recommend it to them—maybe leave a review. I would very much appreciate it.

<3,
SRF

The Chaos grows stronger in The Forgotten Years: The Coming Storm.

ABOUT THE AUTHOR

Sean R. Frazier is the author of The Forgotten Years series. He was inspired to write in elementary school but did not seriously consider publishing anything until he graduated college. Though he had grandiose visions of churning out nonstop novels, those dreams were shelved for a while... until now.

Sean lives in Missouri with his wife, two daughters, and assorted pets. He is a father, a husband, a gamer, a runner, and a total dork. Also, his cat can beat up your cat.

Made in the USA
Monee, IL
07 May 2022